G
gu
ti
in

B
he
po

Ju
c
f
t

A
t
t
l

s
p
l
b

SPENCER CLINE—His dream is to escape rebel territory and join the Union army. But no matter how hard he runs, he can't escape his past and the dreadful secret that pursues him.

MERRIMAN SWANEY—His war is with anyone who stands in his way, Confederate or Union. He leads a group of bush-whackers who supposedly fight for the Union . . . but plunder and kill for themselves.

JOEL—As the times change and war rages all around him, he must choose between his comfortable life as a house slave and a coldhearted daughter who will sacrifice any-thing and everything for freedom—including her own child.

Also by Cameron Judd

BOONE: A Novel Based on the Life
and Times of Daniel Boone

CROCKETT OF TENNESSEE:
A Novel Based on the Life
and Times of David Crockett

PASSAGE TO NATCHEZ

THE SHADOW WARRIORS

Available from Bantam Books

The Phantom Legion

BOOK II IN THE MOUNTAIN WAR TRILOGY

A Novel of Unionist Resistance
in Tennessee and North Carolina
February ~ December, 1863

CAMERON JUDD

BANTAM BOOKS
NEW YORK • TORONTO • LONDON • SYDNEY • AUCKLAND

THE PHANTOM LEGION

A Bantam Book / June 1997

ISBN 0-553-57389-6

Published simultaneously in the United States and Canada

Bantam Books are published by Bantam Books, a division of Bantam Doubleday Dell
Publishing Group, Inc. Its trademark, consisting of the words "Bantam Books" and
the portrayal of a rooster, is Registered in U.S. Patent and Trademark Office and in
other countries. Marca Registrada. Bantam Books, 1540 Broadway, New York, New
York 10036.

PRINTED IN THE UNITED STATES OF AMERICA

OPM   10   9   8   7   6   5   4   3   2   1

To Laura

AN INTRODUCTORY NOTE . . .

During the grim days of the American Civil War, there was in the hills and mountains of western North Carolina and East Tennessee a large population of people, mostly rural and agrarian, who remained staunchly loyal to the Union while living within the bounds of the Confederacy. Some of these loyalists struggled, often vainly, to remain publicly neutral. Many others risked their freedom and even their lives to "stampede" through rebel-occupied territory and reach the Federal lines to volunteer service to the Union military. Others went underground or under cover within the Confederacy itself, acting as citizen insurgents, burning railroad bridges, fighting as irregulars, serving as Union spies, smugglers, bushwhackers, or "pilots" for those fleeing north for Union military service. Some smuggled both escaped slaves and fleeing loyalists along the Underground Railroad. For such "Tories" the war experience was often not so much one of great battles between formal armies on vast battlefields, but gritty, brutal, underground warfare fought at their very doorsteps, often by men and women who never wore uniforms or held military commissions. These loyal hill people and mountaineers, isolated in the midst of a rebel-controlled region, saw the ugliest underbelly of the Civil War. Many were deprived or abused, or conscripted into military service for a cause they opposed. Some were imprisoned for their political beliefs, some were murdered, some were hanged under authority of the Confederacy.

Some endured and ultimately forgave. Others never did, and learned to dole out bitterness for bitterness, brutality for brutality.

Their story is seldom told. It is told here.

Wherever the vandal cometh,
Press home to his heart your steel,
And when at his bosom you cannot,
Like the serpent, go strike at his heel.

Through thicket and wood go hunt him,
Creep up to his camp-fire side,
And let ten of his corpses blacken
Where one of our brothers hath died.

In his fainting, foot-sore marches,
In his flight from the stricken fray,
In the snare of the lonely ambush,
The debts we owe him, pay.

—S. Teackle Wallis
"The Guerrillas" (1864)

THE MOUNTAIN WAR
1860–1865

VIRGINIA

Clinch River

N. Fork Holston R.

Watauga River

EAST TENNESSEE AND
VIRGINIA RAILROAD

Elizabethton

Lick Creek

Colter
*

Jonesborough

Greeneville

River

Shelton Laurel Cr.

Warm Springs

Marshall

NORTH CAROLINA

Asheville

0   20   40

Scale of Miles

* fictional sites

Part I

THE STAMPEDERS

Part I

Chapter 1

Two miles east of
Nashville, Tennessee, February 1863

Nearsightedness ran in Mary Gresham's family and had commenced its inevitable assault upon her vision right after her tenth birthday a month before, though it would be another month before she would notice it. As she peered now through crystal-cold forest air, she was too astonished and afraid to be aware that she was squinting or to notice that the prone human form that held her attention was vaguely blurred.

She stood as unmoving as the trees around her on this cold winter day, and stared, scarcely breathing. The figure did not move, either, she did not think . . . though perhaps the bloodied shirt rose up and down just a little to indicate breathing, or maybe was merely stirring in the breeze. She was not about to go closer to investigate. What if he should move? What if his hand should suddenly spear out and close around her ankle? What if he was a rebel bushwhacker, feigning death to draw her close so he could snatch her and kill her because her father had fought for the Union, had lost his left leg and left hand doing battle for the Union?

Mary Gresham stared a few moments more, then turned and ran back toward the barn a hundred yards behind her.

The prone and bloodied figure lay as before, not rising while she was gone. When she returned two minutes later with Bill, her twelve-year-old brother and now the main workman of the farm since his father's incapacitation, the body looked no different than before, though perhaps, Mary thought, the blood clotting in the shirt fabric had soaked out a little farther.

"I think he's dead," she said in a whisper. "But I ain't sure. He seemed like maybe he was breathing a little when I looked before."

Bill stared, frowning, saying nothing.

"Think he's a bushwhacker?"

Bill shrugged. His voice was wavery, shifting between a boy's tenor and a man's baritone. "Don't know. But I do think he's been bushwhacked."

"You going to get close to him?"

Bill was doing his best to sound brave. "Reckon I'll have to, won't I!"

"What if he grabs your ankle?"

"He can't grab nothing. He's hurt bad. See the blood spreading?"

"If it's spreading, does that mean he's still alive?"

Bill paused a moment. "I don't know."

"Don't get close to him, Bill."

But Bill did get close, stepping slowly toward the figure. The face was turned away, the hat remaining on the head, the hands hidden beneath the body itself.

Mary Gresham watched her brother creep closer, and began to cry without knowing it. Tears streamed down her face; she locked her hands together and held them tightly over her mouth.

Bill stopped about a foot from the body, looked down a few moments, then moved around to the far side and looked at the face, what he could see of it. He knelt, not being so cautious now, and Mary relaxed a little.

"He's dead?"

"No. No. Still breathing."

"Oh, Bill, get away from him!"

"No, you come here."

"I don't want to!"

"I need you to. Come on, quick!"

Mary trembled, wanted to run. But she obeyed her brother. She made a wide circle around the body and came in at Bill's side. She stared down at the face, which she could see only in profile. No beard. Just a half-grown boy.

"What do you want?" she asked.

"I'm going to roll the body over. I want you to look under the shirt."

"I won't touch him!"

"Listen to me! You got to. And you've got to be the one to look under the shirt. It wouldn't be fitting for me to do it, I don't believe."

"I don't want to see a bullet hole!"

"It ain't that you need to look for. Here . . . help me."

"I don't want to!"

"Damn it, Mary!" Bill had taken up swearing since his father's injury, because it made him feel more manly, and it took manliness to cope with the trials of a life that had changed utterly when his father lost his limbs. "I need you to get some grit in your craw and help me out here! Here now, kneel down beside me, like this, and we'll roll her over gentle."

"Her?"

"That's right. Or so I believe. That's why I want you to look down the shirt. That way we'll know."

The injured one made the softest of groans as they rolled the body. The dirty face that was exposed to their view was indeed feminine in its lines and countenance. A pretty face, possibly, though too filthy just now to tell for sure. Bill motioned for Mary to make the investigation beneath the checkered, worn shirt, and turned his head away while she did. He was tempted to sneak a look, but knew that Mary would tell their mother if he did.

A moment later he looked back at his sister, who had just let the shirt fall back in place. "Well?"

Mary's mouth was trembling. She was about to cry again. "Yes. It's a woman, Bill." She burst into tears.

Bill wondered why the mere fact that this was a woman

made his sister weep. "Well, we've got to get her help. She's been shot, it appears to me."

"Why is she wearing man's clothes, Bill?"

"Don't know. On the run, I guess. Trying to hide that she was a she."

"Is she going to die?"

"She might if you set there blubbering all day instead of fetching help."

"Who should I get?"

"Run over to the Smith farm. Get Nigger Bob. He's good with wounds and such. He'll know what to do."

Still crying, Mary Gresham ran away. Bill swore to himself, stood, walked about, swore again, to show himself just how disinterested and in control he was in the midst of this troubling situation. A wounded woman! Who'd have thought it? He wondered who had shot her, and why. And who she was, and what they would put on her tombstone if they never found out.

He paced about, swearing to himself, glancing down at the pale, bloodied woman from time to time and hoping to high heaven that he didn't burst into tears like his sister had, because Lord only knew he felt like it.

Mountain graveyard, Madison County, North Carolina

They came into the place of the dead slowly, following six bearded men who carried a pine coffin. A long, narrow hole had been dug into the hillside, and facing it, a line of hand-made chairs stood awaiting the immediate family of the deceased. The center chair was a quilt-draped rocker—a special chair reserved for the most honored of the mourners.

The bereaved, some wiping tears and others merely somber, lined up before the chairs but did not sit immediately. They stood with folded hands until the eldest of them, a bent old woman with a shawl over her humped shoulders and a big tin earhorn in her right hand, shuffled over to the rocker and sat slowly into it. She adjusted the shawl, put the earhorn into her right ear, and slowly began to rock, lips pressed into a tight white line over a hollowed, almost toothless mouth. Only when she was settled did the others of the family sit, chairs popping and creaking beneath them. The remaining mourners, made up of secondary kinfolk and various friends and neighbors of the family, gathered in a little crowd behind the seated ones, men standing stony-faced, women wiping tears, children fidgeting more than they should.

The preacher was long of beard, long of face, long of years. His hands, which gripped a well-worn, leather-backed Bible, were not the smooth hands of a city clergy-man, but the gnarled ones of a working man. His eyes were surrounded by wrinkles and lighted by an inner sorrow. He had laid away too many dead these past months, most of them men who should have outlived him by decades. War was a demon and a slayer. The preacher had come to hate it.

The pallbearers laid the coffin on the ground on the far side of the hole from the family. The preacher positioned himself behind it. He stood silently a few moments, the cold wind blowing his white beard as he studied the faces of his people. A light snow, remnant of a bitter winter, began to fall. Straightening himself, he opened the Bible to the Gospel of John.

"Let not your heart be troubled," he read, though he could as easily have said the words by heart. "Ye believe in God; believe also in me. In my Father's house are many mansions. If it were not so, I would have told you. I go and prepare a place for you. And if I go and prepare a place for you, I will come again, and receive you unto myself, that where I am, there ye may be also."

The old woman listened through her earhorn. There were no tears on her face, which was as leathery as the preacher's Bible. "Speak up, Orvil," she said in a voice as weathered as her features, but very clear.

The preacher read on, louder. His breath made white gusts in the air. "And whither I go ye know, and the way ye know . . ."

The half-deaf old woman removed the earhorn, leaned to the right and spoke to a much younger, weeping woman beside her in what she obviously intended to be a whisper, but which was more than loud enough to be clearly heard by all. "Millard knew the way, but he strayed far from it at the end." She straightened again and put the horn back to her ear.

The preacher, jolted by the intrusion, resumed reading: "Thomas saith unto him, Lord, we know not whither thou goest, and how can we know the way? Jesus saith unto him, I am the way, the truth, and the life; no man cometh unto the Father but by me . . ."

The horn came out of the ear. She leaned and spoke again in her loud whisper. "I don't believe Millard's gone to heaven, much as I despise to say it."

People in the crowd glanced uncomfortably at one another and fidgeted. A boy among them whispered to his father, "Has Mr. Millard gone to hell, Pa?" and got a firm nudge of reproval for the question. The younger woman sobbed louder. The old woman was oblivious to it all. The earhorn rose, went back into her ear.

The preacher closed his Bible. "My friends, we've come to lay to the earth the remains of a young man who grew up amongst us and was a friend of us all."

The old woman leaned again and said, "Millard made his friends among the wicked this past year."

The preacher shifted his weight and cleared his throat. "Lizzie, everybody can hear what you're saying."

She leaned toward him, horn in place. "What's that?"

"I said, everybody can hear what you're saying."

"Oh. I'm sorry. I'll keep quiet."

He cleared his throat again. "Friends, there's sadness at our loss. But we know that our Father above looks down on us in love and gives us comfort to pass all understanding. 'My peace I give unto you, not as the world giveth.' That's what he has promised to those who rely on Jesus."

The deaf woman spoke again to the weeper. "I wish Millard hadn't took up with Merriman Swaney. It ruint him, riding with bushwhackers."

"Granny, please do hush!" the crying woman whispered urgently, through tears. "Millard was your grandson! He was my own brother! I don't like to hear you talk so."

"Truth is truth, Myra. Millard went bad, and God allowed him to be struck down."

The preacher increased his volume, trying to prevail over a woman who didn't even know she was giving him competition. "Millard McCormick was a good young man. He was a hard worker. He loved his neighbors and would have become a fine citizen, had he been given the chance to live past this cursed war. He was a Christian, baptized by my own hands whilst yet a boy, and the corpse we lay away in this soil is but the husk and shuck of a soul gone to glory. Someday that husk will rise again, filled anew when Jesus comes, rising in a new world where there's no more tears. No more dying. No more war. Most of all, no more war. Millard will be part of that new world, saved and preserved for it by the grace of God."

The old woman frowned. "Who's he talking about?"

"Hush, Granny!"

"Can't be Millard. Ain't none of that applies to Millard."

The preacher struggled desperately now. "Millard lived in a time of trouble, neighbors dividing against theirselves, armies riding through and shooting and killing. He was caught up in this time of dying, trapped in it . . ."

Again the old woman spoke to her granddaughter. "He warn't trapped. He was just mean. I believe it was Millard himself who made Fallon Blake squat by that stump to be shot in the head. They say Fallon wasn't even given time to pray."

The preacher, seeing his defeat, surrendered. He stood unspeaking, looking at her.

Lizzie McCormick, unnoticing, held forth again in the silence. "I got no use for rebels, Myra, but I don't believe bushwhacking and murdering is how to fight them. Many a time I said to Millard, I said, 'Millard, in my opinion, this is a war not worth fighting. Leave it be.' I said it many a time."

The preacher spoke softly. "Lizzie."

She did not hear.

Louder: "Lizzie."

"What is it, Orvil?"

"Lizzie, Millard was your grandson. I believe maybe

you've got something you'd like to say about him. If you do, I'll step aside and let you speak."

The old woman considered, and nodded. She stood carefully, steadying herself with a hand on the rocker until her permanently bent old frame was as upright as it could be. She lifted her head, looking beyond the preacher toward the sky, her back to the crowd.

"I been told I can speak, and from what I've heard Orvil saying, I believe I should," she said. "Orvil speaks kind words. I don't fault him. He's a kind man. But truth is truth, and if it's to be spoke here today, I reckon it's me who must speak it."

She pointed at the pine coffin with a gnarled and knobby finger. "There in that burying box lies my youngest grandson, Millard McCormick. His mother died when he was tiny, his father dead even before that, and I raised him like he was my own born child. He was a good baby when he was little, hardly crying, never giving me no trouble. He was a good boy whilst growing. He helped his grandfather work his land and was a comfort to him in his last days. Millard professed Christ when he was ten year old, and Orvil himself baptized him. I was proud of Millard, believing he had made a true profession, though now I see it was a false one. If it had been true, he wouldn't have strayed, wouldn't have changed." She paused. "But he did change. When the war came to these mountains, Millard changed much. Grew hard and mean, like so many. I'm grateful he never married, never took no wife nor had no children to have to grieve over the sorry ways he took up."

For the first time, she showed sign of emotion, her voice cracking. "Millard's dead now, shot through the head by a cowardly reb bushwhacker, and it grieves my soul. But Millard was no better than the man who killed him. He earned what come to him."

A murmur of astonishment at her frankness ran through the crowd of mourners.

She turned to face the group, head still high, looking beyond them to the line of trees at the top of a nearby overlooking hill. Her eyes narrowed suddenly; there was a pause of several moments. When she resumed speaking, her voice was louder and aimed over the heads of the mourners. "My boy Millard chose to live by the sword and the gun. He took up with a sorry bushwhacker band who kills and murders and justifies theirselves by saying they do it for the sake of the great American Union. But I testify to you that a bushwhacker is a bushwhacker, and a murderer a murderer, no matter what flag he claims."

A boy in the crowd turned, looked behind him. His eyes grew wide. "Look! Look, Pa, yonder on the hill!"

Heads twisted about; muted outcries of surprise arose.

On the cambered hillside, looking down on the mourners below, was a line of about twenty ragged men, all visibly armed, some mounted, others on foot. A few wore portions of Union uniforms, some a mix of Union and Confederate garb, others civilian attire.

"That's Merriman Swaney's band!" the boy declared, pointing. "There's Colonel Swaney himself, come to see the laying away of one of his own!" His father, staring at the line of men, put an iron grip on the boy's shoulder, eliciting a wince.

"Shush, boy! You stand quiet, you hear? You stand quiet, and don't you point that finger no more! Not at that bunch, boy. Not at that bunch."

Lizzy McCormick's old but clear-sighted eyes had been the first to see the watching bushwhackers, and clearly she was aiming her words at them now, more than at the crowd at hand. She spoke in a near shout. "Them that stray off the right path do so only to show they was never truly on the path to begin with. It was that way with Millard. He went out from amongst us to show he was never one of us. If his heart had been pure, he would have never become a vile thief and murderer like bushwhacking Merriman Swaney."

"Lord have mercy! Somebody shut her up before Swaney comes down here and shoots us all!" someone whispered.

"Swaney ain't going to shoot nobody," another replied. "Swaney's no murderer. He's a good Union man and a protector of loyal Union folk all through these mountains. Them he's killed have all deserved it. I cherish Granny

McCormick as much as any of us, but as far as I'm concerned, her grandson died a righteous martyr, whatever she thinks about it. I been standing here biting my tongue, and I feel compelled to say it."

Murmurings among the crowd revealed several inclined to agree, but Lizzy McCormick continued her oration undeterred, her eyes locked on the line of armed men.

"My Millard was drawed to bad and cruel men, like a house dog drawed to a pack of curs. The wickedness of war was too great for him. He became wicked himself." She lifted a hand, gripping her earhorn with the other, as her voice became a trembling, camp meeting kind of warbling shout. "I stand here today to testify that there's no goodness in this war, no righteousness at all. It's a dirty stream that sullies all who wash in it, and it flows through these charnel hills to hell! My boy's gone now, and there's many who will foller him down the path to destruction. God have mercy on them! God have mercy on us all!" Her eyes became wet, her voice lowering and softening. The uplifted arm trembled. "And God have mercy on my poor, poor Millard. God have mercy on my sweet boy, who's been took from me."

She broke down and sobbed, lowering her face. The earhorn dangled at her side, barely retained in her weakening grasp. "Oh, the times I've held him when he was a baby, all nestled against me! Oh, the times I held his dear little self in my arms!"

Her children gathered around her, trying to comfort her.

High on the hill, the lanky, black-bearded Colonel Merriman Swaney tugged at his whiskers and grunted. He addressed an equally lean and ragged, but much younger, man beside him. "Well, I reckon she's told us what she thinks of us, eh?"

"Yes sir, I reckon so."

"Just one sad old woman's opinion, eh?"

"Yes sir."

The bushwhacker sighed through his long, hooked nose. "Fare thee well, young Millard McCormick, and God rest your soul. We'll continue the fight you helped us wage, despite babbling old women who can't distinguish the good from the bad. There's blindness in some folk, eh? But I'm inclined to be charitable. She is in grief, after all."

"Yes sir, Colonel."

Swaney tugged his whiskers again. He was distinguished and authoritative, even pompous, despite his bedraggled clothing and grooming. "Let's be gone, men. I daresay there's some down yonder who'll directly tell rebel ears that we're in the vicinity. Thus I suggest we remain no longer, eh?" He turned his horse and rode slowly back into the woods, his men trailing after him until the hill was empty.

Below, when the old woman had wept herself dry, they lowered the pine box into the hole. The preacher bowed his head and prayed. Lizzy McCormick sat on her rocker, looking even older and more stooped than before. She did not listen to the preacher. She stared at the grave, rocking slowly, humming an old mountain song softly beneath her breath, cradling the earhorn in her arms as one would cradle a baby.

Chapter 2

Near the Doe River,
Carter County, Tennessee, April 1863

He watched the final embraces in the moonlight, the last kisses, the last good-byes. Stifled sobs of parting filled the grove. He pondered how much he despised these moments—despised them mostly because they tended to drag on, and if he didn't step in to shorten them, no one else would. But he always hesitated to force the final separation. It seemed cruel, and Greeley Brown was not a cruel man.

A few moments more won't hurt. I'll give them that much. Some of these folks may never see each other again, after tonight. As he watched the emotional scene, he recalled the time he had enjoyed the pleasure of having a woman to fret and worry over him. It seemed long ago. *A few moments more, that's all.*

Those moments had stretched into minutes before he cleared his throat, raised his voice slightly and said, "Time to end the farewells. We need to cover some miles tonight."

At once the kisses and embraces became fevered, and no more were the sobs stifled. Sighing, fingering the tie-down strap on the holster bearing his prized Navy Colt revolver, Greeley repeated, a little more loudly, "Time to commence our journey, men! You women and young ones, don't you worry—and make sure no one sees no big band of you heading home together, hear? They'll know what we've been about if you do, and come tracking us. So you go home different ways, one or two at a time."

No one was listening. Tears and moans sounded in abundance in the wooded grove. The families of this particular band of stampeders were the most emotional Greeley had dealt with yet. He hadn't observed such sorrow since the funeral four years before of one of his cousin's children, a small child who had fallen off a high porch and died over in Jewel Hill, North Carolina.

"For God's sake, let's move on!" Carter "Ivy" McDermott called at Greeley's right ear. Greeley admonished him at once for speaking so loudly.

"I'm sorry, Mr. Brown. I'm tired of all this gush and slobber, that's all."

Bulbous-nosed McDermott, who had a red and oddly scarred face, was a man all of muscle and sinew developed over years of blacksmithing. McDermott was one of the other two men there, besides Greeley himself, who had no one to embrace him or shed tears over his impending departure. The other unaccompanied man, Spencer Cline, was McDermott's opposite: small, thin, bespectacled, with a nervous twitch in his narrow face. Greeley knew almost nothing about Cline, who had come to him a stranger, seeking his services with ready money in hand. He had Cline figured for a store clerk, or maybe a scholar from some college or academy.

"How long, Mr. Brown?" McDermott asked in a tone of frustration. "Are we going to let the rebs find us right here, drowned in tears, or are we going to Kentucky?"

"Simmer down, Mr. McDermott," Greeley said. "We're going to Kentucky. I'll take care of this situation."

He strode to a man whose wife clung to him fiercely, and gently grasped one of her wrists. "Please, Miz McCloud. Let him go now. We got to leave."

She was big, broad of face, red of hair. She looked at Greeley bitterly a moment, but the expression softened. "Take care of him for me," she said. "See he makes it safe all the way."

"I'll do my best."

She pulled her wrist free of his grip, then grasped his wrist in turn, squeezing so hard it hurt. Her eyes were hidden from him in night shadows, but he felt the sudden intense fire of them. "You see he makes it safe! You hear me? You see he makes it safe!"

He could not promise; surely she knew that. There were miles of wilderness between this place and the safety she desired for her man. "I can only do my best," he said, prying his wrist from her grasp. She held silence a moment, then sobbed loudly, collapsing to her knees at her husband's side, face buried in her hands.

"Kate . . ." the man said. "Oh, Kate, don't go on so. Ain't nothing going to happen to me."

"Let's go, Jim," Greeley said. "Let's go now." He put his hand between the man's shoulders and gave a gentle but authoritative push. The man, face grimacing with emotion, reached out and touched his wife's lowered head a final time, then turned and stalked away, sobbing softly and trying to hide it.

"Jim McCloud," Greeley said.

The fellow swung around, irritable in sadness. "What?"

"You're going the wrong way, and you've left your haversack and hat on the ground."

Through his tears, McCloud grinned self-consciously. Somehow that smile managed to bring a touch of levity, a lightening of the pervasive heavy atmosphere in the grove. McCloud came back for his pack while others chuckled— not including McDermott, who glared over the scene like an offended minor god, and Cline, who seemed cut off from it all and lost in thoughts of his own.

Greeley seized the moment and mood. "Folks, I'll keep watch over them as close as I would my own people," he said, displaying his most assuring smile for the women and children. "I can make no pledge but that I'll do my best, and guard them with my own life. I ain't lost a stampeder yet, and don't plan to lose none this time." He winked at a sad-faced boy standing near at hand. "Besides, my own back-side's in a sling if them rebs catch us—so I don't believe I'll let that happen. Right, partner?"

The boy grinned and nodded. Greeley rumpled his hair.

"God bless you, Greeley Brown!" an emotional feminine voice said somewhere in the group. "God bless you, and be with you!" Murmurings of agreement rumbled from the others.

"God bless all of you, too," Greeley replied. "Now, men, let's start to walking. We've got many a mile ahead of us."

"Confound this talk," McDermott said, resettling his well-stuffed knapsack between ham-sized shoulder blades. "We could have had many a mile *behind* us by now if we'd left when we should've."

"Caesar Augustus, I wish it was darker," was all Greeley said in reply.

Thanks to incoming clouds, the darkness did thicken, for which Greeley was grateful, though it forced the group to slow considerably and pick their way along. Hard as it was to travel in deep night, darkness at least was a shield. Yet the men following him, fifteen in number, cursed the blackness, cursed the rough forest trail that tripped them again and again, cursed the Confederate government from which they fled, even cursed Greeley himself for moving too swiftly. Greeley gave no reply. He had heard all this from prior stampeders. The first night was always trying, tiring, frightening. It would only grow worse later—but the stampeders themselves would grow stronger, and that would make the crucial difference.

They had traveled two miles when the wind kicked up and a light rain began to fall. "I hope the women and children made it in before they got wet," one of the stampeders said. "I worry for them more than for us."

Ivy McDermott, who had kept close pace with Greeley and didn't seem at all tired from the effort, gave forth in reply a peevish sounding grunt. Greeley wondered if McDermott disdained families, having none himself. He seemed a gruff and unpleasant man. Greeley didn't know him well, but did know something of his situation. A capable Elizabethton blacksmith, McDermott had been put to work smithing for the Confederate army the prior

November, after being caught in a roundup of suspected Unionist insurgents that had occurred after the burning of several key railroad bridges across East Tennessee. Greeley himself had been one of the bridge burners, helping Colonel Daniel Stover burn the bridge at a community called Union by the Unionists, Zollicoffer by the rebels. McDermott's only alternative to serving the army he hated had been incarceration in the dreaded Confederate prison at Tuscaloosa, Alabama.

The tale of how McDermott had managed to get out of his fix was becoming Unionist legend in the region. Deeply allergic to poison ivy, he had found a good, drying patch of it and rolled in it stark naked for nearly an hour, giving himself a rash that made him sick almost to death and puffed his face so badly that he had been blind for a week. Ugly pancake scars had marred his visage ever since. McDermott declared to the army doctor that he was obviously dying of the same rare malady that had killed his father, and had begged to be furloughed home to Elizabethton to die in the presence of his family . . . a family he in fact didn't have. The doctor, mystified by the severe rash and afraid the mystery disease would spread among the other soldiers, quickly approved the furlough, and McDermott was hauled home. There he suffered away the rash in baths of brine, erected a tombstone near his house with his own name on it, and went into hiding until he could flee north to the Union lines. Folks who knew what he'd done had called him "Ivy" ever since. McDermott was proud of the nickname. Asking him to tell the story of his escape from the rebels was one of the few things assured to make him smile.

Calls for rest came after the stampeders had covered no more than four miles. "A bit farther," Greeley responded, eliciting groans.

Two more miles and the complaints grew too many to ignore. Greeley called the halt as rain began to pepper down steadily. The men huddled beneath trees, eating from the supplies of food in their knapsacks, trying vainly to stay dry and get some rest. They were no more than a mile from the town of Elizabethton, the proximity of which elicited longing talk about dry, warm beds, enclosing walls, well-laden supper tables. Such luxuries would probably not be theirs for a long time to come, which only made them all the more alluring.

Most of the men ate more of their food than they should have, though Greeley encouraged conservatism. A few managed to fall asleep fairly easily, mostly those who had already been refugees in the wilds, afraid to sleep in their homes because they knew the rebels were watching for them. Greeley was aware that before this northward flight was through, every man there would probably develop the ability to sleep well on hard ground in heavier rains than this one.

But tonight even Greeley, the most wilderness-acclimated of them all, didn't sleep much. The stirrings of the restless men and his awareness of the great responsibility upon him kept his mind turning and stole his rest.

Daylight broke on a cloudy, dripping day. Though they were eager to move on, the stampeders stayed where they were, hidden in the forest, again eating too much of their food out of sheer boredom. McDermott grew even more cross than usual, not liking this sitting about. "We can't do nothing for it, Mr. McDermott," Greeley told him. "Too dangerous to travel in these parts during the day."

Many of the men passed the hours writing letters to their families at home, which Greeley found amusing in that they had left those families only the day before. He noticed that Spencer Cline was among the letter writers. Greeley wondered to whom he was writing, and why the letter's intended recipient, whoever that might be, had not seen Cline off at his departure.

At last the seemingly eternal day ended, the clouds breaking about dusk. When it was sufficiently dark, the stampeders set out again. They made better time tonight, moving about twelve miles, safely crossing the railroad and finally coming to a campsite Greeley had used before, near the Pactolus ferry. The men were weary, hungry, and complaining of sore feet. "God, I wisht I had my horse!" one declared. But men sneaking off for the Union lines seldom used horses. Horses were big, hard to hide, and not prone to keep quiet when rebel patrols passed near their hiding places.

The next morning, Greeley informed the group he had decided to risk moving on a little farther, despite the daylight. "There's a good Union man in these parts. I want to hear from him how things lay hereabouts with the rebs."

They moved like fugitives through weedy fields, along overgrown fencerows, and for a brief, tense stretch down a shaded and narrow public road. Reaching a little cabin perched on the side of a low hill, the stampeders hid among some cedars, and Greeley approached the house alone.

The man inside, old and patriarchal, greeted him at the door with a curt nod, a glance around the landscape to Greeley's rear, and a quick flick of the head to invite him in.

"You've picked a right bad time to stampede," the informant said, his toothless gums gripping a bone pipe that flicked up and down with each word, bobbing out perfect rings of smoke with each downward motion. "Two miles from here, Mr. Brown, there's no less than five hundred rebs, maybe more. They been beating the bushes for stampeders and conscript dodgers. The talk is they're looking for you in particular. You've had a price put on your head, my friend."

Greeley muttered, "Caesar Augustus." He had expected this would happen, but had hoped for later rather than sooner.

"You'd best keep hid out by daylight," the old man went on. "Yonder way"—he nodded leftward—"there's a good thickety field you can hide in. You'll be able to see the road from there, too, so you can keep an eye on any rebs moving on it. Got much food in your pack, Mr. Brown?"

"All I could round up. Not enough to last me all the way."

"That's too bad, for I got not a bite to spare you. If you'd come before yesterday, I could have fixed you proper. Had a larder full. But ten big rebs stopped by yesterday at breakfast time with bellies rumbling. They left here full, and now it's my belly growling."

Greeley returned to his group and shared the news.

Several had grumbled earlier about sore legs and blistered feet, but knowing there were rebels in the vicinity quieted all complaints. The group Greeley led up to hide in the thicket-covered field was somber and frightened.

They waited out the day in the brush, sometimes sleeping, mostly watching the road, along which frequent rebel patrols passed. One patrol that came by in late afternoon was prodding along five men before it, in civilian dress. No one had to be told that the five had probably been caught fleeing northward, just as they were doing. Greeley felt bad for the captured men, whomever they were, but was glad in another way that his group had seen them. It made for a warning more effective than his mere words could ever be.

"What will happen to them?" Spencer Cline asked in a whisper.

"They'll be conscripted into the Confederate army, most likely. Or if they won't be conscripted, they'll probably be sent off to prison somewhere. If they're lucky, they might come out of it alive someday. Plenty don't. A reb prison will kill a man quicker than a battlefield. Especially farther south. East Tennessee folks don't fare well in such places. Like the poor old pap of William Pickens over in Sevier County. William tried to burn the Strawberry Plains bridge back in 'sixty-one, and when the rebs couldn't catch him to punish him for it, they arrested his old pap instead and sent him off to Tuscaloosa. He didn't last long there. Died right in that prison, not having done a single thing to merit being there, and him being a state senator at the time besides. You'd a thunk they'd have treated a senator with more respect than that, wouldn't you? 'Twasn't right, what they done to that poor old man."

They pressed on when darkness came. Reaching a stream, they drank, bathed their feet, ate. The men were beginning to conserve their food now, Greeley noticed. It wouldn't matter that much; they'd all run out well before they reached the Union lines.

Pushing themselves harder and farther, they came to a river; Greeley proceeded to a covelike little indention in the bank and from among the concealing brush there produced a canoe, an act that brought muffled vociferations from the watching men, as if he had just performed a particularly neat conjuring trick.

"I keep it hid there most all the time," Greeley explained. "Or over on the other side, depending on which way I'm traveling. I always expect to find it stole when I come here, but so far I've been lucky."

Helped by Ivy McDermott, Greeley conveyed the men across in small groups. There was little noise but the dip of the paddles and the gasping breathing of tired and nervous fugitives. At length all were across. Greeley hid the canoe and they went on, plunging into a forest as the sky grew cloudy and the darkness more inky, particularly so beneath the trees.

Travel the rest of the night was difficult because of poor visibility, yet under Greeley's guidance they moved with surprising speed and silence for so big a group. Over flats, fields, and ridges they progressed, whispering whenever conversation was necessary. "How far will we get tonight, Mr. Brown?" McDermott asked when they were deep into the woods.

"I hope to make the North Fork of the Holston."

"Have you a canoe hid out there, too?"

"Nope. But if fortune smiles, the water will be low enough for us to wade."

Fortune did smile. In the gloom of the hour before dawn, they found the Holston waters relatively low and slow-running. Though the night was chilly and the black river as uninviting as the Styx, the weary stampeders complied uncomplainingly when Greeley ordered them to strip to the skin and plunge into the water, holding their bundled clothing and knapsacks above their heads. The water felt like ice, and sixteen sets of teeth were chattering audibly when they emerged on the north side.

Shaking off all the water they could, they quickly dressed and sought instruction from Greeley. It would be light soon; would they go on, or wait out the day here?

"I want to go farther," Greeley said reluctantly, knowing he was pushing the limit of their endurance. "I know a good hidden sleeping place for us maybe a mile or two ahead, but to reach it we've got two roads to cross. I'd as soon get that done and behind us, if we can make it there before the sun's up."

"I don't know I can go another step," Spencer Cline said. "I'm unaccustomed to this. My feet are blistered bad, Mr. Brown. I can scarcely stand on them."

Greeley had feared Cline might prove a weakling. He had that look about him. "Mr. Cline, you can indeed make it," he said. "You've come this far, and you can make another mile or two. Then you can rest your feet all day tomorrow, and we'll grease your blisters."

"I don't think I can go on. I'm not sure I should have started to begin with."

"I don't want to leave you behind for the rebs to find, Mr. Cline." Greeley wouldn't have in fact left Cline or anyone else behind, but there was no reason for Cline to know that. "Remember them prisoners we saw."

Silence for a few moments. Cline pulled off his spectacles, rubbed his nose, and put them on again. He sighed very sadly. "I suppose I can make it a little farther, if I must."

"Good." And they went on. Cline whimpered a little at first, but McDermott swore and told him to keep down the noise, and from then on Cline was quiet.

Chapter 3

Since the outbreak of war, Greeley Brown had grown very familiar with the peculiar mad state of the section of the world in which he lived, but never would he be accustomed to it. How was it that, by simply remaining true to the values and patriotism he had been taught since birth, a man could see what had been friendly turn hostile, what had been familiar turn strange, and what had been home turn to alien territory?

So it was for Greeley Brown, but certainly not for him alone. The majority of the people of East Tennessee, as well as of Greeley's original home region of mountainous western North Carolina, had held fast to the Union while their own states moved into the Confederacy. While there was near unanimity of pro-Confederate feeling in many parts of North Carolina and Tennessee, the mountain country was the exception—an inconvenient exception too, as far as the Confederate leadership was concerned.

Through East Tennessee ran a crucial railroad system, the loss of which would hamper greatly the movement of Confederate soldiers and supplies into the critical region of Virginia. In order to protect this system, as well as to hold back a regional Unionist counter-rebellion within the bounds of the Confederacy itself, East Tennessee had become occupied ground almost as quickly as the secession of Tennessee had come about. Similarly, western North Carolina, though more remote, isolated, and somewhat less strategically essential than East Tennessee, was also kept under the rebel fist. The Unionist majority in those regions found itself held under the thumb of rebel overlords sent in by the Confederate leadership.

In Greeley Brown's opinion, one of the greatest twisting ironies of a war of ironies was that Nashville, over in the pro-Confederate center of the state and originally the headquarters for a pro-Confederate state government, was now in Union hands. Its situation as a Union-controlled pocket in the midst of a rebel state was a reverse image of the situation in which the East Tennessee Unionists found themselves.

But it would not be so forever, or such was the hope and conviction of Greeley and his fellow Unionists. For a long time Unionists had anticipated a Federal invasion of East Tennessee—Greeley and many other Unionist insurgents had tried, fruitlessly, to open the door for that invasion as far back as November of 1861 with the burning of several key railroad bridges in the region—and someday, Greeley remained confident, the hope would become reality.

In the meantime, there was tribulation, particularly so since the passing of the Confederate conscription law the prior April. That law provided for exemption on a variety of grounds, Unionist convictions not among them. So Unionist men and even boys became fugitives in their own homeland, hiding in the hills and hollows to avoid the draft, or "stampeding" north, ideally in the company of an established Union pilot such as Greeley Brown, to reach the Union lines and enlist. Those who came from East Tennessee had one great ambition: to be specifically a part of the Union force that would invade their home territory and liberate it from rebel control. For Union soldiers from the North, the war was one of ideology and abstract duty; for Union soldiers from East Tennessee, it was a heartfelt,

intensely personal war whose end was the liberation of a
homeland in bondage.

Sometimes Greeley Brown grew hopeless and restless,
and felt that day of liberation would never come. Too many
times it had seemed at hand, as it had in late '61, only to be
blown away in the winds of changing strategies.

In more analytical and patient moments, however,
Greeley was able to believe that factors were shifting and
making the liberation day more likely. Surely it would not
be long now. The rebels had yielded up Nashville more than
a year ago, and despite bushwhacker attacks, the raids of
rebel stalwarts such as John Hunt Morgan, and internal
sabotage efforts, that city still remained firmly in Union
control. President Lincoln himself was said to still hold a
personal interest in the welfare of the Union loyalists of the
mountain regions. Surely the great Federal advance would
come before too many more months had passed!

But until then, the rebels held the day in East Tennessee,
and a Union man moved through their territory only at the
greatest of risk. And so it was that men such as Greeley
Brown were needed.

Greeley soon began to doubt they would make it before
daylight to the hiding place he had set his hopes upon.

The first public road they would have to cross lay on the
far side of a tall and rocky ridge; the men climbed the ridge
with difficulty, then removed their shoes for silence's sake
and crept down the north slope toward the road, moving in
single file with Greeley at the front. As he neared the road,
however, he saw a fire burning near a fencerow. Halting, he
sent whispered direction back up the line for the men to turn
back; they would seek a crossing farther down.

Yet again they encountered the sight of a fire, and as
Greeley crept closer, he made out an entire line of such fires
along the road. Rebel guards were stationed all along it,
strung out in a wide, loose net designed to capture just such
stampeding groups as their own. A man's cough sounded so
near to Greeley that he felt his scalp pull tight on his skull as
his mouth went dry. Dismayed, he crept back to his men and

hurriedly ordered them back up the ridge; they would have to pass the day hidden on its side, a far from secure position, and not at all comfortable.

The daylight rose and seemed intensely bright; the stampeders hid in the thickest brush they could find, which provided a sense of safety from the rebel outposts below, but little physical comfort. Most ate, working up a thirst before they realized there was no water here. It would be a long and dry day. Grumbling and miserable, most lay down as best they could in the undergrowth and tried to sleep.

Greeley was almost asleep himself when someone came to his side and gave his shoulder a gentle shake. Perturbed, he sat up and frowned into the thin face of Spencer Cline.

"Mr. Brown, sir, I'm thinking I ought not go on."

"You must go on, Mr. Cline."

"I don't believe I'll make it, sir."

"Grease your blisters. Your feet will toughen."

"It isn't my feet, sir. It's just . . . I don't know what it is. I just know I won't make it if I go on. And I don't know I should have come to begin with. There's a situation I'm leaving behind that has come to worry me."

"I can't have you turning back. You'd have to backtrack alone, and then you'd probably be caught, and unless you were mighty resilient, they'd gouge it out of you about the rest of us here and what route we're taking, and that'd bring danger to all of us. You've launched your boat with us, Mr. Cline, so to speak, and you're obligated for the full voyage. I don't want you nor anybody else turning back now."

"But I won't make it, sir. I can tell I won't."

"How can you know that? You've made it this far. You don't look to be no soothsayer nor Gypsy. You can't tell ahead of the game what the end will be."

Cline seemed about to respond, but instead clamped his lips together so tightly they whitened. He was shaking and seemed about to cry. Normally Greeley would have felt sorry for such a nervous, scared man as Cline, but on the stampede there was little room for sympathy. One weak and uncertain man made the entire group weak and uncertain. If Cline dwelt on thoughts of failure, then fail he would, and endanger the whole body of them in so doing.

"Cline, you're wore out. Go grease your feet, eat a bit, and sleep. You will make it. You hear me? You will make it, because I ain't giving you no choice."

"I shouldn't have come to begin with."

"But you did. And you'll finish what you started."

"I'm scared, Mr. Brown. I feel like the worst kind of thing will happen to me."

Greeley was weary, and hated Cline's whining, defeated manner. The image of himself delivering the sallow fellow a ringing slap played appealingly through his mind. But he figured a slapped Cline would shriek loud enough to bring the rebels running up from the road. He sighed.

"Where you from, Mr. Cline?"

"I'm from . . . I live in Sevierville, sir."

"Sevierville! You came a few miles that day you sought me out, then. What are you? Store clerk?"

"A . . . lawyer, sir."

Greeley tried to imagine such a timorous man arguing a case before a jury. He couldn't. "You got family?"

"No. No family at all."

Cline seemed uncomfortable with the questions. Greeley did not relent, however. Once already two brothers on the run because of crime had taken advantage of his piloting services, and he didn't want that to happen again. "You ain't married?"

Cline averted his eyes. "No. No I'm not."

"Got you a girl anywhere?"

"Well, there's . . . yes, I've got . . ." He faded out and looked more uncomfortable than ever. "Mr. Brown, I'm not one to talk about myself a lot."

"Are you running from the law, Mr. Cline?"

"No, sir. I swear before God, sir, that I'm not!"

Greeley stared a silent challenge at him.

Cline locked onto his gaze and held it. "Sir, I'm no criminal. I swear to you."

"I hope not, Mr. Cline. My purpose is to help guide Union men, not men running from things they've done."

"I'm a Union man, Mr. Brown. I am."

"I believe you. Now, how about let's get some sleep."

"Yes . . . but let me ask you one more thing. About that

letter I was writing. They tell me you sometimes carry letters from East Tennessee soldiers and such to their people
back home."

"I do."

"The letter I was writing, would you deliver it for me?"

"Where to? Sevierville?"

"No. North Carolina. Near Warm Springs."

"Well, I know that area very well. Where precisely does
this letter have to go?"

Cline didn't seem eager to answer. "Have you heard of
the Josiah House?"

"Colonel Josiah's place? The house he painted Confederate gray three days before he died, just to show what a
Secesh he was?"

"That's the place, yes."

"It would be right dangerous for me to deliver a letter
there. Me and rebs don't get along, you know. I hear I've
got a price on my head."

"It's important, Mr. Brown. Please. I'll pay you every
extra dollar I have, if you'll do it. And there's a slave there,
an old man named Joel, who can carry the letter in for you.
You needn't try to do it yourself."

If I can find this Joel, that is, Greeley thought. He
regretted this matter had come up. He had obvious good reasons to shy away from rebel havens such as Josiah House.
At least the old colonel, an old Mexican War veteran who
had built himself a mansion in the heart of his own small
wilderness empire, was now gone on to whatever reward
awaited hardened old souls such as his. Greeley had met
Colonel Josiah only once, back when he was a boy, hunting
on some of the colonel's property. Colonel Josiah had
turned out hounds to run him off.

"I'd like to help you, Mr. Cline . . . but I have to consider
what's reasonably possible. Who's the letter to? Your
sweetheart?"

Again the averted eyes. "Yes. That's right." Cline's chin
quivered and Greeley expected tears at any moment.

Greeley was weary. He wanted Cline to go away and let
him rest. He wished Cline hadn't decided to stampede, or
had chosen to do so with a different pilot. For that matter, he

would have been perfectly happy for this particular fellow not to have been a Union man at all. The Confederacy was welcome to all such tremorous weaklings. Greeley had brought in some fine recruits for the Federals, but in Cline's case he felt he had hooked a carp.

"Let me ask you something, Mr. Cline. You aim on becoming a soldier?"

Cline's expression transformed so suddenly, so abruptly, that Greeley was actually startled. The narrow, bespectacled face lifted and gazed firmly into Greeley's. "Indeed I do, Mr. Brown. I'll give my service to Mr. Lincoln's army, and proudly. I made the decision to become a soldier the moment I learned what had occurred on the twenty-second day of September in the year last."

September 22, '62 . . . Greeley dug in his mind for the significance of that date. His brows flicked upward. "Ah, yes! That's the day Lincoln signed his free-the-slaves proclamation, ain't it?"

"Yes sir. And the moment I learned of that grand act, I vowed that I would fight for Mr. Lincoln's army and see the carrying out of his proclamation. That was the moment that this war became *my* war. I knew then that I would become a soldier."

"Caesar Augustus! You speak like an abolitionist, Mr. Cline."

"I am indeed. I despise slavery, sir. I praise the day it was ended."

Across Cline's shoulder Greeley saw McDermott rise up on his blanket and stare at Cline with loathing.

Greeley said, "Slavery ain't truly ended, of course. The Confederates don't go by Lincoln's law."

"Which is why we must strip the power from their hands, sir. Which is why I'm heading northward."

Greeley marveled at Cline's new demeanor. Whining and weak moments before, he now had the spirited tone and fiery eye of a zealot. Greeley was hard pressed to decide if that was an improvement. Zealots of any kind had always made him wary. But a motivated, determined Cline was more likely to complete a successful stampede than was a fearful and defeated one, so perhaps this new fire was worth stoking a bit.

"I'm glad to hear you speak with such determination, Mr. Cline. Mr. Lincoln needs determined men for his army. So do thousands of colored folk still waiting to be set free. So you forget this nonsense about not making it. Put some grease on your feet and keep some of that fire in your boiler, and you will make it through."

Cline's iron expression, though, dissolved into wistfulness; he gave a flickering little smile with nothing behind it. "I don't believe I will," he said. "It's a conviction I can't shake off. And if I don't make it, if something should happen to me . . . you'll still deliver my letter . . . won't you? It deals with a situation I wish I could have resolved before I left. A situation having to do with the welfare of two people very important to me, and which I may not be around to deal with later, should the worst happen."

Greeley saw that he'd misunderstood Cline's concern. When Cline spoke of not making it, he wasn't talking about turning back. He was talking about dying.

Greeley had talked enough. He was ready for rest. "Mr. Cline, don't worry about your letter. I'll get it to the Josiah place one way or another. What was that slave's name you mentioned?"

"Joel. He enjoys a free rein and is in Warm Springs very often; you should be able to make contact with him without much difficulty."

It already sounded like a lot of difficulty to Greeley, but all this was future concern in any case, and he was ready to forget about it for now. "Let me say one more thing to you, Mr. Cline: I don't want to hear no more talk from you about not making it through. You understand me? Not a word. It ain't good for you to say, for me to hear, nor for the others to hear, either. I want men with me who have their eye on living, not dying. You fix your mind on the things that put that spark in your eye a moment ago, and don't think of nothing else."

"I'll do that, Mr. Brown. But just to be sure, I'd like to go ahead and give you my letter."

"No. I don't want it. You give it to me once we reach the end."

"But if something should happen . . ."

"There you go, talking that way again. You see, this way you *have* to make it through to the end, so you can give me the letter."

Cline pursed his lips. "Treating me a little like a child, aren't you, Mr. Brown?"

"Only because you've been talking childish talk."

"See it how you want, sir. But if . . . if something *should* happen, the letter will be in my pack."

"Go lie down, Mr. Cline. Get some sleep."

Cline nodded. "Right. Yes. About the letter . . . thank you."

"Thanks accepted."

Cline headed back for his own resting place.

"Oh . . . Mr. Cline . . ."

"Yes?"

Greeley lowered his voice. "I'd . . . well, I'd not be so inclined to speak so freely about your abolition beliefs and such. There's plenty who begrudge that kind of talk. Not many folk in these parts hold a very high view of the coloreds." He glanced toward McDermott, who had laid back down but did not seem to be sleeping.

Cline replied, "Believe me, sir, I'm aware of the unpopularity of my views."

"Right. And sometimes a man gets by better keeping some of his beliefs to himself."

"Indeed, Mr. Brown." Cline studied him through the thick lenses of his glasses. "I daresay you're no abolitionist yourself. Am I right?"

"I ain't give it much thought. I reckon it ain't my concern either way."

"I see." Cline smiled knowingly to himself in a way that Greeley found vaguely insulting. *Dang moral types always think theirselves better than the average man,* he thought.

He lay down, thinking about the letter Cline was so worked up about having delivered. What kind of woman would he have, especially at a place like Josiah House? An odd one, probably. She'd have to be odd to link herself up with a strange fellow like him. Strange, and an abolitionist to boot! Greeley had encountered few authentic specimens of that rare breed. He'd known only one other fellow he suspected strongly was an abolitionist, that being young Sam Colter, who had started out as his piloting partner. Unlike Cline, Sam kept his views mostly to himself. Also unlike Cline, he didn't have a holy attitude about himself.

Tired though he was, Greeley decided a final check of the rebel situation was called for. He rose and crept to a place where he could see down onto the dirt roadway below without being spotted himself. A handful of uniformed, mounted Confederates rode by, trailed by a drummer boy doing his best to keep up with the striding horses. Greeley shook his head. More rebels about than he had encountered while guiding prior stampede journeys.

He went back to his blankets and lay down, wondering if maybe Spencer Cline's pessimism was more reasonable than he wanted to admit. Maybe Cline wouldn't make it . . . maybe none of them would.

Below, the drummer boy began beating his drum, pounding out a steady military cadence as he paced along behind the mounted soldiers. Greeley put his hands over his ears. Rebel drums always sounded like the music of hell to him, bringing to mind chains and hangings and firing squads. He waited until the drumming was distant and faint, then unstopped his ears, closed his eyes and let his aching bones settle into the earth as sleep came on.

Chapter 4

Greeley got his stampeders across the road come night-fall, but felt he had surely scared himself out of another year or two of life in doing it.

They had moved along the ridge until they found a place where the rebel guard camps were far apart, and crossed directly between two of them, the light of the guard fires flickering within their view on both sides. Scarcely had they made it over the road when the sound of oncoming horses sent them all flat onto their stomachs in the roadside brush. At least ten mounted Confederates rode past, one acciden-tally veering off the road and into the brush, passing directly over Ivy McDermott, who was last across. Had one of the horse's hooves found any portion of McDermott's body, not even so strong-willed a man as he would have been able to stifle a yell. They had been lucky, and Greeley knew it.

As soon as the rebels were past, the stampeders came to their feet and plunged into the woods beyond the road, run-ning so hard that branches and brush grabbed their clothing and pulled hats from their heads. Greeley smelled near-panic among his men and knew they would not heed any command to halt. The only thing to do was run with them.

The deeper they plunged into the woods, the more panic declined. Finally they all stopped, waiting for hearts to pound more slowly and breath to come more lightly. "We sounded like a buffalo herd, running like that," Greeley said, gasping. "We're blasted lucky the rebs didn't hear." It was all the chiding he felt inclined to give. He'd been as scared as any of them.

"I almost got stepped on," Ivy McDermott said.

"I know. I saw it. Now come on. Let's put some space between us and them rebels."

"Where we heading?"

"For Clinch Mountain. Let's go."

Clinch Mountain was more than a mountain, really; it was a long, high ridge lying like a great spiny snake with its head in southwestern Virginia and its tail almost at Knoxville. This ridge was virtually unbroken, its only significant gap being at Estillville, southwest of the current location of Greeley's band.

The stampeders hiked along the mountain base, paused in a deep hollow for a half hour or so of rest in the deepest part of the night, then began their ascent, Greeley leading. Memory of the close encounter earlier on the rebel-guarded road made the difficult climb less intimidating, though each knew that similar dangers lay beyond the ridge.

Partway up the mountain, they found a good sheltered spot, and there yielded to exhaustion, thirst, and hunger, settling down to wait out the rest of the night. Greeley didn't begrudge this cessation of progress. The evening's difficulties had drained the energy and spirit from them all. And they were in a region more remote and untraveled than any they had passed through so far, meaning they could reasonably risk travel over the mountain come daylight. At the moment rest was of more value than progress.

Those that had food remaining brought it out and shared it with their fellows. Ivy McDermott was among those who had already eaten up their own provisions, but Cline shared with him. McDermott seemed reluctant to accept it. Greeley knew why. McDermott had overheard Cline's abolitionist talk, and seemed the kind to despise abolitionists as much as he probably despised the race whose welfare was the abolitionist's concern.

Daylight found them all sleeping beneath the trees. Greeley awakened first and roused the others. The prospect of actually being able to *see* the way ahead cheered them all enough to overcome the natural dread of travel in such rugged terrain, and they pressed up and across the mountain, eating up most of the day with their passage.

Traveling down the north slope, Greeley recalled the time he and Sam Colter had led an early band of stampeders, and found on this very mountainside a poor lone fellow with a wounded and infected hand that they had been forced to cut off just to save his life. What had been that man's name? Greeley didn't remember. It all seemed very long ago, though in fact it had been mere months back. Greeley had observed that wartime had a way of doing that to his mind. Events seemed to move with unusual speed into the darker corners of memory, to seem more remote than they should, sooner than they should.

In mid-afternoon the journeyers reached a remote spot with a splendid, far-ranging view, and there stopped to eat and rest, awaiting darkness. A stretch of valley traveling lay ahead. Greeley dreaded it. In the valleys they were the most vulnerable, the most easily captured.

Night carried them across Poor Valley, over Copper Ridge and through Copper Creek. More laborious journeying across hills and forested terrain brought them to deep-running Clinch River. They stripped, tied their clothing and packs to the ends of sticks, and plunged in, holding the sticks up like banner poles. The water was so high that most had to turn their faces up to keep their noses above water, and the current threatened to sweep them away, yet somehow they made the cold crossing without losing a man or even a bundle of clothing. Once over, they ran into the woods and continued on a mile without even pausing to dress, just in case any had seen them. Greeley eventually decided they were safe, and allowed them to stop.

Putting on their clothing, they aimed for Powell Mountain. "Getting close enough to Kentucky to smell it,"

McDermott said, the encouraging words bringing forth positive commentary from the others. Greeley welcomed this brightening of spirits, but wasn't about to become overly hopeful yet. They still had Powell Valley to face beyond the mountain, where they would be in the greatest danger so far.

Powell Mountain loomed before them; they began picking their way up its side, ants on a vast boulder. This was the hardest exertion yet to Greeley, and harder still for the less experienced men following him. Time and again he turned and took a quick voice count of those there, making sure none had collapsed in the rear and been left. Each time the count revealed all still present, but weak and quavering voices revealed how swiftly they were moving toward hopeless exhaustion. Greeley pitied them, yet forced them on, ever a little farther and then a little farther again, until they reached a small, level meadow on the mountainside and found a pool of water. They collapsed around it, drinking, moaning, feeling pain like few of them had known before. Complaints and moans of suffering rose in the grove, countered only by the stern remonstrance of Ivy McDermott, who had known much of hard living and wilderness existence over the past months and had no patience for weakness.

Greeley stretched his legs, rubbing his feet, and glanced at Spencer Cline. The man looked miserable, almost deathly tired, yet he managed a weak smile back at his guide. "Told you that you could keep going," Greeley said, smiling back.

There was virtually no food left. Once it was divided among them all, each man made do with about three meager bites. "Just enough to remind a man he's starved," Jim McCloud observed.

They did not move from that place all the following day. Though without food, they at least had water and a safe place to rest, and as best they could they readied themselves for the further exertions ahead.

Night came and they went on, crossing the mountain and heading down its far slope. A tiring climb faced them as they reached rugged Wallin's Ridge. They were approaching dangerous country, heavy with rebels, but about this they thought little, concentrating instead on the more immediate challenge of the climb.

They reached the top of Wallin's Ridge. Powell Valley lay ahead. Greeley looked down upon it in a weary slump, rifle in hand, knapsack heavy on his back despite its near emptiness, heart even heavier in his chest. The valley by night looked like an expanse of rumpled black velvet over which sparks had been strewn.

"Why so many fires in the valley?" Cline asked at Greeley's side.

McDermott answered before Greeley could open his mouth. "Because there's so many cussed rebs, fool! Them's Confederate campfires, every one of them."

Greeley said, "Mr. McDermott, I'd be obliged if you'd not insult your fellows here. We're together in this, all of us, and it's together we'll have to make it through this valley."

"And how do you propose we do that, Mr. Brown?" another man asked.

"One step at a time, that's how. We'll avoid the fires, be careful crossing the roads, stay in the darkest and emptiest parts . . . that's all we can do. And hope we don't run upon dogs. I swear, sometimes I believe half the dogs in the world live in this valley."

They picked their way down the ridge side, moving into the valley in the somber and frightened spirit of children passing by some reputedly haunted graveyard.

" 'Yea, though I walk through the valley of the shadow of death . . .' " someone in the group whispered.

"Hush up!" Greeley demanded. "No talk beyond what's necessary."

They put a mile behind them. Rebel fires burned on both sides of them now, and voices and occasional ragged laughter drifted in the breeze from the camps. From time to time the stampeders heard horses on the move, men riding; then they would freeze in place, or drop to the ground if there was time, fearing even to breathe. The riders would pass on by. Each time, Greeley was sure someone would hear or see, and they would be caught. He thanked God for creating darkness, virtually the only thing at the moment that his hungry and worn-down band of stampeders could view as an ally.

Greeley appreciated the darkness for more than its protection. It kept his own followers from seeing his face and the look of uncertainty upon it. He was picking his way along at this point, well off the course he usually followed through this valley. The placement of the rebel campfires had forced him to veer northeast.

They came upon a road unexpectedly, simply walked right out onto it. A break in the clouds above let moonlight spill through at that moment and revealed their situation: to their right, the road humped up in a blind hill; to their left, it cambered off to the left, creating an equally blind curve. Greeley felt like he was caught naked in a public place; at any second a rebel patrol might ride over that hill or around that curve and catch them there.

Crossing the road took no more than ten or fifteen seconds, but when they hit the tree line on the other side, they encountered a crude, irregular, but very tall fence made of rails nailed onto the trunks of saplings. One man struck it so hard it knocked him back like a child's air-filled toy bladder rebounding off a barn wall. He hit the ground with a grunt and lay there stunned.

They heard the sound of an approaching rider coming over the hill—he would be upon them in a moment . . . and they were all in plain view.

"Down!" Greeley ordered as loudly as he dared. "Drop to the ground!" Setting the example, he fell facedown by the roadside, wishing the worst kinds of ill fortune upon whomever had built that tall plank fence.

Not one stampeder followed Greeley's example. Panic had struck them like a cold wind. Some scrambled for the fence, climbing upon it three and four men at a time, breaking down rails and falling clumsily in all directions. Three made it over and darted into the forest beyond, generating quite a racket as they ripped along through the brush.

Others ran in the opposite direction, back across the road. But fully half the men were still in view on the moonlit road when the rider came across the hill. They could make nothing out of him except his dimly limned form. One of the

stampeders yelled in fright; the horse spooked and reared.
The rider fought to remain in his saddle. Greeley came to
his feet and took the precaution of raising his rifle in case
this man proved dangerous. He sighted as best he could in
the dark, but the rider's figure kept bouncing around on the
bucking horse, and Greeley could not hold his target. Then
one of his own men ran into Greeley and knocked him down
hard, trampling right across him in a mad race for the fence.
Greeley dropped the rifle.

The rider was swearing and shouting, as frightened as the
stampeders. Greeley came again to his feet and ran right at
the man, not sure just what he intended to do but feeling
compelled to try something, anything. The bucking horse
veered toward him, almost kicking him in the face. He
reached out, grasped its halter, and managed to bring its
bucking under control.

The rider slid from the saddle and fell to his knees beside
Greeley. He lifted gnarled, clasped hands. Greeley saw he
was no soldier, but merely an old man, probably some
valley farmer frightened out of his wits by the phantoms of
flesh and blood he had encountered on this lonely road.

"Oh, please, sir, please, don't bushwhack me!" the old
man pleaded. "I got nothing, nothing at all but this horse
and the rifle, and you can take both! I'm no partisan, sir. I
treat both sides equal and don't want trouble with neither!
Spare me, sir, I beg you!"

Greeley felt such a wave of relief he laughed. The old
man seemingly found something diabolical in the laughter,
buried his face in his hands and started to weep. Greeley
reached down, put his hand on the gray-mopped head and
made the man look up at him.

"We ain't bushwhackers, mister. We ain't going to hurt
you. Just you don't betray us—you hear? You betray us,
and we won't be friendly at all."

"No sir, no sir, I won't betray you. Oh, thank you, sir.
Thank you for not being no bushwhacker."

"You live around here, old fellow?"

"Yes, I do, I do indeed, not half a mile up this road."

"Are there soldiers about?"

"Lots of them, sir, lots of them, but none between here and my home, as I know of."

"I'm glad to hear it," Greeley said. "Old man, you're going to host us tonight—if ever I can round up my men. We're hungry and tired, in need of food and shelter."

"What are you, sir, if I might ask? Union or Secesh?"

"I'll ask you the same."

"I told you, sir, I take no side. I'm neutral."

"Ain't nobody left these days that's neutral. Tell me straight out: What are you, old man?"

"Well, sir, I admit I lean toward Jefferson Davis's side of things. My sons, all three of them, they're wearing the gray and butternut, off in Virginia. But if you're Union, I'll not hold that against you, not a bit. I can see the Union side too, indeed I can."

Greeley was glad to know this fellow's leanings, though he would have preferred that he leaned in the other direction. Either way, though, he perceived that in this scared old codger he had found a potential source of help.

"We're Confederates ourselves," Greeley said, playing it safe. "Under Colonel Slemp, or so we're supposed to be, but we're weary of this army life and worried about our families. We asked for leave and they wouldn't give it—so we took our leave ourselves, and that's why we don't want none of them catching us."

"I don't blame you, sir, I truly don't. God knows I wish my own boys would do the same as you and come home. I fear for their welfare every day and pray for them every night."

"You'll feed us, then?"

"I will, as best I can."

"Then get up from there, old fellow. Show us the way to your house, and no tricks."

"How many of you are there?"

Greeley looked around. "There was fifteen or so, but all I can make out just now is eight . . . no, nine. God only knows where the others have run off to. No, wait, I see them coming back in through the woods."

The old man rose creakingly. "Follow me, Mister . . ."

"Smith. That's all the name needs knowing. Just Smith."

"It's a fine name, Smith," the old man said. "Fine name. And if your name is Smith, then mine is Jones."

Greeley nodded. It appeared they understood one another. He wasn't sure the fellow could be trusted, but sometimes all a man could do was follow the strongest of his gut feelings, and at the moment that happened to be gnawing physical hunger.

He said, "Lead the way to your house, Mr. Jones. We're right behind you. Me, my men, and my rifle."

In the mountains of
Madison County, North Carolina

He felt that he'd been running forever. Ten minutes ago he was certain he could run not a step farther. One more exertion, one more pace, and he would collapse and die, his heart bursting in his chest. But he'd run anyway, despite exhaustion and the ache inside of him, and the blood that spilled from the superficial bullet would in his side. The wound had hurt when it was first inflicted, but now there was no pain in it at all, or perhaps it was merely that the pain of throbbing muscles, hammering heart, and aching lungs was so great that the other vanished in comparison.

He stopped now, because this time he truly could not go another step. Dropping to his knees beside a fallen tree, panting, and vocalizing with each pant though he tried not to, he laid his head over on the rotting, mossy bark and closed his eyes, sucking in air. His heart slammed against his ribs.

Less than a minute passed before he heard them. Still coming, still pursuing. Whimpering in fear and suffering, he forced unwilling leg muscles to push him up again. He paused only a moment to examine the amount of blood coming from the bullet wound. It was flowing as richly as ever, staining him all the way down his left side.

He went on, heading up the ridge. How many ridges were there between himself and his home? Three . . . no, two, only two! For the first time he felt hope, slim though it was. If he could keep going long enough, he could reach his house, barricade himself inside.

No . . . that wouldn't do. They would burn the cabin down, or riddle it with gunfire. Mabel and the children were there; they might be hurt.

But still he ran, still aiming for his house because there was no other place to go. Maybe he would get there in time to fetch his rifle and shotgun. He could take the guns with him up to the ridge beyond the cabin and fight it out with his pursuers there. Mabel and the children could get away, hide in the woods until the bushwhackers were done with him and rode on. . . .

Cree Henderson gripped his side and ran, hearing the hoofbeats slamming, muffled, against the forest floor somewhere in the trees behind.

He crossed the ridge with lungs threatening to burst, then fell and rolled halfway down the far side. It was hard to rise, harder than anything he'd ever done, but he made it. Staggering down the rest of the way, he began running up the next and final ridge when he heard them thunder up onto the ridge top he'd just crossed.

"There he is!" It was Swaney's voice, unmistakable. The most hated voice Cree Henderson knew. "He's heading for his cabin!"

Someone fired at him; the bullet slapped the treetop above him. He ran harder. Another shot popped and his right leg went out from under him. He looked at it and saw it was bleeding and broken. The ball had entered just below his right knee and snapped the bones cleanly in two.

He groaned and pushed up, dragging the wounded leg behind him. He saw the cabin. "Bryant!" He tried to holler the name, that of his eldest son, but his voice failed him. He tried again, with more success. "Bryant! Fetch the rifle, Bryant!" Then he wondered what kind of man he was and what he could have been thinking, calling for a boy of eleven years to come out with a rifle while bushwhackers approached. They would kill Bryant as quickly as if he were full grown.

"No, Bryant! Stay inside!" he called. 'Don't come out!" But he saw the door moving, Bryant coming out onto the porch, rifle in hand. "No!" Henderson yelled, staggering now, unable to run. "Go back inside!" But Bryant came outside anyway.

"Throw me . . . throw me the rifle!" Henderson could barely get out the words.

Bryant stood frozen, rifle in hand, as his father collapsed twenty feet from the porch and a band of armed horsemen rode into the yard behind him.

"Drop the rifle, boy!" Colonel Merriman Swaney ordered, lifting his pistol and aiming it at the boy.

Cree Henderson rolled onto his back and looked through bloodshot eyes at his pursuers. "Leave him be! You got me . . . leave my boy alone!"

"Have him drop that rifle, then."

"Put it down, Bryant," Henderson pleaded. "Please just put it down and go back inside." He twisted his head and saw his son letting the rifle slide down to the porch at his feet. He stepped back, but stopped, and ran forward. "Pa!" he cried. "Pa, what are they going to do?"

Henderson expected to hear shots and to see his boy fall, but for some reason the bushwhackers held fire. Bryant dropped to his knees at his fallen father's side and wrapped his arms around his neck.

"Go back, boy . . . go inside . . ."

Merriman Swaney rode his horse over close and looked down at father and son. "Move away, boy."

Bryant Henderson reluctantly let go, stood, backed away. Swaney turned and motioned to one of his men, the same lean young man to whom he had spoken the day of the McCormick burial. The man heeled his horse and rode up beside the bushwhacker chieftain, looking down at the panting, bleeding Cree Henderson.

"Is this the man who murdered Millard McCormick in cold blood, before your eyes?"

"It is, Colonel."

"You know it to a moral certainty?"

"Yes, sir. That's him, no question."

Henderson pleaded, "I didn't murder him—he had a gun, was threatening me! I swear it!"

"Did you see a gun in Millard McCormick's possession when he was murdered?"

"No, sir. He was unarmed. That man on the ground there shot him down when he was returning to camp from the woods. Millard McCormick had gone to the latrine there, sir, and had not a weapon about him when he was shot."

"Can you rise, Cree Henderson?" Swaney asked.

"No . . . I'm hurting bad. Please, have mercy on me!"

"We'll have no mercy. We are not in the business of mercy. But your hurting will soon end." Swaney twisted his head and turned to the mounted men behind him. "I need a rope up here! I want this man tied under the shoulders for dragging."

The cabin door opened; Henderson's wife stepped out with a shotgun in hand. Swaney drew his pistol and leveled it at her. "Drop the weapon, ma'am, or I'll kill you before your children."

She sobbed, trembled, and let the shotgun fall. "Oh, Cree!" she said, sinking to her haunches on the porch. "Cree!"

The rope was produced and looped around Cree Henderson's chest, pulled tight under his arms. Swaney tied the other end to his saddle horn. They dragged him away, and the staunchest among them had to admire Cree Henderson for enduring the torment without a scream.

The lean bushwhacker looked behind as the cabin receded. "The boy's following, sir," he said.

"Let him follow," Swaney said. "It will be a fine lesson for him, not to follow in his father's ways."

They dragged the half-conscious man out of sight of the cabin and into a clearing, and removed the rope from his chest.

"Over that limb should do it," Colonel Swaney said.

The hanging wasn't easily accomplished, Henderson being in the shape he was, but with effort they made it work. Swaney himself led the horse out from under the doomed man, who sat astride it with noose around his neck and his hands tied. Death came slowly, with much choking.

"Justice is done," Swaney said. "Millard McCormick, you are avenged."

Before the bushwhackers rode away, the one who had identified Henderson turned and looked at the edge of the clearing. Young Bryant Henderson stared back at him, tears in his eyes, hate in his expression. He had watched it all. The bushwhacker held his gaze a moment, then turned and rode out after the others. Somehow he managed to stifle his heaves and hold back from vomiting until he was out of the boy's view.

Chapter 5

The stampeders sat crowded into the little log and clapboard house of "Jones," gathered around his table with rumps nestled on anything that would bear a man's weight. The old fellow got a few glances from his distrustful guests, but only a few. There were far more interesting things here than he.

Old "Jones" had five buxom, fine-looking young daughters who, along with their fat old mother, were serving up a meal so fine not a man of the fugitive band could have imagined anything better on the dining tables of heaven itself. Never mind that it was mostly leftovers and that the pork was cold and coated with hardened grease. The men ate with fevered appreciation, eyes shifting around the room, following the flow and sweep of the beautiful femininity orbiting around them.

The young women, clad in nightgowns and bonnets with shawls thrown over their shoulders or tied skirtlike around their waists to add a touch of modesty, seemed to be enjoying the provision of service quite as much as the men enjoyed the reception of it. The eldest daughter, a plumpish but pretty married woman who had introduced herself as

Mary Samuels, formerly Mary Poteet—thus betraying the true surname of "Jones" before the old man could stop her—had taken charge and was flitting about like a hostess in some big-city restaurant, talking all the while about the "honor" of serving "men who have stood against the wicked Lincolnites." The men nodded and agreed with her. McDermott revealed a new aspect of himself—an almost impish sense of humor—telling Mary Poteet how right she was about the Yankees and their southern sympathizers; how in fact she, as a well-bred young woman, didn't know the half of Lincolnite wickedness, and how such a houseful of beautiful women had best watch out for themselves if the Union army ever swept into the region.

"I can speak for myself and my sisters when I say that I would sooner die than let a Lincolnite so much as touch my hand," the young woman declared, face blushing with anger. "I would as soon let my lips touch those of the blackest buck slave as those of a heathen Lincolnite. I'm proud to say that my own husband, my dearest Ollie, is off at Richmond with my brothers, serving the noble cause. It is only to true patriots of the South that I and my sisters will give heart and hand."

"Why, let's drink to dearest Ollie, then," McDermott said as solemnly as a preacher, raising his cracked mug of water. "May dearest Ollie serve the South long and well, and never get shot nor bayoneted by no Union bluebelly. May he not take the measles nor the pox, and may the worms shun his bowels and the lice his topknot. May he never be blown apart nor blinded by no Union cannonball burst, nor may he starve in no Union hellhole prison. May Ollie's bones never go to dust in some distant battlefield trench, nor the birds peck him while he lays a corpse. Here's to dearest Ollie. Long life to him, and to Jefferson Davis!" He tilted back his cup and drained it, water leaking out of either side of his mouth and washing grime out of his beard and down his neck.

As McDermott reeled off his toast, several of his fellows had to lower their heads a moment to hide smiles. But all managed the proper solemnity as they raised cups and gravely drank to the absentee husband, while the wife stood looking on with a feeble smile that said she didn't know quite what to make of a toast like this one.

Greeley was not at the table but standing by the door, nibbling a slab of pork wedged into a cold biscuit. He winced and shot a withering look at McDermott when he heard the toast. Much more of that mischievous talk risked destroying their pretense of southern loyalty.

The patriarch of the family tugged at Greeley's sleeve; Greeley turned and looked into angry eyes. "Sir, I don't appreciate your man's talking like that, all this about the bad things can happen to a soldier. My gal, she worries enough as it is. What's he trying to do? Scare her more?"

Greeley slipped an arm over the man's shoulder and drew him close to receive a surreptitious whisper. "Pay him no heed, Mr. Poteet . . . Mr. Jones, I mean. The poor man's not right in the head. A whole big charge of powder blew up in his face a while back, and his mind has been ruint ever since. See them scars on his face? It's from that powder blast. All he thinks about now is getting hurt and killed and so on. He didn't mean nothing bad, saying all them dreadful things."

"Well . . . I'll forgive it, in that case. But I don't much like it."

"I don't fault you for not liking it, sir. I'll have a word with him and see if I can't get him to do at least some better."

"Why you keep peeping out the door, Mr. Smith?"

"It's because I've still got a man missing," was Greeley's truthful reply. After scattering in panic on the road, all his band had come back together again on the way here—all but Spencer Cline. He'd been among those to go over the fence and headlong into the woods, and no one had seen him since.

"What do you aim to do if he don't appear?"

"Don't know. Can't spend my time looking for him. If we're caught as deserters, that'll be hell to pay for us with Colonel Slemp."

One of the young women approached and took Greeley

by the arm, pulling him toward the table. "Set yourself down and rest a bit," she said. "Ain't good to eat standing up. It sours the belly."

Greeley took a last glance out the door, then complied with the invitation. He took the only empty seat remaining, a nail keg, and scooted in beside McDermott.

"Any sign of Spectacles?" McDermott asked a few moments later beneath his breath and behind the masking noise of loud conversation going on around the table.

"No. I fear we've lost him."

McDermott bit off a chunk of pork, settled it into his jaw, and whispered between chews, "Well, it's harsh of me to say it, maybe, but I don't care. I didn't like him no-how. I heard him talking that abolition bilge to you. Let him fend for hisself, that's what I say. At least the rest of us are all right."

"We may not be all right much longer if you don't watch your tongue better than you have so far this evening," Greeley whispered. "You nearly give us away with that toast of yours. That poor gal didn't know what to make of hearing you reel off all them bad things that could happen to her man. I believe she nigh saw it for the mockery it was, and I know her pap was angered by it. Now I'm going to have to keep an eye on him all night to make sure he don't go slipping off while we're asleep to fetch soldiers on to us."

"You worry too much," McDermott replied. "But I'll mind my tongue—though God knows it's hard to keep quiet, hearing all this 'Lincolnite' talk. I hope that gal's husband *does* get blowed up or shot down. I hate the rebs. Purely hate them. Every reb that dies, the world's a bit better."

"Caesar Augustus! Not so loud!" Greeley glanced around at his host and hostesses, grinning. "Good victuals, folks. Mighty good."

"Glad you like it, sir," Mary Samuels said. "Giving good southern men food makes me feel I'm doing my part to help my dear Ollie." She paused, her eyes filling. "Oh, I miss him! I hope he's not been shot, or blinded, or took prisoner!"

"God watches out for them who fight on his side," Greeley replied.

"Here's to Ollie Samuels, hero of the South and fighter of the Lord's battles!" McDermott raised his cup again.

"To Ollie Samuels!" the others declared, and Greeley went along because he could do nothing else. They drank and went back to their food, the young women hovering all around. Greeley ate more slowly than the rest, keeping his eye on the door and wondering what had become of Spencer Cline.

The next day felt longer by six hours than the normal day, and McDermott made the hours all the more tense by his continual grim and pointed jokes. He managed to reduce Mrs. Ollie Samuels to tears three times before darkness fell, and on the third occasion Greeley was hard-pressed to keep her father convinced that McDermott was in fact "witless" and not merely trying to toy with Mary's feelings.

Greeley, like most stampeder pilots, performed his service for a fee, payable in advance, and out of his pocket he covered the expenses of the group, paying the household twelve dollars for the food they all had consumed, and a bit extra besides to cover the cost of some cornmeal and bacon for their journey. Bidding the family farewell, and with McDermott telling Mary Samuels in parting that he'd keep "praying for Ollie every night, that he won't be snakebit nor afflicted with the night blindness from eating bad food," the stampeders left the cabin to continue their fugitive pilgrimage across Powell Valley.

Greeley made a point of watching to see that their former host didn't follow them. He was more sure than ever that Poteet had realized their claim to be rebel deserters was untrue, and even yet might turn the Confederates upon them. But he detected no sign of anyone following. The stampeders traveled without incident through the woods alongside the road upon which they had met the old man, and came at length to the place where the encounter and the wild scramble over the fence had happened.

Here they turned right and headed deeper into the forest,

some of those who had scrambled through here the night
before pointing out places they had hidden or stumbled.
"And right yonder," said one of them, "is the place I last
saw Mr. Cline running. He was scared like I ain't never seen
no man scared before, whimpering over how he'd lost his
glasses and the rebs was going to kill him."

"You say he ran that direction?" Greeley asked.

"That's right."

"Hold on here a minute. I'm going to go look."

"Why, he wouldn't still be hiding hereabouts, would
he?"

"Maybe. He might have been too scared to leave the
woods." Greeley picked his way through a thicket, in it
finding a shred of cloth torn from a woolen shirt. He thought
back . . . yes, Cline had been wearing wool. Farther on yet
and beyond the thicket he kicked something in the darkness
and found it to be Cline's pack.

Greeley held the pack under his arm and looked about.
Darkness was thick. He risked a soft call: "Mr. Cline?
Spencer Cline! Are you about? It's me, Greeley Brown."

No answer. Greeley shook his head. It appeared he was
going to have to forget about Spencer Cline. The entire
group couldn't be endangered for one man's sake. He wondered if Cline had been captured by a rebel patrol. If so, he
might have broken under questioning, revealed that he was
a stampeder, revealed the Greeley name and role, and the
names of others. . . .

Unnerved by these thoughts, Greeley turned to head back
through the thicket to the waiting men, more eager than ever
to make it through this last valley and up to the final range
of mountains. As he turned, however, he caught the faintest
glimpse of something, a vaguely human shape that delin-
eated itself more clearly the harder he stared. A man, it
appeared, standing silently beside a tree not ten feet to
Greeley's right.

"Mr. Cline?"

Silence, like that of a tomb. Greeley felt the back of his
neck grow tight and cold. "I say, Mr. Cline? Is that you? If
not, then who are you? Speak up—I've got a repeating rifle
here."

Again no reply. Greeley was overcome by a most uncanny feeling. Something was amiss here, numinous and strange. He probed his rifle out before him and advanced slowly upon the standing figure. Still no movement, no sound. No noise of breath or whisper of life. Greeley knew the man was dead by the time he reached his side. Feeling that ancient, innate human awe roused by the near presence of the dead, Greeley reached a tremoring hand into his coat pocket and produced a match case. Striking a flame was somewhat dangerous, close as he was to a road upon which rebels patrolled, but he had to confirm this was Cline and determine what had happened to him. Slipping off the lid of the match case, he removed a match, struck it on the case's rough bottom, and lit the tiny candle embedded in a holder built into the side of the match compartment. Shaking out the match, he lifted the little candle and illuminated the figure against the tree.

Spencer Cline stood facing the tree, a maple that forked just at neck level. His face was wedged between the forks, so that the fork held him by the chin, which accounted for the body remaining upright even though he was dead. His eyes were open, two dull marbles reflecting candlelight.

"Poor young fellow," Greeley muttered. But he was puzzled as to what had actually killed Cline. Was it possible for a man to die of pure fright? If so, the tremorous Cline would have been a good candidate for such a fate.

Greeley held the match case by its bottom in his teeth, tilting up his head so the matches wouldn't spill, ignoring the hot drip of candle wax into his beard. He freed Cline's chin from the pinching tree fork. Surprisingly, the body still did not fold and fall. Taking the match case in hand again, Greeley examined the upright body closely, beginning at the head and moving down toward the feet. About half-way down he squinted, looking closely. Straightening, he put one hand on Cline's shoulder and gave a gentle back-ward push.

Cline's body tilted back, stayed poised that way for a moment, then fell to the ground. Candlelight spilled onto the sharp, broken shard of limb upon which Cline had impaled himself. He had simply run upon the sharp stob in the darkness, ramming it so deep into his torso that it had almost come out the other side of him.

"Caesar Augustus!" Greeley murmured. "You picked a sorry way to die, Mr. Cline."

Greeley looked down a few moments more at the crumpled body, noting the dried and brown blood that covered almost every inch of him below the point of the wound. The poor fellow had probably knocked himself cold when he hit the tree, and bled to death slowly as he hung skewered and senseless.

Cline had been right all along. He really had been destined not to make it.

"I wish I could bury you," Greeley whispered to the dead man. "But I'm afraid I'm going to have to leave you where you are. There's just nothing else to be done. I'm sorry."

Shaking his head, he blew out the candle, put the lid back onto the match case, picked up his rifle and Cline's pack, and headed back toward the waiting stampeders on the far side of the thicket.

Chapter 6

Cumberland Mountain,
near the Virginia-Kentucky border

Greeley Brown paused for a few moments simply to gaze up at the high outline of the Cumberland Mountain, dimly visible against the dark sky. Since the Confederates had turned East Tennessee into the kind of place a Union man longed to leave, seldom did Greeley see that blessed, long, stony-topped ridge without having to fight back tears. So it was now. He knew what this mountain meant, what it marked. Beyond it lay the officially neutral but Union-dominated state of Kentucky, a promised land for men such as those with him, who had lived as refugees in their own homeland for so long that Kentucky had become an almost mythic, mystical place in their minds, as it had, for other reasons, to their ancestors of a century before.

"Is that it, Mr. Brown?"

"That's it indeed. That's the Cumberland Mountain there, and beyond that high ridge is our destination."

"Thanks be to God. And to you too, Greeley Brown."

"*Waaaugh!* I'm cold, gentleman. And damp. Wouldn't mind a good drying. What do you say we build us a fire?"

They were all as sodden and chilled as Greeley was, having

waded the Powell River before beginning the final hike toward Kentucky.

"Is it safe?"

"Safer than staying cold when you're as weary and run-down as we are. We'll all get sick as dogs if we don't warm ourselves up some. We're past the real danger of rebels, I believe."

The blaze, once fully built up and stoked, was beautiful to see and feel. The men dried their clothing and gazed into the flames, letting relief bathe over them with the heat. A few made cakes of water and cornmeal and baked them on heated flat rocks, while others whittled out sharpened green sticks upon which they impaled slabs of bacon to roast above the blaze. The sizzle and scent of the dripping fat was almost fine enough to bring tears.

"I have to say, Mr. Brown, that you've done for us just what we asked," McDermott said. "You've brought us to the very borders of Kentucky. I reckon you've earned your money."

"I'll not consider the task finished until I've put you safe into the hands of the Union army," Greeley replied. "And the fact is that I won't have fully succeeded even then. I've lost a man. For the first time, I've lost a man who put himself into my care."

McDermott replied, "What you lost was a darky-loving abolitionist who was fool enough to run hisself against a sharp stick in the dark. Warn't your fault, Mr. Brown."

"An *abolitionist*?" another asked. "Is that what you said?"

"It's true," McDermott answered. "I heard him say so with his own mouth. Spectacles Cline was an abolitionist straight out. Acted *proud* of it, too!"

"He was a fool, then. I'm loyal to the Union, but I've got no use for a bunch of freed darkies running around, taking work from white men, and I regret that Mr. Lincoln has made that an aim of his war," the other man said.

"Gentlemen, I'd much appreciate it if you wouldn't talk bad about Mr. Cline, now that he's dead," Greeley said.

"Where was he from, anyhow?"

"Sevierville," Greeley replied.

"That's your town, ain't it, Freddie?" The question came from Jim McCloud, aimed at the man who had just vented his low view of abolitionists.

"That's right," Freddie Ogle replied. "But I never knew this Cline fellow."

"That surprises me," Greeley said. "He was a lawyer, so you figure his name would be known."

"A lawyer! In Sevierville?"

"That's what he told me."

"No, no. He was telling you a tale, Mr. Brown. I know every lawyer in Sevierville. There ain't none of them named Spencer Cline."

Greeley frowned, puzzled. Why would Cline have lied to him? Or maybe he hadn't; maybe Freddie Ogle simply thought he knew all of Sevierville's attorneys.

It didn't really matter now, of course. Spencer Cline, whoever he was, whatever he'd been, was dead and gone. Whether he had been running to, or running from, made little difference. For him the running was over, forever.

They rested out the remnant of the night around the fire, sleeping long past sunrise in the morning and not getting on the move again until about ten o'clock. Greeley took a good look at his band in the bright morning light. What a bedraggled group they were! Ragged, thin, emaciated, unwashed and uncombed—yet they had an energy and fire about them today despite their poor condition. They were almost on Union-held ground. The ordeals they had endured on their own home ground were almost over.

The actual passage over the line into Kentucky came in mid-afternoon and generated celebration from some, tears of relief from others. A few knelt and kissed the soil. One or two preached sermons toward the south, chiding the rebels for their wickedness and swearing to be part of an anticipated righteous vengeance against them. McDermott gave no sermon, merely stood on a rock and flung obscenities and curses at a government he had put behind him. A subtle man he wasn't.

For his part, Greeley held his silence, but breathed more

easily than he had in weeks. Though he himself would soon return to rebel-held East Tennessee, at least those who entrusted themselves to him had made it safely across the line. All, of course, but Spencer Cline.

He declined to dwell on that matter. There was still traveling to be done. It was not enough merely to be on Kentucky soil. The stampeders needed the refuge of the Union army, who would welcome their service. Many a Tennessee Union man wore Union blue on Kentucky soil these days, and each had one eye always turned south toward the home he longed to see freed from Confederate control.

Greeley had thought about donning a Union uniform a time or two himself, becoming a regular soldier. So far he'd resisted the impulse, not out of any cowardice, but because Union military leaders, in particular Colonel Daniel Stover, had confirmed to him many times that he was performing a far more effective service as a civilian stampeder pilot and unofficial recruiting officer than he would as a regular enlisted man. As a civilian, Greeley enjoyed a certain independence of decision and motion that he would not have possessed working under a chain of military command. He moved outside official channels, making his living from the fees paid him by those he piloted, shuttling back and forth like a shadow across rebel territory. It was a trying and dangerous life, but gratifying in that he knew the Union forces were stronger for his efforts.

But this was a wearying life as well. Sometimes he wondered how long this war would go on, and if the good luck that had followed him so far as a pilot could possibly hold out much longer. He hoped that the death of Cline was not the beginning of a change of fortune.

They pressed on, moving deeper into Kentucky, feeling safer with each step. Coming to the house of a Union man who had given refuge to earlier bands of Greeley's stampeders, they settled in for the night, but received news that washed away almost all the sense of relief and freedom they had been feeling.

The man told them that of late, rebel activity in this

portion of Kentucky had been almost as great as in Powell Valley. He told stories of rebel raids, atrocities committed against Union families, of food and livestock stolen, houses burned, even a few men shot down in their very yards as they attempted to defend what was theirs. Most such offenses the man attributed to rebel soldiers under Humphrey Marshall, a man who had once led the fight for Kentucky neutrality but had since cast his lot with the southern cause. "I despise Humphrey Marshall," the man declared. "A Kentuckian himself, yet he lets his men treat folk of his own state in such a way. I know the preachers and the Good Book say it's wrong to hate, but I hate that man and feel no regret for it."

Greeley accepted the news stoically before the others, but as he fell asleep that night he fought back tears, cursing the day war had come even as he prayed for the day it would end.

As they continued their quest for the Union lines, Greeley's band found evidence aplenty that their most recent host had spoken truth about suffering in the region. Moving through the mountain country, they found families residing in rough shelters in the yards of burned-down homes, and fresh graves that held the corpses of men and even boys slain in the defense of those homes.

There was little food to be found, but the Unionists they encountered shared what they had freely. So pitiful were some of their situations that the stampeders no longer viewed their own situation as badly deprived. At least they had a destination ahead, a Union army that would accept and provide for them. These people had almost nothing, and no guarantees that should they rebuild and restock as best they could, it would not all be taken from them again in like manner.

At length the stampeders began finding evidence of immediate rebel presence, and after that saw actual rebel raiders. The first two such encounters were frightening, but not particularly close. The stampeders managed to stay out of view. As they moved toward Greasy Fork on their way to Manchester, however, they met one force face-to-face while crossing a road, and had to scatter as the rebels pursued. Several shots were fired—one barely grazed Greeley's shoulder—but the rebels did not chase them far, and when the stampeders regrouped some hours later, they found not a man of them had been lost or even seriously hurt. But their awareness of the danger all around them was greatly heightened, and their movements became furtive and nervous. Greeley began to look forward to the sight of a Union flag above rows of tents and masses of blue-clad soldiers with the fervor of a hungry man aching for food.

Federally occupied Nashville, Tennessee

His name was David Calvin, and as hardworking newspapermen went, he worked harder even than most. His title at the *Nashville Sage* was editor, but in fact he spent far more time producing his own copy than editing that of others. This was mainly because there usually *were* no others contributing to the *Sage*, except for the publisher, Adam Hanover. Occasionally Adam allowed the hiring of a reporter to help carry the load, but none had lasted; always the main workload fell back on David Calvin.

Though Calvin grumbled about it, he didn't really mind. He thrived on hard work, loved to immerse himself in it, to lift his eyes after uncounted hours of labor and find an entire day had somehow slipped past. Adam Hanover had hired him because of his devotion to work, and was no different himself in that regard . . . or had not been until earlier in the year, when *she* abruptly entered the picture.

Now Adam Hanover, publisher, friend, and boss of David Calvin, was a changed and still-changing man, and this was the subject upon which Calvin was holding forth in this rare moment of leisure, shared over a café table with the only woman for whom he had time in his busy life: his mother. They shared a midday meal, often hurried, once each week at this same café, usually at this same table. Seldom did they see one another beyond that, their mutual schedules being too prohibitively busy.

The widow Marjory Calvin was a big woman, had been

since her childbearing years, and her own strenuous daily labors in the hot kitchen of a restaurant down the street had done nothing to diminish her bulk. Now she leaned forward, elbows on the table, which creaked beneath the burden of her weight. Her very ample bosom pressed against the corner of the table, and her eyes glittered in response to what her son had just told her.

"*Marry* her?" she declared. "You really think such a devoted bachelor as Mr. Hanover would go that far with a young woman he's known such a short time?"

"No question about it in my mind," David Calvin replied. "I've known Adam for years, and never have I seen him like this. Never. He talks about her constantly. He's convinced that she's the finest and grandest of women, not to mention the bravest."

"Well, I know nothing about the fine and grand part, but he's right about the bravery. What an adventure that poor young woman has gone through! Shot by bushwhackers while trying to make her way to Nashville, and that after already making an escape from the rebels and fleeing over half a state. . . ."

"Not to mention the smuggling she was involved with to begin with," Calvin added. "Not a job for the excitable person. It was the smuggling that got her arrested in the first place."

"Currency smuggling, wasn't it?"

"Counterfeit Confederate currency, to be precise. Printed by the United States government and smuggled into the Confederacy to weaken the rebel economy." Calvin sipped from his cup of water, the only beverage that, for reasons of his eccentric notions about health, ever passed his lips. "She was recruited for the job by some special government agent, or so she told Adam."

"I don't recall reading that part."

"It wasn't in the story. She wouldn't allow Adam to use it. Wouldn't even tell him who the agent was, off the record. Trying to protect the man, I suppose."

Conversation lagged a few moments. David Calvin picked up a folded, rumpled copy of the *Sage* from some weeks before and glanced over it in the silence. His mother had asked him to bring this copy to her, having had her own copy picked up by some sticky-fingered party unknown while she was laboring away in her own restaurant a few doors down.

This edition was indeed a "keeper," one of the most widely distributed and devoured copies of what was a basically unpopular Unionist newspaper in a Confederate-supporting, Federally held city. The reason was wrapped up in a lengthy story Adam Hanover had written and published in that edition, detailing the exciting and remarkable story of a young, female, Union spy who had been found shot and unconscious by a couple of children early in the year, just outside Nashville. She had been clad in male's clothing at the time, her long hair hidden beneath a man's hat.

Brought into Nashville for medical treatment, she had before long found her way into a military hospital. Why a civilian woman shot under unknown circumstances was taken under military custody for treatment was unclear until rumors began spreading. This young woman, it was said, was one Amy Deacon, formerly of Knoxville, and the daughter of the late, great original Secessionist and propagandist, Dr. George Deacon. And reportedly she was telling the Federal authorities that she'd been wounded by pro-Confederate bushwhackers just when she was on the verge of reaching Nashville after making a long flight from Knoxville, where she had been arrested, while bearing counterfeit currency, by Confederate soldiers. Also arrested was the man to whom she had been assigned to deliver her contraband. This fellow, apparently not as sensible as Amy herself, made a wild escape attempt, and thus bought himself death. But Amy took this as an unexpected opportunity to make a flight of her own. While the guards pursued the fleeing man, she was able to slip away, hide, then leave Knoxville altogether. Stealing some man's clothing off a drying line, she disguised herself and undertook a long, covert journey across the countryside, mostly on foot and off roads, toward Nashville and the safety of its Federal occupying force. She was two miles away from her destination when rebel bushwhackers shot her down and left her lying on the cold ground. Even the staunchest Confederate sympathizers in Nashville were dismayed that a woman had been treated so, though they were quick to point out that she had been dressed as a man, and whoever shot her probably had no idea of her true sex.

Adam Hanover found the Amy Deacon story intriguing, and he promptly went to meet and interview the woman. What had come of that was not only the most widely read story ever published in the *Sage*, but also what appeared to be an unexpected romantic affair between writer and subject. Adam Hanover was utterly smitten with the pretty, young civilian spy. Once she was past the first stage of her recovery, he even made arrangements for her to be transferred to the house of an elderly aunt of his, to be nursed and tended like royalty itself, at his expense.

The expense of Amy Deacon's care was no strain for Adam Hanover. His late parents had been well-off and left him a comfortable fortune. David Calvin, for one, was grateful for this: If not for Adam Hanover's private subsidization, the *Sage* would have folded long ago. Few indeed were the advertisers in this city eager to support a newspaper that almost invariably took a hard pro-Union line.

"Have you met Amy Deacon?" Marjory Calvin asked her son.

"Only once," he said, setting down the water glass. "She is quite a striking young woman, I must say."

"Ah, me! Too bad you can't snatch her for yourself!"

Calvin smiled; his perpetual bachelorhood was a common obsession of his mother's, a common obsession of the mothers of unmarried young men the world over, he supposed. "I'm not looking just now," he replied. "Anyway, I don't think I'd have a single chance with her if I was. She only has eyes for Adam."

"Ah, well, that's to be expected, I suppose. He is handsome, wealthy, influential, all that."

Calvin smiled, finishing his mother's thought in his own mind: *All that . . . unlike you, David*. She was more transparent to him than she thought, and what he saw in her mind wasn't always flattering to him. But she was his mother. He loved her anyway.

"I don't think it's so much the usual things that attract

her to him," Calvin said. "She has something about her, some sort of . . . *need*, I suppose. Something you can sense. I swear, Mother, I got the feeling, just watching her and Adam while they talked, that one of the things she likes about him is his age."

"Really? I'd think she'd prefer him a touch younger."

"Well, so you'd think. He's got a good fourteen or fifteen years advantage on her."

Marjory chuckled. "Maybe she's looking for a father instead of a husband."

David Calvin cocked a brow. "I've had precisely the same thought. You know who her father was, don't you?"

"Yes, that dead Secessionist newspaper publisher in Knoxville, right?"

"Right. And did you know that he and she had quite a falling out in his last days? That he evicted her from his house, sent her off to live with his brother in another town?"

"Yes, I know. It was all in the story."

"Right, so it was. And also in there, you'll recall, was what happened to that uncle. The rebels hanged him as a Unionist bridge burner, and Amy took it hard. She had become very close to him. He became a kind of father to her, replacing the real father who would have nothing to do with her, and who then ended up dead and gone."

"So you've figured out the workings of her mind, have you?" Marjory said. "Poor girl loses a father and an uncle, goes through an ordeal as a spy, and now she's ready to marry a newspaperman who's more than a decade older than she is, just because he has gray hair and can be a father to her."

"I'm not saying that's the only things accounting for it. I believe she truly does appreciate Adam for himself. But those things, I think, do come into it. Some, at least. I mean, why else would she be so quick to turn a warm eye on such an old coot as Adam?"

Marjory cocked a brow of her own now; her face became an older, rounder image of her son's. "Old coot? He's only in his mid-thirties, David. Might it be that my son is a bit jealous that it wasn't himself who gained the young woman's heart?"

He glowered and took another sip of water. "Maybe. Just a little."

She chuckled, victorious at having plumbed his secret.

He looked away, offense visible in his expression.

She sighed. "I'm sorry. I shouldn't have said that. But maybe it's best. A young woman like that, she's too reckless. I mean, think of it! Spying, smuggling, getting herself captured, being shot at by bushwhackers . . . there's no telling what kind of trouble such a woman would find for herself. You need a more calm and stable kind of young woman, David."

He stared at his plate, nibbled the last bite of his bread. He pulled out a pocket watch and glanced at its face. "Need to get back to work, Mother."

She folded her napkin. "So do I. Same time next week?"

"I'll be here."

Chapter 7

By the time they reached Greasy Fork, Greeley was ravaged by hunger. He chewed elm bark and hickory sprouts to fight the pangs in his belly. He and his men suffered much, encountering a populace distrustful of any band of strangers. They met many an avowed Unionist, most of whom told them that rebel bands often came through, passing themselves off as men on the way to the Union lines. Thus, these impostors gained knowledge of who and who was not Unionist in sentiment, and then passed the information on to rebel raiders and bushwhackers. So Greeley's best pleadings did little to gain trust.

He was down to pondering doing some raiding of his own when he finally met a woman who, though cautious, seemed ready to give him a better hearing than anyone they had met in the area so far. When he'd managed to persuade her to give him the benefit of her doubts, she agreed to lead him to a secret encampment where her husband was hiding from the Confederates. He had little food with him there, she said, but might be persuaded to guide Greeley to where better fare might be found. He had to come with her alone, however, and without his weapons.

With the other men taking to the woods to hide and wait, Greeley followed the woman up a winding mountain trail that grew all the more rugged as they went along, then virtually disappeared.

"Your man must be right fearful, hiding out this far," Greeley said, then wished he hadn't used the word "fearful," thinking the woman might take it as an insult to her husband's courage.

He was sure that she had when she turned abruptly and faced him with a small pistol leveled at his chest. "My husband is a brave man, sir, but yes, he is fearful, and for good reason. He watched his own brother be dragged off into the woods by reb bushwhackers, and we've not seen nor heard nothing of him since. And the poor man was not even fit for soldiering, being one-legged from a sawmill tragedy, and he held no notions either for or against the rebels. It was pure cruelty and meanness that led them to do him harm, and it's that my husband fears."

"Ma'am, I didn't mean to insult him. I hope you don't aim to kill me for misspeaking."

"I'm not showing you this pistol because of what you said. I'm showing you that if you prove to be what you say you ain't, I'll kill you my own self before I'll see my man hurt. You understand me?"

"I do. And I am what I say, ma'am. I'm a Union man, and you and your husband have nothing to fear from me."

She put Greeley in front of her and directed him from that point on by words. His heart pounded hard, as much from his fear of what she might do as from the exertion of climbing this hard trail.

"Ma'am, you reckon your husband might shoot me, walking in on him with you hid behind me?"

"He might. I reckon you'll have to take that chance, won't you?"

Five minutes later they crested the ridge and came upon a small hollow between two hills. The average man might have noticed nothing unusual there, but Greeley knew the woods better than most and almost immediately spotted a small, hidden tent nestled between two oaks. There was no fire, nothing to indicate human presence.

The woman came to Greeley's side, keeping the pistol turned his way. "Oman!" she called. "Oman! It's Caroline! Where are you?"

From somewhere in the trees a voice called out, a very young man's voice, to Greeley's surprise. "We're here! Who's that with you?"

"A man named Brown, says he's a Union pilot. He's got a passel of men with him, but they're hid out back near the house."

"You believe he's telling the truth?"

"If he ain't, I'm ready to kill him my own self." She paused, then added, "But I reckon I believe him. He talks the right talk. Where's Oman?"

"He's here. Ain't got no voice—weather's got into his throat. You really think we can trust that man?"

"I believe so. We got him outweaponed, anyhow."

Silence. Greeley felt like a prisoner awaiting a verdict. Finally the brush moved and a one-eyed man stepped out, carrying an ancient shotgun. Following him was a thin, typical-looking mountain youth, bearing an even older-looking firearm, also a shotgun, sawed off short.

The pair walked across the camp toward Greeley and the woman, stopping about ten feet away. "You say you're Union?" the elder one said. His voice was whispery, raspy as dry leaves crunching underfoot.

"I'm Union to the heart of me, sir. I'll swear on anything you want me to swear on."

"Swear on the barrel of my shotgun, then." He thrust the weapon out, cocking it at the same time.

Greeley walked forward and laid his hand on the barrel, which was aimed at his face. "I swear that I'm a loyal Union man, a foe of the rebellion, and true to the Stars and Stripes till the day I die."

The shotgun stayed where it was a moment more; the man glared more harshly with his single eye than most could manage with two. "Swear on your mother, too."

"I swear on my mother that I'm a Union man."

The shotgun held, then slowly lowered. Greeley almost wilted in relief.

"Brown? Is that your name?"

THE PHANTOM LEGION 69

"Yes sir. Greeley Brown."

"Greeley Brown! I've heard of you, sir. They say you are a man of honor."

"I'm glad folks feel that way."

"Yes, sir. Man of honor. And a man's honor, that's all he's got that he can keep, the only thing a man can have that he can truly hold his head up for. Not wealth, not fame, not none of that. Honor. That's the key."

"Yes, sir."

"I've heard also that you've piloted many a good Union man out of Tennessee and Carolina up to the Union lines. I've heard you are the best among the pilots."

"I do my best."

"That's what a man is honor-bound to do. His best."

"Yes, sir." Greeley was beginning to note a certain obsession with honor on the part of this man.

"I've been told you are a trusty man, Mr. Brown."

"I am. You can take my word."

"Your word of honor. That counts for much. A man's word of honor is what decides whether he is false or true."

"I agree with you, sir."

The man laid the shotgun aside and stuck out his hand. "Name's Killefer. Oman Killefer. Born in Tennessee, doing my best to live an honorable life in Kentucky."

"Pleased to meet you, sir. This your boy here with you?"

"Yes, sir. That's Julius. He's a good boy, sir. An honorable young man. I've raised him to be true and honorable, or otherwise to die. Life ain't worth living if a man has sacrificed his honor. That's what I've raised my sons to believe. Julius, step up here and meet a fine Union man."

The young man, maybe eighteen years old, whose voice had made him sound so grim and threatening from the brush, now looked like any shy young mountaineer. Wordlessly he approached Greeley and stuck out his hand. It was a thin hand, but callused and strong. Greeley shook it and said, "Howdy, Julius. I appreciate you not shooting me."

Julius Killefer grinned very slightly and backed away.

"Killefer . . . that's a name I've heard in my part of the country," Greeley said to the father. "You're a Tennessee Killefer, you say? I've heard tales of the first of the

Tennessee Killefers, a man with the first name of Owen who got well-known for some of his adventures amongst the Chickamaugas when he was a boy."

"Owen Killefer was my grandfather, Mr. Brown."

"Is that right? I'll be! And call me Greeley."

"You call me Oman, then, and tell me what I can do for you and your men."

"We need food, Oman. Most of us are nigh starved. We didn't know the rebels had been so much afoot in these parts when we came."

"They've drug off my brother already," Oman said. "I figure they've killed him."

"I heard about that from your missus."

"I got little food to offer you, sir. How many in your group?"

"Fifteen with me . . . no, fourteen now. One died on the way. An accident in the woods, running from rebs."

"All the food I got here is meager, what we've hid out for Julius and me."

"I realize that. But your missus said that maybe you might be able to guide us to some place where we could find some."

Oman Killefer squinted his one eye and scratched his bearded chin. "I can't leave here, Greeley. I got a wife and home to keep watch over. But Julius, he could do it . . . if you'd do something for me in return."

"If it's money you want," Greeley said, "I'm willing to pay whatever's reasonable." In fact he was so hungry he would probably have been willing to pay more than was reasonable.

"Ain't money I want. It has to do with my Julius here. There's something I want him to do, someone he wants to see, and you could be the one to help him, to pay him back for helping you."

Greeley took a guess. "You want me to pilot him to the Union lines with my men?"

"No. Are you going back to Tennessee once you deliver your stampeders?"

"Yes."

"Then when you go, I want you to take Julius with you."

• • •

Greeley Brown, leading his men, trudged along behind Julius Killefer, noting how the youth's lean legs moved with the distinctive long stride of the mountaineer as he picked his way along what seemed a trackless forest. A capable young man, this one; he reminded Greeley of himself when he was about half his present age. He couldn't say he really knew Julius yet, but he had a good feeling about him. Julius Killefer was clearly at ease in the wilds, confident in his movements and bearing. He'd make a good soldier.

Yet he wasn't planning to become one, at least not immediately. Greeley thought over the bargain he'd made with Julius's father and thought how odd it was going to be to pilot someone *away* from the Union lines and into rebel territory. Quite a reversal from his usual work, but an understandable one in this case. Given the situation Oman Killefer had described, it made a certain sense for Julius to do what he was planning. Greeley knew that if he, like Julius, had a brother who had gone missing without explanation in rebel territory, he would want to go look for him just as Julius planned to do.

He wondered if the young man really understood how perilous his task might be. There was a conscription law in southern territory, and many of its officers were not overly scrupulous in who they swept in, or how.

McDermott came to Greeley's side, keeping stride as usual, and whispered, "Are you sure we can trust this boy?"

"I ain't sure of nothing these days, but I believe we can. If they'd wanted to do us harm, they had the chance. Besides, did you see how the old man made his son raise his hand and swear on his honor that he'd be brave and faithful and all that? The old fellow seems like he's got notions about honor that go way beyond the average man. I never seen somebody talk so much about one thing."

"That's what worries me," McDermott replied. "I believe that talking up your own honor and such is kind of like talking up how much consorting you're doing with the females: Them that talks it the most does it the least."

"I believe that old Killefer was true blue," Greeley said. "I believe he meant every word he said, and that his boy there does, too. Don't worry. I perceive we can trust him."

Ten miles of trudging brought them to a river settlement; here, Julius said, they might find food. But hardly had they come into view of the little town before they saw a big body of gray-clad soldiers come riding out, followed by a herd of livestock and a wagon laden with goods of all kinds. As the stampeders hid and watched, McDermott swore endlessly. They'd come too late. Whatever this place might have offered was certainly already taken.

Julius and Greeley did some scouting about the settlement after the rebels were gone and found it just as they had guessed. The people were all but destitute. But there was a man there, a former East Tennessean who knew Greeley, who said he had a store of corn the rebels hadn't found and the stampeders were welcome to all they needed.

Greeley and Julius carried back a bushel of corn to the waiting men. They were so hungry they ate it raw, and would have paid any amount for more.

They moved on after a day's rest and came into Manchester, where news was flying about a battle that had occurred in the area the day before. Though it had been a rebel defeat, a bad result was that rebels were dispersing in all directions, and some were taking out their anger over their defeat at the expense of the citizenry. But one positive circumstance greeted the weary men: a tavern, with a roof they could sleep under and real straw ticks to rest upon. The food they bought was far from sufficient, but the night's rest was the best any of them had experienced for days. The next morning even McDermott was in a good mood. After eating a sparse breakfast and paying the tavern keeper two dollars each in greenback currency, they headed toward Richmond.

They traveled main roads once they were well away from Manchester, because here they were out of rebel range. A farmer put them up for the night at the cost of a dollar a man, food included, and they traveled in increasingly high spirits throughout the next day. They stayed at a hotel the next night—an authentic, good quality hotel, complete with a café and a maid who eyed the ragged, dirty men with

obvious suspicion, and shook her head sadly at the sight of
the dirt they tracked in with them. The next day the mood
was so exuberant that they actually hired a pair of coaches
to convey them to the town of Lexington, where their
journey was completed.

It was a joyous occasion when Greeley Brown strode
forward at the Union camp to shake the hand of Colonel
Daniel Stover. Stover was the son-in-law of Senator
Andrew Johnson of Greeneville, Tennessee, a senator so
devotedly Unionist that he was allowed to keep his seat in
the Senate despite the fact he represented a seceded state,
and whom Lincoln had named "military governor" of the
still-embattled state about a year before. Further, Stover, like
Greeley, had been involved in the Unionist bridge-burning
conspiracy of 1861, and that, coupled with Greeley's piloting and recruiting work for the Union forces, created a
strong bond between the pair.

Stationed at Lexington was the Fourth Tennessee
Infantry Regiment, comprised largely of East Tennessee
men who had stampeded north just like Greeley's current
band of followers. In fact, he'd led many of them across the
mountains himself. They warmly greeted him and his followers, many of whom they knew as old friends and neighbors. Greeley received a complete new outfit of rugged
civilian clothing as a gift from the regiment and was regaled
with letters, many containing money, that he was asked to
deliver to the soldiers' families back in East Tennessee. He
accepted them all, promising to do his best to see they all
came into the right hands. His own most recent pack of
stampeders now gave to him the letters they had been com-
posing during the tense and lonely hours of hiding all along
the way north, and he promised to deliver those as well. The
letters went into his pack.

Lying down to sleep that night, Greeley remembered yet
another letter he would have to deliver: Spencer Cline's. He
rose and found Cline's pack. It felt odd to be digging into
the personal luggage of a man now dead, but he had to find
the letter. And he did, tucked into the bottom of the pack

under the extra clothing, razor, matches, and so on, which made up the rest of Cline's personal effects. Nothing out of the ordinary.

And there was nothing out of the ordinary about the sealed letter itself, except for the name of the woman to whom it was addressed: Nanny Josiah. Nanny. Odd-sounding name for a woman.

Greeley put Cline's letter into his own pack, among the others. He didn't dwell on how difficult it would be to get those letters delivered, though he would certainly dwell on it aplenty once the actual labor of it began. But now was a time for celebration and rest, for food, fellowship, and safety in this temporary refuge of the Union military. Tomorrow's burdens and sorrows would be entirely sufficient for their own day. He lay down to sleep, looking forward to a day of fellowship and rest to come with the morning.

Chapter 8

On the same May day that Robert E. Lee drove back the Army of the Potomac in a battle at Chancellorsville that generated more than ten thousand casualties, Greeley Brown and Julius Killefer said their farewells to the Union soldiers among whom they had been mingling in Kentucky and began the journey back to East Tennessee.

Greeley had mixed feelings about heading back. East Tennessee was his home, yet it was occupied by an army and government that wanted him imprisoned. He had lost his home to rebel-set fire back in late '61, and since then had resided several different places throughout the mountains— old hunter station camps, rugged shelters, caves, and so on. At the moment he resided in a tiny log hut on a ridge over-looking a remote portion of the Doe River. He really hadn't minded the wilderness lifestyle that much, truth be told. Even when his house had still been standing he'd spent, by his own choice, at least as much time hunting and roaming in the mountains as sleeping beneath his own roof. He enjoyed living in the wild country, and had always pre-sented himself to people as a "man who needs a house much less than most."

The aspect of his life that wore on him was the awareness of constant danger, the feeling of never being free to relax his guard for a moment. Now that he knew there was a price on his head, relaxation would come even harder once he was back in Tennessee. Though he would make the best time he could, he wasn't all that eager to leave Kentucky.

Julius Killefer, on the other hand, was openly excited about the journey, which was for him a welcome exodus from a somber situation. There was nothing for him here in Kentucky but subsistence as a restless, hungry, constantly endangered refugee in the shadow of his own home. There would probably be danger as well for him in Tennessee as he searched for his missing brother, but Tennessee was still enough miles away to not quite seem real to him. And in the meantime the young mountaineer was about to take the first train ride of his life.

Greeley privately enjoyed young Killefer's obvious, nervous pleasure as they rode the rails together toward Lexington. "Might as well enjoy the ride while you can," he said. "We'll be on foot again before long."

At Lexington they ate at a restaurant—and Greeley had the strong impression that this also was a new experience for Julius Killefer—then hired out a wagon driver to haul them to the town of Richmond. Spending the night in a hotel, they hefted their packs onto their backs the next morning and set out on foot southward and slightly east. With the excitement of new life experiences now giving way to the familiar drudgery of walking, Julius Killefer grew a bit somber and preoccupied. Thinking about his missing brother, Greeley figured. As they trudged through the increasingly rugged Kentucky countryside toward Tennessee, Greeley sparked off a conversation, hoping to learn more about the Killefers in general and Julius in particular.

"What'd you say your brother's name was?"

"Crowell. He lives somewhere on a river called the French something or other. . . ."

"The French Broad?"

"That's right. The French Broad River, somewhere near a town called Newport. I never been there so I don't know much about it. You know where Newport is?"

"Yes. Is Crowell married?"

"Yep. Never met his wife, though. We never heard much from Crowell since he left home, you see. He and Pa had a falling out. The truth is, they ain't had nothing to say to each other for a long time. But Pa still worries about him. I guess a father always loves his boys. And if I know Crowell, he still loves his family, however he might act."

"How did you find out he's gone missing?"

"His wife—Susan is her name—sent a letter, asking if he was with us. She said he had just disappeared all at once, leaving her alone, and she said there was a baby."

"Nobody knew of the baby, I take it?"

"That's right. They'd never told us. I don't have any notion of how old the baby would be. The letter didn't say."

"So Crowell's wife thought he'd stampeded to Kentucky or something, without even letting her know he was doing it?"

"Well . . . I don't know what she thought. I believe she really hoped he was with us, though."

"She was *hoping* to find he'd abandoned her and gone back home?"

"Well, you see . . . there was more Susan told us in the letter. Him coming home must have seemed better to her than some other possibilities. She said in her letter that . . ." He seemed reluctant to go on.

"Listen, Julius, you don't have to air all your family laundry on my line. I'm just making talk with you, that's all. Don't say more than you want."

"No, I don't mind you knowing. It's just that some things are kind of embarrassing, you know, if your family's had a good name through the years. What she wrote was that there was some 'bad men,' that being what she called them—'bad men'—who Crowell had 'had dealings' with sometime before. She didn't call them bushwhackers, but Pa believes that's what she meant. And we ain't sure what she meant by Crowell having 'dealings' with them. It could be that he was being threatened by them, or maybe was taking up with them. You could read it either way. Anyhow, Susan was hoping that she'd find that Crowell had come up to Kentucky, because if he hadn't . . ."

Greeley finished the thought. "If he hadn't, that meant

either he'd gone off to become a bushwhacker himself, or maybe the bushwhackers had . . . had done something to him so that he couldn't come home."

"That's just what we've been thinking, Pa and me. That's why he wanted me to go to Tennessee, so that somebody from the family could see with their own eyes what's going on."

"Does Susan know you're coming?"

"No. We ain't had no contact with her. It was a . . . well, a queerish, worried kind of letter. Like maybe she's a little odd."

"How'll you find her?"

"Well . . . I don't know exactly. Somebody will surely be able to steer me to her."

"Julius, I do want to warn you. Once you get in Tennessee you'll be on dangerous ground. Poking about and asking too many questions about anything or anybody can get a man in trouble. You'll need to be careful."

"Don't forget, Mr. Brown, that I already know some about trouble. We've seen aplenty of it lately right here in Kentuck."

"That's surely true."

Julius kept silence awhile, thinking, before speaking again. "You know, Crowell must not have told his wife much about our family, or else she'd have never even thought he could have come back to Kentucky without her. That would be dishonorable, you know, deserting your own wife, and Pa would never let Crowell come home if he'd done a thing like that. Crowell would know that, too. He'd never try to come home if he'd done a thing so dishonorable as that."

"Your pa has some strong notions about honor," Greeley ventured. "I could tell it from how he talked, and how he made you swear on your honor to stick with me and all that."

"Pa believes in honor really fierce. Believes in it right down to the core of him. He raised me and Crowell to believe the same way. With me, it took."

"But not with Crowell?"

"No. No, not so much as with me." Julius shook his head. "Pa has molded me pretty much the way he wanted.

He'd drilled his honor notions into my head so far that I know I'll never be able to think no other way. I reckon that's good."

"I reckon. There's not so much honor to be found these days, with the war and all. Plenty of folks take loyalty oaths and such, but don't stick with them. There's a lot of good Union men who have took the rebel oath but don't mean it. They do it because they have to."

Julius shook his head. "That ain't right. If they don't mean it, they ought not say it. And if they do say it, they ought to stick with it."

"Wait a minute, Julius. Are you telling me that if some rebel forced you to join his army, made you vow to support Jeff Davis and all that, you'd feel obliged to stick with it?"

"I surely would, sir. That's how my pa raised me."

"You'd go into battle for the Confederacy because of a forced oath? Fight for something you don't even believe in?"

"If I'd took an oath, I would. The Bible says to let your yea be yea and your nay be nay. If you say it, if you vow it, then you do it, no matter what. That's honor."

"Things ain't that simple in wartime, Julius. There's higher duties and lower duties."

"Honor's honor. That's all there is to it."

Greeley studied his companion's rock-jawed expression. "I reckon your pa really *did* mold you in his image!"

"He did."

"But you say Crowell was different?"

"He was. He wasn't always so honorable as Pa would have wanted. He stole something once, and got caught in lies quite a bit. That's what drove him and Pa apart."

"Nothing against your pa, Julius, but I'm betting he can be a hard man to live with."

"If you ain't honorable in his eyes, yes sir, he can."

They walked in silence a minute more. "Well, all I can say to you, Julius, is that I hope the reb conscription folks don't get to you while you're in Tennessee. They'd make you vow an oath to the great Confederacy, and you'd feel honor-bound to follow it, and next time you seen me, Caesar Augustus, you'd probably feel it your duty to shoot me." Greeley grinned to let Julius know this was banter, but underneath it was a serious point. It seemed to Greeley that Julius had some too-starkly defined notions, some rigid ideas that needed to be flexed just a little. Anyone who insisted on seeing all things in black and white was going to face some serious difficulties when he encountered such a gray-shaded beast as war.

"I wouldn't shoot you, sir," Julius said.

"Why? That wouldn't be honorable? What would you do?"

Julius thought about it and shrugged. "I reckon the only honorable thing a man could do in that kind of situation was to shoot himself."

Greeley didn't reply, but inwardly he felt shaken. He'd never met anyone with such firm moral notions as this Kentucky mountain youth. Absurdly firm, it seemed to Greeley.

They went on the next several miles with no further words.

It required two days of steady, fast walking to reach Manchester. Exhausted, they put up with a battalion of Union soldiers stationed there, remaining for two days. Three of the soldiers were from Washington County, Tennessee, and provided Greeley three more letters to deliver. Though delivering what he'd already been given seemed an overburdening responsibility, he'd accepted the additional letters graciously.

"What's in them letters they give you?" Julius asked.

"Mostly just news, and them telling their families how they love them and will be back with them soon, just as quick as the Federal army can come into East Tennessee. And there's money, generally, at least a bit of it. There's no greater a burden on a soldier's mind than the welfare of his kin. Most of them worry a lot more about their folks at home than about theirselves. So they send what money they can."

"Seems like it's dangerous, you carrying all that money in your pack. What if somebody should rob you?"

"I worry about that sometimes. But what can I do? Oftentimes me or some other pilot is the only means these soldiers have of getting news and money back to their homes. So I just watch my back and move on the sneak, and nobody's robbed me yet. But, sorry to say, that ain't the case *after* the money gets delivered. Most of the time it never gets spent by the families it was sent to. Bush-whackers and such break in and take it at gunpoint."

"That's awful mean."

"It is. There's always meanness in wartime. And it's on both sides, sorry to say. Right now in East Tennessee it's the Union folk who suffer, for the Confederates have the upper hand, but when things turn about, you wait and see if you don't see it all reverse itself. The Union folk, I'm afraid, will be just as cruel as the rebs are now. You know why I say that?"

"Why?"

"Because it's a fact of human nature that folks are cruel and spiteful. Don't matter what color of uniform you wear, what color of skin you got, what flag you salute. If you're a human being, you've got in you the potential of being mean as a snake. It's like the Good Book says: Ain't no one right-eous, no, not one. Every man is fallen. Every one of them, including me and you. The prospect for turning mean and sorry is real for us all. And ain't nothing brings that out like wartime."

They hiked the craggy, forested landscape until they reached the Cumberland River, and proceeded on to the Clover Fork. There they looked up a Union man of Greeley's acquaintance, spent the night safe under his roof, and left the next day with extra provisions he sold them at a bargain price.

They reached Powell Valley by night and in a rainstorm. Greeley had developed a cough that was beginning to hurt. Recalling that the last time he had taken up a cough like that it had gone to lung trouble and laid him flat for more than a week, he decided to seek decent shelter for the evening if it could be found—a house or tavern if possible, a barn or shed if not.

They found no taverns, and Greeley heeded a troubling and instinctive mental alarm that told him not to approach any residents of the valley this night. He was about to resign himself to a night beneath the trees when the flash of distant lightning illuminated a big barn standing on a hilltop, well away from the farmhouse with which it seemed to be associated. The farmhouse was completely dark. Greeley and Julius crept cautiously to the barn, cursorily examined its interior and found it empty of livestock. But there was old hay in the loft, warm and softened with age. They climbed into it, spread their blankets, ate some biscuits and jerked beef, and settled in for sleep as rain fell harder outside. The barn leaked, but not over their resting place, and they were nearly as content there as they would have been in more legitimate lodgings. A lightning storm was coming their way and they were glad not to be awaiting its arrival outdoors.

"I might like to be a Union pilot my own self," Julius said as they lay awaiting sleep to descend. "It's a good thing you do, moving men up out of hostile country to where they can fight for the right side of things."

"It's also dangerous—and Lord willing, something that won't have to be done much longer. I'm tired of this war. I hope it's over soon and there'll be no more need for men like me." He scratched and yawned. "Besides, Julius, to be a pilot you have to know the country real well. You know Kentucky, but not much of Tennessee."

"You're right. But I wish I did know all the country so I could do what you're doing. You're an honorable man, Greeley Brown," Julius said. "My pa was right about you. I'm proud to be traveling with you."

Greeley grunted and nodded, self-conscious at having received so fine a compliment. "I'm proud to travel with you too, Julius Killefer. Good night."

"Good night."

The storm awakened Greeley sometime later. He sat up, looking around the loft as lightning flashed and wind howled under the roof above him, tugging at shingles that might hold or might give way. Rain pounded down, running off the barn in small rivers.

He lay back down but couldn't fall asleep again. Eventually he got up and paced about the loft. Julius remained fast asleep. The storm abated after a while. Greeley went back to his blankets, paused to check the loads in his Navy Colt, then lay down again, making sure the pistol was within reach.

He slept lightly the rest of the night, opening his eyes each time a mouse scurried in one of the empty stalls below or through the hay upon which they rested. As best Greeley could tell, Julius never awakened at all.

Morning broke. The sky had emptied itself in the night and was clear and blue. Greeley, already awake and moving about the loft when Julius woke up, nodded a good morning, went to a knothole in the nearest side wall and peered down at the farmhouse below the hill. He watched for several minutes, while behind him Julius slowly roused himself, scrounging in his pack for food, yawning, emptying his bladder over the side of the loft into one of the stalls below, scratching a thousand itchy spots created by a night of sleeping on hay.

"You going to eat something, Greeley?"

"Done ate. Know what, Julius? I believe that farmhouse down there is empty. We could have slept there instead of up here."

"Probably no furniture in it. I'd say we was more comfortable right where we was."

"Maybe. But I woke up in the night and felt the oddest kind of uncomfortable. It was during the storm. I had the feeling we weren't alone in this barn."

"I don't remember the storm."

"You were sleeping like a drunk. I never saw nobody sleep as hard as you."

"You really think there was somebody in here with us?"

"I doubt it. But I think I'll look around."

Greeley explored the barn from corner to corner and found nothing relevant to his suspicion. Yet he couldn't shake off the memory of that odd and tense sensation that had kept him awake. Greeley's instincts were well-honed by years of mountain life. They seldom failed him.

They left the barn and headed toward the house, which did turn out to be empty. In fact, the entire back half of the house was gone, burned away so that only the front remained. They hadn't been able to see the burned portion the night before. Greeley wondered if the house had been set afire by bushwhackers or raiding regular soldiers, or had caught fire in some more mundane fashion.

He explored what remained of the dwelling on the slim chance of finding something useful or edible inside. But the only thing he found was the butt of a cigar that had been smoked recently enough to still have a freshly burnt smell. There was even some remaining moisture where its smoker had chewed on the butt of it.

"Whoever smoked this thing was surely in this house last night," Greeley said. "And maybe if he was here, he was at the barn first. He could have come in the barn because of the storm, detected me and you was there, and come on down here instead."

"Well, he's gone now, whoever he is," Julius said.

Greeley noted something else on the floor and picked it up. "I'll be."

"What's that?"

"A whittled stick . . . whittled down narrow in the middle, wide on the ends, kind of like an hourglass shape." He frowned. "Where've I seen this kind of whittling before? Somebody I've known in the past always whittled, like a nervous habit, and the sticks always come out looking like this." Try as he would, however, he couldn't call up either the face or the name. "Well, no matter, I suppose. Like you said, whoever it was is gone now."

"We heading for Powell Mountain now?"

"Not until tonight. We're in the rebel lands now, Julius. Any traveling we do from here on out will be after dark. Right now we're heading back up to the barn, and that's where we'll sit out this whole dang day."

"That's going to be mighty dull."

"Better a dull day of being safe than an exciting one of getting captured."

They left the house and headed back up the hill to the barn. The day seemed infinitely long, and they passed it telling jokes, chewing tobacco, and whittling—Greeley still straining his memory to recollect who it was who whittled out those hourglass shapes such as they had found in the old house. It was a failed effort.

When night came, they ate, settled their packs on their shoulders, and headed across the darkening valley for the big mountain of Powell.

Chapter 9

The valley crossing was difficult and frightening, and when it was done, Greeley figured Julius Killefer held a less exalted view of the life of a Union pilot.

They crossed the Powell River holding clothes, packs, and weapons above their heads, and were running for the far woods to dry and dress themselves when they heard a call to halt. They didn't halt; the militaristically barked order told Greeley unerringly that it had come from a Confederate throat. The shots that followed when they kept on running confirmed the conviction.

As he ran naked and river-drenched through the night, dodging trees and brush in front of him and bullets pouring in from behind, Greeley again thanked God for the marvelous gift of darkness, the shield of besieged men. He heard Julius crashing along slightly behind him, snapping sticks and whipping the brush as he ran. Their best hope was to lose themselves in the woods, and if they were lucky, they wouldn't run up against any lethal impediments like the sharp shard of tree branch that had killed Spencer Cline.

How far they ran Greeley could not accurately estimate, but he figured it at nearly a mile. When he sensed they had evaded their pursuers, he slowed, and collapsed panting and naked on the ground. A fit of coughing seized him. It was nearly a minute before he was able to speak: "Julius, are you still with me?"

"I'm here." The voice indicated Julius was maybe thirty feet behind, and also lying breathless on the ground.

"Come up where I am," Greeley said. "I'm way too tired to move."

"No more than me. . . . I ain't got the strength . . . to come up there yet. Give me . . . a minute to catch my breath." He gasped a few times. "Your cough sounds . . . bad."

"I'll get over it."

A little later brush moved and crackled, and Julius came up, clutching his wadded clothes. Greeley, who'd overcome his coughing and was breathing normally again, had to squint to see him.

"Well, at least we got our hides dry, running so hard," Julius said, beginning to dress. "Dang clothes are still soaked, though." He put on his shirt and shivered at the wet touch of it. "You know, that was the most scared I've ever been, but there was something sort of . . . well, soul-stirring about it, too. I ain't never been shot at by soldiers before. Coming through alive makes you feel sort of victorious. It's kind of fun in its way."

Greeley stood and began putting on his own sodden clothing. "*Fun?* Caesar Augustus! Tell me, boy, did you lose anything else besides your mind?"

"Don't think so. Still got my shotgun and my pack, all my clothes. Lord have mercy—I'm glad I didn't lose my pants. I'd hate to have to walk home without pants. Have you got all your stuff?"

"I've dropped nothing but one more year of my life, out of pure fright. I lose three or four years that way every time I make a stampeder run. My life span's getting rubbed down thin."

"I don't believe it. You'll live forever, Greeley Brown."

They didn't linger where they were. A determined rebel patrol might come in after them, or circle around the woods and wait for them to simply walk out the other side into their hands. Listening closely, Greeley believed he heard movement in the woods behind them. With minimal conversation they picked their way painstakingly through the overgrown terrain. At the woods' edge they paused, looking out across a wide meadow. No sign of anyone.

"Is it safe?"

"I think so. Come on. I want to reach Clinch Mountain tonight, if we can."

Time dragged on. Their feet moved steadily, carrying them through night, hours, miles. After a while Greeley grew less worried that they'd been followed; most likely the rebels had given up on them as soon as they ran into the woods. He voiced this opinion to Julius, who had been quiet for the last two hours.

"I don't know," Julius replied. "I keep getting the feeling that somebody's still behind us."

As soon as Julius said it, Greeley felt it, too. The feeling was almost identical to that undefined sense of unseen human presence he'd felt in the empty barn. He looked back the way they'd come, wondering if there really was someone there, or if he was merely reacting to Julius's suggestion.

"You hear anything?" Julius asked.

"No . . . I don't think so."

"Should we go on, just in case?"

"If we're going to be running across all God's creation, I want to know there's really something worth running from. Besides, we need rest, and it'll be day soon. This is a good place to camp. We're staying right here."

There was no doubt now. There really *was* someone in the woods behind them.

It was pitch-dark, daybreak maybe an hour away. Greeley sat up.

"That you, Greeley?" Julius whispered.

"Yes . . . but what I'm hearing in the woods is sure 'nough somebody else," Greeley whispered back.

"The rebs! They've followed us!"

"Somebody has. Stay where you are—I'm going to slip into the woods with my rifle."

In a moment he was gone, vanishing with no more noise than a shadow would make. Julius sat alone. He reached for his shotgun, cocked it, and held it in his lap, ready to use it if need be. But he could see very little, and with Greeley in the woods, he realized he wouldn't be able to fire, out of fear of hitting him by mistake.

Greeley crept away from the camp, toward the area where he'd heard movement. Stopping, he sniffed the air. Like the long hunters who ranged this same countryside a century earlier, he had learned to hone and use his sense of smell, an ability that could stand a man in good stead when visibility was poor. Just now it was telling him there was a man not far away, hidden in the veil of darkness.

"Greeley Brown."

Greeley spun toward the left, raising his rifle. "Who's there?"

"So it *is* you. I thought so. I know you, Greeley Brown."

"Who's talking? Show yourself!"

"I also know what's in that pack you carry. Lots of letters. Lots of money sent from soldiers to their kin."

Greeley opened his mouth to reply, but just then a shot ruptured the night, and he dropped to the ground like a stone.

Back at the camp, Julius Killefer vaulted to his feet, throat catching, the blanket he'd been using for cover crumpling at his feet.

"Greeley!" he yelled, lunging in the direction of the shot. He tripped over the blanket and slammed facedown into the ground, grunting in pain. One barrel of the shotgun went off, blasting a load of shot into the ground. Julius pushed up to his feet again, gingerly feeling his chest to make sure he hadn't shot himself. He'd been almost on top of the shotgun when it fired.

"Shoot at me, will you?" a voice just in front of him said.

"Greeley?"

"Nope." A pistol fired, flashing orange flame at Julius, who fell onto his back, screaming as his shoulder spasmed and the hottest of fires began to burn inside it.

• • •

Greeley had come up shooting, though he could see no one at whom to shoot. He heard a curse, then the sound of someone scrambling in the woods. He fired again in that direction and heard the bullet smack into a tree. The scrambling continued.

He heard Julius's shout, the blast of the shotgun. A pause followed, then a shot that sounded like a pistol, and Julius's scream. . . .

Greeley yelled, "Julius!" and ran toward the camp. Whoever had shot at Greeley—it was their bullet singing just past his ear that made him drop—was still scrambling away. But Greeley didn't pursue. He cursed himself for a fool. He hadn't considered that there might be two or more followers, that they might divide, one luring him away from the camp while the second moved in.

Greeley reached the camp and heard Julius moaning. He dropped to his knees, putting out his hands. Finding Julius's shoulder, he felt the hot, sticky wetness of fresh blood.

"Julius . . ."

"Good-bye and fare thee well, Greeley Brown." The voice came from behind him. Even as he was pivoting to face the unseen speaker, he recognized the voice.

Something burst hard against the back of his skull and for a moment the night was day. Greeley pitched over atop Julius's bloody form, his last fragmented thought being that this was not how he'd intended to die, shot in the head in a remote forest cove. He'd planned to survive the war, to find a good woman, to marry again and grow old. . . .

The thought dissolved into nothingness.

When Greeley was next aware of anything, it was daylight and he was lying on his side. He pried open his eyes and saw a pale-faced Julius Killefer sitting nearby, grimacing and wrapping a torn shirt as best he could around a wounded shoulder. From the bloodied look of the shirt and the drained expression on his face, it was evident he'd made several failed efforts to get the makeshift bandage in place.

"Julius . . ."

"Hello, Greeley. You got struck on the back of the head. I wouldn't move much if I was you. It'll hurt if you do. I rolled you onto your side so you wouldn't be lying on the bruised part."

"Struck . . . I thought I was shot."

"No. Just hit. It was me who got shot. But not in the head, just the shoulder."

"Is it bad?"

"Hurts, but it's really no more than a crease. The bullet just kind of plowed through me there—feels like it grazed my shoulder bone. Greeley, they took your pack, with all the letters you was to carry back."

Greeley closed his eyes against the intrusive daylight. "I know . . . I know who did it, too. From a voice I heard. The Fayettes. They're the ones."

Julius was wrapping the most sorely wounded part of his shoulder just then and had his teeth clamped shut against the pain. This time the bandage stayed in place. He let out his breath in a long sigh, then asked, "Who are the Fayettes?"

"A pair of brothers I piloted to Kentucky sometime back. They were from North Carolina and claimed to be good Union men, but folks warned me they really weren't nothing but—" He cut off with a yelp of pain, having rolled slightly onto his back and suffered the consequences Julius had warned him of. "Lordy! Oh, that hurts . . . The Fayettes, they were nothing but two men who'd got themselves in hot with the law and were trying to get away from Madison County. Soon as I got them over the Cumberland Mountain they ran off on me, and from what I hear, they've been a bane to Kentucky just as they was in their own home. Nothing but a couple of thieving outliers, maybe worse. It was Tiller Fayette, I now recollect, who whittled out them funny hourglass sort of shapes all the time."

Julius said, "They intended to kill us, Greeley. I fell after they shot me and pretty much passed out, but come to enough to hear them talking about the mail pack. From what they said, I could tell they thought me and you both was dead, and that suited them fine."

"I believe if I *was* dead I'd feel a good deal better than I do."

"I ain't never been shot before, Greeley."

"Just be glad you're alive . . . oh, Lord. Them letters . . . what'll I tell the folks who was supposed to get them? What'll I tell the men who sent them?"

"Know what they'll think, Greeley? They'll think that you and me took the money and made up a story about being robbed."

"I hope not . . . I hope they trust me more than that." But Greeley wasn't sure. It was easy these days for dark suspicions about almost anyone to rouse up more easily than in peaceful times.

"Julius, would you put my blanket over me?" Greeley asked. "I don't think I could abide trying to sit up just now."

Julius rose, wincing. "I believe I may sling up my arm," he said. "It hurts so much to hold the weight of it." But he managed to get Greeley's blanket across him with his good arm. Greeley closed his eyes and slept.

When Greeley awakened, it was afternoon and Julius was gone. He was puzzled by this until he found a note tucked under the corner of his blanket. Julius had written it with some of his blood. Greeley knew this was no attempt to be morbid or dramatic, but merely reflective of the fact that Julius had no other available ink. From the way it was crusted, Greeley figured the note had been written some hours before.

"GONE TO see iF I kin find sum of the Mail."

Greeley laid the note aside, sat up, and groaned. Quite a knock he'd taken! His head hurt very much. Remembering how a boyhood friend of his had been head-injured and come out of it with his ability to read and cipher numbers completely gone, Greeley did some sums and spelling in his head, traced back his family tree a few generations, and summarized the progress of the war, just to reassure himself he hadn't lost any faculties.

He hadn't lost his rifle, either. It was leaned up against a tree nearby. He guessed the Fayettes had overlooked it in the darkness, because they had taken his pistol.

He rose, drank from Julius's water bottle, took up his rifle and tried to find and follow Julius's trail. Find it he did, but following it proved too much for him just yet, and he returned to the camp. He was very hungry, and so dug a bit of food from Julius's pack, figuring the youth wouldn't mind.

Fifteen minutes later Julius came striding into the camp, carrying Greeley's pack across his unwounded shoulder. He looked poorly, the wound obviously having begun to hurt because of his exertions, but he was grinning. Rather triumphantly, he plopped down the pack, which seemed as well-stuffed as the last time Greeley had seen it.

"You look awful, Julius."

"I overdone it. My shoulder's hurting and making me feel sick at my stomach."

"Is that pack still full of letters?"

"Yes, but don't get your hopes up. They opened every one of them, and if there was money inside, they took it. The letters are all out of the envelopes and jumbled up together, but I believe I found most all of them. They were scattered all around the woods. We'll have to piece together which letters go in which envelopes. I'm sorry about the money."

"You shouldn't have gone to that trouble. It could have been dangerous if the Fayettes had been lingering about." Greeley grinned. "But thank you all the same. I'm glad I'll at least have the letters to deliver."

"What are we going to do, Greeley? I don't know that either one of us is in shape to push ahead just now."

"We'd best stay put a day or two, if our food can hold out. I ate a few bites of yours, by the way."

"What I have is yours, Greeley Brown. Tell you what— why don't I set a few rabbit snares about and see what we can get that way. If there's a stream within reach, I could put out a line for some fish, too."

"You're a capable fellow, Julius. I'm sorry they shot you. But I'm glad they didn't put that bullet through your head."

"Would've bounced right off my rocky skull, Greeley." He grinned pensively. "Crowell always used to tell me that. He'd rap me with a knuckle on the noggin and say, 'Julius, you got a rocky skull.' "

"Good brother, was he . . . *is* he, I mean?"

"Yep. Yep, he is. I hope he's not hurt or dead or nothing."

"I'd help you look for him if I could. But I'll have letters to carry about, and I bet you there's already a new gang of men hoping for me to pilot them to Kentucky. Back and forth, that's pretty much it for me. Back and forth, rebels breathing down my neck both ways."

"Sounds no worse than squatting out in the mountains, jumping at every shadow and crow call. Maybe better," Julius replied. "Me and Pap have done enough lying out to suit us both the rest of our days. At least you get to move around. You get to *do* something"

Chapter 10

Julius proved himself capable of getting on quite well with one arm bandaged and slung up. His snares fetched in three rabbits, and an improvised fishing line hooked a whole panful of trout. They had no pan to cook them in, however, Greeley's having been taken by the Fayette brothers. So they spitted the fish on green sticks and roasted them near a slow fire.

Meanwhile, they worked on matching letters to envelopes. It was mostly a matter of matching up addresses, handwriting, and so on. Greeley handled most of this, going through the letters one by one, fitting rumpled papers with their proper envelopes, trying his best not to read more than he had to. What he did read was all the same kind of thing—warm greetings to "much-missed, much-beloved dear ones," or "darling wife and children," and declarations that all was well, victory was coming, the "foul rebel foe" would soon be driven down, and all would be well again. There were occasional references to humorous events that had happened in camp, occurrences of battle, or some quote from the camp chaplain that had made the writer think of his loved ones at home. All typical material . . . but it made

Greeley feel strange, isolated, cut off from the best aspects of life. Alone.

He'd been married once, and had buried her. Not a day passed that he didn't think of her, and hurt.

Right now he would have given anything he owned, what little that was, to have a real home waiting for him at the other end of this journey, and a real, living, loving wife to welcome him, pet him, worry over him, maybe shed a few tears over his bruised skull. Real children to tousle and laugh with and fret over. There wasn't a man who had written the letters he carried who didn't consider himself in a hard and terrible situation, being away from his home and loved ones—but there wasn't a man of them Greeley didn't envy.

He picked up the final letter and immediately revised that thought. This letter was written by one man he did not envy at all: Spencer Cline.

He didn't intend to read any of Cline's letter. It wasn't necessary to do so even to match it to its envelope, the process of elimination having already taken care of that. But Greeley's eye fell randomly on a portion of the second page, and he read silently, guiltily, until he forced himself to stop and glanced up to make sure Julius hadn't seen him doing it.

Greeley went to sleep that night thinking about the lines he'd read, feeling deeply troubled. What he gleaned from those few sentences he would have rather not known.

The next morning they broke their camp and continued on their journey. Greeley's head still throbbed and Julius's plowed shoulder was slightly infected and ached. Neither complained. They were equally eager to plunge deep into East Tennessee and put behind them a trek that had proven far more troublesome and dangerous than expected.

They reached Clinch Mountain and crossed to its southern slope, where they remained throughout the next day. That night they pushed themselves particularly hard, making about half the distance to Greeley's home. They spent the night in the home of one of the families whose patriarch had been among Greeley's most recent stampeder groups;

Greeley handed over a letter, with an explanation about why it had been opened and why no money was included. To his relief, his story was accepted here without evident suspicions being cast his way. He hoped it would be that way when he carried the ravaged letters to other homes.

They went on. Julius was eager to go to the French Broad and begin his own personal search, but had decided to lay up at Greeley's place for two or three days until his wound cast off its infection. Greeley admitted he would be glad for the company. Fate couldn't have thrown to him a more compatible—or honorable—young companion than Julius Killefer.

They reached the base of what was to Greeley a familiar and welcome ridge, and the foot of a hidden trail that ran up to his lodgings. They climbed, so eager for the end of the journey that they hardly felt injured skulls or bullet-plowed shoulders. But eager steps came to an abrupt halt when Greeley saw that his little cabin, a tiny hut that was the most recent in a series of hidden mountain dwellings, was no longer there. All that remained were charred timbers, cold and black.

Greeley stared numbly. Julius kept total silence.

"Greeley! Is that you, Greeley?"

They turned. An old, nearly doubled-over man with a long beard white as clean lamb's wool came striding toward them.

"Who's that?" Julius asked.

"Mathen Ricker," Greeley replied. "An old fellow who lives by himself across the ridge."

"He's a Union man, I hope to God."

"Nope. Mathen's a strong-minded rebel. But he's a friend of mine, and that counts more to him than politics." Greeley raised his hand and waved at the oncoming old fellow. "Hello, Mathen! Glad to see you well!"

"Whose that there with you, Greeley?"

"This here's Julius Killefer, from Kentucky. Julius, meet Mathen Ricker."

"Pleased," Julius mumbled, looking very distrustful.

"Killefer . . . that's a name I've heard hereabouts," Ricker said as he reached them. He was so bent that he had to tilt his head up to look at them. Had his spine miraculously straightened, he would have been staring straight up into the heavens.

"Julius's ancestors come from this area," Greeley said. "Mathen, what the deuce happened to my hut? Was it rebs?"

"It was. They come a day, two days maybe, after you left. Injuns. Red-skinned, Cherokee Injuns, out of Carolina. Come looking for you, aiming to take you in, or maybe to kill you, and when you waren't to be found, they set fire to your place and left. Burned some other places, too. Committed wicked acts aplenty among the Union folk." He leaned over and spat tobacco amber across his right foot. "I despise Injuns. Always have. I don't care if they are fighting on my side."

"Did they bother you?"

"Nope. Never come over the ridge, even. They seem to know who was Union and who wasn't. But I watched them destroy your place. Made me feel bad, Greeley. I wish you'd turn Confederate. Your life would go a mite easier if you did."

"Maybe—until the Union army sweeps in. Then I'll be glad I've stood by the old flag."

"T'ain't going to happen, Greeley. T'ain't going to happen. But be that as it may, they've sure 'nough burned you out. I saw it going up in flames from up on my setting rock."

Greeley saw Julius's look of puzzlement and explained, "Mathen's 'setting rock' is a kind of natural stone chair up atop the ridge. He goes up there and sits, looks around at the world. Sings, too, at night. I've gone to sleep many a time hearing him sing."

"I got a voice like a mockingbird," the old man said.

"Injuns did this, you say?"

"Yep."

"Some of Thomas's Highland Legion, I'll bet."

"So I feel sure."

"Well . . . what would you think of putting up a couple of good Union men for a spell, Mathen? Otherwise we'll be sleeping in a cave somewhere."

"You know you're always welcome, Greeley. And your young friend, too."

"Thank you, Mathen."

Julius turned his back on the old man and whispered sharply, "Greeley, you're putting us up with a rebel?"

"I told you, Julius, Mathen puts more stock in friendship than political allegiance. He won't betray me any more than I'd betray him if the situation was turned about. Believe me, we'll be safe with Mathen." Greeley grinned a bit. "He's an honorable man."

Before they set off over the ridge, Greeley looked sadly at the remains of his home one more time. "Well, at least it wasn't big and well-finished, like the first place of mine the rebs burned. Caesar Augustus, Mathen, I'll surely be glad when this war's over."

"Don't say that, Greeley. When the war's over, the victorious Confederacy will be obliged to hang you for all the treason you've done against it. I, for one, dread seeing it."

Greeley strode up the hill at Mathen Ricker's side, Julius hanging back and looking very uncertain but following all the same.

Part II

THREE QUESTS

Chapter 11

The woman was clearly trying to maintain an expression purely of sympathy for the bearded, dirty, maimed man who stood slumped before her where the alley joined the street, but obvious repulsion kept intruding, making her wrinkle her nose against the stench of his unwashed person. She cringed particularly when the organic reek of the ugly rag bandage that wrapped the stump where a hand should have been wafted to her nostrils. It was an old bandage, soaked through with blood that had long ago blackened into a permanent stain. She looked away from it as the man told his woeful tale, but he was prone to wave the stump about while he talked, often sweeping it beneath her nose.

". . . and along that cannonball came, just a-bounding along the ground," the malodorous fellow was saying. "It was as spent as could be, just bouncing like a ball, and I says to myself, 'Slow as that's coming, I can catch that cannonball barehanded.' It was just like a ball that had been throwed, you know. I loped out and stuck my hand out to do it, and next thing I know, that cannonball's just a-loping along on past me as if I hadn't even touched it, and there ain't no hand on the end of my arm no more. Oh, the blood just a-squirted! I never found that hand, though I looked hard. I swear it was as if that cannonball just ate it." He looked at his feet, scuffed his boot toe on the dirt. "Now I ain't nothing but a poor discharged Confederate soldier with nothing to my name, no home, no people, no money. Nothing to eat . . . nothing to drink."

"What battle was it you lost your hand in, sir?" the woman asked, her face having gone pallid at mention of the squirting blood.

"It was . . . it was . . . tell you the truth, ma'am, once I lost my hand, I lost all my memory of that battle. The shock and terror of it, you see. I don't rightly know what battle it was."

Her expression changed. "That's odd. You seem to have a remarkably clear memory of how you lost the hand."

"It's everything after losing it I don't recall, ma'am."

"Then you still should be able to recall what battle it was. You would have known prior to the fight where you were, wouldn't you?"

"Well, I . . ."

She shook her head. "Sir, I'm sorry, but I think you're lying to me, trying to get me to give you some money."

"I'd never do such a thing, ma'am."

A new voice spoke. "Ma'am, if I was you, I'd walk away from that man. He's a liar and a drunken beggar, and he ain't never been a soldier. As I hear it, he lost that hand after getting it cut on a busted water bottle he'd dropped while fleeing Tennessee so as not to be conscripted."

The woman turned to the man saying these things. He had come up behind her unnoticed. He wore a Confederate corporal's uniform and had a boyish, freckled face and bright red hair. "My name's Curtis Delmer, ma'am. I live in the Harpeth Valley over at Nashville now, but I grew up right here in Knoxville. That there's Ben Scarlett, the worst of the local drunks."

She wheeled to the one-handed man. "Is this true, sir?"

"I, uh . . . well . . . ma'am, the fact is, whether I was a soldier or not, I'm still one-handed and pitiful, and could use any help you might spare."

Curtis Delmer stepped around the woman, grabbed the

rag on Ben Scarlett's wrist and yanked it off. Revealed was a stump that had thoroughly healed over. "See there, ma'am? He lost that hand long ago. All this blood on the bandage, I expect it's cow blood from the slaughterhouse, or from a dead dog or something. Disgusting, ain't he? And a liar besides."

The woman grew haughty. "I do not appreciate you lying to me, sir," she said to Ben. "I'll give you nothing. Not a thing! Good day." She turned to the soldier. "Corporal, I thank you for intervening. I might have wasted good money on this scoundrel had you not come along. You are to be commended."

He smiled and touched his hat. His boyish face, if only a few years younger, could have been a Sunday school book portrait of the proverbial Fine Little Gentleman. "Just trying to be helpful, ma'am. Good day to you."

She made a wide circle around Ben Scarlett and headed down the street. Ben, meanwhile, ducked back into the alley and began walking very swiftly away from Curtis Delmer, whose gentlemanly manner vanished once the woman was gone. He took three long strides after the fleeing beggar and grabbed him by the collar, yanking him around. Ben Scarlett looked for a second into Delmer's meanly grinning face and quickly averted his eyes.

"I ought to trounce you, Ben Scarlett," Delmer said, shaking him by the collar. "Still the same sorry old drunk you've been for years."

"Let me go, Curtis. Please."

"Who gave you leave to call me by name? I'm Corporal Delmer to you!"

"Yes sir, Corporal Delmer."

Delmer brought up his free hand and slapped Ben on his bearded cheek. "That's for begging." He slapped him again. "That's for being Ben Scarlett the drunk." A third slap followed. "That's for making me have to take time out of my day to deal with you." Yet another slap fell, hardest of all. "And that's for stinking. The reek of you makes me sick!"

Ben was older and bigger than his abuser, yet he lifted not a hand to defend himself. Instead he cringed and pleaded for the soldier not to slap him again.

"Listen at you beg! You're a puke-eating dog, Ben. Naw, you ain't even good as that! You're lower by far."

"Let me go, Curtis . . . Corporal Delmer. Please just let me go."

"All righty, I will." He shoved Ben off his feet.

Ben fell on his rump, catching himself partially with his one hand, but unfortunately chancing to put that hand right into a fresh pile of dog manure. Delmer cackled with laughter.

"Found you a prize, Ben?" He strode up and pushed the toe of his boot into the smashed manure pile, reached down and grabbed Ben by the hair, hard. He lifted his fouled boot before Ben's face.

"You think you're worthy to kiss a real man's boot, Ben?"

"Don't be so bad to me! I ain't never hurt you." Ben pulled away from the boot, and caught the glimpse of something falling from the soldier's coat. It landed just behind Delmer, who didn't appear to notice it.

"Don't be bad to you? Why, I'm *supposed* to be bad to you, Ben! I been bad to you since I was little! Don't you wish you had a dollar for every rock I've throwed at you when I was just a sprout? Huh?" He laughed. "I'll bet you danced for joy the day I moved away from this town, didn't you? Well, guess what, Ben? I'm back!"

"Let me go."

"Kiss my boot first." He shook the manured foot in Ben's face and yanked his hair.

"No. No!"

"You kiss that boot or I'll make you eat what I stepped in. I mean it. I'll make you eat every bit of it."

"Curtis Delmer!"

The startled soldier turned, letting go of Ben, who sank back onto his rump—and surreptitiously extended a foot out to drag back toward him the object he'd seen fall from Delmer's coat.

At the end of the alley stood Daniel Baumgardner, a long-time Knoxville merchant who had known Ben Scarlett most of his life and Curtis Delmer all of his. At the moment, the florid-faced storekeeper, with his characteristic underbite, stood tall with fury as he stared at the abusive soldier. "Curtis Delmer, what I've just witnessed makes me ashamed of you. Your parents must be turning in their graves if they can see that their boy is down to torturing downtrodden souls like poor old Ben."

"Mr. Baumgardner, I was only having a bit of frolic."

Ben got his hand onto the object he'd snared and slipped it into the pocket of his coat, unnoticed by either of the others.

"I don't favor that kind of frolic, and won't stand by and let you do it."

Ben stood, backing away. He thought about running, but it was fun to see Delmer squirm under Baumgardner's scolding. The hierarchy of relative dominance in the little society in that alley had undergone a major change with Baumgardner's arrival. Delmer's uniform and military status held no sway with the merchant, who had employed him in his store when he was a boy and still held a residual authority over him that wouldn't have been lessened had Delmer been the president himself. Delmer was in the position of the schoolyard bully just confronted in the act by the headmaster.

Ben himself assumed a schoolyard role: the tattler. "He was trying to make me kiss his boot, Mr. Baumgardner."

"I saw, Ben. Delmer, I'm ashamed of you. You get away from here and leave him alone."

"Hell-fire, Mr. Baumgardner, he's only a drunk!"

"Better a drunk than a cruel man," Baumgardner replied. "And don't you go cussing around me."

"He was trying to get some woman to give him money, claiming he had lost his hand in battle. Look there! He's got part of somebody's old uniform on! He shouldn't be allowed to do that kind of thing, Mr. Baumgardner."

"You're not his keeper. Get on out of here, Delmer. Haven't you got anything better to do than roam this town? I'll bet you ain't where you're supposed to be. Maybe if I told some of your superiors just how much time you take roaming the streets, bothering the town drunks and such, they'd find you better ways to keep busy."

"No need for you to do that, Mr. Baumgardner," Delmer

said. "I'll go." He fired a quick glance back at Ben that said: *Later*, as clearly as if he'd spoken it aloud.

Delmer strode off, past Baumgardner, turning right at the alley's end. Baumgardner watched him go and shook his head. "He was no-account when he was working for me, and now he's no-account as a soldier, either. That Delmer's got a mean streak longer than a scold's tongue."

"I thank you for your help, Mr. Baumgardner."

"Ben, when in the world are you going to change your ways? You know you'll always have to put up with such abuse as long as you live like you do."

"I know." Ben wished Baumgardner would go away so he could examine the item he'd secretly confiscated.

"I don't know how you've managed to live as long as you have. Most of your kind is dead before they hit your age."

"The Lord's been good to me."

Baumgardner took that one in, digested it, then laughed. "The Lord's been good to you! Ben Scarlett, what other kind of drunkard but you would say something like that!" He laughed again. "Well, maybe you ought to consider trying to improve yourself. That'd be a good way to thank the Lord for all those blessings huh?" He paused, studying Ben, growing more somber. "You got a place to sleep these days?"

"Yes sir, I do."

"Is it decent shelter?"

"Decent enough."

"Well . . . you take care of yourself, Ben. Have you any food?"

"Yes sir." This was the truth; he had recently stolen half a smoked ham from Baumgardner, though the merchant didn't know it. He also had a loaf and a half of stale bread filched from a local bakery. All these foodstuffs were stored safely away in the secret, snug refuge where he made his home now, unknown to all.

"You get hungry, Ben, you come see me. You hear? And try to stay clear of Curtis Delmer."

"Yes sir. Thank you, Mr. Baumgardner." He ducked his head. The merchant had become the closest thing to a friend he had in Knoxville. In past years Baumgardner had been more of a scourge, chiding him, preaching at him, running him out of his shed. War had brought death to Baumgardner's sons, however, and since then he'd changed. He was much kinder now, forgiving, generous. Ben would never know how to say or show it, but he had come to love the man dearly.

Baumgardner walked away, humming to himself. Ben stayed where he was until the merchant was gone, then dug from his pocket the item he'd hooked. It was a man's leather purse, well-stuffed. Ben glanced quickly inside and saw a few coins and some folded Confederate currency, along with a few other items he would go through later, when he was safe in his refuge. Realizing that Delmer might have lingered on the street, waiting for Baumgardner to leave, Ben put the purse back into his pocket and left the alley by its opposite end, and began winding his way through the streets of Confederate-occupied Knoxville toward the big old warehouse building where he made his secret domicile.

Ben whistled idly and peered about to make sure no one was nearby to see him as he turned around the rear of the warehouse and into a little overgrown patch of trees and brush that had grown up in the months since this building had fallen into neglect. At one time this big structure had housed the offices of a local pro-secession newspaper called the *Secession Advocate*, but that journal's publisher, Dr. George Deacon, was dead now these many months, and the building was locked and empty. Its front right section had been badly damaged by fire and the building was considered a collapse-prone hazard, and so had escaped use by the occupying Confederate military.

A ladder hidden among the brush made for Ben's staircase. He mounted it and climbed, reaching the top of the building's rear. Just beside the ladder's top was a big wall panel that stayed in place only by merit of a single nail at the top. Ben pulled the panel slightly out and swung it aside, opening the unseen door into his private refuge. Carefully he slipped from the ladder into the opening—this being the single truly dangerous part of entry, during which he had to swing his body out for a moment across empty space—and once inside, swung the panel back down and pulled it as best he could back into place.

It was dark here, but he dug out his matches and lit the coal-oil lamp that had once burned on the desk of the *Advocate*'s editor. Light flooded a little upper room in which Ben had a cot, an old chest of drawers he'd found elsewhere in the warehouse, a three-legged stool, and a few crates turned on their sides and stacked for shelving. The crates also made up one wall of the bottle-strewn room, which was really just a portion of a big upper storage loft, now empty. Old copies of the *Advocate*, glued in layers against the walls, made for good insulation, and Ben even had a small, square heater of iron, vented through scrounged stovepipes into the main part of the empty warehouse. There the smoke could disperse unseen. Ben couldn't vent it outside because somebody would be bound to notice it eventually.

He loved the warmth, security, and solitude of his makeshift room. The empty warehouse beyond the stacked-crate wall could seem haunting and grim by night, but he had merely to draw the curtain door shut to block it out and feel protected.

Apart from the etchings on the pages of newspapers papering the walls, there was but one picture in Ben's room. He had found it inside George Deacon's old desk in the enclosed office area at the warehouse's front. It was a photograph of a pretty, dark-haired, young woman, Deacon's own daughter Amy, whom Ben had come to deeply admire. He'd actually helped her smuggle counterfeit rebel currency into Tennessee from Cumberland Gap—she was acting as a Union espionage agent at the time—and when last he saw her, she was entering a Knoxville hotel to deliver the contraband money. He'd wandered off, leaving her there, and returned to his haunts in the streets. Now he didn't know where she was. She was supposed to have gone on to Nashville from Knoxville, and he supposed that she had, to return again to her spying and smuggling. He worried about her often, and prayed for her at night, though he didn't know if the prayers of a drunkard counted for much. He wondered if she ever thought of him. He doubted it. It didn't matter. He would love her just the same.

Ben sat down on the stool and pulled Delmer's leather pouch from his pocket. He counted out the money—seventeen dollars and a few cents—and began probing through the rest of the contents. To his delight he discovered a woman's ring, made of gold and set with a jewel. Ben eyed it with a smile, wondering how much it was worth and where Delmer had gotten it. Stolen, probably. Delmer seemed the kind who would steal something if he had the chance.

Other than the money and the ring, the purse contained nothing of value. There was a scrap of a letter, a few personal notes that made no sense to him, and various other scraps of this and that. Then Ben felt something stiff inside the lining of the wallet and scooted over closer to the lamp to examine it. He found a tear in the lining, poked his fingers in and pulled out a stiff piece of cardboard with a gold border around its edges and a photograph in its center. He looked at the picture and gaped, for odd though it might have seemed, Ben Scarlett was a quite prudish, almost puritanical man when it came to women.

Shown in the picture was a woman posing on a fancy parlor chair, her face at semiprofile and her arms reaching down to pull up her skirts to an indecently high level, showing a white expanse of thigh. Ben shook his head in disapproval—but also stared quite closely at it. He had seen a few of this kind of picture before—the soldiers in and around Knoxville were prone to have these, and flashed them about sometimes—but Ben had never possessed one himself.

"Shame on you, you hussy!" he said to the woman in the picture. "Shame on you, showing off yourself that way!"

All at once he began to frown. Pulling even closer to the lamp, he studied the woman more closely. He set the picture aside, stood, and paced around the room a time or two. His stomach grumbled and he fetched some of his bread. Gnawing at a hunk of it, he looked at the picture, lying on the floor, his brows knitting. He squatted, picked it up and studied it awhile longer, looking closely at the woman's face.

"No," he said. "No, it ain't her. Couldn't be."

He put the picture on one of the shelves, built up a small fire in his stove, and sliced up some ham to fry. As it sizzled in the pan, smoke belching out through the pipe into the dark warehouse beyond his makeshift wall, he took the picture in hand again and continued to examine it. When he ate his supper, he hardly tasted it, being preoccupied with the picture and the hauntingly familiar face of the fallen woman it pictured.

Just after midnight Ben Scarlett sat up on his bunk and sighed. Sleep usually came easy for him, but then, usually he was drunk, and tonight he hadn't touched a drop. Hadn't even thought about it, oddly enough, his mind being too filled with another matter.

He rose and lighted his lamp. Crouching with lamp in hand, he slipped out through his curtain door and into the warehouse. At once the lamplight was swallowed by the pervasive blackness; its flicker was feeble and small, but gave sufficient illumination to guide Ben across the loft and down the stairs to the main level below. He walked toward the front of the building and pushed open the door that led up to the old office of the *Advocate*. Though the press was gone now, taken over by the Confederate authorities and moved elsewhere, some of the furniture and other items remained, among them an old ink barrel. Ben went to the barrel and pried off its lid. Poking around the old office section, he found an empty inkwell, which he thrust down into the barrel, dipping into the meager remnants of ink that hadn't yet dried up. He capped the little well shut and carried it back with him to his upper room, closing the curtain behind him.

He removed the little cardboard picture from its place on the shelf, stuck a finger into the inkwell, and carefully dabbed ink onto the portion of the picture showing the woman's thigh. He covered that portion thickly, looked at it and nodded.

"There, Angel. Now you're decent, like you ought to

be," he said. "That's better. That's the Angel I remember. Good and sweet, like her name."

He sat the picture up on the shelf, beside that of Amy Deacon, and looked at it a long time before blowing out the lamp and crawling back onto his cot. This time he fell asleep almost at once.

Chapter 12

The next evening

It had been a long day for Daniel Baumgardner, nothing going right from the moment he opened the doors of his store. He'd been looking forward to closing time since midday, but now that it had come and he was totaling up the day's receipts, he was faced with a realization that somehow, part of his money was missing. Gritting his teeth as best his snow-shovel underbite would allow, Baumgardner thought back on a group of seven Confederate soldiers who'd come bursting in earlier, spreading across the store, two of them making quite a racket toward the front and distracting his attention while the others fanned through the place. . . .

He seemed to recall that one had been in the vicinity of the cash drawer. His florid face grew even redder. Thieves! These days a merchant was hard-pressed to get by at best, with merchandise hard to obtain, growing even more expensive, and with the law requiring the honoring of increasingly low-valued Confederate currency. To be robbed atop of all that, by soldiers, of all people, was unbearably galling. Baumgardner instantly made plans to make a timely visit to the city's top military authorities and have a few words with them about the behavior of some of their soldiers. He might even mention what he saw Curtis Delmer doing to poor old Ben Scarlett.

The front door rattled. Baumgardner rose from his seat in the rear office room, took off his reading spectacles, and stuck his head out into the store. He saw a figure at the door and was about to yell at the fellow that the place was closed—as the sign in the front window clearly stated, anyway—but noticed that it was Ben Scarlett. He gave a snort of displeasure, not being in the mood to fool with Ben just now.

Baumgardner walked up to the door and through its paned window said, "Ben, I'm closed for the day."

"Can I come in a minute? Just to have a word?" Ben said back.

He's come for food, I suppose, Baumgardner thought. *Well, I did make the offer.* Sighing, he opened the door, let Ben in, and closed the door behind him.

"Ben, you stink." The merchant was in no mood to mince words.

"I know. Everybody tells me that. I don't smell it, myself. I reckon a body gets used to itself."

"What do you want?"

"Just wanted to see if you could tell me anything about where a certain kind of thing comes from."

"What are you talking about?"

Ben dug into his pocket, pulled out the picture he'd taken from Delmer, and handed it to Baumgardner.

"What's this?" The merchant put his spectacles back on and peered at the photograph. His eyes went wide and he thrust it back at Ben as if it had become hot in his hand. "Why are you coming in here showing me French pictures? I'm not the kind of man to look at such filth as that!"

"French pictures? So it's France they come from?"

"I don't know—that's just what I've heard such rubbish called. That's indecent, Ben! I'm surprised at you, showing me such a thing!"

"The bad part's inked over, Mr. Baumgardner."

"Well . . . yes, I see that." He took back the picture and looked at it again, more closely.

"You won't be able to see through the ink. It's laid on thick."

"I am *not* trying to see through the ink!" Baumgardner grew more red even than he'd been, and thrust the picture back to Ben again. "Are you drunk again, Ben? Why in the devil have you come here? I'm busy."

"I thought that you, being a merchant and all, might be able to tell me where these kinds of pictures comes from."

"How should I know? I don't market in trash."

"But I need to find out."

"Well, as best I know, it's mostly soldiers that carry them. Foul fellows, so many of these soldiers are. You get them away from home, away from their families and their churches and such, and the indecent side of them comes right out. And dishonesty, too! Confounded soldiers will steal a man blind, and him just trying to make a living—"

"I know it's the soldiers that carry them. I want to know where they come from *before* that. Where they make these pictures."

"I have no idea. I'm offended you'd think I *would* know." Baumgardner paused, his redness decreasing as curiosity began to take over. "Ben, where'd you get that?"

"A soldier . . . give it to me."

"Why'd he smear ink on it?"

"He didn't. I did."

"May I ask you why?"

"I didn't like seeing her show her leg that way. It made me feel bad that she'd do such a thing."

"Ben, women like that one probably would do a lot more than just show their leg to a picture box. I'd think a man of the world like you would be aware of that."

"She wouldn't, I don't believe. I don't want to think she would."

"You *are* drunk. You're not making any sense. You talk like you know this woman."

Ben said nothing. He fingered the picture, looking at the face.

Baumgardner, puzzled, found his harsh feelings softening further. Ben had a way of bringing out the soft side in him, though for the life of him, he didn't know why.

"Ben, I doubt you'll find out where that picture was made, unless there's a photographer's mark on the back. Have you looked?"

"No. I don't know much about pictures." He flipped the picture over and examined the back. "What's a photographer's mark?"

"Here, let me see. I doubt anyone who takes this kind of picture puts his name on them. . . ." Baumgardner squinted through his spectacles. "No. Just as I thought—it's blank . . . no, wait a minute." He grasped a corner and began to peel off a layer of paper pasted atop the cardboard mounting.

"Don't tear it up!"

"I'm not, just peeling up the backing. Well, I'll be! Look there! 'Henson Belle Fine Photography, Nashville, Tennessee.' You see?" He held it up for Ben to examine.

Ben read the words and nodded. "So that picture comes from Nashville?"

"I suppose it does." Baumgardner did some quick deduction. "Know what I think? I think this Henson Belle probably runs your usual kind of photograph studio in Nashville, but does these foul kinds of pictures on the sneak, and covers over the back of them with paper to hide the fact it's him doing them. Not very smart of him. It's easy enough to peel off and see his mark, plain as day."

"Henson Belle," Ben repeated. "Henson Belle."

"Might I ask why you're so curious about this picture?"

"Just curious, that's all."

"Ben, *do* you know that woman?"

"Why, no, no. Of course I don't. How would I know her?"

Baumgardner had learned to read Ben long ago, and saw there was more here than was going to be said. He smiled slightly. "Ben, you are indeed a strange bird. I've never known any man with as many confusing qualities as you have. I don't know another man who'd be so intrigued by pictures like that, and then smear ink across them. It makes no sense to me."

Ben pocketed the picture. "I'm just a drunk and a fool. I never claimed to make sense."

Baumgardner laughed. It felt good to laugh after a day

like his. Unexpectedly, even to himself, he issued an invitation: "Ben, would you come eat supper with me this evening? And maybe take a look through some of my old clothes and see if there's any you'd want? Nobody should walk around in stinking rags like you do."

Ben smiled brightly. "I'd be glad to eat with you, sir." Baumgardner had fed him many a time, good and tasty meals, all of them.

"There's a price, though. If you're going to eat at my table, you're going to clean up first. If you'll wait around a few minutes, I'll finish up here and we'll go to my house. I'll fill you a good bath there."

Ben didn't care much for the bath notion, but it seemed a small price to pay for one of Baumgardner's meals, and a new suit of clothes besides. "Fair enough, Mr. Baumgardner."

It was late in the evening by the time the meal was done. Baumgardner gave Ben a pipe and some tobacco, and they sat up late, talking about the war. Ben wanted liquor badly, having had little that day, but Baumgardner was a teetotaler, so there was no point in asking.

He fell asleep on Baumgardner's couch. The widower merchant knocked out his last pipeful of tobacco, pulled a quilt up over Ben's sleeping form, and headed for his own room, blowing out the light as he went. It was raining softly outside, pattering down gently on the roof, washing the soot from the Knoxville skies.

The next morning

Ben had just made the turn around the rear of Deacon's old warehouse, heading for his ladder, when they jumped him. He was on the ground before he knew what was happening, his new clothes being soiled by mud, his face mashing into the ground beneath the weight of a boot pressing the back of his neck, and his ribs taking a pounding from several kicking feet. He let out a cry that was muffled by the ground and writhed, trying to move out of reach of the kicking feet. He was on the verge of passing out from suffocation when at last the boot sole left the back of his neck and the kicking stopped. He pulled his head up, sucking in air, and someone rolled him over.

"Where is it, Ben?" Curtis Delmer asked in his usual snide tone, but with an edge of hate beyond anything Ben had heard from him before. "Out with it, now!"

"I . . . what . . ."

They started kicking him again. There were three of them, all gray-uniformed and young, Delmer their obvious leader. Ben grunted and yelled, and this time Delmer put his boot over Ben's mouth.

"You're kissing that boot now, ain't you, Ben? I ought to jam it right down your throat! Don't you yell no more, hear?" He lifted his boot. "Tell me where it is, Ben."

"I don't know . . . what you're talking about. . . ."

Delmer said to the others, "Kick him some more. Break some ribs if you have to." He fished a cigar out of his pocket, lighting up and watching through the smoke while the others pummeled Ben again.

"No . . . stop . . . I'll give it . . . to you. . . ."

Delmer smiled around his cigar. "Now, that's what I wanted to hear, Ben! A little cooperation earlier on might have saved you a few bruises."

Ben lay gasping, hurting, face toward the sky, eyes closed.

Delmer walked up and kicked him, but not as hard this time. "Well, where is it?"

With eyes squeezed shut, Ben reached a trembling hand up and dug beneath the old coat—a new coat to Ben—that Baumgardner had given him. He brought out the picture and handed it up toward Delmer. He felt it snatched from his hand. He opened his eyes in time to see Delmer firing down a fiercely angry look at him. Ben braced for, and received, another kick, this one in the thigh and very hard indeed. He yelped in pain despite himself, providing Delmer an excuse for a follow-up kick.

"It ain't the picture I want, you reeking old drunk! Where's my purse? My money? My ring?"

"I ain't got them . . . on me . . . up in my room . . ."

"Up yonder?" Delmer waved toward the upper rear of

the warehouse, and Ben realized that the place he thought was his secret alone was in fact not a secret at all. He could only guess that Delmer had seen him entering or exiting sometime in the past, or had gotten information from someone else who had.

"Yes . . . I'll get them for you."

"No you won't. You don't appear in no shape to climb. I wonder why?" Delmer laughed. "I'll get it myself."

Ben, who seldom felt emotions beyond general feelings of sorrow or, when drunk, warm numbness that approximated a sense of well-being, now felt angry. The idea of Curtis Delmer entering his private haven and going through his possessions was rankling beyond words. He tried to sit up, pain notwithstanding, but Delmer kicked him down again.

"Don't let him get up," he ordered the others. He chewed the cigar while stomping off toward where the ladder was hidden. Ben heard him climbing, the panel being moved. After that came a couple of minutes mostly of silence. Ben lay in pain in the mud, the two soldiers grinning down at him, looking for an excuse to abuse him again. Occasionally, muffled crashing and cracking sounds came through from above—Delmer tearing up his refuge. It was all Ben could do to hold back tears.

A minute later Delmer descended the ladder again, looking very happy with himself. He walked over and looked down at Ben, smiling brightly, and flipped a hot cigar ash down on Ben's face.

"I found it! Every cent still there, and even the ring. I'd have figured you'd have spent it all on liquor by now."

"You tore up my room?"

"Yes indeedy. Kicked down all them crates, smashed it all up really fine. I thought about setting fire to it, but figured that might buy me more trouble than you're worth. So I just satisfied myself to make a bit of water all over it all." He guffawed, the others joining in.

Delmer knelt, bringing his face closer to Ben's. "Let me tell you, drunkard, that it's a good thing you hadn't spent my money. If you'd spent even a cent of it, even a cent, I'd have killed you, right here. And there ain't nobody in this town would have bothered to even figure out who done it, because there ain't nobody cares a bit about the likes of you. When you die, it'll matter no more than some stray dog getting run over by a wagon."

"Leave me alone . . ."

"I will, I will. You know why? Because I ain't never going to see you again. You're going to leave town, Ben Scarlett. You should never have took anything that was mine. You thought I wouldn't figure out you had my purse? Where else would I have lost it but in that alley with you?"

"I'm hurting . . ."

"You'll be hurting worse if ever I lay eyes on you again. You crossed the line when you stole from me, Ben. You done spit in the silver chalice, my friend."

"Look here what he's done to your leg picture, Curtis," one of the others said. "He's smeared ink all across the good part!"

"Yeah, yeah, I noticed that!" Delmer said, reminded. He took the picture and glanced at it. Abruptly he kicked Ben again, in the shoulder. "Why'd you ruin my picture, Ben?"

"I didn't . . . it was . . ."

"Ah, keep your mouth shut! I don't care about that picture no way—I've seen a lot better than that one. But what's wrong with you, anyhow, Ben Scarlett? Ain't you a man? Don't you like seeing them female legs and such?"

"He's sweet, bet you anything!" one of the others said.

"I ain't . . ." Ben didn't finish. He was hurting and beginning to feel very sick.

"Here—keep your picture," Delmer said, throwing it down atop Ben's heaving chest. "Every time you look at it, you think about me and how I'm going to kill you dead next time I see you. You'd best get out of town, Ben. And don't come back, not as long as I'm around."

The trio turned to stride off, each one giving Ben a final kick. One of them spat at his face and missed, tried again and hit him on the forehead. Ben lacked the spirit even to wipe it away.

They were almost gone when he sat up. "Wait . . ."

Delmer turned, obviously surprised Ben had called to him. "You talking to me, worm?"

"That picture . . . where'd you get it?"

Delmer looked incredulous. "Why do you care where I got it?"

"I got to know."

Delmer said, "It was give me by a Nashville boy. There's a feller there takes a lot of them pictures and sells them. Why you asking, you old sot?"

Ben laid back down and gave no reply.

"Get out of town, Ben!" Delmer said again. "I mean it!"

As they departed, Ben listened to the receding sound of them laughing and mocking at him, describing happily to each other how they'd kicked him here, there, and felt his bones straining with each blow. Their voices faded and were gone.

A few minutes later he managed to stand. He examined himself by feel, running his hands over his body. His new suit of secondhand clothes was almost ruined, and that made him sadder than he would have thought. He'd never cared much about clothes. But at least he still had Angel's picture.

He went to the ladder and managed to climb it, very slowly. He hurt badly and would hurt worse later on, he knew. With great difficulty and a near fall he made it through the makeshift door and into the room. The place reeked of urine; Delmer had wet the place like he said. Though this was a smell the drunkard Ben was more accustomed to than he would like to admit, this time it nearly made him sick, knowing it was Delmer who had caused it, and caused it out of pure meanness. He didn't miss the fact that Delmer had made a point of urinating on his food supply.

The room was destroyed. The stove was kicked over, the piping broken down, the crates shattered and splintered and kicked down. Two of the cot's legs were broken. The old newspaper with which he had insulated his walls were ripped down in shreds, and the picture of Amy Deacon, printed on a metal plate, had been bent, scratched, ruined.

Ben gathered up what he could salvage of his possessions, including the ruined picture of Amy Deacon, and packed them in a burlap feed bag. Groaning, fighting tears, then with a force of hard will, he forced himself to rise again. He descended the ladder with difficulty, dropping his bag in the process but making it safely to the ground.

He picked up his bag and threw it across his shoulder. His thigh ached from the kick it had received and he felt his face beginning to swell.

"I'll make quite a pretty sight, staggering down the road all bruised and banged," he muttered aloud.

He walked out onto the street and looked sadly around. "Well, I reckon it's good-bye to Knoxville," he murmured. Sorrow drained down over him. This was his town, a place he'd once left but had returned to, and now didn't want to leave. He thought briefly of going to Baumgardner, telling him what had happened, and seeing if Baumgardner would protect him—but no. Delmer's threats had been quite clear and sincere, and if he caused even more trouble for Delmer by reporting what he'd done, it might delay but would not halt Delmer from carrying out his threat sometime down the road.

Well, maybe it's all for the best. I got to go to Nashville anyhow. And I don't like some of the changes I'm seeing hereabouts. It's starting to look a little too much like war.

This was true indeed. Ever since late April, when Major General Simon Bolivar Buckner, the distinguished Confederate leader recently named commander of the Confederate Department of East Tennessee, had set up his headquarters in Knoxville, things had been changing. There were defensive posts around the depot and railyard, and an earthwork fort, called Fort Loudon, up on a hill near the university. Ben didn't like the looks of that. Knoxville hadn't seen much real war yet, and he'd hoped to see none here at all, but the forts and defense outposts and so on didn't bode well. Ben didn't follow the war news very closely and had no clear notions about what was going on, but it sure looked like the Confederates were getting ready for a fight. He didn't like fights. Maybe it was a good time to leave Knoxville for a lot of reasons, even if it was hard on his sentimental side.

He set out on a limping, slow stride, heading west, saying his mental good-byes to his city as he went, and thanking providence that at least his abusers hadn't broken any of his bones. He was at the edge of town before he finally broke down and began crying in earnest, hurting and humiliated, wishing he could be someone, anyone, besides Ben Scarlett.

Chapter 13

Stony Creek, near Elizabethton, Tennessee

Greeley Brown stood, hat in hand, and nodded a tense farewell to the woman who sat facing him, her expression melancholy, a freshly read letter held loosely in her hand.

"I'm mighty sorry, Mrs. Frakes," he said. "I regret the loss of the money you was to have received. If I had it to give you myself, I would."

"It's not your fault, Mr. Brown. You can't help it you was robbed." Her voice was soft, almost a whisper. Greeley turned the hat in his hands, fidgeted where he stood, and eyed the door.

Iron-faced July Frakes, seventeen-year-old eldest daughter of the family and a girl as thin as a sapling and taller by two inches than Greeley himself, looked at him piercingly. "I never heard of you being robbed before, Mr. Brown. They always told us you was a reliable man who always brung both letters and money through."

"I ain't been robbed before. This was the first time."

"It does seem odd, you still having the letter, but the money being took out."

Greeley tried to squelch a rising anger born of frustration. He had heard this refrain several times now from other families to whom he'd carried letters. The worst of it was that he could hardly blame them for being suspicious, and his defense, true though it was, had no evidence but his own word and visibly injured head to back it up. "I already told you, miss. The letters was stolen, tore open by the thieves, and the money took out. They threw the letters onto the ground, not caring about them. All they wanted was the money."

"What'd you say their names was?"

"Fayette. Two sorry brothers I piloted to Kentucky, not knowing them to be as bad as they was."

"So you've been friendly with the very thieves you say robbed you. Maybe you're *still* friendly with them—if there even are such men. It could be you made them up. I believe you might have just took that money out of them letters yourself."

Greeley thought, *Caesar Augustus! This girl ought to be in a court of law, prosecuting cases.* "I understand how you might be suspicious, Miss Frakes. All I can do is swear to you that I'm telling you the truth. I ain't a thief."

"Well, you took my father's money to pilot him north some months back, and promised him you'd carry back any money he sent to us. And you ain't done that. So I reckon you *are* a thief, that far at least! Maybe farther."

"July, please don't talk so to Mr. Brown," the mother chided, but there was no heart in it and Greeley knew she held the same suspicions as her more forthright daughter.

"Miss Frakes, I did for your father all I promised him. It ain't my fault I was robbed."

"Perhaps, Mr. Brown, it would be best if you just left," the mother said wearily. "Thank you for bringing Henry's letter to me."

"Yes, ma'am. And again, I'm mighty sorry the money's gone."

"Seems to me you ought to make it up out of your own pocket, being as how it was you who got it stole," July Frakes said.

"The truth is, Miss Frakes, I've done made up all the money I could to other families in just your same situation. But I ain't wealthy, and there's none left I can give."

"I don't believe you."

"You go ask some of these other families I've brought letters to, then. They'll tell you I gave all I could."

"I *will* ask. And I'll ask why they was privileged and we wasn't."

"July, that's enough!" Mrs. Frakes said. "Good-bye, Mr. Brown."

"Good-bye." He gave a final glance around at the faces staring back at him, the sad faces of the younger children and mother, the angry face of July Frakes. He felt a welter of emotions from sorrow to anger. He understood their situation, their skepticism toward him, and wished they could understand him in turn, and know he was speaking the truth.

Without another word he left the house, picked up the rifle he'd left leaning against a porch post, and walked across the road and into the woods.

He put a mile between himself and the Frakes house before sitting down beneath a tree to smoke a pipe of tobacco and try to calm down. In his mind he cursed the Fayette brothers, despising them not only for what they had done to the impoverished families of the good Union men he sought to serve, but also to him. Word would spread among the Unionist populace of East Tennessee about what had happened; distrust toward him would grow. It might well be that he would no longer be trusted to pilot other stampeders north, bringing an end to a career that was not only his personal moral calling, but his profession.

Well, it's been a worthy effort this far, and I can take pride in knowing that I've done it well, whatever folks may think. And at least I've carried all the letters through to all the families . . . all but one.

He dug into his now nearly empty pouch and pulled out the final letter: Spencer Cline's. He had put this one off until last mostly because he would have to travel far to deliver it, but also because he dreaded delivering it more than any of the others. Hard as it was to tell people about the stolen money, it would be harder yet to give word that this letter's writer had never even made it to Kentucky at all, and never would.

And there was that other aspect too, perhaps the most troubling one of all . . .

I wish I'd never read a word of this letter. It would have been better not to know.

For a moment the thought of simply putting a match to the letter and being done with it crossed his mind. He'd never been tempted to do anything like that before, but had never been faced with such a burdensome situation as this one. It would be a relief to simply put it all out of mind, let Spencer Cline be forgotten, along with the woman to whom this letter was addressed.

Maybe I'll really do it. Why should I take Spencer Cline's burdens on myself? He's the one who created the situation—wasn't my fault!

He lay his pack down for a pillow and stretched out on the leaves, wanting a brief nap. Generally, a few captured moments of sleep did him almost as much good as a night's rest, but this time his mind drifted into a dream: an infant lying on a railroad track, a train bearing down, closer, closer, the baby crying . . .

He awakened with a start, sitting up. *Just a dream, thank God.* But as he thought back on it, he knew what the dream meant, and that he could not run from the responsibility it reminded him of.

Greeley sighed, stood, and picked up his pack. *Confound me, I probably should have delivered this letter first, before the others. Yes, I should have. There's the child to think of. That child's more important than ungrateful and distrustful folks like the Frakeses. Don't you worry, Mr. Cline. I'll do all I can for that child. Lord only knows what it will be, though.*

He stood, weary and laden with a weight of responsibility that felt heavy enough to crush him to the ground. Many a hard mountain mile lay ahead before he would reach the little western North Carolina community of Warm Springs. He might as well get started, and get all this over with.

He sauntered off, wondering how Julius Killefer was getting along. They had parted days before, Greeley setting out with his letters, Julius to go seek his missing brother's family on the French Broad River. Julius's quest had its burdensome aspects, but at the moment Greeley felt he could trade his burden for Julius's in the span of a heartbeat.

Near the French Broad River, outside Newport, Tennessee

Julius Killefer stopped in his tracks, peering through the trees at whatever it was that had just moved somewhere among them. A free-roaming cow, maybe, or a hog. Maybe a deer . . . but then the movement came again and he saw it was in fact a sleek black mare, sixteen hands high at least. He was surprised. Horses were a highly protected commodity these days, the military having possession of most of the best ones, and farmers making do with whatever old and poorer animals were to be had.

This horse, however, was not poor at all. Julius knew horses well, and this was a fine one, strong and young. Why it was roaming loose in the woods he couldn't guess.

He clucked with his tongue and gave a gentle, soothing call: "Hey girl, hey girl, come on girl, hey girl." It was his father's way of calling his own mare, and imitating it struck an unexpected little pang of homesickness into Julius. He wondered how his father was doing right this moment, and if he was still having to hide out in the hills. "Hey girl. Come on now."

The mare was looking at him and didn't seem inclined to bolt. He approached quietly, slowly. "Hey girl."

"Please, sir, if you don't care, sir, I'd like to ask you not to take that horse, sir."

Julius heard the speaker's voice and saw him at the same moment. A small-built black boy it was, who had just emerged from behind a big oak. He was dressed in dirty but decent clothing, had on a good pair of brogan shoes, and a handmade straw hat that looked new. From his right hand dangled a rope halter. A young slave, Julius figured, and from the healthy and clear-eyed looks of him, one who enjoyed better circumstances than many of his counterparts.

"Hello, boy," Julius said. "What's your name?"

"Caleb, sir."

"That horse ain't yours, is it?"

"It's my master's, sir. It broke from the barn sometime last night and I been looking for it all day."

"Well, you've found it. Where do you live?"

"Yonder way." He pointed northwest, back up a ridge down which he had apparently descended as Julius had been traveling lengthwise along its base. "I'm from the Green Hill Farm, if you've heard of it."

"You think it safe to be out roaming alone with no pass?"

"I'm still on my master's land, sir."

"Is that right? I reckon I'm a trespasser, then. I thought that trail there was a public road."

"Ain't no true road, sir. Just a cow trail." He bowed his head a little, face growing humble, as he continued. "Sir, you mind, sir, if I go fetch that horse now?"

"You go ahead. I ain't a horse thief."

"No sir, no sir, I don't doubt that at all. You look an honest man, sir."

"I am. But I tell you, you'd better fix that barn so that horse don't get loose again. That's a fine animal, and there's many a man this day and age, in a uniform or out of one, who'd steal her in a minute. There's too little honor among folks these days."

"Yes sir. It's only been by cleverness we've kept her from being took already."

"How've you done it?"

"With molasses, sir. We pour it on her back and lay a blanket across it, so the molasses sticks it down. And when the soldiers and such comes looking for horses, they go to tug on that blanket and she ripples her back, and they say, 'This here mare ain't broke yet,' and so they don't take her. You know how an unbroke horse will always ripple its back that way."

"That's a clever trick, Caleb. You think it up?"

"I helped."

"Maybe you can help me, too. I'm looking for somebody."

"Sir, you ain't no bushwhacker or nothing, are you? You ain't looking for somebody to hurt them or nothing?"

That was an unexpectedly forthright bit of talk to come

from a slave, it seemed to Julius, whose views on slavery and the relative stations of white and black humanity were not by any standard progressive. "I ain't no bushwhacker. I ain't looking to hurt nobody. I'm looking for the house of Crowell Killefer. I was told in Newport it lay out in this direction."

Two eyes grew wide and fearful. "Sir, if I was you, I'd not go nowhere near that house!"

"I'll go where I need to go. That's my concern alone. Does it lie yonder way or not?"

"Yes, sir, it does. This trail forks where the ridge breaks, and if you'll turn the right hand way, sir, it'll take you up by the back way to the Killefer house." The youth looked like he wanted to say more, but clamped his mouth shut.

"You know if Crowell Killefer is home?"

"He ain't home, sir."

"Why'd you say I shouldn't go near his house?"

"Well, sir . . . 'cause of *her*, sir."

"Who? Crowell's wife?"

"Yes, sir."

"I'm supposed to be afraid of a woman?"

"Sir, I . . . I don't know how free I am to speak such truck to you, sir."

"Say what you want. I want to hear it."

"They say that Miz Susan, she a crazy woman."

"Crazy? What kind of crazy? And who's the 'they' saying all this?"

"The colored folk, sir. They all say she kilt her husband. They say she sit up there and sing lullabies at night just like the baby was there, but there ain't no baby. Maybe a *ghost* baby. That's what I think."

"I'd think you would have better to do than to sit around and think up spook stories. But tell me: Why do they say she killed her husband? Is it known he's dead?"

"No, sir. But he ain't there no more, so everybody just figures, you see, sir."

"Well, let me set you straight, and you can go back and tell all them doing this gossip-mongering: Crowell Killefer ain't dead, but just gone away. Maybe run off from home by bushwhackers and become an outlier. And his wife didn't kill him, for she don't know where he is and is worried about him. And there ain't no ghost baby or nothing like that. There's a real baby, living and breathing. I know that because I have a letter telling me about it."

"Yes, sir. Whatever you say, sir, I figure it's the gospel truth."

"More truth than you'll get listening to a bunch of gossip. 'Ghost baby!' Why you slaves so quick to believe such foolishness?"

"I don't know, sir."

"You'd best go fetch your horse. It's straying off down the ridge."

"Yes, sir. Good day to you, sir."

"Oh, and boy . . . no need to tell nobody you seen anybody in these woods today. Nor to say nothing to nobody about what we talked about. You hear?"

"Yes, sir."

"You take good care of that mare, all right? It's a fine one."

"I will, sir."

Julius wandered on, perturbed at the slave boy and at himself. The boy's talk had gotten to him far more than he'd let the young fellow see. His heart had jolted the moment he heard mention of rumors that Crowell was dead. And despite all he had said, for all he knew Crowell might indeed be dead, and the baby, too. Even Susan Killefer herself might be dead or gone, for all the information he had. Or she might in fact be as crazy as the boy had said. The letter she sent did have an unsettling quality about it. It was the boy's self-assured attitude that had angered Julius . . . and that the boy was saying things he didn't want to hear but couldn't really refute.

As he traveled along, following the trail and looking for the branch of it that would lead him toward Crowell's cabin, Julius began to regret the sharp way he'd talked to the boy. Though he was far from an abolitionist, and indeed accepted without question that his own race was the highest and best of all the world's varieties of people, Julius was able to feel a certain sympathy for slaves. It would be hard to live under the thumb of someone else, always having to do what they said, being able to make no real plans for one's own life. It didn't seem fair, he was able to admit . . . but, on the other hand, most of the preachers he'd known had said that God had set up whites to lord it over the "lesser races," and he had no grounds to question them. He had been told that some preachers, mostly farther north, said differently. But who could trust a northerner? As his father said: A man can support the old Union without loving Yankees.

Julius noticed the ridge beside him beginning to peter out, the tree-crested line of its top descending more to his level the farther he went. At just where it met the flat forest floor, the trail forked just as the slave said it would. Julius looked up the right branch of it. The path crawled along the forest floor for a hundred yards, then cut up the side of another, smaller ridge. On the other side of it he should find Crowell's house.

I hope she really ain't a crazy woman, and ain't really killed nobody. I hope Crowell's home, and that everything is good and fine.

He shifted the weight of his haversack, put his shotgun into his other hand, and set out along the branch of the trail leading toward the ridge.

Chapter 14

Evening, the same day

*T*ill the day I die, I'll never forget what it was like when
she come running at me. I'll dream about it every time I
close my eyes.

Julius Killefer lifted his spoon and tried again to hold it
steady enough that the soup wouldn't slosh out before he
could get it to his mouth. All prior efforts had failed almost
utterly, and this one went only a mite better. He managed to
get perhaps a third of the spoon's contents onto his tongue,
the rest being trembled out back into the bowl, onto the
table, or into his lap. *I won't be able to stand for a while,* he
realized. *I've sloshed so much into my lap she'll think I've
wet myself.*

He thought back to the moment, receded only an hour
into the past, when he met his sister-in-law face-to-face—
actually, face-to–rifle muzzle, the face being his, the rifle
hers—and wondered if maybe he really had wet himself.
She came as if from nowhere, rising from behind the well
when he strode into the yard, calling Crowell's name over
the fearsome barking of a chained hound that looked big as
a mastiff, and which had leaped and pulled at its bond,
trying to get at him. Retrospect was even now telling Julius

he'd made an error of judgment, approaching the house that way, and the thought that the error might have gotten him killed contributed mightily to the shaking of the spoon.

"Is the soup hot enough?" Susan Killefer asked him, turning up her blond-framed, plain face, looking as wide, freckled, and pale as a very old and well-used china plate. He'd already noticed that she seemed to look down most all the time, lifting her face only when addressing him. It seemed odd . . . *Maybe she really is crazy, like the slaves say.* He wished he hadn't heard so much from that little horse hunter. He would be eternally nervous around his sister-in-law from now on because of it.

"Soup's just fine, thanks."

"You're shaking pretty bad. Are you cold?"

"You made me nervous, coming up at me with that rifle like you did."

"You scared me, coming into the yard. I thought you was another of the bushwhackers who drove off Crowell. You look like Crowell a right smart, you know that? You look a lot like him."

Finally surrendering, Julius laid down his spoon, picked up the bowl, and imbibed the soup by drinking it. It tasted good, though it was thin.

He wiped his mouth on his cuff. "You know for a fact he's run off?"

"I'm told he has fled the state. Gone in hopes of getting to the Union lines."

"He just up and left you? Walked out?"

She abruptly began to cry, her breath suddenly coming in hard jerks accompanied by weird, moaning exhalations that matched Julius's imaginations of what the death keening of mourning Indian squaws must sound like. She had cried that same way a little earlier, when he'd told her, while staring wide-eyed and dry-mouthed down the barrel of the rifle she had poked into his nose, just who he was and why he'd come. "Yes, he just left me all alone. Oh, it was hard of him to do that!"

"I hate to ask it, but you think maybe he might not have run off at all, but got killed by these bushwhackers you say was bothering him?"

"No. No, he ain't killed. He *ain't*!" Now she seemed furious, her manner having altered in a second or less. Julius wondered if that was a sign she was crazy, or if he was just spooked toward her by the slave rumors the boy had told him.

"All right, all right, he ain't killed. I'm sorry I said it."

She stopped being mad and went back to crying.

"These bushwhackers, I reckon they're rebel, huh?"

"What?"

"These bushwhackers who run off Crowell. I reckon they must be rebel, since he was Union."

Her voice trembled with her weeping. "No. They're Union."

"Why would a Union man bother another Union man?"

Once again the anger. "Why do you think *I* would know? Why are you asking me that?"

"I'm sorry." He looked into his soup bowl and wondered if it would be safe to ask for another helping. So far he seemed to be saying all the wrong things, though he couldn't quite see just where he was going astray. The things he was asking seemed sensible enough as best he could tell.

Her tears stopped. "You want more soup?"

"Yes, if you can spare it."

She smiled, that previously cold, china-plate face now as warm as the sun. "Of course I can spare it! You are my own brother, ain't you?"

"Brother-in-law. Yes, ma'am."

She was up, filling his bowl out of the kettle on the wood stove. "And so much like Crowell! I'll bet he looked just like you when he was your age."

"My parents say that's true, yes, ma'am."

She brought him the bowl, still smiling. He studied her eyes. A cheap novel he had read had once mentioned the "light of insanity" burning in the eyes of a crazed character. Julius didn't know what such a light would look like, but didn't see any light in her eyes in any case. If anything, they seemed vacant, like the eyes of a blind person.

He tried eating with the spoon again and did better this time. "Baby's asleep, I reckon," he said.

She burst into tears, burying her face in her hands.

I believe that little darky was right. She really is crazy.

"I'm sorry. Did I say something bad? The letter you sent mentioned there was a baby, you see, and—"

"The baby's dead!" she sobbed out. "Dead! I laid his little form away with my own hands! Dead!"

"I'm . . . I'm sorry. I didn't know. It must have happened since you wrote to us."

She sobbed a minute more without speaking, then got some degree of hold upon herself and said, "Yes. Two weeks and three days ago. My poor little Charles! He seemed so fine and healthy, and then I went to get him come morning, and he was lying cold and dead in his cradle. The Lord had seen fit to take him from me. The Lord gives and takes away, blessed be His name, but oh, it can hurt when the taking time comes!"

"I'm sorry." Julius wished he had kept count of how many times he'd said those two words in the brief time he had been here.

"My baby's dead, my husband has abandoned me . . . but I do have you, don't I! My dear young brother, come to see to my welfare!"

"Yes, ma'am. Brother-in-law, ma'am."

"God bless you, Julius. May I call you Julius?"

"Yes. May I call you Susan?"

"No."

"No?"

"It's too forward, Julius, you calling me by name. I believe Miz Susan is better."

"Oh." *Here I go again.* "I'm sorry."

"I expect you not to be forward with me. Crowell will be furious if he finds out you've attempted in any way to disgrace my honor."

That one made him mad. "I'd never do such a thing! All I done was ask to call you by your name because you'd asked to call me by mine. I wasn't being forward, and if you feel like that, then I don't want you calling me by name, either."

She began to cry.

"I'm sorry. You can call me what you want to." He wondered why his brother had ever married a woman like this. Had she been this way always, or turned this way sometime after the marriage? He was beginning to see how Crowell might have been led to abandon her. Not that abandoning a wife was in any way right. But maybe understandable, in this case. In fewer than two hours Susan Killefer had worn his mind half threadbare. It was impossible to imagine how hard it would be to endure such emotional ebbings and flowings unendingly.

He finished his soup. An awkward moment had come. Up until now everything about this quest had been uncertain, nebulous. He had half expected, and strongly hoped, to find that matters had changed since Susan mailed her troubling letter, and that Crowell was back home with his wife and baby, all being well. It hadn't proven out that way, and now he was alone in a cabin with a woman that might actually be insane, maybe even dangerous. Maybe even a killer. Those slave rumors didn't seem so hard to believe now.

What should he do? Would she let him pass the night here? If so, what would happen come morning? His notion had been to come here, and if Crowell did prove to be gone, to make some arrangement to bring mother and child back to Kentucky, into the care of their extended family. The child would have been blood kin, after all, and a family responsibility. Now matters weren't so clear. There was no child anymore to be rescued, and Julius wasn't sure it would be a good idea to bring such an unstable woman as Susan Killefer into his family.

"Well . . . I can wash these dishes up for you," he offered, mostly just to have something to say. He despised washing up plates and bowls and hoped she'd refuse him.

"Oh, you're a dear young man. Thank you."

He muttered, "Welcome."

"I appreciate you helping me, Julius. It's hard for a poor woman, her child fresh in its grave, and her husband so recent dead."

"Dead? What do you mean, dead? You said Crowell was just out of the state!"

Her reply didn't miss a beat. "He's dead to me, Julius. He's abandoned me, left me to suffer alone. But now you've come along to help me! God has sent you. What a dear, good brother you are!"

"Thank you." He started to point out yet again he was her brother-in-law, not her brother, but there seemed no point.

To his relief, she left the cabin while he washed the dishes, as best he could, in a basin of unheated water, with nothing but sand to use for scouring. The basin sat on a table facing an open window, a burning lamp perched on the windowsill for light, and as he worked he peered out and could see nothing because of the lamp. Eventually, however, he shifted the lamp farther away after some water splashed onto the bowl of it and sizzled, threatening to crack the glass. Soon his eyes adjusted to the darkness in the window.

She was out there, standing at the edge of the woods, watching him. No expression, no movement, no sound. Just a silent, unblinking stare. He looked right back at her, but she didn't react. It was as if she did not realize he could see her, or maybe didn't care.

He finished the dishes as quickly as possible and moved away from the window. Sitting down in a rocker beside the fireplace, he waited for her to come back inside, but she didn't, and before long he was asleep, wearied from his earlier long hike to reach this place.

When he opened his eyes, the cabin was dark except for light that glowed off the coals in the fireplace. She had banked the fire, apparently, with him still asleep in the chair at the fireplace. It bothered him to think she'd been that close to him, no one else about, him asleep and helpless.

They say she kilt her husband, and her baby. . . .

He scooted the rocker a little closer to the fire, feeling cold all at once. As he resettled himself, the chair squeaked.

A nearly identical squeak sounded above, in the loft of the cabin. Then more squeaks, rhythmic and thrumming, making the boards above him groan softly. There was another rocking chair up there, obviously, and she was in it.

And singing. So soft he could hardly hear it above the gentle hiss of the fireplace coals. Singing . . . a lullaby.

They say she sit up there and sing lullabies at night just like the baby was there, but there ain't no baby. Maybe a ghost baby . . .

That was enough of that. He wouldn't succumb to

foolish slave ghost tales, rocking chairs and lullabies notwithstanding. He rose, bumping the chair and making as much noise as possible so she would know he heard her, and went to another chair nearby and from the back of it took a quilt. He sat back down, throwing the quilt over himself, and took off his brogan shoes. He dropped them loudly onto the floor, one at a time.

She was still singing above, ignoring the noise he was making. For some reason that made him mad, and he wondered if she was toying with him, trying to scare him for fun or for whatever reason a mind like hers might come up with.

"Good night!" he called out, more loudly than necessary.

She didn't answer, and didn't stop singing. He rocked for an hour, listening to it, before he finally heard her stop, get up, and climb into her bed in the loft above.

Chapter 15

Julius sanded and rinsed the residue of egg and pan-fried potatoes from his plate and stared out the window to the place where she'd stood watching him the night before. He had the most uncanny feeling in this house and around this woman. The world seemed askew, out of focus.

At the moment, she was gone to the spring, and even that simple act had given him cause to question and ponder just what was the truth about Susan Killefer and her situation. "Why are you going to the spring when there's a well in the yard?" he'd asked.

"That well's no good. The water is fouled. A critter fell in there and drowned. Don't try to drink nor use the well water," she replied.

So the well was fouled . . . Julius instantly had a vision of the little body of a dead child down in that well. Maybe even the body of Crowell! It required no great imaginative stretch to picture so bizarre a woman as Susan committing murder.

He dried his hands on a rag hanging by the basin, picked up the basin and carried it out to the yard for dumping. Glancing around to make sure Susan was not yet returning, he went to the well, opened its wooden cover and peered down into it, taking a sniff. There indeed was a scent of decay rising from below, masked and muffled by the water that surrounded whatever "critter" was there. He quickly closed the cover. Could it be? No, no. Surely not. He couldn't let himself accept such a terrible idea.

He set the basin aside, realizing that this was a fine chance to explore the cabin's surroundings by daylight. It took only a moment to circle the little structure and poke his head into the storage shed, the smokehouse, the privy, the corn crib. Nothing unusual or amiss that he could see. Yet by the time he completed the circumference of the cabin, he sensed that something was missing, though he couldn't put his finger on what it was. He looked around, pondering, then shrugged and went back to the well, fetched the basin and took it back into the cabin. He glanced up at the loft, and only then realized what it was he hadn't seen in the yard but should have.

Putting the basin back on its stand, he sat down in the rocker and went back and forth, letting the cadence of the motion lull his mind and open the door to thought. He had decisions to make, duties to balance, and little time to get it all done.

They were seated together at the little table, eating a cold lunch, when Julius brought up the question that occurred to him during his tour of the yard.

"Where's the baby buried?"

She dropped her fork. "Oh, look at me! I'm clumsy as I can be."

She leaned down, picked up the fork, and wiped it on the tail of her skirt. She returned to eating again without having answered him.

He felt a hot surge of irritation, and asked again, "Where'd you bury the baby?"

Her eyes lifted to his, unreadable. If anything, they masked an irritation equal to his own. "Why do you ask that?"

"I walked around the yard this morning and figured I'd find the grave, but there was no sign of one."

"The baby's buried beside a church."

"Close by here?"

"Why? Are you wanting to go mourn?"

Why was her tone scornful? His mystification at her deepened. "It seemed fitting to go pay respects. It was my nephew, my blood kin."

"You Killefers put a lot of account on the notion of blood kin, don't you? That's the way Crowell was. The way he is, I mean. Angry at his own father, not seeing him for years, nor writing him even a letter, but always talking about how when the pinch gets tight, it's blood kin you stick by." She shook her head at the seeming rankling nature of that thought.

"That's the way we were raised to think, Crowell and me. But you ain't told me where the church is that the baby's buried."

"It's miles from here. Two, three miles. No, more like four."

She's a liar. I don't know why she'd lie about such a thing, but she's a liar. "How would I get there?"

She didn't drop the fork this time. She slammed it down. "You don't go. I don't want you to. That's my baby, and it's me who'll visit the grave. Not you! Do you hear me?"

"I'm sorry I upset you. I meant no wrong. I won't go if you don't want me to."

"I don't." She picked up the fork and began eating again, her face virtually buried in her plate. Julius picked at what remained of his own food, having lost his appetite.

This time she washed the dishes. He sat in the rocker and pretended to read the only book in the house, a volume of English stories that employed many words he couldn't understand. His schooling had been limited, only a couple of years, and anything but basic reading, writing, and ciphering was beyond him.

When she was done she shook her hands dry, walked toward him, and sat down in a chair. She stared at him openly, making him uncomfortable.

"How long are you going to stay?" she asked.

"Well . . . I ain't. No need to. But I'm glad you asked, for I need to tell you what I've been thinking."

"Go on."

"Times look right bad for you here, with Crowell away, and your baby gone to heaven. When we got the letter you sent us, it was the thought of all of us back at home that one of us ought to come down and fetch you and the child up to join us, at least for the duration of this war, or until Crowell came back. Of course, we didn't know the child was to die . . ."

"You going to take me up to Kentucky to join your kin?" she asked.

"Well, I don't know what to do, really. You're Crowell's wife, so that makes you one of us, I reckon, as long as you're married. Of course there would be no question if the baby was living, him being—" Julius chopped off his statement, realizing it wasn't going to sound quite right, but she finished it for him.

"Him being blood kin, where I ain't. I'm just *married* kin."

Julius reddened. She might be insane, but she was also perceptive. "That's pretty much what I was thinking, I guess. I'm sorry."

"You say 'I'm sorry' an awful lot."

"I know. I'm . . . sorry."

"So you going to take me to Kentucky or not?"

"If you want me to, I will."

"How would we get there? You can't just travel into Kentucky no more, you know. There's a war on. They guard the roads."

"You can get there if you've got a pilot to take you the secret ways. That's how I got down here: coming back with a pilot who had just run some stampeders up to join the Fourth Tennessee in Kentucky. If we can get back to him soon, I'd say he'd let us go along with his next stampeder group. Might be awkward for a woman, going with all them men, but this is wartime, and that's probably the best can be done. Up in Kentucky you can live with us. We ain't got much, and right now Pa is having to be an outlier in the woods because of the rebs, but at least you wouldn't be alone, and we could keep you fed."

"I don't want to go to Kentucky."

He felt an instant wave of relief. The truth was he didn't want her to go, either. The idea of having such a woman about the homeplace was too much to bear. But relief quickly mixed with worry. How was she going to live here alone? Was she capable of keeping herself alive? How would she obtain money, food? Like it or not, she was his brother's wife, and therefore his concern. He didn't relish the idea of going back to his father and telling him he'd found Crowell's wife, struggling to get by on her own, then turned around and left her behind, no better off.

Her next words provided his answer. "I've got kin of my own, an uncle. I've found out they've moved just recent over near Greeneville, to farm as tenants on some big farmer's land. I want to go to them. They'll take care of me." She paused, then added with a certain ironic emphasis, "They are *blood* kin, after all."

"Greeneville . . . I seen it on a map. It ain't too far from here, I don't believe."

"Yes, I want you to take me there. I was ready to go alone, but then you showed up, and I figure it's better for me to travel with a man." She eyed him up and down. "I reckon you're the closest to a man that I've got handy at the moment."

She was surely the strangest woman he'd ever met. Warm sometimes, then cold as a stone. "I'll go with you," he said. "I may not want to take the main roads, though. I've heard tales of fellows being conscripted by the rebels right out of cornfields or right on public roads. I don't want to be a soldier."

She smiled only with the corners of her mouth. "Crowell had a touch of the coward about him, too."

His throat grew tight and his blood surged. He didn't dare respond immediately, for fear of what he would say. Coward! How dare she call him that! But he recalled his father's frequent advice: *When somebody insults you, consider the source.* Susan Killefer, he decided, was not a source worthy of credence. She was just a mountain woman, probably insane, whom he'd be glad to dump off on her kin and bid farewell to forevermore. No wonder Crowell left her behind! It would take a saint to endure Susan Killefer for long.

A countering thought, however, whispered something that gnawed at the back of his mind, and had been gnawing at it since he came: *Crowell would never abandon his wife, no matter how she behaved. That wouldn't be his way. If he ain't returned to her, it's only because he couldn't. He's either been conscripted, or bushwhacked, or killed. Maybe by soldiers. Maybe by her, like that slave boy said.*

It was hard to keep his voice level, but he did it. "I'm no coward, Miz Susan. I just rode hundreds of miles through dangerous country to make sure you were safe and well. That's no coward's act."

"You didn't come because of me. You came because of Crowell and the baby."

"But I came all the same, and I've made you the same offer of help I would have made even if the baby had lived."

"Well, I don't want you taking me to Kentucky. Just to Greeneville."

"They'll be willing to take you in?"

"I believe so."

"Have you been in contact with them?"

"They'll take me in. Quit fretting about it."

Lord in heaven, she was wearying! "I'm not fretting, just asking. But forget about it. All right. I'll take you."

"Good." She got up and walked out of the house without a word. He went to the door, watched her vanish among the trees and wondered where she was going. To the baby's grave, he guessed. Going to say a final good-bye.

For a moment he was able to overlook her ways enough to feel sorry for her.

He looked about the cabin in her absence, and with a vague sense of guilt for his nosiness nagging at him, climbed to the loft. He hadn't been up here before. There was only one small window, and light was dim.

Her bed was rumpled and unmade. The rocker he'd

heard creaking up here in the night was hung with dirty clothing she had tossed onto it. The cradle, likewise, was filled with castoff clothing and so on. And over in the corner, near a closed wardrobe that leaned out from the wall because the loft floor was uneven, stood Crowell's rifle, the same rifle his and Julius's father had given to him many years ago. It had been a flintlock, but Crowell had since converted it to percussion cap.

Julius frowned, whispered to himself, "Wait a minute . . ."

Why was Crowell's rifle here? Would a man flee the state and not take his rifle with him? He tried to make sense of it. Maybe Crowell had a better rifle and had taken it, leaving this one for his wife. No . . . he wouldn't do that. This rifle was a gift from his father, not something to be abandoned.

Julius turned his eyes to the wardrobe. He went to it, threw open its door.

It was filled with clothing, as much man's clothing as woman's.

Crowell had left not only his rifle, apparently, but his clothing as well? It made no sense at all.

He closed the wardrobe door and descended to the level below, feeling shaken and hoping it wouldn't take long to get to Greeneville, and that Susan's kinfolk wouldn't balk at taking her in, for he wanted to be rid of her as quickly as possible.

Chapter 16

Madison County, North Carolina;
near Warm Springs

Greeley Brown puffed his pipe, letting the smoke curl up and divide itself into twin streams on either side of the low-hanging brim of his hat. Leaning back against a tree, hat turned low on his brow, pipe burning evenly and giving off an aromatic smoke, he felt more comfortable and content than in many a day.

The course he'd followed to reach this pleasant spot had increased in difficulty and danger the farther he went. From a point northeast of Elizabethton, he veered southwest, crossing the Watauga and Doe rivers and entering the embrace of the mountains, where Buffalo Creek flowed between the ridges. He passed through Greasy Cove, where many years ago a young and cocky Andrew Jackson had lost a horse race. Following the converging mountain waterways, Greeley reached the French Broad, and in the Laurel Creek region had left Tennessee behind to enter western North Carolina, and the country of bushwhackers. He kept a close watch there, for a man could walk into trouble before he knew it. The North Carolina mountains could swallow an entire army and look unchanged for it. Many said they had done just that.

The terrain had grown more rugged the farther Greeley traveled, but at last he crossed a long-sought final gap and saw before him, through the trees, a distant glimmer of the flowing French Broad. He was close to Warm Springs, and to the gray-painted Josiah House that stood nearby, a defiant rebel haven that he would normally have nothing to do with, if not for Spencer Cline's letter addressed to that place.

Greeley had longed to go into Warm Springs, but he was known in this area and had to be wary. This was divided, hotly contested country with plenty of Unionists about, but held by the Confederates. The town of Warm Springs itself, a major attractor for years of tourists who came from New York and even more distant major cities—to bathe in and drink of the natural hot and therapeutic springs—had as one of its most distinctive features a huge, two-story hotel in which five hundred guests could easily reside with comfort. The hotel was struck a hard economic blow by the coming of the war, but had been purchased the prior year by a stage-coach operator from Greeneville, over across the line in Tennessee. That man, James Rumbough, was strongly Confederate and reportedly came to Warm Springs because he was made uncomfortable in the heavily Unionist environs of Greene County. Greeley had no ambitions to meet such as Rumbough, and so didn't enter Warm Springs at all.

Instead he had stayed hidden by the road, like a highwayman, and kept watch for passersby. Several went by him, unaware of his presence, before he finally saw one who looked promising for his purposes. Greeley then stepped out of the trees and smiled into the startled face of a middle-age black woman who had come walking up the road with a pushcart full of firewood in front of her.

"Hello, there," he said. "I'm looking for a slave man name of Joel, from the Josiah House." He waved toward the gray-walled structure, partially visible through the treetops. "You know him?"

The woman nodded, her face untrusting.

"I need to see him. Can you arrange to have him come to me?"

"Who are you?"

"You tell him, without anybody else hearing, that I have something for Nanny."

The woman's eyes grew veiled. She nodded quickly.

"Tell him to meet me under the big oak by the road, the oak there, the one you can see from that tower on the Josiah House. Tell him to come as soon as he can, and if he can't do it, you come back and tell me so. You understand?"

"Yes, sir."

"Good." He gave her some money, and settled down to spoke his pipe and wait, his thoughts drifting free.

An hour passed, and he began to wonder if something had gone wrong.

He didn't so much hear another human presence as sense it. Lifting his hat, he found himself looking into the broad face of a black man of sixty or so. Greeley tried not to look surprised, though he was. He always prided himself on being impossible to sneak up on, yet this old fellow had done it with seeming ease.

"Here I am," the man said. He was unsmiling, wary.

"You're Joel?"

"I am."

"My name's Brown. Greeley Brown. You heard of me?"

"Yes, sir. You're a pilot for the stampeders what go out of Tennessee and Carolina up to the Union lines."

"That's right. And so I'm a man who has to lay low. You won't betray me, will you, Joel?"

"No sir." The face didn't change at all. The same hard, probing frown lingered, a virtual auger of a stare that prickled the skin. "You got something for Nanny?"

"I do. A letter, and a message."

"Who from?"

Greeley might have laughed. Joel was a novel kind of man. Unlike most slaves, he didn't act deferential or subservient at all. "It's from Spencer Cline. You know who that is?"

"Yes, sir."

"Were you friendly with him?"

"I reckon you could say that, sir."

"Then it's my hard duty to tell you that Spencer Cline is dead."

Now the face did change. It was as if Greeley had

stepped forward and kicked Joel hard in the ankle. A kind of vague ripple seemed to pass through him from top to bottom, making the ends of his fingers twitch and his lips press tight together for a moment before the earlier look of wariness came back. "Dead, you say? Mr. Spencer is dead?"

"That's right. Dead by accident. He . . . we, all of us . . . we were running from rebels, or what we thought was rebels, in the dark woods. He had the misfortune of running upon a sharp tree branch and stabbing himself to death."

The shudder passed through the slave again. Greeley knew Joel was imagining how it must have been for Spencer Cline when the unseen branch had pierced him. He'd imagined it many a time himself, and shuddered in the same way.

"The letter . . ."

"Yes, I've got it." Greeley reached into his pack and brought it out. "It's been opened, Joel, but not by me. I was robbed on my way back from Kentucky. The Union soldiers from Tennessee, they always give me letters to take back to their folks at home, and there's often money in them. Thieves robbed me, took the money out of the letters and threw them on the ground. There was no money I know of in Mr. Cline's letter, but they opened it all the same, along with the others."

Joel stepped forward and held out his hand. Greeley laid the letter into it. It felt good to be rid of it at last.

"I'll take it to Nanny, sir."

"Yes. Do that."

It came to Greeley just then that he could turn away at just this moment and declare this task finished. The temptation was strong . . . until he remembered the dream of the train and the child on the tracks. He couldn't turn away if a child truly was in danger.

"May I go now, sir?" It was the first thing Joel had said that sounded slavish.

"You may . . . but if you'd stay a mite longer, I'd like to talk to you."

"What about?"

"I saw a few lines of the letter. While I was putting it back into the envelope after the robbers had torn it out."

Greeley paused, studying Joel's face. Defensiveness that had built up over days of accusation and mistrust colored his perception, and he abruptly lashed out at Joel. "I see you doubt me. But it's true. There were thieves. I don't open other folks' letters, no matter how it looks to you."

Joel seemed surprised at the sharp tone. "I ain't said nothing, sir."

Greeley saw the error of his perception and was embarrassed. "No, you didn't. I'm sorry. Can you stay and talk to me a few minutes more?"

"Yes, sir." Joel slipped the letter into an inner pocket of his coat. "I expect you're going to tell me you know the big secret."

"I know part of it. Come up and sit down. You got a pipe on you?"

"Yes, sir."

He and the slave withdrew into the trees and sat down on the other side of the big oak. Greeley filled Joel's pipe for him and held a match for him to light with.

Shaking out the match, he said, "I know about the baby. I know that Nanny is a slave, and that Spencer Cline fathered her child. That much I saw in the few lines I happened to see. After that I didn't read anymore. I didn't think it was right."

"That's all you know?"

"That . . . and that Mr. Cline seemed to have fear about something bad happening to Nanny and the child in Josiah House." Greeley drew a thick stream of smoke through the stem of his pipe and let it blow out through his nostrils. "Mr. Cline grew fretful on me as we progressed along the stampede. Wanted to turn back, and had notions that he wasn't going to make it. I believe the turning back part was because he had begun to worry about Nanny and the little one, that he thought he'd made a mistake, leaving them behind without his protection. So tell me, Joel, is Nanny still in Josiah House, and is she safe? And the baby?"

"They're both in there, sir. Well enough for now. But they ain't safe. Not with the Old Missus there, worrying about the 'scandal.' That's her way of talking about the baby, sir. The 'scandal.' White man, dark girl, mulatter baby . . . it's shameful to her."

"The 'Old Missus'—is that Mrs. Josiah?"

"Yes, sir. Colonel Josiah, he dead now. Died last year. Now it's just Old Missus left running the place, and she's a fearsome woman. Mighty fearsome."

"You think she'd harm that baby, and Nanny?"

"If she believed she'd get away with it, I believe she would, sir. I believe she'd kill them both, no lie." He reached up to the place his coat covered the pocketed letter. "If she learns about Mr. Spencer being dead now, I don't doubt she'd kill them right quick. It's him that's kept her from it up until now."

"Tell me something. How does a Union-loving, abolitionist Sevierville lawyer wind up falling in love with a North Carolina slave girl in a household as rebel as the one in Josiah House?"

Joel took the pipe from his mouth. "Sevierville lawyer? Who you talking about?"

"About Spencer Cline. He told me he was a lawyer in Sevierville."

Joel chuckled. "He was lying, then. I reckon he was doing it to cover his tracks. He ain't no lawyer, not at all, and he didn't live in no Sevierville. And I may as well tell you his name isn't . . . wasn't, no Spencer Cline, neither. That was only part of his name. He was Spencer Cline Josiah, the one and only living son of the late colonel and the Old Missus, and that was why the shame of it was so deep, all that happened with him and Nanny."

Greeley blew out his breath and shook his head. "Lord have mercy! So the very son and rightful heir of the Josiah household up and got a slave girl in the family way. Caesar Augustus! A big, well-known, distinguished family with a wayward son and a bastard mulatto baby . . ."

"Oh, no bastard, sir. Not a bit of it. Mr. Spencer and Nanny, they married."

Greeley dropped the pipe. "Married? Legal married?"

"I don't know much about the legal part, sir. But they stood up together and said their vows."

"Papers and such? A real preacher, and a real wedding?"

"A colored preacher. No papers I know of. But they considered theirselves married. I believe it was learning of the marriage what killed old Mr. Josiah."

"I'll be . . . I'll be . . ." Greeley picked up his pipe and watched the burning coals that had spilled from it burn themselves out on the ground. "Nanny and the child need to be gotten out of that house, Joel."

"I know, sir. 'Specially now that Mr. Spencer is dead. Lordy! I can hardly think of him dead . . . knowed him since he was born."

"Was he the only true protection for Nanny and the child?"

"Yes, sir. The Old Missus, she's knowed that bad things would come from Mr. Spencer if anything happened to his woman and his baby. He loves Nanny, as deep as any man has ever loved a woman." Joel paused, looking sad. "Or he did love her. When he was alive."

"I confess to you, Joel, it don't seem right to me, a white man and a colored woman being together."

"I don't know how to judge such things, sir. But I do say that it surely also don't seem right that a child should be put in danger just because it was born of two different kind of parents. Sure 'twasn't that baby's doing."

Greeley couldn't argue with that. It was the very point he'd been dwelling on since he stumbled across this bizarre situation.

"Joel, tell me about Mr. Spencer. He seemed an unusual kind of fellow."

"He was, Mr. Brown. Has been since he was a boy. The colonel, he was a big, strong man, loved to hunt, loved his guns and his horses and dogs. Mr. Spencer, he never took to that kind of thing. When he was little I seen him cry over pigeons his father shot, his father just a-standing and glowing mad like a red-hot stove. Called Mr. Spencer a 'girl,' and a 'petticoat boy.' Said hurtful things to him, many a time, and acted ashamed of him. Mr. Spencer, he tried to act the way his papa wanted him to, but he couldn't. Not for long. It just warn't in him, sir." Joel glanced at his pipe. "My fire's gone out—might I have a bit more of your tobaccer?"

Greeley shoved the pouch and match case to Joel and waited for him to go on.

"Well, sir, what that boy went through with his father was nothing to compare to the way his mother treated him. She seemed thrice as shamed by his weakish and girly ways as the colonel was." Joel leaned over close and spoke in a lower voice, though there was no one nearby to hear. "Once I heard her call him a sodomite, Mr. Brown, and say she was ashamed that she'd give birth to such a one. But Mr. Spencer was no such thing. He was just different than his parents, and he had a heart in him. His feelings, they run deep. His folks couldn't understand that he just plain old cared about people. Even colored people.

"It was over colored folk, matter of fact, that the biggest trouble rose between him and his parents. Mr. Spencer decided early on that he didn't have much use for slavery. He walked up to me when he was no more than ten year old and said, 'Joel, you're free.' I says, 'What'd you say?' And he says, 'You're free. I'm 'mancipating you here and now.' Says I, 'I thank you, but I believe it'll be up to the colonel to do the 'mancipating,' and that really seemed to let Mr. Spencer down, for he knew the colonel would never let any of his slaves go free. He was a big one for slave owning, the colonel was. Bought and sold slaves like cattle. Me, I been luckier than most at Josiah House. The Josiahs kept me with them since they bought me. I was a very young man at the time and had been a field hand, and when they made me a house servant it suited me good, the work being easier, and I done good for them. I must have suited them, for they never got rid of me. Living under the Josiahs, I've been given a pretty loose leash. I've married, had me a little house there on their land, and me and my wife was right content there, long as she lived. Raised us a good healthy child in that house, me and her."

Living under the Josiahs . . . a loose leash . . . Greeley sat trying to imagine what it would be like to be bought and sold like property, to enjoy the privileges of marriage and living in a house of one's own only at the pleasure of others who regarded you as an inferior. He couldn't grasp it. For a few moments the things abolitionists said made a bit more sense to him than they did in less reflective times.

"But let me tell you more 'bout Mr. Spencer. When he was a young man, he cast his eye on Nanny. The Old Missus and the colonel, they never seen what was starting to happen, I reckon 'cause it was just a thing they'd never conceive of their own selves. But I seen it, and some of the other slaves. We kept our mouths shut around Mr. Spencer, but we spoke hard to Nanny, telling her it wasn't suiting for her to act like she was around Mr. Spencer. She wouldn't listen. She said he'd pledged to marry her, and take her off with him so she'd be free. And Nanny, she wanted to be free, wanted it bad. Always has. Wants to be free more than she wants to breathe or eat.

"Anyways, time went by and Mr. Spencer up from the table one night at suppertime and declared himself an abolitionist. His old papa about died on the spot. The Old Missus stood and cussed Mr. Spencer up and down, and he just stood enduring it, smug-looking grin on his face. He'd finally found a way to slap back at them for all the things they'd said and did to him over the years. After that night, the colonel run Mr. Spencer off from the house for a time, and by and by Mr. Spencer came back, all cringing up and acting sorry, saying he'd not be an abolitionist no more if they'd take him back to live with them again."

"Why would he want to come back to a place where he was treated so bad?" Greeley asked.

"Couple of reasons, sir. One is that he warn't never able to make a living for hisself. He just didn't have it in him to go into business, and he wanted to be a lawyer, even studied it some, but he warn't a good student, neither. He was smart enough, just not able to handle the work. Mr. Spencer had a few weak spots, sir, if I can speak so free. Now, the second reason he come back home was—"

"Let me take a guess," Greeley interrupted. "Nanny."

"That's right, sir. He'd gotten really took by her by that time. He come back, brought in that colored preacher, and had him a wedding. Starting sneaking out and sleeping with Nanny at night, right in her room in the slave house, and calling her his 'wife' while he was among the slaves. He never called her that before the colonel and Old Missus, though. He knowed better. Knowed they'd kick him out of there again.

"But when Nanny turned up pregnant, they did find out what was going on. Warn't no hiding it then, and Mr. Spencer, he did the manly thing and went and told them himself. The colonel took sick and died just a while after that, and the Old Missus, she turned into a more fearsome woman even than before. I saw her take up a fireplace poking iron and swear she was going to kill Nanny before she could give birth to a 'yaller baby,' and Mr. Spencer yanked that poker out of her hand and said if aught ever happened to Nanny, or the baby, he'd tell a few certain secrets about the colonel and the Old Missus out in public. That stopped her cold, I'll tell you."

Greeley had to ask. "What secrets?"

"I don't know, sir, and if I did, I wouldn't tell. Old Joel knows when to keep his mouth shut, Mr. Brown."

Greeley refilled his pipe, nodding.

"The war came along and had Mr. Spencer stirred up from the start. Naturally, he went the way opposite his parents. And when Mr. Lincoln signed his 'mancipation paper, Mr. Spencer got extra much worked up. Declared himself an abolitionist again, said he was going off to fight for Mr. Lincoln and the freeing of the slaves, and got his ma so mad that she told him he'd best get out of the house. And he did, but swore he'd be back to get his wife and child when the war was done, and warned Old Missus one more time that she'd better take good care of them if she didn't want every dirty spot on her under-britches showed to the world. I ain't being disrespectful when I say that, sir—just quoting the words Mr. Spencer used."

"I understand. Sounds like the Josiahs are one hellacious family."

"They are indeed, Mr. Brown." Joel looked off through the trees toward the house. "They've been fair to me, in one way. Never sold me off, always fed me good, didn't work me too hard. They've give me the run of town, and I come and go pretty much as I please, doing whatever needs doing. I married and shared a good little cabin with my wife long as she lived. I been as good off as a slave can be, I suppose. So in that way the Josiahs, they been good to me. But I do worry, now that Mr. Spencer is dead. There's nothing left to keep Nanny safe, without him. Nor her baby."

"What's the baby's name?"

"They wanted to call him Cline, but the Old Missus wouldn't have no 'yaller baby' called by her son's middle name. So you know what they done? They named him Joel. After me." The old slave turned his head and quickly touched a finger to his eye.

"That's nice," Greeley said. "Very thoughtful of them."

Joel turned his face back toward Greeley. His eyes were moist and red-rimmed. "What am I going to do, Mr. Brown? How am I going to keep Nanny and Little Joel safe, now that Mr. Spencer is dead and gone? There's no safety for them in Josiah House. Not a bit."

Greeley had made up his mind sometime in the midst of Joel's narrative. All the inner struggle and dread that had revolved around this entire affair up until then had simply died away, and he knew what he would do, as if the decision had been made for him. So there was no hesitation or second-thinking when he put out his hand and laid it on the old man's shoulder.

"We'll get them out of that house, Joel. Me and you. And I'll get them away, to where they will be safe, and where they'll never have to go back to Josiah House at all."

Joel looked at him in awe. "You'd truly do that, sir?"

"I would, and I will."

"You know a place they can go? A safe place?"

"I do. It's a place they can stay, in secret, until this war is done. It's a big rich kind of place, sort of like Josiah House, and the man who owns it owes me a favor from way on back. He's got slaves of his own; Nanny and Little Joel can lose themselves among them, and he'll keep the secret. The South isn't going to win this one, Joel. Mr. Lincoln's army is going to be the victor, sooner or later, and when that happens, Nanny will have that freedom she wants. And Little Joel, too."

Joel's tears spilled out freely. For several moments he was unable to speak. "God bless you, sir. God bless you.

You must be an angel in the form of a man, sir. You're helping this old slave man more than you know."

"What do you mean, more than I know?"

"Because Nanny, she's my own daughter, Mr. Brown. And Little Joel, he's my grandson."

Chapter 17

Of all the odd things about Susan Killefer, this seemed the oddest to Julius: She insisted that they take the cradle with them.

He didn't question her about it, not much, at least, because he knew nothing himself of what it would be to lose a child and did not think it his place to challenge anything she said or did that touched upon that matter. But the brunt of difficulty her insistence brought about fell upon him, for they had no horse or mule, and he had to carry the cradle on his own back, along with his pack. It was heavy, cumbersome, and threw him off balance so that his legs ached with each step and his feet, which tended to flatness, grew tender and sore under the extra weight.

Making matters no easier was the fact they traveled off the main roads, but this was Julius's own decision, made over her protest, because he feared the rebel patrols who rode the highways. He'd heard many a tale of men and even boys drafted into the rebel army by force, legal niceties be hanged, simply because they looked able and strong and happened to stumble upon a rebel patrol at the wrong time.

They brought along a folded tarpaulin, carried by Susan,

that they used to make a kind of tent by night. Susan slept beneath it, but by mutual agreement Julius made do with whatever nearby natural shelter he could find. The idea of sleeping near his own brother's wife, even in the thoroughly sexless context in which they interacted, was deeply uncomfortable to him, and apparently to her, too; he would have kept well away from her even if she hadn't insisted upon it.

The physical ordeal of travel kept him from paying much attention to her ways, but at length he noticed that she seemed less odd than she had, more like a normal woman. He attributed this to her being away from the scene of her losses, and to the hope of a new and better life ahead.

They made poor time. Their route was northeasterly and passed through relatively level terrain, mostly small hills and valleys, but the necessity of avoiding observation caused them to travel slowly. By the first nightfall they had gone only eight or so of the twenty-odd miles they needed to cover.

Susan declared herself feeling poorly the next morning, and from her pallid look, Julius had no cause to disbelieve her. He spent the day setting rabbit snares and fishing from a nearby creek, and that evening risked a small fire to roast up a fine supper. She ate heartily and seemed to feel better.

They went on the next day beneath increasingly cloudy skies. The wind rose and smelled of moisture. The rain began softly, and before it grew hard they chanced upon an old abandoned church building that stood in a weedy clearing beside a small graveyard. The road leading to it was overgrown with saplings; this place had not seen use for a long time.

The roof leaked in several places, but one corner was dry and snug and they made their quarters there. Julius would have been willing to press on right through the rain, figuring they'd have maximum safety from potential observation while most folks were taking shelter, but Susan was unwilling and he did not press the matter.

The rain stopped by night, and Julius put forth the idea of going on by darkness, stampeder style, but again she would not hear of it. Forcing down impatience, reminding himself that soon enough he'd be rid of her, he again held his peace and found a sleeping place in the far corner of the church from her—a dampened corner, but comfortable in the sense that it was far from hers.

He awakened in the night to hear her crying. Opening his eyes, he saw her kneeling where the church altar would have been, crying with her head pressed up against the back of an old rotting bench pew. The empty cradle rested before her. He sat up, rubbing his hands through his hair, blinking away the fog of sleep.

"Miz Susan, are you sick again?"

"Oh, the weight is hard to bear!"

He took her to mean "wait," and assumed she was talking of the slowness of their progress. "Don't worry—we'll make good time tomorrow."

"But the weight, the weight of guilt I feel—oh, it's heavy on me tonight!"

Guilt . . . "What have you got to be guilty about?"

She cried more but did not answer. He lay back down, full of concern and doubt, but fell asleep despite all that and the sound of her sobs. What rest he received thereafter, however, was meager and unsatisfactory.

The next morning she seemed more a normal woman than he had seen her at any prior time. She was cheerful, and eager to get under way. He was eager as well. They ate what remained of the meat he'd provided earlier and set out, Julius determined that today they would make the rest of the journey, even if they had to walk until midnight. He'd endured enough of this woman and was eager to be through with her.

They were traveling along a small creek with high banks when they encountered the man with the gun. He wasn't much of a man, hardly older than Julius, and it wasn't much of a gun either, just an old rusted flintlock that looked to be loose and wobbly in its stock, but he had the advantage on them all the same. They stopped, wordless, as he eyed them with the wildest, most fearful eyes Julius had ever seen.

"Who are you?" he asked. His voice surprised Julius. It was high and quavery, like that of an agitated woman.

"My name's Killefer," Julius answered. He set down the cradle, which the high-voiced fellow looked at with a question in his eyes. Julius waved toward Susan. "This here is Susan Killefer. My sister-in-law."

Julius glanced back at Susan after he introduced her. She was staring at the gunman with no expression of fear, no expression of any kind at all, in fact.

"Why are you coming through here?"

"We're traveling, looking for some of Susan's relations. Their name is . . ." His mind blanked. "What did you say their names was, Miz Susan?"

"Weston. The Richard Weston family."

"I ain't never heard of no Richard Weston family."

"They live near Greeneville, on the farm of . . . what was that name, Miz Susan?"

"Fellows. J. W. Fellows." Her voice was as blandly fearless as her look.

"Why did you come down here to surprise me?" The rifle was moving around, one black hole of its muzzle making a mesmerizing pattern of motion that drew Julius's eyes.

"We didn't. We're just traveling."

"You ain't on the road." The voice was still just as quavery, the kind of voice Julius might have laughed at in other circumstances.

Julius saw no reason not to be honest—and with his obsessive sense of honor, he doubted he could lie, anyway. "We're traveling off the roads because we don't want nobody to see us. I don't want to get conscripted by the rebel army. I'm a Union fellow. Maybe you ain't, and if you ain't that's fine by me, but I am Union."

The rifle lowered. "That's the God's truth?"

"I swear it. And we didn't know nobody was down here. It just looked like a place we could travel without being seen." He glanced behind the rifleman and saw a small cave in the high bank of the creek. Matters suddenly grew a little clearer. "You're hiding out here, ain't you! Living in that cave."

"That's right. I don't want to get conscripted, either."

"That's a damp-looking cave."

"It is damp. The damp of it's got into my throat and ruint my voice."

The voice didn't sound funny to Julius anymore. He felt pity. "I know what it is to be an outlier myself. I been doing much the same as you, up in Kentucky. That's where I'm from."

"You come down here from Kentucky? Why?"

"I came to fetch my sister-in-law here. She's in need of help. Her husband is—"

"My husband is dead," Susan said flatly. Julius flashed her a disturbed glance. Dead?

Susan spoke again. "My husband's brother is taking me to live with some of my kin who've moved onto the Fellows farm near Greeneville."

"Fellows . . . I know that place. It's big. Mr. Fellows has a lot of land, and a lot of money. He's a Confederate by sympathies, though he don't own a single slave. Don't believe in owning slaves, he says."

"Can you tell us how to get there?"

"I surely can." The fellow put the rifle completely down and his eyes no longer had their wild fire. "You got any extra food about you?"

"Nothing, not now. We ate the last of what we had this morning."

"Oh. I'm hungry, you see. I stay hungry most the time."

"Is somebody coming to feed you?"

"My uncle comes as often as he can. Gets him a pan of salt and goes out pretending to look for his sheep, but then he slips down here and brings me food."

"But not enough."

"No, not nearly. But I'd rather starve than join Jeff Davis's army."

"My husband, God rest him, was a Union man, too," Susan said.

They stayed with the fellow a half hour more, mostly because he seemed so starved for human company. He talked ceaselessly, his ruined voice telling stories of woe and suffering on the part of himself and others like him. He listed an endless string of cousins, first, second, and third ones, who were either lying out like he was, gone to the north and the Union lines, or serving against their will in the Confederate army.

At last, after some further inquiring from Julius, he gave directions to the big farm of J. W. Fellows, and even named the location of the tenant house where they could probably find Susan's kin.

Julius felt very sorry for the outlier as they left him. He stood holding his rusted flintlock, looking sad and lonely. As Julius and Susan crossed the hill and were about to go out of his sight, Julius turned and waved.

"God go with you!" the high and wavering voice called.

"And you, too," Julius called back. Then they went over the hill and the lonely fellow dropped out of sight.

"There it is," Julius said, pointing. They were in a field about halfway between Greeneville and the little community of Blue Springs. Based on the outlier's description, they'd spotted and identified the big stone house of J. W. Fellows, then traced their way unseen along a narrow creek toward the tenant house, which had just come into view.

Susan wiped a tear. "My new home," she said.

"If they'll take you in," Julius added. He caught her glance, and tacked on, "And I'm sure they will."

"Let's go on down," Susan said. "I want so bad to see Uncle Richard."

"Wait." He set down the cradle. "I want to ask you something first."

"What?"

"Why did you tell that fellow that Crowell was dead?"

She opened her mouth but did not speak at once. He studied her eyes, looking for the shifting and veiling that often went with deceit, but could tell nothing. "I figured he would feel more sorry for us, thinking of me as a widow."

"Is that it? Really?"

She arched her neck, looked defensive. "You doubt me?"

"Maybe. Let me tell you what I heard from a little slave boy outside Newport. He said there's rumors about you."

"Rumors . . ."

"The slaves talk among themselves that you killed your husband. They even say you killed your child."

Her eyes grew wide, then she lowered her face and cried. "Is it true?"

"No, no . . . how could anyone . . ."

"When you were up in the night in that church, you talked about guilt. The 'weight' of guilt. What guilt did you mean?"

The tears stopped with surprising speed. "Up in the night? Whatever are you talking about?"

"You remember. You and me, we talked to one another, right there in that old church."

"I did *not* talk to you. I slept the night through."

"No you didn't."

"I did! If you talked to me, you did it in a dream. I didn't rise once the entire night."

He saw there would be no prevailing. Either she was lying now or she'd walked in her sleep and didn't recall it. Or maybe he really had dreamed it, though he would have sworn he hadn't.

"Never mind," he said. "Let's go on."

It went better than Julius had dared to hope. Susan's kin recognized her even as they approached the little tenant farmhouse and rushed to meet her, eyeing him with suspicion that lasted only as long as it took for the situation to be explained—this time Susan going back to her original story that Crowell Killefer was merely missing rather than dead. Richard Weston, a balding, thin man who limped on one short leg, and his corpulent wife, Daisy Anne, gave him a welcome that would have hardly been exceeded had he been one of their own blood kin himself.

They sat now around the supper table, which was crowded by the Westons' houseful of children, the eldest several years younger than Julius. There had been an older son, Julius was told, about his own age, who would have occupied the chair in which he sat if he hadn't caught measles more than a month before, while the family was living near Greasy Cove, and died just before their move to

Greene County. A cold had set in with the measles, the combination proving lethal.

"Jimmy would have liked to meet you, Julius," the rotund Daisy Anne Weston was saying. "He was a friendly young man, just as kind and gentle as can be, and so hard a worker!"

"I'm sorry to hear he's gone," Julius replied, and took another bite of chicken. He had eaten two chicken legs already, and could have eaten ten more had there been any to spare.

"I miss him bad," Richard Weston said. "And I'll miss him worse in my work. He was a great help and benefit to me."

"Looks like you've got a houseful of other good helpers," Julius said.

"Yes. We're blessed with children. It's the greatest wealth a man can have. Probably the only wealth I'll ever have."

"Jimmy was deaf," one of the children piped up.

"Is that right?"

"Yes," Daisy Anne said. "Deaf from his birth. But it never seemed to hold him back." Her eyes misted; she looked down at her plate.

"It's better he should have died as he did than to die in this war," Susan said, and everyone at the table looked at her, a little shocked, uncertain what to make of such a comment.

She's going to turn all strange again, Julius thought. He looked at her out of the side of his eye. *I'll bet Crowell is dead, and I'll bet she killed him. And the baby, too.* He was eager to be away from her, though it was indeed pleasant to be among the friendly folks to whom she had brought him.

That night, in private, Julius and Richard Weston had a lengthy talk. Julius felt it only fair that the Westons realize Susan's odd ways, and even the rumors that aired about her. Before it was through, he even expressed his own fears that the rumors were true. He told of her rocking and singing in the night, of her strange activity at the abandoned church and her subsequent denial. He awaited Weston's reaction with trepidation; what if the man decided Susan was not fit to be in his household, and sent her off? Then he would be right where he didn't want to be, stuck with taking Susan with him back to Kentucky.

"These things you say, they worry me," Weston said, gnawing on the stem of his pipe. "I'll keep a close eye on her. Murder! Merciful heaven, what a rumor!"

"What has Susan been like through the years?" Julius asked. "Has she always been . . . odd?"

"No, no, not in my experience, though that is limited, I admit. I saw her occasionally while she was growing up. Just a normal girl, as far as I've known."

"I hope it's nothing but the trials she's endured that have made her different," Julius contributed. "Maybe among you folks she'll be her old self again."

"We'll hope so, Julius."

"You're willing to take her in?"

Weston thought about it before he answered. Julius awaited the answer with true fear, but was relieved when Weston said, "I am willing. She's my kin, more than yours. We'll take her in."

That night Julius slept very well indeed, though the little tenant house was stuffed to overflowing with humanity, and Richard Weston snored like a pit saw.

Chapter 18

Julius Killefer anticipated the briefest of stays with the Weston family, but two days passed and he remained, held there by an unanticipated development. Richard Weston, who had so far avoided military service because of his age and partial crippling, twisted his ankle badly the morning after Julius's arrival while walking toward the nearby barn, leaving him temporarily incapable of much work. Julius, feeling pity, stepped in to take his place, a little reluctantly at heart, though not letting that show.

Another day's labors through, he was standing and reading one of the newspapers Daisy Anne had used that day to paper a drafty wall. She was cooking a stew in a kettle over the fire, the delicious scent of it filling Julius with an almost lustful hunger. Maybe it's the food that's keeping me here, too, he thought wryly. Certainly it was better fare than he would have once he set out on his return trip home.

There were other reasons he lingered as well, ones he scarcely admitted to himself. He couldn't get Crowell off his mind. It troubled him deeply to not know if his brother was alive or dead. And Susan . . . she was a related concern.

What if she really had killed Crowell and the baby? The notion that she might do such a vile thing and get away with it through bland lies rankled him deeply. Perhaps, if he stayed about for a time, he could discern the truth.

The pasted-down newspaper he was reading was the January 1, 1863, edition of the *Tri-Weekly Banner*, Greeneville's pro-Confederate newspaper. The headline of the main story read: BURNSIDE'S DEFEAT—COMMENTARY OF THE PRESS—UTTER DESPAIR OF THE NORTH. The story itself, a commentary on Burnside's disastrous efforts at Fredericksburg back in December, was written in a way that annoyed Julius to the point that he wondered why he was making himself read it. He wasn't heavily literate, and reading was a strain at any time, but he read on for lack of anything better to do at the moment, and because the irritating nature of the story kept his attention, like an itchy scab keeps the attention of a child.

One of the little Westons came up to him and grabbed his sleeve. He looked down at the household's second Daisy Anne, the youngest daughter of the Westons and proud bearer of her mother's name. "You can read, Mr. Julius?"

"Yes. Fairly well."

"Read the story to me!"

"Well . . . all right." He cleared his throat and went back to the beginning of the months old story, reading the simple words quickly and tripping over the bigger ones.

" 'The defeat of Burnside has given a wide scope to the comments and strictures of the press in the North. The general tenor is one of despair and censure, and so universal that even the administration papers confess the hopelessness of an advance against Richmond. No attempt is made to disguise the extent of their disaster. The New York World, in a fit of deep melancholy, cries out, while commenting on the result of the battle:

" 'It is a terrible spectacle. A ship, the grandest that ever sailed the tide of time, freighted with interests for the race passing all calculation and beyond all price, the marvel and glory of the whole world—we say it is a terrible spectacle to see this peerless argosy in the *hands of chattering idiots and blind, bumbling imbeciles, driving straight upon the breakers and quicksands, while the crew, the stoutest and the most faithful that ever trod deck, are compelled to look passively on, and in sheer helplessness, await the engulfing fate.'* "

"What's all that mean?" the child asked.

"I ain't sure."

"Read some more."

"Let's see . . .

" *'How can the country be saved with such men in charge of its destiny? Human reason hopes in vain for an answer. But is there any prospect of a change? How can it come? The president is blindfolded and obstinately confident in these men. Of public opinion he takes no heed . . .'* "

"Who they talking about?"

"President Lincoln, I reckon."

"My papa likes President Lincoln. Do you?"

"I reckon so. I like the Union."

"The Union's going to win. It's going to whip the rebels. But papa says we shouldn't talk about that much, for the man who owns this farm, he's a rebel."

"Your papa's right. You got to be careful what you say these days."

"You believe the Union will win?"

"Yes. I don't know how long it'll take, but I think they'll win."

"Are you going to be a soldier in blue?"

"Maybe so. Probably, if it comes to that."

" 'Soldier in blue, tried and true; soldier in gray, run away.' My brother Jimmy made that up. He's dead now."

"Yes, I know. So he could talk even though he couldn't hear, huh?"

"Yes. He sounded funny. A lot of folks couldn't understand him. But I could."

The elder Daisy Anne called them to supper about then, ending the conversation. After the meal was through, Julius went out into the yard with Richard Weston, who settled himself onto a bench and propped his twisted foot up on a section of log awaiting splitting for firewood.

"I believe my ankle will be in good shape come morning," Weston said. "I reckon I can quit imposing on your good grace."

"Aw, I don't mind the work. I've worked hard all my life."

"You got a home to get back to, though. You know it won't be easy, neither. How you plan to do it?"

"I came down here with a pilot. I figure I may have to make my way back without one."

"That's dangerous. I wish you could find you a pilot this time, too."

"The only pilot I know is in Carter County. It don't seem worthwhile going that far when I could put the same number of miles behind me heading north. I can't pay no pilot anyway."

"I see your problem, but you shouldn't underestimate the danger. In the short time I've been here I've heard of three forced conscriptions myself, right here in this community, and of another one over near Tusculum, where the fellow had his exemption papers, all legal and signed. His daddy was a county tax agent and he worked for him. According to the law he couldn't get conscripted. It didn't make a bit of difference. They took him right off anyway."

Julius thought it all over that night. Maybe he ought to go seek out Greeley and wait to head back home with Greeley's next stampeder band. But for all he knew, Greeley had already gone on with a new group and might not be back for days or weeks to come. And there was the matter of money. Greeley did his work for pay, for which Julius couldn't fault him. But he also couldn't pay him. His prior travel out of Kentucky with Greeley had been compensated by the food his parents had provided and the Kentucky guidance Julius himself had given to Greeley and his stampeders. He had nothing to offer in return this time.

Julius awakened the next morning with his decision made. He would not seek Greeley's guidance, he would go on alone, and he would do so at once. He'd been away for many days, his parents surely worrying much about him, and his father probably suffering there alone, hiding out in the Kentucky woods without his companionship. As for Crowell, Julius realized there was no realistic hope of tracking him down, if he was alive. And if Susan had killed him, she wasn't likely to own up. He would have to leave that matter where it stood, like it or not.

He made his announcement after breakfast: One more day, and he would be gone. His plan was to rise while it was still dark in the very early hours of the following morning and get a healthy start on his journey. Richard said he was pleased to hear this, despite his wish that Julius could find a pilot, and told him he'd seen two men he believed to be Confederate conscription agents riding by the farm the evening before . . . which he hadn't mentioned for fear of spooking Julius. After breakfast he and Julius sat down with an old map and, as best they could, planned as seemingly safe a northward route as possible for Julius to follow back toward the Cumberlands and Kentucky.

Susan Killefer remained silent all morning, reacting not at all to Julius's announcement. She studied him closely, however, and he felt sure she was thinking about the questions he'd asked her concerning the dark rumors about her spreading near Newport. *If she's guilty,* he thought, *I hope her conscience pangs her deep until she confesses. If she killed my brother and his child, I despise her.*

Daisy Anne Weston declared herself vexed that she had no good farewell supper to offer Julius that evening, nothing but greens and vegetables without meat. No matter, Julius told her. He wasn't hard to please. The Westons had been more than gracious enough to him already.

The supper was cooking, and Julius was at the barn helping Richard repair a broken stall door hinge, thinking with a combination of dread and eagerness about the coming night's journey, when the two conscription agents rode up into the yard. Richard saw them through a barn window before Julius did, and reached out to clap his hand hard around Julius's shoulder. "Look there."

"That's them?"

"It is."

"Who do you think they've come for?"

"I don't know. If they've seen you, maybe for you. You stay in the barn, out of sight. I'll go out and speak with them."

Julius spent the next five minutes crouched at the edge of the barn door, peering around and trying without success to hear what was being said. Richard Weston talked calmly at first, then louder and with increasing hand gestures, and the two agents also seemed to be growing stirred. An argument was under way, clearly, and that didn't strike Julius as good. Julius glanced behind him at the arched, open door of the barn. If he left that way, and ran along just the right line, he might be able to reach the woods beyond while keeping the barn between himself and the conscription agents. His rifle and haversack were still at the house, however, and he was loath to set out without them. Maybe he could hide in the woods until night and return to fetch them then.

He looked around the door again and sucked in his breath. They were coming! Marching straight for the barn, and one had his hand on his holstered pistol.

From out in the yard Richard Weston yelled, "Run! Run hard!" and Julius knew the game was up.

He loped out the back of the barn and took off as hard as he could toward the fence that intervened between him and the field. It hadn't seemed all that big a field before, but now it appeared vast, the woods on its far side distant and unreachable. He ran harder, hearing one of the agents yelling for him to halt, and was reminded strongly of the flight he and Greeley had made from the rebels on their trip southward.

He didn't halt, of course, and was not surprised when a moment later a pistol shot slapped the air behind him and a ball whistled over his head. He fancied he heard the smack of it as it hit a tree in the woods beyond the field. *That could have been me it was striking.* He reached the fence and leaped it with the grace of a gazelle, and normally he was far from graceful. Fear had taken control of his leg muscles and made them pump harder than they had ever pumped before. Another shot fired, then another. The scoundrel had a revolver! Julius felt a sudden strong, nostalgic affection for the single-shot, cap-and-ball pistols that were now being replaced by more modern and lethal weapons.

He was bearing as hard as he could across the field when his feet hit a stone concealed by the dried grass of the prior year's summer and the new growth of the spring. It kicked his feet out from under him and he fell headlong, chest slamming the ground. For several moments he could neither breathe nor move, and those several moments were all it took for the conscription agents, who had leaped the fence as easily as he had, to reach him. A hand grabbed his collar, another his belt, and he was hauled up to face their angry faces.

"Think to run away, do you? You'll not run no more. A young and healthy man such as yourself belongs in the service. Let old men and darky slaves run the farms!"

Julius tried to speak but could make only faint grunts. He still could not catch his wind, and the breathlessness was making panic start to rise in him.

"Listen at him! I believe maybe he *is* deaf!" one captor said to the other, and by those words revealed that Richard Weston had told them Julius was his deaf son, hoping to stop them from taking him. Weston had in effect resurrected his departed son in the person of Julius, for Julius's intended benefit.

Julius would not feign deafness, though. His pride and overblown sense of honor would not hide behind someone else's identity. "Not . . . deaf!" he gasped. "Leave me . . . be!"

"Well, well! It appears we been lied to!" The agent grinned a very cold grin. "So young Mr. Weston has ears, and a voice, too! You'll make a soldier after all, boy."

Julius pulled loose from their grasps. His ability to breathe had returned and he sucked in precious air so hard he had to struggle to talk. "I'm not . . . a Weston. My name's . . . Julius Killefer, from Ken . . . tucky. Neutral . . . ground."

"From Kentucky? Then why are you down here, working in the barn of a Tennessee tenant farm?"

"I came down . . . to check on my brother." No reason to give more details than that.

"So you got family here, do you? Then you're a local boy as far as I'm concerned. And you can consider yourself conscripted, Mr. Weston, or Mr. Killefer, or whatever the devil your name is. Come on. Get back to the house and fetch your coat and such. You've got a train ride ahead of you."

Julius sat in a locked room in a block storage building near the train station at Greeneville, feeling as if all the good things in his world had been snatched from him all at once. The events that had transpired since he was herded back to the Weston house, where words and tears from the Westons had mixed with curses and orders from the agents into a great unintelligible blur, seemed in retrospect to have happened in a deathly rush.

The agents had herded him back to Greeneville between their two horses, kicking at him and reminding him of their pistols whenever he looked about to run. There, he was placed in the care of what appeared to him to be off-duty soldiers getting ready to depart after being home on a leave, and the agents talked to uniformed officers while he was forced to sit out of earshot. They waved in his direction and looked over at him several times during the course of conversation, and finally he was told to rise and marched here to this little room. "We don't quite trust you to stay with us out of your own free will just yet," he was told. "This here's the place for you to spend this night, till you've calmed down some."

Calmed down. Julius couldn't figure how he could have given any impression other than already being calm. Calm he was, a frozen, rigid, disbelieving kind of calm that left him cold inside. He figured this must be a bit of what it would feel like to be told you're going to be hauled out and shot come sunrise.

He glanced up at the barred little window in the room and saw that night had come. He wished the window was lower so he could look out, but it was out of reach, and the bench he was seated on was built into the opposite wall and couldn't be moved. All he could do was sit, stare out the window at the little rectangle of black sky visible through the bars, and wonder what would happen next.

He actually slept some, though no more than an hour or two, and by the time light came through the window, it felt like he'd passed three nights tacked together, beginning to end. He stood and stretched and fancied the walls were scooting closer together, making the room smaller by the moment. The air was close and musty.

The lock rattled; the door swung open. A bored-looking soldier motioned him out. "Somebody here to see you."

He stepped blinking into the morning light. "I need to pee," he said to the soldier.

"Do you? Let it fly right here, for all I care."

"I kind of need to do the other, too."

The soldier, looking as if all this put him out very much, sighed and motioned toward a privy standing down near the tracks. "Don't you try to run," he warned.

Julius went to the privy, and when he came out again, the soldier was standing there waiting for him, with Richard Weston beside him.

Julius, filling with more hope than he knew was reasonable, walked up and stuck out his hand toward Weston, who shook the hand and his head at the same time. "Oh, Julius, what have we got you into! It's my fault, letting you stay around and work when you should have been going."

"It's Jeff Davis's fault as far as I'm concerned," Julius said, forcing a smile. He didn't feel at all brave or nonchalant about any of this, but was determined to act as if he did.

"They're bound and determined to go ahead and conscript you, Julius."

"Where will they send me?"

Weston looked like he didn't want to answer that. He licked his lips and said, "Last year they started East Tennessee boys off to Mississippi."

"Mississippi!" Julius exclaimed. "I've heard what happens to mountain folk who get sent to Mississippi. They take sick and die. It's the air and all down there. Swampish and sickly."

"I know, I know. I've heard all the same. And I've already tried to see if I can do something about it. Not me directly, but Mr. Fellows. He owns the land I'm on, and he's got a lot of influence with the Confederates. I told him about what happened, and though I don't know if he can keep you out of the army, I believe he can have you sent to a place you might be better suited to."

"Where's that?"

Weston glanced at the bored-looking soldier, who didn't appear to be listening, and said in a whisper: "Cumberland Gap, I'm hoping."

Julius felt a thrill of hope. Cumberland Gap was at least on the brink of his home state.

"Don't try to desert," Weston warned. "They shoot deserters sometimes, or whip them until they wish they were dead. You stay put—don't go trying to desert. But at least you could keep your health at Cumberland Gap."

"Thank you, Mr. Weston. I know you've done your best for me. I'll remember all your advice."

"Don't thank me. I feel it's because of me, at least partly, that you're in this fix. And you have to understand, I can't assure you that Mr. Fellows will be able to affect your station. But he has a good likelihood of it, I believe."

"You've been hospitable and helpful to me, Mr. Weston. I appreciate it."

"You'll be in our prayers."

The soldier, who had been standing like a lump, suddenly stirred to life. "They're a-motioning," he said. "Time to go."

"Where am I going?"

"Where all the little soldier boys go to start with. The instruction camp."

"Where's that?"

"Knoxville. Now get up to that platform. And you, mister"—he nodded at Weston—"get on back home."

There was only time for a quick grasping of hands. "Good-bye, Julius. For now, at least."

"Good-bye, Mr. Weston."

Part III

★ ★ ★ ★ ★ ★ ★

THE BUSHWHACKERS

Chapter 19

Deep in the mountains near Marshall,
North Carolina

Greeley Brown trudged along through the unpathed forest, walking in the midst of a driving, hard rain, thinking he must surely be doing the most foolish act of his life. It was one thing to lead Unionist men north to the Federal lines, another entirely to be guiding escaped slaves away from their legally bound stations. They were heading south, ironically, to the environs of the town of Hendersonville, which lay among the hills and mountains only a handful of miles above the upper boundary of South Carolina.

He glanced back at his followers, the outlines of their forms made murky by the rain. Even so, he could clearly see the obvious strain attending the progress of old Joel, who had come along because he was unwilling to see his daughter and grandchild carried off without him, and because he knew there would be a great price for him to pay had he remained at Josiah House after the escape was detected. Greeley understood Joel's motivation, yet saw clearly how great a mistake it had been to act in accordance with it. The old man, bringing up the rear, lacked the strength to move fast enough and the stamina to keep at it long enough. But on his face, underlying the lines and creases generated by the agonies of travel, was a look of determination to keep going.

But the determined manner of the lone woman in the group exceeded Joel's by fivefold. From the moment Greeley met Nanny Josiah, he was overwhelmed by the sheer mental will this young woman exuded. Her eyes, intense and black, were like those of a caged animal sensing an unexpected chance to escape, and ready to take it or die. Greeley had been intimidated by a few women in his life, but never until now by a woman of a race he'd been taught was subordinate to his own. Nanny, "wife" of the late Spencer Cline Josiah and mother of his child, did not act as if she felt subordinate to anyone. She was not at all the frightened, quailing creature Greeley expected Joel to bring to the rendezvous he and the old man worked out together. If anything, she came to that meeting, child in arms, as if the rendezvous was one she'd awaited all her life, and over which, all appearances to the contrary, she exercised the true control. She had claimed her opportunity for freedom with the aura of a newly coronated queen accepting her rightful throne.

Greeley spoke to her through the veil of rain. "We need to slow again, and let your papa catch up."

She glanced behind her, brows lowering, eyes narrowing, pretty face framed by the sodden ringlets of her hair. The child she carried whimpered and protested the insulting intrusion of the rain. In the baby's coffee-colored face Greeley saw the looks of both mother and father. The eyes, the nose—they were Nanny's, but the jaw, the general shape of the head, those were her late father's. Greeley was intrigued by this tiny boy, whom Nanny called Little Joel, but uncertain just how to react to him, to feel about him. He had trouble getting past the fact of the child's mixed race, and the first thing he said upon being presented with the child by Joel had come out sounding gratingly inappropriate: "Handsome little mulatter pickaninny you got there, Joel!"

"Come on, Pap!" Nanny urged her struggling father now. "We're moving too slow!"

"I believe he's doing the best he can," Greeley said. He paused, then admitted, "But we are moving too slow. That's true. Your mistress probably already has searchers out on our trail."

Nanny's face, streaming with rain, snapped about to stare into his. "*Not* my mistress. Ain't no Old Missus my mistress no more! I got no mistress but myself from now on!"

Greeley could have told her that this defiant rejection of the servitude she had endured since birth was too adamant and too early. They hadn't escaped yet, and even when they reached their destination, she would not be truly free. In fact, he did not know certainly that she would even be accepted there. But she had to be. There was no backup plan. All his hope was staked on Phillip Thornwell, and the mutual memory he and Thornwell shared of a moment of danger and a daring rescue that had put Thornwell into Greeley's debt. Greeley had never planned to collect the debt, but that changed when Nanny Josiah and Little Joel came into his life.

Nanny's words angered Greeley, and he turned his attention past her to her father to keep himself from boiling over. "Joel? Are you going to make it?" Then, while Joel struggled up toward them, he said with a forced calmness to Nanny: "We ain't gone far enough for you to be spouting your own personal emancipation proclamations. I'm taking quite a risk, helping you like I am, and I expect you to talk civil to me. Understand?"

If she did understand, he couldn't tell it from her look, nor her silence.

The old man reached his daughter's side. He gave a quick, forced smile, but was gasping for air and looked ready to collapse.

"Pap, we've got to go faster," Nanny said. "You got to walk faster, got to keep up."

Greeley spoke in Joel's place. "He's doing his best—can't you see that?"

"His best ain't good enough," Nanny said.

I don't care for your wife, Spencer. "His best was good enough to get you away from Old Missus and out of Josiah

House, and maybe to save the life of you and your child," he reminded her. "Show some respect for your father."

"You going to show him respect when they catch us 'cause we go so slow because of him?" she threw back.

Greeley, furious at her attitude, and—if he'd admitted it—angry to be addressed in such a manner by a black woman, opened his mouth to chide her, but Joel found his voice and spoke before Greeley could. "She . . . she got a good point there, Mr. Brown. I am going too slow. Dragging us down."

Greeley, eyes still locked on Nanny, swallowed all the ire he could. He would not let her gain control for herself by angering him out of his control over himself. He broke his gaze from her with effort and turned to Joel. "If you want, I can try to carry you a spell, give you time to rest." It wasn't as wild a notion as it sounded. He'd carried many an exhausted stampeder on his back for two and three miles at a time.

"I can't have you do that, Mr. Brown. I got way too much meat and bone to be carried. I'm a heavy man. And it wouldn't be fitting for you to carry me, no sir. No sir."

"Caesar Augustus, it ain't fitting for me to be helping slaves escape neither, but here I am doing it. I'll carry you if it needs doing. It's my neck on the block here too, you know."

"No, sir. I won't have you carry me," Joel insisted. "I'll not have you do that, sir."

But Greeley did carry him, because it was the only thing that made sense. They made better time for it too, and Joel was able to find his breath.

"Never thought I'd be riding a white man's back," Joel said into Greeley's ear when they were nearly a mile on. "No sir. 'Twas the other way around before now. There was a time once I had to tote Colonel Josiah this way."

"Why's that?" Greeley said between puffs. Joel was indeed heavy and he wouldn't be able to go much farther with him in this fashion.

" 'Cause his horse was lame. He'd rode to Marshall, me

walking with him, and halfway back to Warm Springs the horse, he go lame, and the colonel made me put him up on his back and tote him. I done it too, though it made me feel a fool. We met some folks on the road, and they just laughed and laughed! The colonel, he grinned and raised his hat to them and says, 'Riding me a dark horse today, gentlemen! Giddup, nigger! Giddup!' He grinned and they grinned and I grinned too, but oh, I was so ashamed down inside, so ashamed, being rid for a horse. You ashamed to be carrying me, sir?"

"Don't know why I should be. Ain't nobody but Nanny and the baby to see us." Diplomatically, Greeley didn't add that he would certainly dump Joel off in a second should a white man appear.

"You a good man, Mr. Brown. I do love you, sir, yes I do. I do love you for what you're doing for my girl and my grandbaby."

A picture of the little farce he was playing out suddenly played through Greeley's mind, and if he hadn't been so exhausted, he could have laughed. All at once it seemed ridiculous and funny, walking through mountain woods in bushwhacker-infested country in the driving rain, an old slave riding his back and declaring his love, a sass-mouthed fugitive woman toting a mulatto child right behind. He couldn't imagine anything more dreamlike, absurd, surreal.

They went on in this manner for several minutes more. The rain fell harder.

When Greeley could carry Joel no farther, they rested and ate some of the food Joel had brought with him from Josiah House when he and Nanny had escaped to make their rendezvous. Nanny nursed her child while she ate, her eyes flitting back and forth without pause, eternally animal and cunning. There were depths in this woman Greeley could detect but not see the bottom of. Serving as her guide was as disconcerting as it had been to pilot her late husband, though her personality seemed very different than his. In fact, he could hardly imagine the seemingly weak and easily overborne Spencer Cline Josiah being able to deal with Nanny's forceful manner.

They went on as the rain lessened and the sun moved

west, and spent that night in an abandoned cabin among the ridges. Little Joel was fitful and fussy the night through, and Greeley kept imagining he heard noises, as of men and dogs moving through the forests, though none appeared.

The next morning Joel was weak and suffering a vague but disabling pain that seemed to spread across his back and down both arms. "I can't go no farther," he said. "You all will have to go without me. Leave me to rest, and maybe you can come again for me, Mr. Brown."

Greeley was displeased to hear this idea, having no desire to make any portion of this journey more than once. He was also suspicious of Joel's sudden display of ill health. "Are you trying to make us leave you, old fellow? Because I won't do it. I'll carry you all the way if I have to."

"I ain't lying to you, sir, I swear before God. I feel poorly. Never felt so weak as this."

Greeley looked him over and could tell that Joel did feel bad. "I don't want to leave you. You never know if your Old Missus may not have slave catchers on our trail already."

"You can't carry me all the way, no matter what you say, and I can't go on by foot, sir," Joel said. "It's Little Joel and Nanny that matter, not me. Leave me some food, and I'll be fine."

"Not if slave catchers come along, you won't. And you do matter."

"If they come, then I'll lead them astray 'bout which way you've gone. If they take me back, I'll 'scape again, somehow. I like this breaking off the chains, Mr. Brown. I decided I don't want to die still a slave in that big gray house. I want to die free."

"He's right, Mr. Brown," Nanny said. "He can't go on with us."

Greeley felt the rising of an increasingly familiar anger. Nanny was remarkably ready to abandon her father . . . her *father*, the man who raised her and who had risked his all to gain escape for her and her child! Though Greeley turned a fearsome frown on her, she looked back at him without the slightest evidence of shame.

In the end Joel had his way and was left behind, with Greeley's firm promise that he would return for him as soon as Nanny and Little Joel were safely ensconced. He left Joel a hatchet and knife, the latter marked with his own initials—a tool his late wife had given him. He made Joel swear to guard it well. If Nanny didn't weep at this parting, Joel did, caressing and stroking his daughter's shoulders as he embraced her, and kissing the soft face of his grandchild. "You get them safe where they need to go, Mr. Brown," he said. "Will you?"

"I'll surely do my best."

"God go with you. God go with you and bless you dear."

Greeley led the way, Nanny following with her child in her arms. Little Joel seemed as weakish and puny as his grandfather, Greeley noted, though Nanny didn't seem overly worried. As Greeley was heading out of view of the cabin where Joel stood watching, he gave a final wave. Nanny did too, but mechanically and only after seeing Greeley do it. Greeley did not know what to make of her coldness. He despised her hardened ways, yet knew he could not hope to totally understand the feelings that stirred in the heart and mind of slaves who have caught the hope of freedom. Could he rightly judge her? Rightly or not, judge he did, and harshly. Joel, after all, was a slave too, and had spent far more years in servitude than had she. Yet he cared less for himself than his loved ones. By the standard of Joel's attitude and behavior, he had grounds to judge Nanny, and she fell wanting.

The day evidenced that it was to be a repeat of the prior one. Though the night passed without rain, new clouds were rolling in, a cool and moist wind stirring the leaves and whipping down from the high rocky ridges. They would be wet again very soon, which was good in that it would make pursuit more difficult, but bad because it would slow them and make their travel uncomfortable, and for the sickly baby potentially dangerous.

"If you want, we can try to find a cave or some such to wait out the storm when it comes," Greeley suggested. "Might be best for Little Joel."

"No," Nanny replied. "I want to go on, far as we can. I want to go far and far and far away from the Josiah House. I want to be free."

"You got to realize, Nanny: You won't be free where we're going. You'll be in a different place, safer, better, I believe . . . but you won't be free. You'll still be among slaves. There'll be no true freedom for you and your kind until the Union army comes in and drives down the rebels. That'll happen, but not for a while. You'll have to be patient."

She was looking past him, eager to press on, and didn't seem to listen.

The rain set in at ten in the morning, and made the previous day's downfall seem like a spring shower. Lightning ripped the mountains, splintering trees into fiery ridgetop displays that petered out under the drenching force of the storm. Waterfalls and freshets gushed down mountainsides where no waterways had run. It was too much to endure, and the lone young horseman who had suffered through it for the last forty minutes decided he would have to find shelter.

He sought it in an empty mountain cabin he'd seen before, while riding as one of the company of Colonel Merriman Swaney and his irregular Unionist band. He was not with Swaney's band now, and did not anticipate riding with them again. He'd seen and lived enough of the bushwhacker's life to suit him. For him, it was over.

As he dismounted and led his horse around to a sheltering overhang at the rear of the cabin, the rider recalled a time when an almost identical lightning storm in these same mountains had led him to another little cabin, there to find the unconscious form of an old friend named Greeley Brown, who had been injured by a lightning jolt that came down the cabin chimney and almost seared him alive. He remembered the good conversation he and Greeley had enjoyed once Greeley had come around again, and all the miles they covered together in times subsequent. He wouldn't mind seeing Greeley again, but God only knew how and when that could come about. Folks said that

Greeley was still busy with his work as a stampeder pilot . . . assuming no rebel had yet been fortunate enough to get close enough to him to put a rifle ball through his head. Piloting was a hazardous duty; a man never knew on any of his todays if he would have a tomorrow. And Greeley supposedly had a Confederate bounty on him, to make his life all the more precarious.

He got the horse settled under the leaky overhang and came around the front of the cabin, which he entered, then exited again with a yell of alarm.

There was an old black man in there, lying still on his back, a presence so unexpected that it had frightened him as badly as a springing rattler.

The yell brought the old man jolting up with a yell of his own. The old man drew a knife from somewhere, waving it about. In response, the newcomer fumbled at his belt and yanked out a pistol. The old man groaned, dropped the knife and covered his face with his hands.

"Who are you?" the pistol-wielder demanded, going for the knife.

"Joel, sir. Just Joel, a sick old man. I want no trouble, sir. I'll leave if this is your place."

"Ain't my place. Just getting out of the rain." The speaker slipped his pistol back into its belt holster. "Looks to me like there's room enough for two in here."

"Yes, sir. Yes, indeed."

The lean young man eyed the older fellow up and down, then came toward him to return the knife. He glanced at the knife as he did so and noticed initials on the handle: G.B. He frowned and hesitated a moment, then gave the knife back. "Sorry to have scared you. Joel, my name's Colter. Sam Colter."

"Glad to know you, sir."

"What's a lone black man doing up here so far in the mountains?"

"I been roaming, sir." A deliberately vague answer. "My chest took to hurting me, so I thought to rest myself here awhile."

"Roaming . . . you a free Negro?"

The old face was touched by a half-hidden smile. "I am now, sir. Ain't always been. But I am now. And I intend to die a freeman, sir."

Sam Colter grinned and nodded, perceiving more than required saying. Clearly this man was a runaway. "Good for you, Joel. I ain't got much use for folks being slaves. I've even been called an abolitionist a time or two in my life, and I suppose that's a fair title for me."

"God bless you, sir. I love the abolitionists awful dear."

"Do you know what else I am, according to a lot of folks?"

"What's that?"

"A bushwhacker. That's what folks have said. Sam Colter is a bushwhacker. Rides with Merriman Swaney. You heard of Merriman Swaney?"

Joel had a wary look. "Oh, yes sir. Everybody in these mountains has heard of Colonel Swaney."

"What do you think about him?"

"Well, sir, he is Union, and I like that. The Union, it cares a lot more for folk of my type than do the Confederates, no question of that. Beyond that, well . . . I reckon it ain't my concern. Colonel Swaney and his band, they ain't never hurt me nor mine, and don't think they'd ever have cause to. But I know the rebels, they fear the colonel and his men really fierce. They say that they—" Joel, who was still seated on the cabin floor, cut off sharply and grabbed at his middle with a wince.

"You hurt, old fellow?"

"I think I've pulled a muscle or two, doing all this traveling here lately. Or maybe it's just a bellyache. This old belly, it's eat many a good meal, but many a bad one too, and every now and again, lately, it gives me a stab to punish me."

"Your belly, huh?" It seemed to Sam that Joel was rubbing a bit high on his torso if it was really stomach trouble, and seemed to be holding his left arm strangely. But none of this seemed of consequence and he went back immediately to the themes that filled his mind. Normally taciturn, Sam Colter was for once in the mood to talk. He'd been doing some deep thinking lately and was glad to have an audience to vent some of his thoughts, even no more an audience than an old black runaway with a sore belly. "You're right about the colonel, old fellow. The rebels do fear Colonel Swaney. And for good reason. You know some of the things I've seen done under the colonel's authority over these past few months?"

"No, sir."

"I've seen rebel men, and sometimes men just suspected of being rebels, or sympathizers, begging for their lives, but losing them all the same. I've seen them told to pray, and shot while they were kneeling. I've seen them shot without being given time to pray at all. I've seen men hanged, watched them choke and kick and turn all colors until they died. I've seen all I can stand of the bushwhacking life."

He paced about the cabin, the hammering rain pounding a thrumming cadence that backdropped his voice. "Let me tell you a little tale. Earlier this year, we lost one of our own. His name was Millard McCormick. Millard was killed by a local rebel Home Guard fellow named Cree Henderson, more or less a bushwhacker himself, who'd come after Millard because Millard had made another Home Guard man, Fallon Blake, kneel over a stump so he could shoot him through the head. When they were burying Millard—me and the colonel and all of us watching from the hill—Millard's old grandmother got up and talked about the war, about the bushwhacking and the killing. She said it was all the same, no matter whose side it was on. Said it was all wicked, none of it worth doing. Some of what she said didn't make much sense maybe . . . but some of it did. After I heard her, I thought about it all for the longest time. And the more I thought, the less I wanted to ride with the colonel. We killed the man who had shot that old woman's grandson, Joel. Hung him, with his own son watching . . . and I didn't know then if we was doing right, and still don't. I'm tired. Downright weary of it all. Weary of fighting a bushwhacker's war. I want to be a regular soldier again. Enlisted, fighting the war in the open."

"You been a soldier before, have you, sir?" Joel was rubbing his left shoulder, his voice tight.

"Not a Union soldier. I was conscripted into the rebel army. Then one day me and a whole gang of other conscripts just up and walked away from our post and went into these hills and mountains. We had no plans, nothing beyond wanting to get away from the reb army. But we met up not a week later with Colonel Swaney, and the most of us, we ended up riding with him. Turned bushwhacker, none of us half realizing that it was happening—but so it was. We just sort of fell into doing it, just following the colonel. And you know, after a time or two, you get over the bad feeling that goes with it. You get where you can watch a man die and not think much about it beyond being glad it's him and not you. It strips the soul out of you. Don't matter what your cause is, how right it might be. Bushwhacking strips you of your soul. So I'm putting it behind me. I'm going north, into Kentucky, and I'm going to enlist as a Union soldier. Maybe it won't be a bit better than bushwhacking . . . but no. No. It will be better. It has to be better."

"Yes, sir. I'd say it is." Joel's voice was more strained than before. He lay down again, grimacing. Sam Colter wasn't looking or listening, and didn't notice.

"I've broke away," Sam said. "I'm leaving bushwhacking behind. Leaving off from shooting men in their own yards. In front of their wives . . . their children. That kind of thing, it should have never been. Not on either side of this war. And I never should have let myself become part of it." He paused, musing, and chuckled. "Sam Colter, a bushwhacker. You know what I used to be, old fellow? A store clerk. That's right. Just a young store clerk, in Greeneville, Tennessee, working for a man named Hannibal Deacon. He was an abolitionist to the soul of him. His very house was a depot of the Underground Railroad, right there in town! You know what, Joel? I myself guided slaves on their way north, more than once. Did it for Mr. Deacon, mostly. But also because I knew it was a good thing, and righteous. It led me to thinking that maybe what I wanted to do, once war broke out, was to become a Union guide, like Dan Ellis or Greeley Brown. I rode with Greeley for a time. You heard of Greeley Brown, old man?" Sam turned. "Old man?"

He walked slowly to the unmoving form and knelt,

touching the neck. No pulse, nor any breath moving the chest. Joel had died during Sam's self-absorbed soliloquy, died quietly, like a man falling asleep.

Sam took off his hat. It was a bizarre thing, meeting a man only to have him die within minutes. Yet this death was a better one than other deaths he'd witnessed lately. Joel's death had been natural, quietly brought to him by nature and the passing years, a far better death than the kind that came from the muzzle of a bushwhacker's rifle.

Chapter 20

Thornwell Estate, on the Green River
southeast of Hendersonville, N.C.

Greeley took another sip of coffee from his cup and thought how grand it was to drink the authentic beverage, not the pitifully inadequate toasted grain makeshifts one made do with most of the time since war had come. Count on Phillip Thornwell, the multiply divorced young romancer of every wealthy and attractive young woman within a three hundred mile radius of his big house, to still have real coffee about his place; it seemed to fit his style. If anyone could find a way to keep life's luxuries in supply, Phillip Thornwell could.

"I tell you, Greeley, I bless the dear old substitution law," Thornwell said as he drank big gulps from his own coffee cup, unlike Greeley, who sipped his slowly. They had been talking about the war and Greeley's role in it. Though Greeley and Thornwell stood on opposite sides of the conflict, Greeley knew that here, as at Mathen Ricker's, he was safe and could speak freely. Now Thornwell was speaking freely in turn. "Of all the privileges that come with wealth, the power to purchase myself a substitute has been the greatest for me. If I hadn't been able to afford a substitute, you might have seen yours truly playing soldier.

Can you imagine it? Me carrying a rifle, sweating on some battlefield, dodging cannonballs? Hah!" He gulped down another swallow.

"I can't," Greeley said. "You have nothing of the soldier about you, Phillip." He saw at once from Phillip's look that perhaps the remark had been wrongly taken. "Nothing but courage, of course, and ability. Plenty of ability. You'd certainly make a fine officer. In fact, that's probably what you would have been. An officer. Coming from a background of prominence and all."

Thornwell smiled and pulled a couple of cigars from his vest pocket. He handed one to Greeley, who accepted gratefully. He remembered from long ago days, when he'd served as a mountain hunting guide for Thornwell and his late father, that Phillip smoked excellent cigars. In those days Phillip hadn't been so quick to share them, however. Not until after Greeley saved his life.

They lit up, sending rich puffs of smoke into the fashionably designed and furnished drawing room of this old stone mansion on a mountainside. Greeley had long been fascinated that a family that had made its fortunes in shipping along the North Carolina coast had forsaken the ocean in favor of the mountains. Of course, lots of rich folks had visited and vacationed in this region, particularly over around Flat Rock, for years. Yet still it seemed a man would want to be close to what had brought him wealth. But who was he to divine the mind of the well-off Phillip Thornwell, any more than the mind of Nanny the slave woman? Notions that Thornwell accepted with ease, such as the buying off of one's own war duties by hiring a substitute, or breaking up slave families with no more trepidation than taking a calf from the mother cow, were troubling to Greeley.

Right now, however, Greeley held Thornwell in quite a high regard, because this rich, idle heir of a late father's abundant wealth had minutes before agreed quite readily to an odd and risky proposition. And to get him to accept it, Greeley hadn't even had to play his ace by reminding Thornwell of a certain long ago rescue from a crumbling ledge halfway down a cliff. Thornwell, then barely out of his teens, had acted carelessly during a hunt at Mount

Pisgah, dropped twenty feet over a cliff's edge to a narrow bluff, and broken an arm and three toes when he struck. Greeley roped himself down to the ledge, literally strapped the blubbering and repentant Thornwell onto his shoulders, and somehow managed to climb back up again, with the help of some pulls from Phillip's doting father and the three slaves they'd brought along. Greeley had gotten himself quite a good bonus from the elder Thornwell for that bit of heroism, and a promise from the rescued one that he would do "anything, anything at all" for him anytime he came asking. Greeley had not come asking until now.

Whether Thornwell's acceptance of Nanny and her baby constituted, in his mind, the fulfillment of that old pledge of benefaction was unclear. Greeley accepted the act as such, in any case; he would ask no more of Phillip Thornwell than this. By taking the responsibility for Nanny off his shoulders, Thornwell was lifting a burden that weighed far more heavily than Thornwell himself had that day at the Mount Pisgah cliffs. That a Confederate–sympathizing, aristocratic young slave owner such as Thornwell had been so unhesitant in helping out a known Unionist pilot with a reward on his head was no small thing. Even more significant was his willingness to involve himself in an act that under Confederate law would be quite thoroughly illegal: accepting the runaway "property" that Nanny was.

Greeley, enjoying the rare luxury of good cigars, real coffee, and a big house so fine that he'd hesitated to sit on its furniture, sat talking to Thornwell of old days, of Thornwell's late father—a man Greeley had liked despite the vast difference between their stations in life—and of the war. Phillip Thornwell, though able to give Greeley the latest and best public information about the war's progress on various fronts, seemed oddly aloof to it all, as if it were some great chess game playing out dramatically on the board of the world, but in the end no more than that: a game. Typical Phillip Thornwell. Wealthy from birth, still virgin to any kind of true labor or need, and twice divorced without the slightest seeming concern about the scandal of such a thing, Thornwell lacked the capacity to take any part of life seriously other than his own epicurean pleasures. In that regard the years had not changed him a bit.

Greeley was ready to rise and leave when it came to his mind that perhaps Thornwell had a right to know more of the story of Nanny and her child than he had told. So far he'd revealed to Thornwell only that Nanny was a runaway from the well-known Josiah House over near Warm Springs, and that for personal reasons he would consider it a great favor if Thornwell took her in, mixing her among his own slaves and keeping her identity secret. And if anyone should come seeking her, it would be necessary for Thornwell to hide her and lie about it. To all this Thornwell had readily agreed—Greeley detected that maybe there was some personal grudge against the Josiahs that helped speed his decision—but honesty compelled Greeley to speak further.

"Phillip, there's a bit more I must say, so you'll know why I've asked what I have of you. Nanny had a husband— I don't know whether the law would agree he was her true husband or not—and he was, well, a white man. I see your look. . . . I reacted much the same when I learned of it. In fact this white man . . . he was Spencer Josiah, son of the household."

"Great day of glory! You mean Colonel Josiah's own son was married to a *nigger*?" Thornwell threw back his head and laughed boomingly.

"He was an odd kind of fellow," Greeley said. "Very . . . different. An abolitionist, for one thing, but even beyond that, a kind of unusual human being. He died by accident while stampeding north."

"Oh, I've seen Spencer Josiah a time or two—I know the oddities of that bird! But I never would have guessed he would actually marry a darky," Thornwell said. He had laughed tears into his eyes and wiped them away. He froze for a moment, then said, "Oh, my—this all means that baby is the *grandson* of Colonel Josiah!"

"Yes, though I doubt the old fellow would have claimed it as such."

"Colonel Josiah's legacy—a mulatto grandchild! Oh, how rich! How thoroughly, delightfully *rich*!" Thornwell enjoyed another long laugh and made a show out of slapping the arms of his chair and stamping his feet in mirth. Greeley drew the last cloud of smoke out of his cigar and watched Thornwell guffaw, thinking that maybe Spencer Josiah wasn't the only "odd bird" in these mountains.

When the laughter subsided, Thornwell again wiped mirth tears from his eyes and said, "You know, Greeley, I doubt you need to worry that anybody will come looking here for your runaway friends. I'll bet you old Mrs. Josiah is glad to have them gone. What a scandal! What a delicious, rich scandal—a mulatto grandchild!"

Greeley doubted Thornwell would find it so funny had the scandal involved his family rather than the Josiahs. "Uh . . . Phillip, I need to tell you also that I'll probably be back with another slave, an old man. Nanny's father."

Thornwell's smile faded away. "Her father?"

"Yes."

"Hmmm. Oh my."

"Something's wrong with that notion, I can see."

"Greeley, Greeley, Greeley . . . I owe you a lot, old fellow, and I'm happy to take in the wench and her pickaninny. More than happy! You should know there has been bad blood between the Thornwells and Josiahs for years, and I'm glad to gig those Warm Springs frogs any way I can. There's a bit of adventure and fun in it, taking in stolen goods from the Josiahs, hiding them out like spies or fugitives . . . but a third one, an *old* one at that, meaning he would be probably of little practical use—that's asking a bit much of me, Greeley. And if you wanted me to take him, why didn't you just bring him along with the others so I could see all at once the dose I was being asked to swallow?"

Greeley's dismay mounted, unrevealed. He'd been afraid of something like this. "I had planned to bring them all in at the same time. But Joel—that's the old fellow—he took to feeling poorly and had to stay aback in an empty house to rest. But I'm sure he's fine now. I told him I'd be coming back to get him after I got Nanny and the baby turned over to you."

"Oh my—not only old, but sickly. Greeley, as I said, I do

owe you a lot for you hauling me up that bluff years ago, but *really*, old fellow . . ."

"Phillip, I know it's asking much, but you've got to understand my situation. I have no other place I can take the old fellow. I don't even have a place to live, since Thomas's Highland Legion burned it down, so I can't keep him with me myself. But here you've got other slaves, cabins and such for them, other darkies who could take care of him."

"I don't know, Greeley. I'm hesitant."

"He can't go back to Josiah House, not after running off, and especially not after helping his daughter and grandchild run away. You know why they ran, and why I was willing to help them? Because the late colonel's wife is so hard a woman that it was feared that she might have the baby done away with because of the scandal. I just couldn't see having a child hurt or killed, even if it is a mulatto."

"Well . . . oh, hang it all, I suppose one more wouldn't hurt. Bring the old boy on. Maybe he'll be fit to help us cook at least."

"He's been a house servant for years. He could be very helpful once he gets his strength back."

"We'll hope so. But me taking him—that makes you and me even. Square. All accounts are settled. Right, old fellow?"

"Right indeed, Phillip. I'll ask no more of you."

"And you'll be coming back one of these days to get these darkies, I imagine?"

Greeley had no such plan. The future that he foresaw included a Union victory, an enforcement of Lincoln's Emancipation Proclamation, and the freeing of all the people Phillip currently held in bondage back in his slave huts. So he answered: "If there's a southern victory, then I'll be back to get them."

Phillip's eyes twinkled; he caught the twist in the comment. "Fair enough. I expect I'll see you, say, within a year or so."

"We'll see. Good-bye, Phillip. And thank you."

"Don't go off yet, Greeley. Let me have one of the kitchen girls fix you some traveling food."

Greeley couldn't turn that down. He waited while a

young slave woman packed him some of the finest food he had seen in months. *Maybe all this effort was worth it after all.*

He left about sunset, pausing to look back at the row of slave huts behind the imposing big house. Standing before one of them was Nanny, Little Joel in her arms. She stared at Greeley with a look that told him she at last was coming to understand what he'd been trying to tell her, that here she was not at all free, despite all her big talk. She was away from Josiah House, but not out of bondage. Hers was still just one more dark face among a gaggle of others. Though Greeley didn't like Nanny, he felt sorry for her just now. He lifted a hand and waved; she did not respond in any way.

"I'll be back, with your father, just as quick as I can," he said.

Nanny turned without a response and walked back into the hut, her baby bobbing on her arm.

Greeley headed into the mountains.

Greeley could not make sense of it, and in the gathering twilight pondered the mystery with a combined sense of awe, curiosity, and sorrow. The sorrow surrounded the fact of Joel's death, which had taken him by surprise. He hadn't thought the old fellow was that poorly. But dead he was, unless this fresh grave beside the old cabin really contained no body at all and was merely someone's idea of a joke.

A sniff of the atmosphere around the grave gave the lie to that notion. There was certainly someone beneath that heaped sod, and none too deeply buried. Whoever dug this grave had done so with inadequate or makeshift tools, and barely gotten the body into the ground. But even that inadequate effort had surely required a lot of work, considering the entwining roots that permeated the forest floor would have made grave-digging laborious even with the best of tools.

It was the who and the why of it all that intrigued Greeley most. Someone went to a lot of trouble to dignify the passing of this poor old slave. It couldn't have been anyone who had been sent to catch him. A slave catcher would have merely hauled the corpse back home. And no slave catcher would have placed at the head of this grave the bark marker that was there now, bearing words carefully carved in: HERE LIES JOEL, A FREE MAN.

Weary, Greeley sat down beside the grave. He dreaded having to return to Thornwell's house with news that Joel was dead. Thornwell would probably be relieved to hear it, since he hadn't wanted Joel to begin with, but what of Nanny? Already she had lost her husband. Now her own father was dead as well. The news would hurt her deeply.

Or perhaps not. She seemed quite an unemotional woman. Thinking back, Greeley couldn't recall a single sad word she'd said about the loss of her "husband," and certainly she hadn't seemed concerned about leaving her sickly father behind at this cabin. Nor, for that matter, had she even demonstrated much affection for her baby. She had fed it when it cried, held it while they traveled, yet never had there been much evidence of feeling or deep affection. One generally could feel and see the love of a mother for her child. Greeley had not seen or felt any of that around Nanny.

The only time she showed signs of being emotionally stirred was when she talked about gaining her freedom. That one theme seemed to play in her mind and heart to the exclusion of all else. Greeley wondered if he would be that way, were he a slave. No. He couldn't imagine any personal ambition, no matter how heartfelt and rightful, overriding his love for family and friends. Family, especially. He could think of little that he wouldn't give simply to have a family to sacrifice and work for, and to worry over.

But Greeley Brown had no family, and that was that. His theory was that if it was true God arranged the lives of men, perhaps He had arranged Greeley's own lonely existence for the sake of his piloting work. Greeley realized that if the worst should happen to him and some fortunate Confederate managed to collect that reward on his head, there would be no wife or children to feel the loss. It was best that he was alone right now, hard as it was to endure sometimes.

He went into the cabin, ate, and lay down to rest. Come tomorrow he would begin the journey back toward the

Thornwell Estate and give the news about Joel. His penultimate thought as sleep came was cynical: *I'll bet that Nanny doesn't even shed a tear for him.*

The last thought was a question: *I wonder who buried Joel and scratched out that marker?* It was the most intriguing mystery, as bothersome as an unscratchable itch, made all the worse because he knew it was far from likely he could ever find out the answer.

When he awakened the next morning there were men on horses outside the cabin and others approaching it on foot. He rose and grabbed for his rifle as two men came through the door. They were faster than he and got to it first. One leveled a shotgun at his middle.

"Hello, Mr. Mackafee. It seems we've caught you."

"My name ain't Mackafee."

"We'll see about that. Up and out!"

Greeley knew as soon as he was nudged at gunpoint out the door who in the line of riders was the leader. Though none of the men were uniformed consistently enough for rank to be evidenced—what uniform portions there were, in fact, mixed Confederate and Union garb so thoroughly that Greeley couldn't tell which side these men favored—one sat his saddle in a different manner than the rest and had about him a bearing that said as much as any officer's uniform could.

"You, sir, are Mr. Jesse Mackafee?" the man said.

"No, sir, I ain't."

"Then who are you?"

"I want to know who you are first."

"Not a good answer." The apparent leader drew out a saber and advanced his horse toward Greeley. Pointing with the long blade, he said, "You, sir, are Jesse Mackafee, a damned bushwhacker. It's you, sir, who forced the son of Mr. Mead Chapel back yonder to hack to death his own pet dog on the doorstep of his house."

"That ain't true. I never heard of Mead Chapel or Jesse Mackafee."

"Then say who you are, man!"

Greeley could not say. He was a man with a reward on his head, and it would be foolish to reveal his identity without truly knowing the political leanings of this armed band. Greeley stood there, looking guilty and evasive in his silence. Finally he said, "I have no desire to tell my identity to men who don't tell me theirs, nor am I obliged to bark like a show dog at the flash of your sword, sir."

The man glanced at his fellows; a chuckle rippled down the line of riders. Greeley hoped that was a good sign, that his show of dignified defiance had gained him some respect.

"Well, sir, I'll tell you who I am," the leader said. "I am Colonel Merriman Swaney, commander of this band of good and loyal Union men. Have you heard of me, eh?"

"I've heard of you." Greeley was relieved; a Unionist band shouldn't have any cause to harm him.

"Then who are you?" Swaney demanded.

"My name is Greeley Brown. You've heard of me too, I reckon."

"You reckon wrong."

"Wait a minute, Colonel," one of the others said. "I've heard of Greeley Brown. If that's really who this is, he's a good man who we should leave be. Greeley Brown is a pilot for Unionist stampeders. The rebs have a price on his head, they hate him so much."

"Have you identification, sir?" Swaney asked.

"I've got Federal recruiting papers in my coat." He produced these, and handed them up to Swaney, who examined them with one eye squinted, then handed them back. "Those appear to be the legitimate item, but you might have stolen them. Have you anything else?"

"No, sir. I don't tend to carry identification around, considering that such could get me killed if I fell into Confederate hands."

"The lack of such may well get you killed today," Swaney said. He looked across his shoulder. "Mr. Chapel! Tell me if this is the man who forced your son to kill his dog!"

A man with thick spectacles rode up beside Swaney and peered through heavy glass at Greeley. "It surely appears to be one and the same," he said. "I *think* it's him."

Greeley did not like the way this was going. "Sir, listen to me: My name is Greeley Brown. I don't know you, and

I'm no rebel nor bushwhacker. I'm not guilty of this thing you're accusing me of."

"His voice sounds the same, too. I do believe he is the one," Chapel reaffirmed.

Swaney seemed pleased to hear this. "Mr. Chapel, shall you do the honors, or shall I?"

"What do you mean, Colonel?"

"I'm offering you the chance to take this saber and use it the way your son was forced to use that axe. You have my permission to hack this Secessionist bushwhacker into pieces."

Chapel went pale and swallowed hard. He shook his head. "No, sir. I won't do *that*."

Swaney sighed loudly, as if very put upon. "Oh, well, I suppose it falls to me, then." He swung out of his saddle and regarded Greeley, hand clenching and loosening around the grip of the saber. "Mr. Mackafee, sir, you are about to die, and I advise you to take what time you have left to pray so that your soul may be ready to meet its creator."

"I'm *not* Mackafee!" Greeley declared. "God in heaven, that man there is half blind! You can see it just looking at him! He couldn't identify his own mother at ten paces! I tell you, I'm not any Mackafee! My name is Greeley Brown!"

Swaney shook his head and lifted the saber.

"Tell him, Mr. Chapel!" Greeley said. "Tell him you don't know that I'm the one—for I ain't!"

Chapel's voice was whiny, like a worn-out violin string. "Colonel Swaney, maybe you shouldn't do that . . . I mean, I didn't see the man all that well, and I *could* be wrong. . . ."

The bushwhacker chieftain was not listening. With saber aloft, he suddenly advanced upon Greeley. Mead Chapel, upon whose words Greeley's unjustified condemnation hung, stammered and looked uncertain, then squeezed his eyes shut and turned his head just as the blade descended, flashing in the rising morning light and making an audible slashing swish in the forest air.

Chapter 21

Greeley felt a keen, stinging pain in his upper left arm, followed by an instant numbness that extended to his fingertips. Swaney pulled back his blade for a second swing, its sheen now dulled by a smear of blood. In that brief second between the first swing and the second, Greeley took in an amazing amount of detail—Swaney's grimacing, blood-hungry expression, the dark frowns of the onlooking bushwhackers, his own blood coursing down his wounded arm, the saber going back and then forward again. . . .

Greeley let out a roar and dropped suddenly, the saber slashing over his head. Lunging, Greeley rammed his right shoulder against Swaney's lean middle, folding the man in half and knocking him back. Swaney managed to keep his grip on the saber but was unable to use it for the moment because he was flailing wildly to keep his balance. Greeley, driven by fury and the energy that comes of threatened survival, took a deft leap back, lifted his foot, and kicked Swaney very hard in the crotch. The bushwhacker gave a visceral grunt, his eyes bulging, face going red, hands groping at his injured region. But still he held the saber. Greeley, his head suddenly beginning to swim as the blood gushed in increasing quantities from his arm, backstepped away from Swaney, expecting him to fall at any moment. Swaney did tilt forward as if he were going to collapse on his face, but managed to thrust the tip of the saber into the ground and keep himself propped up. He lifted eyes full of anger and pain to Greeley, cursed so fiercely that drool dribbled onto his beard, and reached for his belt pistol.

Before it could be drawn, however, something big intervened between him and his intended target. One of the bushwhackers had ridden his horse between the two men. "That's enough, Colonel," he said. "You ain't going to shoot that man. He is Greeley Brown. I know it for a fact."

"Out of my way, Butterfield!" the furious Swaney bellowed. "Damn you, move!"

"Colonel, I can't let you do that to that man," Butterfield replied calmly. "That ain't the man you say it is, and he don't deserve to be cut upon."

"I'll see you shot for this, if you keep interfering!" Swaney declared, voice tight with pain and fury. "I'll shoot you myself, right now, damn you!"

"If you so much as try, Colonel, you'll be shot down where you stand."

This was a new voice, coming from somewhere behind and to the side of where Greeley stood bleeding and Swaney propped on his saber. A new voice, yet familiar to all who heard it, including Greeley Brown. Hand gripping his bleeding arm, he turned and saw the lean, lightly bearded man who had spoken, and who now stood with rifle raised and leveled at Swaney. This was the same slender bushwhacker to whom Swaney had spoken the day his band watched from a hillside the burial of one of their own, the same bushwhacker whose eyes had locked with those of the son of Cree Henderson after Merriman Swaney and band hanged the man.

"Sam Colter?" Greeley said, tentative. Then, with assurance, "Sam Colter! Caesar Augustus, son, what are you doing here?"

"Hello, Greeley," Sam Colter said. "I was hoping I'd find you here. But not like this."

Swaney took his weight off the propping saber and stood

on bowed and shaking legs. He lifted a trembling finger and pointed it at Butterfield, then Sam, then Butterfield again, back and forth. "You two, both of you are damned insubordinates! You'll be held to account for this!"

"Your authority over this band is gone, Swaney," Butterfield said. "There's been talk among us, every one of us, for a long time. You've become little more than a madman, sir, as cruel and bad in every way as the rebels we're supposed to be fighting to overcome. When you go so far as to do injury to so fine a Union man as Greeley Brown, then that's a damn sight too far."

Swaney looked wildly at the others. "You hear that? Are you going to sit still and let him talk insubordination to your superior officer?"

Sam Colter, the continuing object of Greeley's disbelieving stare, spoke in reply. "You aren't an officer, Colonel. Not no real officer. Any authority you had was accorded to you by all of us, because you seemed to merit it. But that's over. You've been losing your authority a long time, Colonel. It's been leaking away with every foolish and cruel command, every sign you've showed of this blood lust and wickedness that's ruined you. You were just too blind to see it."

Swaney, looking scared but still trying to maintain the demeanor of a man in charge, said, "Where were you today, Colter? You were absent without leave. Speak up, now!"

"The truth is, Colonel, I was deserting you. I'd had enough. I was riding out. And I wouldn't have come back here now except for having met an old black fellow, sick and dying. The one I buried in yonder new grave. I saw a knife that he had. Initials on it, looking familiar . . . your initials, Greeley. But I didn't put it together until I had already ridden on a few miles. When it came to me whose knife that was, and that you surely must have been the one to give it to that poor darky, I came back, hoping I'd find you."

Greeley was bleeding badly from his arm and beginning to feel faint, but managed a grin.

"Greeley, you're looking mighty pale."

"I'm getting weak."

Swaney cursed and raised his pistol, aiming it at Colter

because the intervening form of Butterfield and his horse still blocked him from access to Greeley Brown. Butterfield pulled a booted foot out of his stirrup and kicked Swaney in the chin, hard, knocking him cold instantly. "Somebody take his weapons," Butterfield said. "I don't want him to wake up shooting or cutting."

As others moved to obey the quietly spoken command, Butterfield swung down from his saddle and approached Greeley. He was a broad, muscular man, with a rich auburn beard and large eyes sporting lashes the most beautiful woman of society might have envied. His belly bulged widely, but one could see at a glance that there was nothing flabby about it. A fist that slammed that belly would find it to be more pillar than pillow.

Sam Colter, rifle now lowered, approached as well, and reached Greeley, who stood grinning, but with a face pale as paper and growing whiter by the moment.

"Old friends, you two are, I believe!" Butterfield said. "This is indeed the same Greeley Brown you've spoke of so often, Sam?"

"It is indeed," Sam replied, reaching out as Greeley staggered toward him, appearing likely to faint at any moment as blood spurted through his gripping fingers and ran down his left arm.

"Better sit down, Greeley," Sam said, and helped Greeley ease onto his rump on the ground.

"We've met before, Mr. Brown," Butterfield said. "The memory and the recognition came back just as Swaney was swinging that sword back the first time. I was introduced to you once, way back before the war, over at Jewel Hill. I'm Jack Butterfield, and I was there for the funeral of that Shelton fellow who'd fell out of the tree and cracked his head open. You remember?"

"I do," Greeley said. The image of Butterfield was beginning to dance and waver before his eyes. "Thank you, sir, for stopping that madman ... from hacking me to death. . . ." Greeley was sounding weaker, fainter. "And you too, Sam . . ."

"We need to stop this bleeding," Sam said.

Butterfield was already at it, tearing off part of the tail of his own shirt to make a tourniquet. "He indeed would have hacked you to death," he said. "Swaney was in the humor to cut somebody to pieces, and by gum, he'd have done it. You heard him talking about that boy, son of Mead Chapel, who's that fellow yonder in the spectacles. The boy was made to chop his dog to death by some rebel name of Jesse Mackafee, and Swaney had him a notion to see Mackafee cut up the same way. He was eager as he could be to believe you was Mackafee—you could tell that, I'm sure. And Mead Chapel yonder is so blind he'd have identified his own granny as Mackafee, with Swaney pressuring him like he was."

"Mr. Chapel nigh . . . got me killed. . . ." Greeley's field of vision took on a shimmering sheen that twinkled out into bursting stars as he slumped to the side. "Sam, I believe I'm going to—" And he fainted dead away.

Two hours later Greeley was sitting up on a log beside a canvas tent that had been pitched, along with many other temporary shelters, in a very secluded hollow. Butterfield was squatted beside him on legs like trunks of two big Tennessee poplars, wincing as a skinny, pale-haired fellow with wheezy breath squinted at Greeley's arm and repeatedly poked into its flesh a bent sewing needle being employed to stitch up the gash.

Butterfield screwed up his face and made a little puckered circle of his mouth beneath that lush auburn beard. Greeley chuckled at him. "I'd never have guessed you for squeamish, Mr. Butterfield. You didn't seem bothered while I was standing there gushing blood."

"It ain't the blood," Butterfield said. "It's the needle. Ever since I run a needle through my hand when I was seven year old, I ain't never been able to stand needles."

"Well, this needle's hurting only when he pokes it above the cut. It's all pretty numb below. Numb all the way through my whole hand."

"Can you move the fingers?"

Greeley made a fist and opened it.

"Don't do that!" the stitcher said. "You're making your muscles pull where I'm trying to sew."

"Sorry."

Butterfield said, "You may not get much feeling back in that arm. An uncle of mine got cut at the wrist and lost the feeling in his thumb and three fingers."

Greeley nodded. He was worried about the arm, but with typical masculine vanity trying not to show it much. What if the feeling really didn't return? Worse, what if the wound festered and mortified, and the arm had to be cut off? That was pretty much the standard treatment in the army: bad limb wound, off it goes. It was the cleanest, quickest, safest way to deal with it. Greeley was glad right now to be among bushwhackers and not regular Union forces. Among the latter he would probably be undergoing the sawmill treatment in a hospital tent rather than receiving the careful stitching being administered here.

Sam Colter strode up, nibbling on a dried biscuit, and eyed the stitchery. "Going to be able to keep that arm, I believe," he said. "That's a good thing."

"Don't I know it. Sam, you and me got some talking to do. I'm burning to know what happened to you since we was parted. Last I saw of you was when you were heading toward Cumberland Gap, guiding that man who we found with that mortified hand."

"I'll tell you the whole tale, soon as I finish my biscuit."

"Well, while we're waiting—ouch! Caesar Augustus, but I felt it that time!—would somebody tell me how it was a madman like Merriman Swaney was ever able to persuade sensible folk like Jack Butterfield and Sam Colter to give him allegiance? Did he hold a true military rank or something?"

"Swaney? Nah," Butterfield said. "He's nothing but an ordinary back-country bushwhacker. As I hear it, he was indeed regular army once, but not no colonel. And there's rumors that I can't vouch for, that he was kind of quietly slipped out of the army because of some of his behavior during the war with Mexico."

"So why the devil did you follow a man like that?"

Sam cut in, having just swallowed the last bite of biscuit. "I can tell you that, Greeley. Because Merriman Swaney like he is now ain't the Merriman Swaney that Jack and me and several of these others met after we came to these mountains. Swaney seemed a good man at the time, a natural-born leader. He was living here in this encampment with three or four other Union men, hiding from the Home Guards, protecting some of the houses of Union men off in regular service, and doing a bit of bushwhacking when it was called for. Swaney was a man looking for someone to lead, and he showed us his best side. We fell in with him at first for mutual protection, but when the Home Guards found us, there was a fight. Swaney showed some true bravery, fought well, saved the life of a couple of us. It was only natural that we followed him after that, but as time went by, he began to show another side of himself to us."

"Who's this 'us' you keep talking about, Sam? You and Butterfield?"

"Me, Butterfield, and most of the rest of this band. We were all soldiers together. Rebel conscripts, until we deserted and fled into these mountains."

"Conscripts . . . I had figured that might have happened to you, Sam, when you didn't return. That, or getting killed."

"I was caught in Powell Valley, coming back from Cumberland Gap."

"I'm glad I left Joel that knife," Greeley said. "Otherwise you'd have never come back. I wouldn't have seen you again. And Swaney might have managed to kill me despite Butterfield's best efforts."

"The others would have moved in to help me, if Sam hadn't been there," Butterfield said. "Swaney's control over us had already been wore down to a thread . . . all I did was go ahead and snap it, a little sooner, maybe, than some of the others expected. But we all knew Swaney was on his way out, and all agreed it should be that way."

"Where is Swaney now?" Greeley asked, wincing as he felt another probe of the needle. The stitching job was almost finished now.

"Already gone. We sent him on his way, and where he goes and what he does is up to him."

"He seemed a prideful man. It must have hurt him bad to be mutinied like that."

"Indeed. The man looked like a living corpse. But I feel no pity for him. He had become hard and ugly, just like this war, and he had notions of being lord over us all. The very reason we were out scouting today was to look for Sam, who'd gone missing. I figured he'd deserted—I'd seen it coming a long time—and I think Swaney suspected the same. If he'd caught Sam, there's no telling what he might have tried to do to punish him. But as it happened, along the way we ran into Mead Chapel and heard his tale about the boy and the chopped-up dog, and after that the colonel forgot all about Sam and took to looking for Jesse Mackafee instead. He had the madness stirred up in him like we'd seen so often lately, and was determined that he'd find Mackafee and chop him to pieces before the day was out."

"And instead he found me, and decided I'd do for a substitute," Greeley said bitterly.

"I don't know how he saw it in his own mind. Maybe he convinced himself you were Mackafee. Maybe he didn't really care. Doesn't matter now. You're still alive, you've still got your arm, and Swaney is gone."

"Who'll lead this band now that Swaney's out of the picture?"

Butterfield cleared his throat and said, "The consensus seems to center around yours truly."

"I ain't surprised. You'd do a fine job of it. Congratulations."

Butterfield's reaction was surprisingly solemn. "Don't congratulate me. There's no honor in this business. This is mountain war we're engaged in. War of the ugliest kind. This is men being shot in their yards, in their very doorways, and women insulted. I've seen old folks treated like I wouldn't treat a mad dog. Back in January I saw a boy no more than twelve shot down protecting a scrawny hog he'd managed to keep alive so his family would have meat enough to make it through to spring. I've watched children crying for their daddies, with me knowing them very daddies are swinging from a tree limb back in the woods and won't never be home again. This ain't no normal war, not in these mountains. It's a ghosty, shadowy kind of war, fought by ghosty, shadowy men. You can look across these hills and see nothing you wouldn't expect to see, but those same hills are hiding a whole legion of phantoms. A phantom legion, fighting a shadowy, hell's-fury kind of war."

"The rebels are indeed cursed cruel," Greeley said.

Butterfield looked him in the eye, a cold and leaden stare. "They are. But it ain't only the rebels. Some of them things I've just talked about, it's us who's done them. Us."

The stitcher leaned back and put down his needle. "You're done."

Greeley examined the work. "You're a good seamstress, friend. And if this thing will heal without festering, I'll be beholden to you forever."

"It'll fester," the fellow said very casually, wiping the needle on his trousers. "I have nary a doubt I'll be chopping off that arm in a week or so." He got up and walked away.

"Cheerful soul, ain't he?" Butterfield said, grinning.

Greeley managed to grin back, but it required a great effort.

Julius Killefer couldn't get over the irony. He had anticipated a long trudge back toward Kentucky, but hardly under these circumstances. Instead of surreptitious journeying over ridges and along hidden mountain trails, hiding out from the rebels, here he was walking right up an open road, Morristown miles behind him and Cumberland Gap miles ahead, in the company of soldiers returning to their own duty at the Gap after a period of leave. And rather than hiding from the rebels, he was heading up as one of them.

The experiences of the past several days had already blended into a surreal blur. From Greeneville he'd been hauled to Knoxville in a freight car with a few dozen other hollow-cheeked, somber mountain boys also being swept into the Confederate forces. Most of them looked so scared they appeared sickly—a look that might be to their advantage, given that they would have to be cleared for duty by an examining physician at the instruction camp.

After dumping its load of conscripts at the Knoxville rail yard, the train went on as the reluctant soldiers were sent to one of the conscript encampments at the edge of town.

Julius was appalled when he saw the camp, which consisted of row upon row of very crude little log huts that were little more than stables made for humans. Open-fronted, unfloored, and even lacking beds, the shelters hardly seemed suitable for human occupation, but fit only for swine. Julius hoped his situation would be better once they reached their actual station at Cumberland Gap.

He held an even stronger hope he wouldn't go to the Gap at all. Maybe the examining surgeon would find some physical defect or previously undetected medical problem, and release him from his conscription. Never before had Julius hoped to be puny, but at this moment he would have hardly cared had the doctor told him he was dying. Forced service as a rebel seemed no less dreadful than death, anyway.

The examining surgeon was a bored-looking man who quickly dashed Julius's hope of a medical exemption. After giving him a cursory examination that included a few very personal pokes and prods Julius hadn't anticipated, having never visited any kind of physician before, he mumbled, "This one's ready," and pushed him through. Julius thought wildly about making up some medical complaint on the spot and seeing if he could actually convince the doctor of it . . . but something restrained him. It was that absurdly strong, utterly inconvenient sense of honor that his father had drilled into him since babyhood. When it came right down to it, Julius simply couldn't lie, not even to save his own skin.

They marched him and his fellow conscripts—all of whom had passed medical muster, including a couple who had obvious physical problems—back to the encampment, lined them up, and brought out an officer with a manual in hand. He thrust his right hand up into the air, and Julius wilted. It was the moment he'd dreaded, the moment when that cursed code of honor of the Killefer family would do him its greatest damage. He bit his lip, full of dread.

"Raise your right hand, men," the officer said, lifting his own in example.

Hands rose all around. Julius's did not.

"Repeat after me," the officer said. He cleared his throat, opened his mouth to read the first line, and only then saw that Julius hadn't lifted his hand as ordered. Frowning, he lowered his own hand and approached the unwilling conscript.

"Didn't you hear me, son? Raise your right hand!"

"I . . . I can't, sir."

"What?"

"I can't take that oath. Because I don't believe in it."

"The hell! You will take that oath, son, because you're a duly conscripted citizen of the Confederate States of America, called upon to do your bound duty, and if you don't do it, there'll be worse hell to pay for you than you've known ever before in your sorry life! You understand what I'm saying to you?"

"Yes, sir."

"Then lift that right hand!"

Julius raised it—halfway. "Sir . . . I want you to know that I don't agree with the rebel cause. And I ain't a Confederate citizen. I come from Kentucky, and I'm only here because of family business. I shouldn't have been conscripted, and I don't agree that I've got a duty to take this oath."

The officer's words were cold as a January night. "You'll raise your hand, now. You'll take the oath, now."

"But if I take the oath, sir, I'll be honor-bound to hold to it. I believe in that, sir. Honor. My pa taught me that way."

"Son, one more word out of you other than the vow to support the Confederate States of America and I'll have you under arrest. You hear me?"

"Yes, sir."

"Raise your hand." He backed away. "All of you, raise them hands again! And repeat after me."

Julius lifted his hand, slowly. There was no way out. He was about to vow to serve the same cause that had forced him and his father to hide for so long, under such bad conditions. He was about to pledge his honor to that which he believed dishonorable. And because of the irrevocable molding of his mind and concepts, he wouldn't be able to do it in the same manner as those people Greeley Brown had talked about, who took oaths but didn't mean them nor stick to them. Once sworn as a Confederate soldier, he would consider it his duty to serve, and to give it his best. He knew that his father, ironically, a man who hated the Confederacy with all his heart, would see it just that same way himself, if he were here.

The officer voiced the first lines of the oath; the conscripts, Julius included, mumbled in echo. When Julius lowered his hand again, he knew his world had just undergone a major change. He was a soldier now. A rebel. He wouldn't be going home until the Confederate States of America declared that he could.

Just now, living hardly seemed worth the trouble.

That night in camp, he talked with a Greene County conscript, a fat fellow of nineteen years named Mickey Cossit. The whining drone of Cossit's voice put Julius's nerves on edge, but he endured it for the sake of having someone to talk to.

"I knew we'd all get through the surgeon's examination," Cossit said. "They put almost every one of them through—except them that come in as paid substitutes. It was like that for a fellow I know from back home. He was exempt from conscription because he was the assistant tax collecting agent for the county, but some conscript officers rounded him up anyway—chased him down, shooting at him with pistols, and one of them being his own kin!—and they hauled him here and declared him fit for service even though he'd been sick a long time and was even spitting up blood when the conscript boys run him down. Well, his father paid a stout young fellow a thousand dollars to come in as his substitute, and the doctor looked him over and said, 'Nope. Got a speck in his eye. Can't take him.' So they sent my friend off to be a soldier and sent the substitute home, and once that substitute got there, you know what they done? They turned around and conscripted him! Hauled him right back here, and the surgeon says, 'He's fit for duty.' So that way they got them both, you see. The rebels are taking about anybody they can now. It's hard to get out of serving. The Confederates got so many deserters, especially in East

Tennessee and North Carolina, that they'll take anybody who can walk ten steps and shoot a gun."

"I ain't shooting no gun for the rebs," Julius answered. "They may clad me up in gray or butternut, but I'll never be a real soldier. Not for *them*."

They marched the conscripts back to the railroad station the next day and rode them by train to Morristown. There they were turned over to a guard of soldiers heading for Cumberland Gap on foot. Fit and strong and used to drilling and marching, these soldiers stepped along quickly. Julius marched along with them easily, but for others, including the overweight Mickey Cossit, it was difficult to keep pace. Julius was afraid on the first day that Cossit would literally drop down dead.

Julius glanced to his right. Cossit was doing a little better today, and it was already evident he was losing weight. From all Julius had heard about the slim rations that went with rebel military service, he figured Cossit would be thin as a rail before his tour of duty was through, and said as much.

Cossit grinned as cheerfully as he could. "I hope I do thin up. There'll be less of me for the boys in blue to shoot at."

"If we're lucky, we won't be in no fights," Julius said. "We'll just set on our rumps there at the Gap, until the Union comes in and sets us free."

"You better not talk in favor of the Union," Cossit said. "It's one thing to think it, but another to say it. I don't covet getting whipped for talking treason." And he dropped away and let Julius pull ahead.

Julius realized that Cossit was right. He would have to be careful now that he was under official Confederate authority. These days even civilians had to watch what they said, and a soldier all the more so.

They trudged on, weary but unresting. "How many miles to the Gap?" Julius asked one of the soldiers. He received no answer but a command to keep marching.

Julius wouldn't learn until later that he'd left Knoxville in the nick of time, or he might have found himself in the midst of a fight whether he liked it or not. While he was settling in to his unwanted duties at Cumberland Gap, things were growing lively in and about Knoxville.

Union General Ambrose Burnside, his eye on East Tennessee, had sent out a young Kentucky–born soldier, Colonel William P. Sanders, and an army of cavalry, to disrupt rebel communications and transportation in portions of East Tennessee. Sanders, riding with his command out of Mount Vernon, Kentucky, had done just that, taking the rebel garrison at Wartburg, Tennessee, burning the depot at Lenoir's Station near Knoxville, capturing an artillery garrison and ripping down telegraph lines.

On June 19 he reached Knoxville itself, where the Confederates awaited him, having been alerted of his activities by rebel pickets who had met him at Kingston. Sanders was in no position to have seen the wild scramble that occurred within the city as news of his approach spread. Regular Confederate forces there had been caught in a moment of disarray, and as they scurried to ready themselves for battle, the authorities put out a call for citizens to step forward and help in the defense. Quite a few did, including some prominent people, such as Confederate Senator Landon Haynes, and even a couple of local ministers.

Batteries on Summit, McGhee's, and College hills were manned; barricades made from cotton bales were thrown up in the streets. Lieutenant Colonel Milton Haynes, in charge of the artillery defense, then undertook a clever bit of stealth and headed out of town toward the Federal lines, dressed as a farmer, using an assumed name and claiming to be a good Unionist who was surely glad to see the boys in blue at last paying a call. The Federals took him at his word when he told them that the city was ripe for plucking and wouldn't put up much resistance. Then the colonel, nodding his acceptance of the thanks given him for this bit of intelligence, returned to Knoxville, put on his military garb again, and prepared to give the invading force far more resistance than they had anticipated.

Colonel Sanders and his Union raiders came into the city after dark and set up their artillery in the Fifth Avenue area, where one Ben Scarlett had laid drunk in alleyways many a time. The battle that followed was about an hour long, dominated by artillery, and relatively bloodless as battles go.

It was not bloodless, of course, for the few who did die. A single artillery shell fired by Sanders's Union batteries killed two men almost simultaneously, ending the life of one soldier who had flattened himself onto the ground, then bounding and exploding again with fatal effect upon a rebel lieutenant who watched the fight from the fence of the local asylum. The same explosion also wounded a citizen who had answered the call for volunteers. Another officer, a captain, died while assuring his cringing men that there was nothing to fear from the flashing guns turned their way.

The Federals put on a good show of fire and struck a lot of fear into the citizens of Knoxville, yet when it was done, the defenders had held on. Colonel Sanders sent in a message to Colonel Haynes, who had skunked him so cleverly with his play-acting as the Unionist "farmer": "I send you my compliments, and say that but for the admirable manner with which you managed your artillery, I would have taken Knoxville today." Then Sanders withdrew, headed to nearby Strawberry Plains to destroy some bridges, disrupt some more telegraph systems, and generally wreak what havoc he could on his way back to Kentucky. He was home again by late June, with only two of his number killed and only a handful more missing or wounded.

The Federal raid upon Knoxville generated quite a bit of flash and fire, and the disruption that had been its aim, but all in all the city had escaped much damage and seen a relatively small-scale fight. The citizens breathed in relief and hoped this artillery duel would be all the warfare their streets would know, while knowing that such a hope wasn't likely to come true.

The day Greeley and Sam left the bushwhacker encampment, Jack Butterfield rode out with them a mile or two. The horse Greeley rode was a gift from Butterfield, given without the knowledge of Colonel Swaney. This secrecy had an entirely reasonable foundation of which Greeley was unaware: It was Swancy's favorite horse. Butterfield had relieved him of it by hiding it; Swaney, eager to leave the camp when he learned he was no longer in command, hadn't looked for it long. He'd left on foot after a brief, dispirited search, no doubt knowing that his horse hadn't vanished by accident.

The three rode on together, talking quietly, until Butterfield declared it time for them to part. "What are your plans, Greeley?"

"Well, first thing is I've got to go back to tell the daughter of old Joel that her father's dead. Then I believe I'll go back to Carter County. Back home. I want to recruit some more stampeders and run them north to the lines. Me and Sam have already talked about it. He's going to help me, just like when we started out." He pursed his lips, thinking of the robbery, the hard duty of delivering those plundered letters. "There was a thing that happened that hurt my reputation. It was a wound just as unjustified as the one Swaney gave me. I need to see if that wound is going to heal, or if I'm going to have to find a new way to serve the cause."

Butterfield obviously didn't fully understand what Greeley was talking about, but he wasn't a man to press. "Good luck, whatever you do, my friend. And if ever you want to ride with me and my men, you're welcome."

"I don't believe I'll do that, sir. What you're doing . . . I reckon it must be done, but it ain't my kind of war."

"It ain't nobody's kind of war, except maybe Beelzebub himself," Butterfield said. Being a southpaw, he stuck out his left hand for a shake, then realized that Greeley's injured arm prevented him from returning the gesture. Butterfield thrust out his right hand instead, and he and Greeley shook.

Butterfield turned to Sam and shook his hand, too. "Sam, I don't fault you for leaving us. I'd leave too, if I had any better options just now. I been looking for you to leave us for some time now, to tell you the truth."

"You could tell, huh?"

"That it was eating on you? Yep. I could tell."

"Despite it all, I'm glad to have ridden with you, sir."

"The feeling's the same," Butterfield said. "Good-bye, Sam. And you too, Greeley Brown."

"Good-bye."

Sam and Greeley rode off, Butterfield watching them for a time, then turning back the way he'd come, heading back to his camp and the bloody war of a bushwhacker.

Chapter 22

Greeley Brown drew in a mouthful of cigar smoke and pondered again how fine it was to know a man such as Phillip Thornwell. He blew out the smoke and glanced out the window to the yard, where Sam Colter paced back and forth. Too bad he hadn't wanted to come in. It had probably been a long time since he'd had so fine a cigar as this one. Maybe Thornwell would let him take one with him for Sam to smoke on the trail.

"So, Phillip, how's Nanny and the baby getting on?" Greeley asked, blowing smoke toward the ceiling.

Thornwell was a different man than the last time—burdened, distracted. "Hmmm? Oh . . . fine, I suppose. The baby is getting on fine. I have a slave woman here, Rose, who has a way with sick children, and she's nursing him into health—though I must tell you the slaves don't know what to make of a baby that's a half-blooded white. We haven't had any mulattoes about the place until now. As for Nanny, from all I hear, she's having a bit of trouble fitting in with the others. I'm told she has a haughty way and some odd attitudes. Some of the slaves apparently think she must be 'witched' in some manner." He smiled and drew in a small puff of tobacco smoke, blowing it out through ovaled lips into a ring that floated upward a few inches and disintegrated.

"She does have a troubling way about her. I can testify to that." Greeley sighed. "I dread telling her about her father. Not that she's showed much sign of caring about him or anybody else, as I can see."

"Well! Now that you mention it, that is another thing," Thornwell said. "The slaves tell me she seems very cold and unconcerned even about her own child. She seems content to let Rose tend the baby; about all Nanny does is suckle it. And even though she expected her father to be here before now, she hasn't seemed worried that he hasn't shown up. She's very centered upon herself, and I won't be surprised at all if you find she doesn't react much when she hears her father is dead." Thornwell paused and smiled stiffly. "I confess, Greeley: I'm not dismayed to hear he's dead, either. To tell you the truth—"

"I know you didn't want him," Greeley said. "I wouldn't have asked you to take him if there had been any alternative."

"By the way, the word is out about runaways from Josiah House. Have you heard?"

"No."

Thornwell picked up a folded piece of paper. "This was brought to me yesterday. It's a broadside that's being hung all over the western end of the state. It says there is a reward for the 'return of an old colored man named Joel, a slave wench named Nanny, and a light-skinned Negro infant, also named Joel.'" He put down the paper. "I'm surprised they've advertised even these facts, considering the scandal they've been trying to hide, but note that they call the baby Negro rather than mulatto. I suppose they wouldn't want speculation to start about who fathered the child . . . and I'll bet you Mrs. Josiah is already worried that these runaways are out somewhere spreading scandalous tales about what has gone on inside her house!" Greeley expected one of Thornwell's big, rich-man laughs at this point, but he merely smiled.

"Phillip, you don't seem yourself."

"Yes. There's bad news, you see, for my side from

Vicksburg. . . . It's been surrendered to Grant—old Useless Ass Grant, I like to call him. Get the joke there? Ulysses S., Useless Ass . . . yes, right. Not all that funny, I suppose. In any case, there's something like thirty thousand Confederate prisoners. And there's fighting at some Pennsylvania town called Gettysburg, though I know not a thing of whether it's still going on or what the result is. I can only hope the dear old gray-clad army has fared well there."

"You need to join the winning side, Phillip. Whether or not the South wins or loses this or that battle, it can't hope to prevail in the end. That's my opinion, leastways, for what it's worth," Greeley said. He stood, pursing his lips for a moment. "Well, I may as well see Nanny now and get it done."

"You may as well. Here—have another cigar. Put it in your pocket for the road. Who knows when we'll see each other again?"

"Who knows?" Greeley replied. "Thank you." He put the cigar in a pocket and headed for the rear door and the walkway beyond it, leading back to the slave houses.

Greeley had hoped she might shed tears, show some sign of normal human emotion, but she took the news of her father's death with hardly a flicker on her cold features. She reacted more to hearing how he'd received his arm injury— a story Greeley was compelled to tell first—than to the news of Joel's passing.

She looked away. "So he's gone. That's bad. But it's one less thing to worry about."

God in heaven! Can anyone truly be that coldhearted? He couldn't restrain his tongue. "To 'worry about'? You show little sign of worrying about anything. I'm told you hardly care for your own baby here."

She did not flinch, but turned to him and said, "Take me with you."

"What?"

"Take me with you, away from here."

"I'm not taking you anywhere. I'm not hauling an escaped slave and her baby across creation."

"Leave the baby. They take good care of it here. Take me alone."

"Leave the baby? Great God in heaven! Don't you care about anything or anybody but your own sorry self?"

"I care about being free. I'll do anything to be free." She stepped closer to him. *"Anything."*

He ignored the obvious implication. "I want to ask you something, Nanny. Spencer Josiah—did you love that man?"

"I loved what he could give me."

"Freedom? Is that what you mean? You saw him as a means of gaining your freedom?"

Her silent gaze told him that the answer should be obvious.

"You stood up beside him, said vows, bore his child . . . all because you thought you could get your freedom through him?"

"Yes."

"And now your father's dead—'one less thing to worry about'—and you're ready to abandon your own child . . ."

She stepped toward him. "Take me with you!"

"No. You're staying right here, with your baby. I'm done with you, Nanny."

"Take me! Don't leave me here!"

He headed for his horse. Sam awaited him, already mounted. Glancing toward the big mansion, Greeley saw Thornwell watching from a window. He waved; Thornwell waved back.

Suddenly she became plaintive. "Mr. Brown, please, sir, take me with you!"

He reached his horse and swung into the saddle.

"I hate you!" she screamed. "I hate you! I hope you burn in hell! You hear me? I hope you burn in hell forever!"

He rode off, joining Sam, and would not look her way again.

It required many miles and several hours of riding before Greeley fully got over the unsettling feeling Nanny Josiah had left him with. In all his days, he hadn't encountered anyone so hardened, so focused on one ambition. He saw no fault in her desire for freedom, but this woman put that desire above familial love, above morality, above maternity. He hoped he would never see her again, and vowed to do his best to forget he'd held any involvement with her at all. She was to him like a bad taste that would be too slow in fading.

They were weary, Greeley in particular, worn down by the stress Nanny had produced and the weakness that came of his arm wound, which now hurt almost continually, though his arm below the wound remained substantially numb. He wriggled the fingers of his left hand again and again, trying to work feeling into them, and sometimes just to remind himself that they were still there and functioning, even if he couldn't much feel them.

Sam, bless him, didn't inquire about how things had gone with Nanny. He'd witnessed and heard enough to know the situation had been tense, and could tell that Greeley had no wish to talk about it just now.

They guided their horses into a little valley and looked around. It seemed as good a place to camp as any they would find. Hobbling the horses to graze, they found a spot to pitch their small tent—another gift from Butterfield—and settled down for rest. Greeley fell asleep, but Sam remained awake and thoughtful. Around sunset they would rise and eat a bit of supper, or such was the plan.

Instead they slept the night through and awakened to the first pale light of morning. Both were brighter and stronger men for benefit of the long hours of sleep. They ate a big breakfast, food brought out of the bushwhacker camp, and talked about what was to come.

"Where will we go?" Sam asked.

"Well, I'm thinking we might go hole up for a time with Mathen Ricker. He'd be pleased for our company, and we can build us another hidden place out in the mountains, one it will take the rebs longer to find than my last one. And I'll put out word that me and you are ready to pilot more stampeders. It shouldn't take me long to see if I've got any reputation left among the Union folk."

"Pshaw! They'll be glad to see you back in business. You'll have stampeders knocking your door down."

"I hope."

The hobbled horses hadn't wandered far. They saddled up and rode out, wanting to cover as many miles as possible that day and reach Mathen Ricker as quickly as possible.

At midday Greeley suggested a change of plan. A fellow he'd known for years and hunted with as a boy lived on a ridge not a mile away. Greeley decided that, Caesar Augustus, they should just drop in and see old John Rumple! It had been too long, and for all he knew, old John might be dead and gone already. If not, the old man likely would be before he was through here again, for he'd be getting well on in his years.

Sam was agreeable and the horses tired, so they veered right and headed up the ridge, taking advantage of the climb to enjoy a steadily improving view of the vast mountains. Mountains were an odd thing; they could seem the biggest, most vast bits of creation, going on endlessly and openly, yet at the same time cramp a man, restrict his vision, make the world hard to see. Many a mountain man and woman in these ridges and valleys lived and died hardly knowing there was even a world out there beyond the next range, or over that occasionally glimpsed distant horizon.

Pausing at the top of the ridge to look over the ranges stretching as far as they could see, they looked for signs of life. They could see nothing except one distant cabin outlined against a field far below them. It wouldn't have been hard to imagine themselves the only humans in these mountains, but such was far from true. It was as Butterfield had said: In these hiding hills lived not only the civilian people of the mountains, but also a legion of phantoms—conscription dodgers, deserters, bushwhackers, Home Guards, renegades, outliers. Greeley had always thought nothing could change the mountains. He'd been wrong. War had changed them. Life here was different, and might never be the same again.

They rode on until he came to the cabin he'd sought. Sure enough, old John Rumple was still living, and greeted Greeley warmly once Greeley was able to make him understand who he was. John was blind now, he saw, but obviously didn't want to admit it, so Greeley never let on that he'd detected it. Maudie, Rumple's wife, was also still living, and the cabin swam with the same scents Greeley remembered from years back—earth, musk, pelts, strings of dried onions, herbs, twist tobacco, and the smoke of a million fires on the flat stone hearth that old John had laid himself when he was just a gangly boy getting ready to marry Maudie, then just a fresh-faced girl. They had little, yet they had much—far more than he himself, Greeley thought, for they had one another to love, and he had no one. To their good fortune, bushwhackers and others had left them relatively alone, perhaps in deference to their ages, not to mention that they had nothing material worth stealing even in the best of times.

John Rumple's knowledge of the goings-on of the mountains had always astounded Greeley, for he never figured out how John managed to pick up all the information he did. That aspect of the man had changed no more than his cabin had. He was full of gossip, some of it striking mighty close to home for Greeley Brown.

"I hear there's quite a stir a-going on over at the Josiah House about Warm Springs," John said in the midst of his long recital of mountain news.

"Why's that?" Greeley asked, suspecting he already knew.

"Some kind of a scandal, something really bad. The Josiah boy, kind of a sissy fellow, they say, he's turned up dead miles and miles away from here. And there's been some niggers to run off from there—and oh, the stories they're a-telling about it all!"

"What kind of stories?"

"They say the Josiah boy, he fathered a baby with a darky wench, one of the runaways. They say that he was an *ab'litionist*"—he put the emphasis of incredulity on that word—"and was heading off to fight for the Union just so as to free the slaves. It's an amazing thing what this world's come to, boy."

"Time's are a-changing, that's for certain."

John Rumple leaned over and spat. Coffee-dark tobacco spittle struck the ground, rebounded up into a brown flower-shaped splatter, and settled down to make mud of the dust. "I never much liked the old colonel, Josiah. He was a snootish, towny kind of man, like the merchants over at Marshall, or the rich northern types you'd find over at the hotel at Warm Springs. Fine-smelling, uppity kind of folks . . . ain't done no good for these mountains, them coming in here."

"You don't care for that kind, huh?"

"No sir, no sir, I don't. I tell you, it's a-getting to be bad, folks not happy with their stations in life and always a-trying to change them. I'll tell you, Greeley boy, if the mountain folk would keep to theirselves, and the northerners stay up where God put them, and the redskins and darkies would keep in their rightful places, then this land would be what it ort to be, by Jacob! You wouldn't have these wars and killings and such, and everybody wanting to *change* everything! It ain't right, I tell you. It ain't. Leave things alone. Let them be. Let folks learn what their place is and stay in it!"

"Times are a-changing," Greeley repeated. He had to grin at John Rumple's words. He was a man who exemplified the viewpoint of many an old mountaineer, a breed who Greeley knew could not last forever. They were an opinionated lot, full of their own prejudices and individual visions of the great chain of being that supposedly should shape and guide the world. Sometimes they seemed to have more feeling than sense. Even so, when such as old man Rumple were gone, Greeley for one would miss them.

They spent that night with the Rumples, sleeping on pallets near the fireplace, an old hound competing with them for the space. Sometime during the night the hound lifted its head, rose and went to the door. Outside, other dogs bayed and howled; the old hound made guttural noises in its throat, responding. Greeley got up and peered out the front window, and in the darkness saw a lone figure stride across. Fearing bushwhackers, he sat up the rest of the night in John Rumple's rocker, rifle across his lap, as Sam slept. The morning came without any further barking or sign of any other passersby, and Greeley didn't even mention the evening's little disturbance to his hosts, though later he told Sam what he'd seen.

• • •

Greeley and Sam discovered later that day who had passed the house. They had ridden out after breakfast and stopped to eat a bite and drink at a spring when, while crouching to pull water to his mouth, Sam sensed another presence. Looking around and then up, he was shocked to see a body hanging from an oak limb on the other side of the spring. He fell back in surprise, just as Greeley also saw the corpse and did the same. The rope around the neck was short and tied with a regular sliding knot, not the proper neck-breaking hangman's noose, so this man had died hard, choking out his life slowly.

Bushwhackers had done it, most likely. Or so they thought until they stepped across the spring and went around to see the man's face.

Colonel Swaney must have taken his ouster hard. It appeared he had not decided what to do for some time thereafter, for he'd walked an awfully long way before finally hanging himself. Greeley wondered if Swaney had come to this spot for a reason, or if it was picked randomly.

A brief examination of the area showed it hadn't been a random selection. Sam pointed out the crumbling remains of an old cabin lost in the undergrowth, and beside it a few graves marked with stones. No names were on the graves, but into the flat stone that had served as a front step for the cabin was chiseled the name SWANEY.

"This was his old home place, Sam. Where he grew up," Greeley said.

"I believe so."

"He came home to die. Walked all this way to this very spot, just to hang himself."

Sam sighed: "Well, I suppose the best we can do for him is dig him a grave here among his kin."

"We got nothing to dig with. And I wouldn't be much help with digging, anyway, considering the cut on my arm . . . the one the good colonel himself gave me."

"Well, then let's lay him out on the ground, among the tombstones. He can at least go back to the dirt among his own people."

It seemed as good a notion as any other. When Greeley Brown and Sam Colter mounted again and rode out toward

Tennessee, Colonel Merriman Swaney, bushwhacker, lay stretched out between the unengraved, rough stones in his old and forgotten family plot. Lying exposed as he was, it would be only a matter of days before little remained of him and he would be part of the same soil that covered the bones of his mother and father, sisters and brothers.

Part IV

BEN SCARLETT

Chapter 23

A few miles east of
Nashville, Tennessee

He was sleeping soundly when he heard the thump, but he didn't fully waken. Ben Scarlett tended to sleep soundly when drunk, and drunk he had been when he crawled into this most unusual bed the night before. The liquor had come from a man who gave him a ride on a wagon, one of the few rides he'd received on his long pilgrimage west from Knoxville. Most of his travel was on foot, and a greater trial he had never known. The worst of it was finding food in a countryside already scoured by armies for whatever sustenance it offered. He begged meals in more houses than he could count, telling one pitiful story after another, and more often than not getting at least something to put in his belly. Occasionally he would get a bit of liquor or wine too, and those days were the best.

A jolt awakened him with a start; he threw up his hands like a frightened baby, and scuffed his knuckles on a level plane of wood directly above him. He was in darkness, enclosed, and there came panic that almost brought a scream from him until he remembered where he was, recalled that half-heard thump that had come in the night, and realized what had happened.

He'd finished his liquor late the prior evening as a storm built, and, after tossing away his bottle, went looking for shelter and a place to sleep. He found both in the unlocked barn, half of which was taken up by a carpenter's shop. A wagon parked in the barn held a hinge-topped coffin, empty, and he'd pushed the top open, crawled into it, and fallen asleep. But obviously the coffin lid had fallen closed in the night, accounting for the thump he heard in his sleep.

The jolting he felt now, though, was more a mystery, but even that came clear when he realized he was in motion. Obviously, the coffin maker had left his house come morning, hitched a horse to the wagon, and was driving off with it, not realizing he had a trespassing, unseen passenger going along.

Now what do you do, Ben Scarlett? You've got yourself into a mess this time! His head ached from the liquor he'd consumed, and he worried about what might happen when he was discovered. Yet despite all this, the humor of it struck him and he stifled a chuckle. He could picture what the driver's reaction would be if he shoved the coffin lid open and came out with an otherworldy yell—and he considered this for a few seconds, but didn't follow through. He'd probably scare the driver so badly the unsuspecting fellow's heart would stop.

So Ben lay there like an entombed vampire and simply rode along, having no idea how he would escape without being caught. Could they throw a man in jail for hitching a ride in a pine casket?

The ride went on for almost an hour, as best he could estimate, until he heard the driver's voice come muffled through the coffin top: "Whoa, gals. Whoa." And the wagon stopped.

Here it comes. I'm caught now for certain. He slapped a smile on his face, ready to greet whoever discovered him in as innocuous and good-humored a manner as possible.

He heard the driver climb down from his perch—only one man, judging from the sound. He steeled himself, waiting for the lid to open or the coffin to move. . . .

Half a minute passed and nothing occurred. *I'll be!*

Maybe he's gone off somewhere! Ben decided to open the lid himself.

He pushed up on it; light came in, the new hinges, well-oiled, moving without noise. He sat up, looking wildly about for the driver, and saw no one. The wagon was in the drive of a very typical clapboard house, and a man—the driver, he guessed—was just then being admitted through the front door by a woman with a red face and a hand-kerchief draped over her hand, dabbing at her eyes.

Ben lighted out of the coffin without anyone seeing him, reached back in to snatch his hat, which he'd used for a pillow, and gently closed the lid. His limbs were stiff, and his clothing—the same clothing Daniel Baumgardner had given him, and more clean than might have been expected since he'd washed it all out at a creek two days before—was rumpled. He glanced at the house, and through a front window saw several people moving about. Nobody was looking back toward him. He trotted toward the road, feeling he'd gotten out of this one pretty well, considering.

He stopped, turned, and looked at the house again, the wheels of his mind taking cunning turns. Everything had just come clear: The coffin he'd slept in had been made for someone, obviously, and apparently that someone was inside this house. The crowd was probably family and friends of the deceased, gathered to comfort one another. And where there was a crowd of family and friends, there was generally food and drink.

Did he dare? He paused, weighing the possibility. Yes, he dared. What was there to lose? At worst, they would run him off, and he'd been run off so much in his life that it wasn't even humiliating anymore.

Ben brushed down his clothes, smoothing as many wrinkles as he could, then punched his hat back into shape and finger-combed his hair and beard. He meandered up the drive as if he'd just come walking off the nearby road, and hoped the liquor he had drunk the day before wasn't still leaving a smell.

The wagon driver came back out the door when Ben was about to mount the front step. "How do, sir," the driver said with a nod.

"Howdy, there. Is this the house of grief?"

"What?"

"The house of grief. The place bereavement has come."
Ben wished he had a name to attach to the deceased.

"You a preacher?"

Preacher! That'll do the job, yes indeed! "I am. I've
come to call on the bereaved."

"They're inside. I just come to bring the burying box."

"I see. Do you need help lifting it?"

"Well, as a matter of fact . . . oh, pardon me. I see you've
got but one hand."

"No matter. I've learned to make do. I can help you."

Ben and the wagon driver hauled the coffin in through
the door less than a minute later. Ben got a few curious
stares, having appeared from nowhere, but he smiled back
pleasantly and took off his hat as soon as the coffin was laid
out between a couple of chairs.

A fat man with bulging, wet eyes and a nose red from
many a blowing came up and stuck out a hammy hand at
Ben. "I'm Jake Trousdale, the husband."

Ben shook the hand. "I'm very sorry for your loss, Mr.
Trousdale. I'm the Reverend Ben Scarlett, come to see if
there's anything I can do for you."

"You're a preacher?" The man eyed Ben up and down,
confused. Despite Ben's hurried efforts to unrumple his
clothes, he still looked very much like the unwashed and
unshorn wayfarer he was. Seeing the fellow's nostrils
twitch, he figured that he probably still put out his usual
smell, too.

"I am. I hope you'll pardon my appearance. I'm in the
midst of a long journey, heading for Nashville, and I've had
a few difficulties along the way. I was . . . robbed."

"No! Were you hurt?"

"No, no, but I did lose my baggage, my money, and a
good pocket pistol. Even my Bible."

"Curse these times, Preacher. Curse these times. Folks
will rob anybody these days."

"They know not what they do."

A girl almost the size of her father, and with much the

same face, came up crying. "Preacher, I'm glad you've come, but we expected Preacher Roach."

"Preacher Roach . . . yes. He's been detained. He'll be on later. He sent me ahead to tell you. Preacher Roach and I are old friends, and I stopped in to call on him while I was passing through."

"Well, I'm sure he was glad to see you," Jake Trousdale said. "Preacher, I wish we could offer you a happier welcome, but we're deep in our grief today. I can't believe yet that she's gone."

The coffin maker, whom Ben supposed might also be the local undertaker, stuck his head out of a side bedroom he'd entered a few moments before. "I'll need some help moving her into the box."

Several lanky, somber-faced boys in their mid-teen years rose and headed for the bedroom. There were sounds of grunting and movement, the bed scooting on the floor, and moments later the coffin maker and his helpers came staggering out of the bedroom bearing the gray-faced body of the biggest woman Ben had ever seen. She was heavier even than her sizable husband. Her fleshy arms dangled toward the floor, the thick fingers already going stiff. The sight of the body brought wails and howls among the women in the room, and Jake Trousdale had to turn his head away from the sight, squeezing his fleshy face into a pinched mask of emotion.

"My goodness, she was a right big old bear of a woman, wasn't she!" Ben said.

"What'd you say?" Trousdale asked.

"Oh . . . that it's right that we bear much grief for this woman. Death is sorrowful."

"Yes."

They settled the massive corpse into the coffin, and the men stood around looking sad, though Ben figured their expressions reflected almost equally their dread of having to heft that overladen box outside and onto the wagon. The coffin looked flimsy with her crowded into it. He was ready to bet she would burst the bottom right out of it when they lifted her up.

The big Trousdale girl, who looked as much like her

mother in form as she did her father in face, came over near Ben, looking down on her mother's still face, and began to talk the rapid-fire talk of the grief-stricken. "Oh, Preacher, it was so sad a thing! She seemed so healthy and strong! And she was all excited and happy, getting ready to go into Nashville tomorrow and visit her sister. Had her pass all signed and ready so the bluebellies would let her in . . . and now she's dead! Oh, Preacher, it ain't fair! It just ain't!"

"We all got to die sometime, miss. It was just your mama's time, I reckon. You say she was going into Nashville?"

"Yes."

"And had her a pass . . ."

"Yes. It's still lying by her bedside. Oh, it breaks my heart! She was wanting so bad to see her sister. She'd just talked and talked about that trip!"

"Yonder comes the Preacher Roach on his buggy," one of the boys said.

"Come out with us and greet him, Reverend Scarlett," Trousdale said.

"You go on ahead. I want to pause for a prayer by the bed of the deceased."

"She's gone now. Bed's empty."

"It's a habit I have." Without awaiting permission, Ben stepped into the bedroom and closed the door.

The bed was the most broken-down, hollowed one Ben had seen, which was no surprise given the weight of Trousdale and his late wife. Ben went straight to the table beside it and dug through the papers there. In a moment he had the one he sought—a duly signed, perfectly legal pass for one Bertha Mae Trousdale to enter the occupied city of Nashville. Ben stuffed it into his pocket, then threw open the wardrobe. It was full of dresses the size of tents. He yanked one down, and a shawl and bonnet, and headed for the window.

Ben heard Trousdale's voice as he greeted the newly arrived, authentic clergyman. "Come on in, Preacher Roach. We ain't even carried her out yet."

Ben pulled open the window, which overlooked the side yard but was also nearly covered by a rose-laden trellis. He hefted out the wadded up clothing he'd taken, then put out a leg.

"Your friend the Preacher Scarlett is in the bedroom praying," he heard Trousdale saying. "We appreciate you sending him our way. He seems a good man."

"Who?" a stranger's voice said. "I didn't send anybody named Scarlett—"

Ben didn't hear the rest, for he was by then out the window, breaking down the trellis and taking some deep scratches in the process. Grabbing his purloined female garb, he ran across the yard and behind a shed, crossed a fence and loped across a field toward the woods. He had gone in hoping for food, and hadn't gotten any, but he didn't mind. What he had would be of much greater value at the moment than food.

The next day, the blue-uniformed occupants of one of the guard stations on a road leading into Nashville watched the approach of one of the oddest-looking women any of them had ever seen. She wore a dress much too large for her that hung all the way to the ground. As she stepped along, what appeared to be a man's brogan shoes made brief alternating appearances from under the long dress, like rats taking turns peeking from beneath a curtain. She carried a bundle, and wore a bonnet that almost entirely hid her face.

The bundle was a man's coat wrapped around a wadded pair of trousers and a shirt. "Who's this for?" a guard asked.

"Pardon my voice . . . I've lost it to a cold," the woman, whose face was hidden in the shadow of her oversized bonnet, replied in a soft, airy, hoarse and voiceless whisper. She pointed at the clothing. "For my sick brother."

"You got a pass?"

She handed over a paper. The guard scanned it, handed it back. "Go on, Mrs. Trousdale. Everything appears to be in order. Take care of that cold, ma'am—you sound bad."

She was already past, moving along with a masculine kind of stride, before they noticed yet another oddity about her: Her left hand was missing.

The sentinel watched the strange woman stride away and

shook his head. He had no idea who was the mister half of the Trousdale couple, but whomever he was, the sentinel surely felt sorry for him.

Ben changed his clothing in the first shed he came to, and also found an empty grain bag into which he stuffed the massive dress, bonnet, and shawl of the late Bertha Mae Trousdale. It had worked even better than he'd hoped. His biggest fear was that the rash on his face, left by shaving off his beard with a knife, would generate suspicion, but the bonnet apparently had shaded him enough to make the rash go unnoticed.

"I appreciate your help, and God rest your soul, Mrs. Trousdale," said the drunk turned preacher turned woman turned drunk again. "I'd wondered just how I was going to get into town."

He threw the grain sack over his shoulder and stepped out of the shed. The city of Nashville! He had never been here before. He was a long way from Knoxville; the land looked different here, a little flatter, more open, and the city had a feel and scent about it dissimilar to Knoxville. Though Ben could see only one part of Nashville from where he was, what he did see looked fairly impressive.

It would take some doing to learn this town—its streets, its buildings, its places where a man without means could ferret out a meal or a drink, or hide himself. But having made the long journey with success, Ben felt he was up to the challenge.

He stepped out and onto the road, heading into Nashville and thinking of the woman he hoped to find here. Maybe it would go easier than he anticipated. Maybe everything would fall into place, as it had with the coffin and the corpse and the dress and the pass.

He was filled with an uncharacteristic optimism, pleased with himself for being such a clever fellow as to walk right past Union guards, and thrilled to think that somewhere out there, in this capital city on the Cumberland River, he might find *her*, after all these years and all these miles.

Chapter 24

July, Nashville

Sometimes when she woke up it took a few moments to remember and make sense of where she was, who she was, and what life for her had become. It had all changed so suddenly and dramatically that she hadn't fully absorbed and accommodated present realities, and occasionally she would wake up and think she was still quiet, studious Amy Deacon of Knoxville, Tennessee, daughter and assistant of the great Secessionist publisher Dr. George Deacon.

This was one of those days, but within three seconds reality had taken its proper shape, truth settling in. Her father was now dead, having suffered both a public discrediting and a mental breakdown before ending his own existence. The house in which she had lived throughout her girlhood, the house wryly labeled Secession Hill because of her father's radical secession advocacy, had burned to the ground long ago. No more did she reside in East Tennessee's Knoxville, but here in the capital city of Nashville in the heart of the state. And she was no longer merely Amy Deacon, but Amy Deacon Hanover, a woman married just a month earlier, after what had surely been the most speedy of courtships. Amy had surprised herself. Was it not she who had told prior suitors that marriage was not an option for her while the war still raged? That there were more important, immediate causes that demanded her allegiance and could not abide at the moment the competition of a husband and domestic life? Empty words those had quickly become when she met Adam Hanover. When he entered her life, and she his, the world had quietly but suddenly begun to turn on a new axis for her. Everything reordered itself all at once in the most wonderful ways. She smiled drowsily, eyes still closed, reached across the bed to where her husband slept . . .

. . . and found his place empty. Opening her eyes, she frowned, yawned, and sat up. He'd done it again: awakening and rising without getting her up, too. She had hinted to him that this annoyed her. Apparently she would have to do more than hint.

She rose, brushed her hair, and washed her face. Putting a robe around her, she descended the stairs toward the old parlor room he had made into a sort of secondary, home-based office. Pausing at the front window, she pulled back the curtain and looked out onto Vine Street, then turned her head to look left toward the imposing, high-towered capitol building, completed only a few years before at the astonishing cost of nearly $900,000. Designed as a center of state government, it now had a militaristic look because of the Federal cannon emplaced on its porticos, pointing out across a city whose population was strongly Confederate in sympathy. The cannon, which at the moment were being undraped by soldiers of the tarpaulins that had protected them through the night from a light, misty rain, served along with the American flag atop the tower as stern reminders that Nashville, though in the heart of a Confederate state, had been firmly under the control of the Union since February of 1862. Amy liked living so close to the capitol; the sight of that flag and those cannon, though hated by pro-rebellion Nashvillians, were to her a comfort and inspirer of hope.

She let the curtain fall and turned to finish her descent, but paused with a sharp wince as pain rippled in her side. She touched the still-tender place from which the pain had radiated and wondered, *How long does it take for a bullet wound to stop hurting?* She hoped she wouldn't have to put up with pain from the wound the rest of her life, but reminded herself that the wounding had occurred only a few months back. With time, the pain would surely entirely vanish.

She descended to the bottom of the stairs and heard her husband's distinctive laugh come undulating out of his office. *What a wonderful laugh he has!* she thought. *It's such a marvelous thing to hear it!* She smiled as she entered the office and saw him seated in his favorite old Chippendale, scanning pages of handwritten notes. Amy recognized the big scrawl on the pages from where she stood—notes from Adam's underling, David Calvin.

Adam saw her and bounded from his chair, letting the papers scatter. "Good morning, wife! How are you today?" He aimed a kiss at her forehead; she tilted her face and caught it on the lips instead.

"I'm furious, that's what!" she said, putting her arms around him. "You know I don't like sleeping in while you're already up and at your day! Why didn't you waken me?"

"What's the harm? You need the rest. You're still healing, you know."

"Yes, and healing quite well, thank you. And I'd like the occasional pleasure of breakfasting with my husband."

"Very well. Mea culpa. I'll do better from now on." He pulled away and began picking up the scattered papers, moving in that ever quick, cheerful way of his that put a youthful veneer on his thirty-six years of age. Adam Hanover was the type who would seem indefinably boyish at fifty.

"What has David brought you this time? I heard you laughing." David Calvin's notes appeared almost daily in the special wooden receptacle box nailed up on one of their front porch columns. Calvin had a penchant for working late at night, and often dropped off memorandums related to his current writings for Adam to peruse come morning.

"What I was laughing at was this new special order that's come down. 'Special Order Number Twenty-nine'—that's the official title. David's doing some writing about it. It came down on the sixth of the month . . . here, let me find it; I'll read it to you." He shuffled papers quickly. "Yes. Here it is. 'July six, 1863. Special Order Number Twenty-nine, Lieutenant Spalding, Provost Marshal, is hereby directed without loss of time to seize and transport to Louisville all prostitutes found in this city or known to be here. The prevalence of venereal disease at this post has elicited the notice of the General Commanding Department who has ordered a preemptory remedy. By command of Brigadier General J. D. Morgan.' " He stopped reading and grinned at her.

"So you find that funny, do you? I personally think it's rather sad, all those pitiful women. Do they really have the right to force them out of the city like so many cattle?"

"Those 'pitiful women,' my dear, are spreading their unique kinds of diseases among the soldiers like the pox. If you've seen a soldier with both his mind and his limbs being eaten away by syphilis, you'd not take so liberal a view of our local prostitutes."

"In fact, Adam, I've seen several soldiers in just that condition. I do spend a good bit more time than you around the hospitals."

"Yes, of course you do. My 'Union Spy turned Healing Angel.' " He laughed as she screwed up her face upon hearing that flowery phrase of appellation, originating from the newspaper, which always both amused and slightly embarrassed Amy.

"So tell me more about this order. How do they intend to convey these women to Louisville—and what will Louisville have to say about it?"

He looked to his papers again. "Well, listen to this. 'July eighth, 1863. To the captain of the steamer *Ivanhoe*. You are hereby directed to proceed to Louisville, Kentucky, with the hundred passengers put on board your steamer today, allowing none to leave the boat before reaching Louisville. Signed, George Spalding, Lieutenant Colonel and Provost Marshal.' "

"So they simply forced these women onto some steamer captain?"

"So it appears. Military authority in action."

"You know, I find that rather troubling. Who can say with certainty that all those women are really what they accuse them of being? And what if they have families here? Are they forcing them off to some distant city without any regard to any of those questions?"

"Amy, believe me, it's known quite well among both the law-enforcing and military circles in this city who and who is not engaged in prostitution. And those kinds of women aren't the family sort, you know. And as for Louisville, I suppose the feeling here is that it's better their problem than ours." He grinned. "I'm sorry, but I do find something funny in all of this. A steamer filled with fallen women, chugging right up the river! Can you imagine it?"

"Well, let me ask you this, Adam: If these women are spreading disease among the soldiers, that can only mean they are diseased themselves. Is anything being done for them on this great floating bawdy house you find so amusing?"

Seeing that Amy was becoming steadily more serious about this matter, Adam let his smile diminish. "Well, that's a good question, one I'll try to get David to find an answer for. I will tell you this: Supposedly, several of the women placed on the *Ivanhoe* were so ill they were bedridden."

"Oh, that *is* a tragic thing," Amy said. "I think it's too bad how people forget the sad side of that kind of life, all the disease and abuse such women suffer. People either want to moralize against them and dismiss them as human vermin, or else they laugh at them, like they are some kind of joke wearing a skirt."

"Or, while engaged in their business, *not* wearing a skirt," he added, smiling coyly.

Amy shook her head. "You refuse to take me seriously, I can see!"

"No, Amy, no. Just couldn't resist the jest. In fact you've raised some good questions and I'll put David right on to them." He pulled out his pocket watch and glanced at it. "Time for me to be going. Will you be by the office anytime today?"

"I doubt it. I have work at the hospital."

"I worry about you spending so much time in those places. The wounded men, that's one thing. The diseased men, that's another. I'm afraid you'll make yourself sick."

"Someone has to do this work. The doctors and nurses alone aren't sufficient. They need volunteer help, much more than I can give."

"Why do you do it, Amy?"

"Because it must be done, and I'm blessed with a certain ability to bring a bit of practical help to the medical workers, and good cheer to the men. So I do it. I know I appreciated all the people who were encouraging to me when it wasn't certain I was going to live."

He kissed her. "Then be off, and do your good deeds—carefully, please. I'll be home by suppertime." He turned to go, reaching for his hat. "Oh, by the way, have you heard of the upcoming grand tour?"

She knew what he meant. "Yes. They're already getting ready for it. I believe it's to happen the fifteenth, isn't it?"

"Yes. And if you're there when Governor Andy comes in," he said, "tell him I'm still 'prone to rabble-rouse.' Isn't that how he put it?"

"I think so. But if I see him, I don't think I'll bring that particular matter up."

"No doubt that would be the best policy. Good day, Amy. I love you."

"I love you, too."

She stood in the doorway, watching him stride broadly and enthusiastically down Vine Street, heading toward Union Street, where a left turn would take him down a few hundred yards to the office and printing facilities of the *Sage*. As always, he paused just before going out of view to give her a big wave; she waved back.

Closing the door, Amy withdrew into the house to ready herself for the day. Thanks to her late rising, she was behind schedule, and eager to get to the hospital and the volunteered labors that were becoming so important to her. Before long Willie would come 'round with the buggy, as he always did on weekdays, and it would take effort to be ready by the time he arrived. She headed into the kitchen for a quick bite, her methodical mind mapping out the day before her.

Willie was a quiet man, very big and possessing the blackest skin of any man Amy had ever known. Because of his reticence, it was widely thought that he was simpleminded, but Amy knew the opposite was true. A slave freed by a master who had converted to abolitionism some years ago, partially under the influence of writings Amy had contributed anonymously to the Knoxville-based abolitionist journal *Reason's Torch*, Willie held Amy in the highest of esteem and gave her a ride each morning to whatever point of the city she needed to reach, usually one of the various military hospitals established since the Union takeover. The rest of his day he spent hauling freight around town, delivering messages, and providing a rough-and-ready, low-cost cab service with his flatbed wagon, which he'd rigged to accommodate a removable bench in the rear. Amy rode free. He wouldn't hear of taking payment from the young woman who had helped, however indirectly, to bring about his freedom.

Amy didn't ride behind Willie, as most did. She sat on the seat beside him, an act appropriate to her abolitionist philosophy, and which lent to her an aura of controversiality that was, in her case, equally appropriate.

They were moving along toward the University of Nashville, where Federal Army Hospital No. 2 had been established in a big Federal-styled building originally designed as housing for the university president and staff members. A short, round, little male pedestrian with thick side whiskers and tiny metal-rimmed glasses touched his hat and nodded pleasantly at Amy. She nodded and smiled back. Many times she had encountered this fellow in passing, always receiving from him a friendly nod and tip of the hat, but she didn't know his identity. This time she glanced back at him after they had passed, and was surprised to see he'd stopped in the street and was looking back at her with an expression quite different than the bland, smiling one he had presented to her face. His look now might best be described as hungry. When Amy's glance met his gaze, however, he quickly slapped on the smile again, then turned and walked in the opposite direction, more swiftly than before.

Slightly unsettled, Amy turned forward again and wished she hadn't looked back. "Willie, did you see that man we passed?"

"Yes, ma'am, I did."

"Do you know him?"

"Yes, ma'am. Know who he is." Willie paused. "He ain't nobody you need to be knowing, ma'am."

"But who is he?"

"His name's Mr. Belle. Mr. Henson Belle."

"I've never heard of him . . . wait. Yes, I have. He's a photographer, I think. Adam has mentioned him. He has a studio in the downtown area."

"That's him, ma'am."

"Why did you say I didn't need to know him? What did you mean?"

It appeared Willie didn't want to answer. Then, reluctantly, he said, "Well, ma'am, it's just that he ain't what you'd call a good man."

"How so? Is he dishonest?"

"No . . . he's—he ain't decent. That's all."

"How so?"

"Ma'am, I don't feel right, talking about some things with you. A man, he ought to watch what he talks about with women."

"I'm not a child, Willie. You've got my curiosity up, and you may as well tell me what you're talking about."

"It's the kind of pictures he takes, ma'am. Some of them ain't decent. He takes pictures of the kind of women they put on that steamship a few days ago. Ain't decent pictures at all."

"Oh." Amy saw now why Willie had been reticent, and felt no desire to further explore the matter.

She thought about that hungry look Belle had given her behind her back, and felt soiled. What kind of thoughts had been coursing through his cesspool mind? A tiny shudder ran through her and she vowed never to give a smile to that foul little man again.

Willie let her off at her usual place at the northwest corner of the university's tract, and she trudged across the tree-shaded yard to the big brick building that housed Hospital No. 2.

Chapter 25

He was troubled, and for more reason than the unending chatter his rail-thin wife was pouring into his ear in that nasal Illinois voice that thirty years in the Southland had done nothing to alter.

Henson Belle was a man suffering the end of a foolish but beloved fantasy, one he'd indulged in so long that it had the ambience of heartfelt reality. He had allowed himself to pretend that *she* admired him, that *she* secretly adored and longed for him.

But now it was clear that the woman he thought the most beautiful in Nashville, the increasingly well-known wife of the *Sage* publisher and darling of the Unionists of the city, the lovely and untouchable Amy Deacon Hanover, no longer cared for him.

It was all rather silly, of course; he knew in reality she had never cared for him at all. She hadn't even known him! To her, he had been, if anything, that stranger she occasionally passed on the street, to whom she always gave a kind and pretty smile. Upon the foundation of that smile his fantasy had been built, a structure made of dreams, lusts, and pretense that had gone almost to the point of belief. He'd imagined that Amy Hanover saw in him something his wife obviously didn't: an appealing, stirring, masculine something that led her to give that smile to him day after day, a smile that almost unveiled her own passion for him, her desire, her need. . . .

But she didn't smile at me today. Just like yesterday, and several days before that! It had him very troubled. The wagon, driven by that same big black fellow, had rumbled by as usual, Amy Hanover at her regular place—and not only had she not smiled at him, she hadn't even looked. Had made an obvious point of ignoring him coldly, despite his tipping of the hat. He couldn't imagine what had made the difference, but it roused a surprisingly deep despair. In the mundane world in which he lived, the smiles of Amy Hanover and the secret fantasies they fueled had meant a lot to him.

He sighed. Reality intruded in the form of his wife's voice, droning in the other room and making him wonder why, if she wished to talk to him, she didn't bother to come into the same room. Not that he wanted her to. Let her chatter off in the back. That way he didn't have to look like he was listening.

He was slumped back on a sofa, staring at the wall, the latest copy of the *Sage*—a newspaper he read not because he liked it, but because he despised it—spread across his ample belly. He glanced over at a mirror on the wall. He saw a fat, bald man looking back at him. He snarled at the fellow, whom he didn't like at all; the fellow snarled right back. He sighed again and looked away. His wife paused in her back-room monologue, and he filled the gap with, "Is that right, honey?" She said it was right, yes indeed it was, and started up again. He pulled the paper up over his face and closed his eyes, planning to nap until suppertime.

A rap at his front door brought him jolting up and broke off his wife's chatter at the same time. He stood, laying the paper aside, and adjusted his loosened tie. Who could be calling at the end of the day?

The old fantasy sparked to life again. He would open the door and *she* would be there, tearful, telling him she could resist him no more, must have him, no matter what, and she would throw herself into his arms, pressing up against his lean form, admiring the way the wind whipped his thick, black hair, and from the fire in her eye he would know that this night would be the finest of nights. . . .

He opened the door and stared into the bleary-eyed face of a one-handed man who looked half drunk.

"Well, howdy!" the drunk said.

"Who are you and what do you want?"

"I'm Ben Scarlett. I'm from Knoxville. I'm hoping that you're a picture-taking fellow I been trying to find here for a few days."

"What 'picture-taking fellow' in particular are you looking for?"

Belle's wife's voice came echoing up the front hallway. "Who is it, Henny?"

How he wished she wouldn't call him "Henny" when other people could hear it! "Nobody, dear. Just a . . ." He erased the planned word "drunk," and substituted, ". . . man."

"What does he want?"

"If you'll be quiet for a moment, dear, maybe I can find out!" He frowned at Ben, whose smell, at its worst summertime pungency, was beginning to waft in through the open door. "What *do* you want?"

"Are you Mr. Henson Belle, sir?"

"I am. What can I do for you?"

"Do you take pictures here in Nashville?"

"Yes. I have a portrait studio downtown. I specialize these days mostly in photographs of soldiers." Imagining how hard it would be to get the stench of this man out of his studio, he made a preemptive maneuver. "Look, if you're wanting a picture taken, I have such a full schedule for the next few weeks I certainly won't be able to fit you in. And besides that, I make appointments only at my studio during regular business hours, not at my front door. Good evening."

Ben said at a very indiscreet volume, "You still take pictures of naked Cyprians?"

Henson Belle's heart jumped toward his Adam's apple, his fingers went numb, his throat closed down, his eyes bugged, and his knees became soft and gelatin. In a harsh and wild whisper he said, "Merciful *God*, man! My *wife* is back there—have you no common sense, have you no common decency and discretion—"

"Is he still there, Henny?" The voice echoed up the hall.

"Just a moment, dear! This is business!" He stepped outside, closed the door behind him and looked about to make sure no neighbors were near. "Sir, I have to ask you to leave. I'll not have some drunk come to my own house and insult me with insinuations that—"

Ben stuck out the ink-blotted picture of the woman he called Angel.

Henson Belle grabbed the picture, covering it with his hand, and looked around again. "How *dare* you bring this around here! Are you trying to ruin me, sir?" He paused. "Not that I have anything to do with this . . . this *filth*. I've never taken such a lewd photograph in my life."

"How can you tell it's a lewd photograph? It's got ink on it so you can't see much of anything but her face."

"I can tell, I just know that . . . get away from here, sir." He thrust the picture back to Ben. "Get away before I call the authorities on to you!"

Ben turned the picture backward, peeled back the paper layer, and showed Belle the mark of his own studio. "Looks to me like this is your emblem, Mr. Belle."

Belle felt like collapsing. He had always been uncertain that a mere strip of covering paper over his studio mark was enough insurance against detection. Now, what meager confidence he'd possessed shivered into ruin. If such a fellow as this drunk had managed to discover what the paper covered, how many others had as well? Perhaps the secret, sideline business he conducted with the underclass of Nashville womanry wasn't as secret as he'd thought.

Belle stammered a time or two, glanced about once, twice, then again and again, compulsively, and after a swiping of his palm over his mouth, said, "All right. Very well, sir. You win. Tell me how much you want."

"What? I don't want nothing."

"You don't want . . . may I ask you why you've come to me in this most, most *distressing* way?"

"I'm looking for Angel."

"Who?"

"Angel. The woman in the picture. That's Angel. At least, I believe it is. It surely looks like her."

Belle hardly knew what to say. "Are you saying that you know that whore . . . that woman, and you're trying to find her?"

"Yes, sir."

Belle almost chuckled with relief. *Maybe this scoundrel wasn't after him or his money after all!* "Why do you want to find her, might I ask?"

"Because . . ." Ben lowered his head. "I'm half ashamed to say it, sir, but at one time I was engaged to be married to Angel. That's right. Me and her, we were going to be husband and wife. We were mighty young then, and everything was different. Then it all started to change, and that was the end of that."

"Ah, I see." So great now was Belle's relief that he was actually starting to feel almost cordial toward this fellow. "Well, sir, you needn't be embarrassed. We all make mistakes, many times involving whom we choose to be our mates. Believe me, sir, I know whereof I speak. You, at least, had the good fortune of ridding yourself of her before you tied the knot. It would have been hard to marry a woman only to find out she was capable of displaying herself in a lewd fashion."

Ben looked confused. "No, sir, you don't understand. It ain't that I'm embarrassed I was engaged to her, but embarrassed that she was engaged to *me*. It's me who's no 'count, sir. I'm nothing but a drunk. I've been a drunk for years and years—though I'm proud to say I put the stuff aside for a good long spell sometime back, and maybe will again, if ever I get the strength."

"Well, if you're so ashamed of yourself that you feel you're lower even than a common prostitute, why do you want to find her?"

"Because I'm worried about her. If she's in such a state that she's taken to doing such as this"—he waved the picture—"then she may be in trouble in some way. Angel, she's a good woman. She wouldn't do this without reason."

"Where did you see that picture? And put it away, would you? I don't want my wife coming out here and seeing it."

Ben put the picture in his pocket. "I got it at home. Knoxville. From a soldier who'd got it from a man from Nashville."

"You mean to tell me you came all the way from Knoxville just to find that woman, based on nothing more than having seen a picture that may or may not be her, and my studio mark?"

"Well . . . yes. I had to leave Knoxville anyway over some trouble I was having, but I'd have come even without that, just to find her. I was engaged to her once, sir. I cared about her. Still do, I guess."

"You must indeed. But I have to tell you, sir, that I have no idea who that woman is."

"Did you take the picture?"

Belle evaluated the man. Was there any reason to lie to such an obvious social worm as this? In Ben Scarlett, Belle saw one of the few human beings he could actually feel superior to. No one would believe anything a drunk said, anyway, so there seemed no reason to lie. "Yes, I took it. I don't recall just when. It was one of many along that line."

"Her name—was it Angel?"

"I never know their names. Most of them use false names anyway."

"Is she a . . ."

"Yes. She is a Cyprian. That's what they call them around here in the newspapers. Cyprians. For the Isle of Cyprus, birthplace of Aphrodite. You've heard of Aphrodite?"

"No. Is she another you've took pictures of?"

"No, no. The goddess of love. Mythology and all that." Belle saw that the man still didn't understand. It didn't matter.

"I want to see Angel. If it is her."

"Then see her. But you'll have to travel many a mile to do it."

"Why?"

"The Cyprians, they've been rounded up like so many cattle, put on a steamer, and sent up to Louisville, Kentucky. It's been in the newspapers. You haven't heard?"

"No. Was Angel one of them?"

"I would assume so, if she's still around Nashville and still active. They rounded up every Cyprian they could find. They tried something like this last year, sending them all up to Louisville by train, but they came back. This time they seem determined to really be rid of them." He looked at Ben, intrigued by him and despising him at the same time. "Take some advice, friend. Forget this woman. She isn't here. And even if she was, believe me, if she's been at the Cyprian trade for any time, the odds are good that she's sick."

"Sick? Then I *have* to find her. I'll need to get her help."

"What makes you think she'd want your help?" Belle paused, cocked his head and looked irritated as he heard his wife's voice sounding out, muffled and uninterpretable, from inside the house. "Listen, I've spent enough time talking this nonsense. I need to go before my woman in yonder asks too many questions. Don't you ever come around here flashing that picture again, hear? And don't you repeat that I took it or any other like it. I'll deny it if you do, and I'll be believed and you won't. Now good evening to you, Mr. Scarlett, and be off."

"How far is it to Louisville?"

"Too far. A long way. Good-bye." Belle turned and entered the house, closing the door behind him.

"Who was that?" his wife's voice called from the other room.

"Just a man looking for directions," he said.

"I thought you said it was business."

"Well, I guess I was wrong, wasn't I!" He sat down on the couch again and picked up the paper.

His wife began to chatter again. He gave the newspaper a shake and straightening and resumed reading. His wife's words passed by him like humming insects flying in from elsewhere in the house, occasionally noticed, mostly ignored.

Chapter 26

Amy thought it ironic and perhaps a little funny that the wounded soldier with the Indiana accent was nervous. Here was a man who had faced an armed foe in battle, felt the sting of a minié ball passing through the calf of his leg, and almost seen that same leg amputated—and he was nervous merely because of the impending visit of three dignitaries! The human mind had its oddities.

The soldier's nervousness displayed itself in chatter at Amy, who stood beside his bed, wearing one of her best dresses and beginning to feel nervous herself. "Is my hair combed good enough, Mrs. Hanover? I want to look my best before the general. But how can a man look his best when he's laid up in a bed?"

"I'm sure the general has no expectations of seeing anyone dressed out in their Sunday best today," Amy replied. "This is a hospital, after all."

"Yes, I suppose you're right. Is my hair combed?"

"Your hair looks fine. You have quite a head of it! My husband's hair is as dark as yours, but it's beginning to thin." She smiled and winked at the soldier. "He hasn't noticed it yet and I haven't the heart to tell him."

The young man grinned; Amy noticed how boyish he was. A war of boys, this all sometimes seemed to her. A game in which gray-bearded men played chess, with living boys as their pawns. "My brother had thicker hair even than me." The grin dwindled. "He's gone now, killed at a place called Baptist Gap, fighting Confederate Indians. Have you heard about that fight?"

"Yes."

"They scalped some of the dead, you know. The Indians did. But not my brother. I don't know why, with him having all that hair. You'd have thought they'd have wanted to take hair like his was."

"It's all very dreadful."

"Mrs. Hanover, I don't want to ask nothing personal, but are all them stories true I've heard about you?"

"Well, I don't know what you've heard, but the stories in my husband's newspaper, those are all true."

He looked at her with admiration and a touch of quick shyness. "You're a true heroine, Mrs. Hanover. Spying, hauling in counterfeit Confederate money for the Union, getting yourself shot . . . you really did get shot, didn't you?"

"Yes."

"It's just like some pond-scum rebel soldier to shoot a woman."

"I was dressed as a man at the time, and running in spite of a command to halt. I suppose whoever fired the shot had the right."

"You're a brave lady. I do admire you. You've gotten well from the wound, ain't you?"

"I'm doing fine. I still feel some pain occasionally, but all in all I'm fine. Just like you'll be very soon."

"I hope so. I hope I don't take the gangrene and lose my leg."

"You'll be fine."

Suddenly there was a great bustle and movement on the other side of a slightly ajar door. It pushed open to admit a delegation of official-looking uniformed military men, a couple of the top surgeons of the Nashville army hospitals, and at the front and center of it all, four men whom Amy knew at once.

Wearing a black suit, looking quite distinguished, and with an expression a bit less severe than the brooding scowl that often lingered on his clean-shaven face, was Andrew Johnson, the military governor of Tennessee. He carried a cane in his left hand, a hat in his right. He smiled at the bedded men in this long, high-ceilinged university lecture room turned hospital ward, and when his eye caught Amy's, they exchanged a silent greeting. Amy had met Johnson only once before, and only briefly, but their lives shared a few common threads that made Johnson seem more familiar to her than he truly was.

Johnson, not being in uniform, did not convey the militaristic aura of his companions, but was in fact as much a military man as the others. When Lincoln made him military governor of the state back in March of the prior year, he'd also made him a brigadier general, giving him authority both civilian and military. In addition, Johnson was a duly elected United States senator, holding the unusual distinction of representing a seceded state in the governing body of the nation from which that state had seceded. An authoritative man all around, this Andrew Johnson, and unafraid to use that authority. And only a few years ago he'd been a mere small-town tailor, sitting cross-legged on a big table in the midst of his log-walled shop, stitching away while his wife taught him to read! He'd come a long way from his impoverished youth as a runaway tailor's apprentice out of North Carolina.

Beside Johnson was General William S. Rosecrans, a dark-haired, bearded fellow with a rather long nose and brooding eyes. Amy recognized him from an etching the *Sage* had published several times, and she knew something of Rosecrans, having heard her human fact bank of a husband expound on the various careers of Union leaders several times. An Ohio native who had graduated fifth in his West Point class, only to leave the military after disillusionment with his peacetime military career, Rosecrans had suffered burns in a kerosene plant fire back in '59, and after recuperation had reentered military service with the coming of war. He was known as "Old Rosey" by the soldiers. Rosecrans was freshly back in town after an absence of several weeks.

Beside him stood General Robert S. Granger, another Ohio-born West Pointer, and a veteran of the Mexican War. Commander of the District of Nashville for the Army of the Cumberland for a little over a month now, Amy had been introduced to Granger at a social event, and with her husband had enjoyed a lengthy conversation with him.

The final man in this quarter of dignitaries was one Amy had never met at all. Bearded and auger-eyed, this was the chief of staff of the Army of the Cumberland, Adjutant General James A. Garfield. He too was an Ohioan, but no West Point man. Garfield had worked his way into wartime military service, as a lieutenant colonel of the 42nd Ohio, after careers as a schoolteacher, lawyer, and Republican state legislator. He'd worked up through the military ranks to the rank of brigadier general. His eyes swept the room swiftly, paused for a moment on Amy, then turned to Rosecrans, who had just stepped forward to address the patients, some of whom were making ill-advised efforts to rise to attention despite their wounds.

"Stay as you are, men," he said. "No need to exert yourselves. You do us honor by allowing us merely to pay you this call."

"Three cheers for Old Rosey and the grand old flag!" a voice at the rear of the ward called out. Whoops rang up from the ranks of the wounded.

"I thank you," he said. "That's damned fine of you." He stepped to the nearest bed and put out his hand to shake that of a one-armed, one-legged bandaged soldier who smiled despite obvious pain.

The other dignitaries, trailed by their entourage, followed. The Indianan soldier beside Amy watched the progress of the group as it made a wide circle around the room. He would be reached only at the end of the sweep.

He said, "Just regular-looking men in one way, but with a way and manner about them. You know what I mean?"

"Yes. It's called 'authority,' " Amy said.

"I hear that you and Governor Johnson are from the same town."

"In a way. I lived at Greeneville at the beginning of the war. He ran a tailor shop there for years. He was a friend of my Greeneville uncle, Hannibal Deacon."

"The one they hanged as a bridge burner? He was your uncle?"

"Yes."

"You do have quite a life story, Mrs. Hanover. And you still so young!"

By now the delegation had almost reached them, and conversation ceased. Andrew Johnson was the first to shake the hand of Amy's friend, then he smiled warmly at Amy, turned to the trio of military leaders and said in a voice that rang with the warm inflections of East Tennessee, "Gentlemen, it's my pleasant surprise to find here a young woman with whom I share a bit of common ground. You may have read, in fact, of Mrs. Amy Deacon Hanover."

"Amy Hanover!" Rosecrans repeated. "So *this* is the valiant lady spy, is it?" He came up and thrust out his hands toward Amy; for a moment she actually thought he was going to embrace her, but instead he merely took one of her hands in both of his. "Ma'am, I'm pleased to have met you."

Amy was embarrassed by the attention suddenly turned on her, but accepted it politely. Rosecrans gave Amy's hand another squeeze, then backed away, allowing Garfield and Granger to give her their own similar greetings.

Granger turned to Johnson. "Governor, in that it's my understanding that Mrs. Hanover has lived in your own town yonder in the eastern end of the state, and given that you and her new husband have had a touch of a tiff every now and again . . ." He paused as light, knowing laughter rippled around the room. ". . . perhaps you will share with General Garfield here some of her remarkable story."

"Gladly, sir, and Mrs. Hanover, feel free to correct me if I should stray from the facts," Johnson said. "General Garfield, it may be that even an Ohio man such as yourself once heard the name of Dr. George Deacon, the great disunionist of Knoxville."

"Indeed. Publisher, I believe he was . . . the *Secession Argosy*. . . ."

"The *Secession Advocate*, to be precise," Johnson went on. "You may be interested in knowing that Mrs. Hanover here—may I call you Amy? Thank you!—that Amy here is the daughter of the late Dr. Deacon."

"Do tell!"

"A daughter—but a promoter of a viewpoint very different from that of her father. Amy has a history of advocacy on behalf of the Union cause." Amy noted that Johnson discreetly failed to mention that her advocacy also included staunch abolitionism, and that the primary conduit of her journalistic contributions had been the hated *Reason's Torch* abolitionist rabble-rousing publication, originally published in Knoxville, now holding forth in Baltimore.

"Amy and her late father, as you might imagine, had a falling out once he learned what she believed, as opposed to what he had thought she believed," Johnson went on, using some diplomatic generalizations to cover what had been an intensely painful rending of a relationship between Amy and her father. "Amy and he parted ways," he continued, "and she came to join the household of her uncle, Hannibal Deacon, in Greeneville. Mr. Deacon, a great friend of mine, was one of the unfortunate souls who paid the ultimate price after the bridge-burning episode in late 'sixty-one."

"I recall that sad business," Garfield mumbled. The bridge-burning effort, a Lincoln-sanctioned act designed to cripple Confederate rail shipments and open the door to an invasion of East Tennessee, had proven a basically failed and tragic effort that most wanted to forget and seldom talked about.

"To summarize as best I can, after some tragic family circumstances, including the death of her father, Amy was recruited into a work of espionage: smuggling counterfeit Confederate currency into Tennessee. Unfortunately, things went awry. She was caught, managed to escape, but wound up shot by bushwhackers near Nashville. A wound suffered in service of her country, as far as I'm concerned. I made an official declaration of such in her honor. Such things inspire the loyal people, you see."

"I hope the wound wasn't serious," Garfield said.

"I'm doing quite well, sir," Amy replied.

Johnson went on. "To summarize, Amy wound up here in our military medical facilities to start her recuperation."

Granger cut in: "And here the story takes a romantic turn, I believe."

"Yes. There's a newspaperman in the city here, Adam Hanover, a good Unionist for the most part, but a bit of a . . . well, how shall I put it in a way Mrs. Hanover will accept? A bit overly independent, maybe, sometimes prone to stubbornness. Would you say that is correct, Mrs. Hanover?"

"Adam holds firm to his beliefs," she said.

Granger, already familiar with the tale, grinned and goaded Johnson with his forefinger. "I do believe that Mr. Hanover rankled you a bit, Governor, if I recall correctly. Wasn't he one of the editors you had jailed?"

Johnson arched his brows. "Yes. Shortly after I came in as military governor, I did have Mr. Hanover briefly committed to jail."

"Why was that, sir?" Garfield asked.

"Because he did his best to undercut my efforts to take proper control of this rebellious city," Johnson said. His voice temporarily lost its levity. "And that at a time when there were bushwhackers and renegades plotting conspiracies to capture or kill me, and a populace that would have cheered to see me assassinated. I was not a welcome man when I came to Nashville. One needs the newspapers to support him at such a time, not carp and criticize."

"But did you not say he was a Union man?"

"Perhaps Mrs. Hanover can explain the odd workings of her husband's mind better than I can," Johnson said, waving his hand invitingly toward Amy.

She cleared her throat. "I wasn't here at the time he was jailed, you must understand, but my husband has told me he declined to take the Union loyalty oath because he objected to the oath being forced upon the ministers and educators of this city, and to the imprisonment of one of the pro-Confederate editors by Governor Johnson."

"See what I mean?" Johnson said. "You push one way and the good editor Hanover will push the other."

"If I may speak in his defense as his wife, I don't believe it was mere obstinance, Governor," Amy said boldly. Granger and Rosecrans glanced at one another in private amusement at seeing this young woman deigning to stand up before the most powerful man in the state. "Adam held no objection to your requirement that city councilmen, officeholders, and so on, be required to take the loyalty oath, in that they are directly involved in the operation of the government. But he objected on the grounds of press freedom to the gagging of the newspapers and the jailing of dissident editors, and to having the oath forced upon schoolteachers and ministers, both of whom should enjoy, in his view, a certain degree of academic and ideological freedom."

Johnson shook his head. "I still say it was merely bull-headedness. In any case, I put the good editor in the jail for a few days to teach him some manners. . . ."

"You also jailed several ministers and forced the oath down the throats of every Nashville lawyer," Amy added.

Johnson grunted and cleared his throat. "Mrs. Hanover, it's my view that if the only way to make a loyalty oath come out of the throat of a man is to force it down that same throat first, then force it I will. In this case," he continued, turning back to the others, "Mr. Hanover and I managed to mend our fences, to agree to disagree, and on the whole he and his newspaper have been generally supportive since then. But forget that for now: The point is that Amy here gained the attention of Mr. Hanover once she reached Nashville. He heard the story of this beautiful Union smuggler who had taken a bullet for her cause, and paid her a call for a story. He got his story, and in the end, a wife as well."

"Remarkable!" Garfield declared. "Remarkable and splendid! Mrs. Hanover, I salute you."

"As do we all," Rosecrans added. He stepped forward, took one of Amy's hands, and kissed it delicately, rousing cheers from the wounded. She felt a great blush spread across her neck and begin a crawl up her face.

"I believe Mrs. Hanover might have the ability to charm the rebels of this city over to our side, if we just put her to it," Johnson said.

"I'm hardly that persuasive," Amy said, ready for all this

to end. Had she realized her presence here was going to divert so much attention from the soldiers, she wouldn't have come. But the soldiers did seem to be enjoying it.

To her relief, the entourage moved on. The young Indianan looked up at her from his bed. "You are a remarkable lady, Mrs. Hanover."

"No, I'm not. I'm just . . . myself. Nothing special."

"You take good care of us. You brighten up these wards. You're special to every man here. Why do you spend so much time with us when you could be home, or out doing the kinds of things regular folks do?"

She had never asked herself that question, and thought about it before she answered. "Because I know what it is to be wounded myself."

That night, when Adam asked her about her day, she told him about the tour, but did not much mention the praise that had been heaped upon her. She did, however, describe some of Johnson's recounting of his own tiff with Adam Hanover the prior year, much to Adam's amusement.

He told her about his own day then, which involved in part a coverage of other portions of the generals' grand tour. Besides visiting the hospital at which Amy volunteered, they had inspected several other hospitals, the convalescent camps, the gunboats then in port on the Cumberland River, and had reviewed troops all about the city. It had been a busy day for the military men, and Adam described in his usual detail what he observed of it while Amy snuggled silent under his arm. He didn't stop talking until he glanced down and realized that his wife had stopped listening some time ago and drifted off into sleep.

He held her awhile longer, enjoying her warm presence and the touch of her fingers, which were extended across his chest. Adam considered himself a fortunate man. Busy, opinionated, and self-involved by nature, he had never anticipated marriage until he met Amy, and from almost that moment on had been unable to *not* envision marriage. She was captivating and delightful beyond any woman he'd seen. It was as if she was made for him, and him for her. He knew she had felt the same; she'd told him so. She hadn't anticipated marriage either, and had turned down two proposals from others, one from, of all things, a Confederate soldier, the other from some young storekeeper she'd known in Greeneville.

Carefully, he slipped his arm from under her; she moved, murmured, turned in her sleep and settled her head onto her pillow. He touched her back gently, feeling the smoothness of her and then the place it was broken by the scar of bullet entry. He thought how she might have died from that wound, and shuddered. Death and Amy Deacon Hanover were two realities that did not belong within the same thought. He was glad she'd recovered, glad she'd let him love her, and glad most of all that she had let herself love him in turn. It was a marvelous miracle of a truth, so good he sometimes had trouble comprehending it was the truth at all.

Someday the war would end. There would be no more soldiers and shooting and worries. They would have children then, and raise them in a better world than this one. He tried to picture what their children would look like, and smiled when he realized he placed upon them all the face of his wife.

He kissed her and lay down. Life was good, and would get better when war was over. God speed the day. Adam Hanover couldn't wait.

Chapter 27

Ben Scarlett's view of himself was about as low as a man could have. On the many occasions through the years that he'd been insulted, sworn at, and generally abused by countless people, he seldom disagreed with the things they said to and about him, as unpleasant as it was to hear them. But one good thing he knew about himself: He had talent. Just one, and maybe not one that counted for much to anybody else, but it was his own, and he was proud of it.

The talent was survival in virtually any situation. Of all life's achievements, that was the only one Ben had managed to accomplish. He had slept in places most human beings wouldn't have been willing to lie dead in, eaten food that a dog might have shunned, and survived illnesses that should have killed him three times over. Somehow he managed to always get by and through whatever situation life threw at him.

In the strange city of Nashville in the summer of 1863, in the sad period after learning that the former fiancée he had hoped to find was at best far away and probably untraceable—if it was even truly she at all—Ben's challenge was finding a place to reside and a way to keep food in his belly and, if possible, alcohol in his bloodstream. So far the latter challenge wasn't being met too well, but he'd managed in the most novel of ways to find a solution to the former—more novel, maybe, than the time just a few months back when he lived in an empty privy house at Cumberland Gap, earning him the nickname "Outhouse Ben" among the Confederate soldiers stationed there.

Ben had become a subterranean dweller, living in a sort of closed-off half cellar beneath the floor of a big double store building in the College Hill area of the city. The portion under which he resided, though built as a commercial structure, was currently in use as a church meeting place. With the Union army in control of almost every formal church building in the city, using them mostly for hospital sites, churches were meeting in all kinds of odd places, store buildings included. The church side of the double building butted right up against one side wall of a big general store that reminded Ben very much of Daniel Baumgardner's business in distant Knoxville.

Ben had first made the interesting discovery, while seeking shelter from rain, that the cellar, which was really not a true cellar at all but merely a rough, big hole never intended for use, inaccessible from within the building itself, could be entered through a hole beneath a back porch. He'd waited out the rain in this oversized crawl space, almost high enough for him to stand up straight in, then found a loose floorboard above him and obtained entry into the church itself. There, he'd taken two or three candles, all throughout the theft fervently asking the Lord to forgive him for plundering His house, and promising his creator that he would pay the church for the candles—just as soon as he could steal some money to do it with. Ben had matches already, and descended back to his cellar, lighted one of the candles, and laid the floorboard back in place above him.

Then had come the most intriguing discovery of all. The foundation and crawl space was as big as both buildings together, so that when he walked, and then crawled, into the area where the uneven dirt floor rose up to within three feet of the floor above, he was no longer under the church at all, but beneath the store next to it. He waited until nightfall came and there was no more noise of footsteps above, and began poking about for another loose floorboard. Not finding one, he hammered up a board with a broken-off piece of foundation stone, and by this means created an upward-opening makeshift trapdoor that gave him access to the rear storeroom of the store above.

And thus Ben had found himself an even more cozy and self-sustaining situation than he'd enjoyed in the upper reaches of the old Deacon warehouse in Knoxville. Beneath the church he had a cool but surprisingly dry place he could sleep—he didn't much mind sharing the space with the three or four big rats that also resided here, especially since those rats might provide him some meat if it came to that—and up above the loosened floorboard of the store he had access each night to food and other goods right off the shelves. Not that he would take much. As much stealing as he did, Ben Scarlett didn't really believe it was right. Besides, if he took too much, it would be noticed, an investigation made, and his handy little living situation discovered and ended.

He busied himself with stocking his new "house" for a couple of days, dragging in some old throwaway blankets he'd found to make a bed, and some empty crates to serve as shelving and furniture. He lived off canned food and so on that he sneaked down from the store a little at a time. The only thing he lacked was whiskey, which the store did not sell.

A thought came to him about midnight on a Sunday, while he lay trying to sleep on his blankets, suffering deeply for lack of liquor: *Just because a store don't sell whiskey don't mean there ain't none there.*

He rose too fast in the pitch-blackness and bumped his head on the bottom of the church floor. One of his fellow-tenant rats skittered off somewhere in the darkness, frightened by the sound. Ben swore and groped his head, then apologized to the Lord for doing so beneath a house of worship. Earlier, he lay on his blankets, listening to the motion and music of the congregation above, hearing a bit of the sermon and feeling awfully weighted with sin and fearful of hell because of the things the preacher was saying. He'd felt very glad when the church emptied at last and there was no more guilt-rousing sermon to writhe beneath.

Feeling about for his matches, Ben lit a candle and let light fill his cavernlike home. He walked in a stoop to where the floor began to rise, his shadow distorted, huge and bobbing before him in the flickering candlelight. He crawled up toward the loosened floorboard, pushed it up, and felt a downrush of wind from the closed store above.

Once inside the store, he stretched to full height and let his spine pop and expand. It was hard on a man, having to walk around in a half stoop for a long time. Then he went to the desk of whoever owned this place and lit the kerosene lamp there, keeping the wick cranked low so it wouldn't give off enough light to be detected easily from outside.

His whiskey craving about to drive him mad, Ben began digging through desk drawers and behind items on storeroom shelves in the faint hope that whoever ran this place kept some kind of liquor hidden about. "With my luck he's a teetotaler like Mr. Baumgardner," he muttered to himself. But hardly had he said it when his hand closed over something cool and glassine. He thrilled with excitement as he drew out a half-full bottle of high-quality whiskey that had been tucked behind a crate on the top storeroom shelf.

"Bless your heart, Mr. Storekeeper, whoever you are. Bless your heart, your home, and your hearth. May you have many fine children and more money than you can count!" He unstoppered the bottle and lifted it to his lips, taking a welcome swallow.

He'd taken a couple of further swallows before a concern came. What if the owner of this bottle noticed some of the whiskey missing? Might he start poking around, find the loose floorboard, and ruin everything?

Ben put the stopper back in the bottle and looked at the liquor by lamplight. Yes, there was an obvious decline in its level. Should he water it down to restore volume? No . . . that would be noticed whenever the bottle's owner sneaked his next drink. . . .

Ben decided he didn't want that owner sneaking any

drinks from this bottle. This was his whiskey now! He not only wanted it, but needed it. He simply wouldn't worry about what the bottle's former possessor would think when he found it missing. The odds he would go poking around at floorboards because of a missing whiskey bottle didn't seem all that likely.

Ben went back to the desk and took out a cigar he'd seen earlier while rifling through a drawer. He had been tempted to take it upon discovery, but hadn't because he figured someone might notice it was gone. But if he was going to live dangerously where the whiskey bottle was concerned, why not with the cigar as well? Carrying the logic a little farther yet, he headed into the store and took more food than he ever had before: a couple of cans of beans, a small sack of flour, and another of cornmeal. Tomorrow he'd go out into some empty lot, build up a fire, and bake himself some hoecakes to keep stored in his hole of a home. Remembering the rats, he looked around on the shelves and took a tight-closing metal bread box, just the thing to keep them from his food.

He went back down into his subterranean dwelling, packed his flour and meal inside the bread box, and closed it tight. Then he drank his whiskey until it ran out, fell asleep, and dreamed about going to hell—a hell that looked remarkably like this dark underground dwelling place, but full of fire and with a lot more rats. He awakened in a sweat, wishing he had more liquor. Finally he fell asleep again, and dreamed this time about Angel, seeing her as he'd known her in younger days when she was girlish and pretty and destined to be his wife, and he'd only just begun to fall under the influence of the liquid demon that lived inside glass bottles and now owned him, body and soul.

When he got up the next morning, he was worried. He'd been careless, stealing that whole bottle of whiskey. He hadn't smoked the cigar yet. Maybe he should sneak back up tonight and put it back in the drawer . . . but a cigar that vanished and reappeared would be just as suspicious as one that merely vanished, so he gave up that idea.

Exiting his dwelling through the hole under the church's back porch, he discovered it wasn't morning at all, but about noon. He couldn't tell much about time down in the everlasting darkness. He looked down at his clothing, all rumpled and smeared with the greasy dirt of the cellar, and in much worse shape than when Daniel Baumgardner had given it to him. Before long he'd have to find some new clothing. Perhaps some charitable organization or church might give him some. Maybe he could get clothes from the church that was his unwitting host, hiding him in its underbelly like a tapeworm living unseen and unknown in somebody's gut.

"That's me!" Ben muttered. "No more 'count than a tapeworm, and just as hard to get rid of."

He wandered around to the street, along which fairly heavy traffic moved today. He slumped back against the front wall of the church, scratching himself and watching people go by.

"You poor man," a woman's voice said. "Here . . . please take this, and use it to buy yourself some food." She put a coin in his hand.

"Thank you, ma'am," he said humbly. "God bless you for helping a poor downtrod soul."

She went on. Ben bit the coin, nodded with satisfaction, and stuck it in the one pocket he possessed that didn't have a hole in it. Not a bad way to start a day, getting money without even begging for it!

His hand touched the picture in his pocket and he pulled it out, eyeing sadly the image he couldn't help but believe was his own lost Angel. Off in Louisville, out of reach. Gone forever, unless he went after her—and maybe he would, after he'd rested up some.

He yawned loudly, and looked through watering eyes to the left just in time to see a policeman enter the store from which he'd taken the whiskey and bread box. This concerned him, and he decided that perhaps he ought to pay a call on the store as a daytime customer, just to see what was going on. He brushed as much filth off his clothing as he could and headed down to the store, slipping in the door as quietly as he could. Meandering about, trying to look like he had business there, he casually drifted back toward the rear of the store, where a man in a merchant's apron was talking in obvious agitation to the policeman.

". . . and not only was my medicine gone, but the things in my desk looked like they'd been gone through, though I didn't miss anything but a cigar that I'd left in the top drawer, though that I can't swear to. But the oddest thing of all was that the desk lamp was burning. Cranked real low, but it was burning."

"Might you not have left it burning yourself when you closed the store yesterday evening?" the policeman asked.

"No sir. I have a strong respect for fire, having lost a store to a fire seven years ago, and I'm always very careful to make sure no blazes are left burning when I close. That lamp was out last night, but burning this morning."

"This medicine, what kind was it, and how much was there?"

"What do you mean, what kind?"

"I mean, was there spirits in it? Might somebody have stolen it to drink it?"

"It was . . . yes, I suppose it did have some spirit contents. And I'd say there was half a bottle left, maybe."

"Big bottle? Small?"

"Oh, about the size of a whiskey bottle, I guess."

I'd say it was exactly the size, Ben thought.

"Most likely that bottle has been emptied by now, sir. My guess is that whoever broke in here must have been looking for something to drink."

"I suppose I'll have to get another bottle now," the merchant said. "I need this medicine to keep my blood purged."

Ben thought, *Me, too. Got to keep the old blood purged.*

The storekeeper was in an increasingly grumpy mood. "I despise having to go out and spend money on whisk—on medicine just because somebody has stolen from me. It ain't right!"

"No, sir. But you can be glad that's all that was taken. No merchandise or money gone?"

"Not that I can tell. I haven't checked the stock yet, though."

Ben realized he should have been far more cautious than

he had been in what he stole, and cursed himself for so stupidly forgetting to extinguish the lamp he'd lighted. If not for that, the merchant might not have detected the theft for many more hours, until it was time to take his daily "medicine" dose.

"Any sign of anyone coming in through a window or door?"

"I checked them all, officer, and there was no sign anything had been disturbed. Not a fleck of dust out of place on any windowsill, inside or out, and no sign the door had been forced. It was locked up tight when I arrived this morning."

"Well, whoever it was must have come through the ceiling or floor, then."

"There are no holes in my floor, and I know the boards are tight. I built this floor myself. And you can look at the ceiling and see there's no way in that way."

"That can only mean that whoever did this was in the store when you closed, hidden."

The merchant paused, thinking about that. Ben studied him from the corner of his eye and saw the worry creeping in. He hoped to high heaven that the merchant would accept the policeman's theory.

"Whew!" the storekeeper said. "That's a thought to put a chill down a man's spine! Hidden in the store, me moving around, sweeping up, closing out the books, and never knowing he was here! It's a good thing I left no cash about the place last night."

Ben turned and bumped a bottle onto the floor, where it shattered with the force of a small bomb. The merchant saw him for the first time then, and the man's brows lowered and a hard and angry look spread across his face.

"You there! What did you just do?"

"I was just standing here, and all of a sudden that bottle tipped off the shelf and busted itself on the floor," Ben said. "I didn't touch it, sir, I swear!"

"Good Lord, man, what's that muck all over your clothes? What are you tracking into my store?" He headed for Ben on a quick step. "I don't care for vagrants coming into here. Your kind will steal a man blind."

"I was just doing some looking around, thinking about buying something."

"I doubt you got a single piece of change anywhere about you. I want you out!"

Ben put on his most haughty look and pulled from his pocket the coin the woman had given him.

The merchant wasn't particularly impressed. "Don't flash it if you don't intend to spend it. But I suggest you put your little coin away and get out of here. I was robbed last night and I'm in no mood to deal with the riffy-raffy varmint level of society today. Off with you!"

"And a good day to you too, sir!" Ben said, heading for the door.

Once outside, he wandered down the street some distance, thinking about what he'd heard. This merchant was awfully upset about having been robbed, and it was still possible he might discover the loosened floorboard despite his professed confidence in the sturdiness of his floor. He would have to lay low for a while. Be careful. He'd have to stay out of the store for a few days, just in case the merchant kept a secret watch for another entry.

He was wandering idly along, lost in thought, when he heard a woman's voice call to him from an alley. He turned, peering into the dark shadows, his eyes seeing nothing because they were at the moment adjusted to the bright midday light on the street.

"Somebody say something to me?"

"I did indeed, mister. I say, why don't you step in here and visit with me?"

He stepped into the alley, and once he was in the shadows, was able to make out the form of the woman who had called to him, and who was even now advancing with a big smile on her face and a more pleasant and inviting look than any human being had turned upon Ben Scarlett in many a month.

"Howdy," he said, responding with the instinctive friendliness he showed to those rare folks who were friendly to him. "My name's Ben. What's yours?"

She was a black woman, wearing a tight dress pulled indecently low. "I got me a heavenly name," she said. "My name's Angel."

Chapter 28

Ben sucked in his breath, jolted at hearing this unexpected mention of The Name.

"Angel," he said. "I knew an Angel one time. I was to marry a woman by that name."

"Is that right? Well, you want to marry me?" Her manner and tone conveyed practiced artificiality and cynicism; this was a woman who had learned to separate herself from her gutter profession, a woman playing a role while the real woman, whoever she was, cringed somewhere inside.

"I have a picture of my Angel, or a woman that sure does look like her." Ben began digging for the picture. "She's been living in Nashville, so I hear, and I come looking for her, but she's gone. They hauled her off to Louisville with all the other Cyprians." He pulled out the picture and handed it to the woman. "Are you a Cyprian?"

That made her laugh. "What do you think, Five-fingers? What happened to your hand?"

"I had to get it cut off for mortification. Look at the picture. Do you know her?"

The woman squinted at the picture, picking with a fingernail at the ink that Ben had smeared on but making no comment on it. She handed it back toward him. "I know her. That woman there, she's Angel Beamish."

Suddenly Ben's breath wasn't coming just right. "You know her . . . she lives in Nashville, then?"

"She did. But she be gone now."

"Sent off on the steamboat?"

"That's right. They sent them all off, all they could find. I know they sent off Angel Beamish—I seen her climbing aboard with my own eyes. You were going to marry Angel Beamish?" She cocked her head and looked at Ben peculiarly, then broke into laughter. "*You* were going to *marry* Angel Beamish!"

He failed to see the humor. "Why didn't they send you off on the steamboat, too?"

"They didn't send off no colored whores. They left us all here, and now the town is ours. We got all the business."

"When you saw Angel get on the boat, was she well?"

"Angel Beamish is bad sick. Been sick a long time. Look, you want to be my friend or not? You going to pay me for my time?"

A side of Ben that exhibited itself rarely emerged. He'd come a long way for the sake of a woman who once had loved him and who might have given him, and herself, a far better life than either had known apart. This was no game to him, no idle bandying of words, and certainly no business exchange with a street-corner Cyprian. He advanced toward the young black woman and grabbed her shoulder with his one hand, very hard. She cringed as his fingers pinched into her flesh. "You tell me, right now: How sick is Angel?"

"I don't know . . . just sick, weak, like a lot of us get to be. She was walking slow, onto the boat, leaning on somebody's shoulder—you're hurting me! Stop it!"

He shook her and squeezed harder. "I want to know all there is to know about Angel. Where did she live?"

"I don't know—no, wait, she lived with another woman, both of them whores—"

"Don't call her that!"

The woman was growing scared now. "I'm sorry, sir. I won't call her that, I won't. She lived with another woman, sir."

"What was her name?"

"She call herself Nectar, sir. Nectar Childs."

"Where?"

"Two streets over, sir. Up in a room above an empty store right on the side of the big alley there."

"Is Nectar Childs still in town, or did she get sent off, too?"

"I don't know, sir. I swear to you, I don't know!"

He let her go. She turned and scurried away, rubbing her shoulder, glancing back twice with frightened and angry eyes to make sure he wasn't following.

Ben walked slowly along the street, studying the storefronts and the layout of the avenues until certain he was at the right place. There was an empty store building—though not really empty, in that the Federals were using it, as they used virtually every available space in the city, for storage of supplies—and beside the storefront the mouth of a wide, upsloping alley, big enough for a wagon, opened onto the street. A blue-clad Federal guard stood sentry at the front of the empty store, looking bored and unhappy at this menial job. Ben could tell the guard was watching him out of the corner of his eye.

Ben looked at the second-story windows above the storefront. The curtains in them were half shut and the glass very dusty on the exterior, as were virtually all neglected windows in a city without paved streets. Though he saw the outline of a lamp bowl through the dusty glass he could not tell from the outside whether anyone now lived on the other side of those windowpanes.

He walked farther, tipping his hat at the unresponsive guard, and looked into the alley. An exterior staircase led up to a second-story door into the rooms above. It was closed tightly, the curtain drawn over the small glass panes set high in the door panels. Ben turned into the alley and headed for the stairs.

The sentinel came around after him just as he set his foot onto the first step. "You there! What do you think you're doing?" The accent was that of a Minnesotan.

"I was going up to see if Miss Nectar Childs was in," Ben replied.

"She isn't. There's nobody up there. The whores that lived there have been sent off by steamer to Louisville. Now be off with you."

"Are you sure that Miss Nectar was among them sent away?"

"I'm sure. She and the other one as well, the sickly one. Now be gone! We've had a couple of theft attempts here, and as a result I've been given the very undesirable task of standing guard when, believe you me, there are plenty of other things I'd rather be doing. I'll not have you loitering about."

"The sickly woman you mentioned, did you know her?"

"Are you asking me if I dally with whores? I take some insult to that, you sorry cracker!"

"I didn't mean no insult. I just think that maybe I know the woman. Was her name Angel?"

"I don't know her name. All I know is she looked pretty miserably ill and had a cough that would make you sick to hear. Now get off!"

Ben went back to the street and turned left, marching off as the soldier took his place at the storefront again. Ben was very worried. He'd found the clearest track yet of his lost love, only to have the matter of sickness mentioned every time her name came up.

"Take care of Angel, Lord," Ben prayed in a whisper. "I know I got no right to ask anything of you, I don't know you even hear me, and I don't ask nothing at all for myself . . . but please take care of my Angel, if you will."

He roamed the streets for hours, having nothing else to do, and finally stumbled across something that made the roaming worthwhile. A group of women wearing white, homemade uniforms and solemn looks of charity were dishing out hot soup beneath a tent in an empty lot. Ben fell into the queue and accepted a hot bowl of it, wandered to the two long tables set up nearby and ate it without enjoyment. What robbed his pleasure in the food, which in itself was delicious, was his worry about Angel. He finished the bowlful, got back in line, and obtained a second helping, which he also ate down to the final drop. One of the white-clad women gave him a cheaply printed New Testament, told him that God loved him and so did she. He thanked her and went on his way.

He roamed some more and headed back toward his subterranean dwelling place. *I live the life of a rat,* he thought, not in sadness, but merely in observation. He had no worries about himself just now; all worries were concentrated on Angel, who by now was probably ensconced in Louisville. He hoped she could find some sort of doctor to treat whatever sickness she had.

He was just squeezing into the under-porch hole that led to his secret chamber when he caught sight of a human figure peering at him—or had he? It was merely a flash, an impression of seeing a part of a human face turned his way, mostly hidden by the corner of the store building in which he'd obtained the illicit whiskey. The face might have been that of the storekeeper, but Ben hadn't seen it long enough to be sure, if in fact he had seen a face at all.

Had he not been so filled with thoughts about Angel, he might have worried more about that possibly imagined flash of a face. He might have pondered how undesirable it would be to have the storekeeper learn that a human vole occupied the space beneath his building. No such thoughts arose. All he could think of was his onetime fiancée, who to all others in this city was nothing but an undesirable, sickly prostitute, but to Ben Scarlett was a living link back to days before he himself was ruined and enslaved by liquor, and life still held the promise of being something good and worth sharing with another.

He was sleeping soundly that night beneath the church end of the double building above when a creaking, wrenching noise awakened him. He sat up in the pitch-blackness and detected that the sound came from the area beneath the store. He sucked in his breath and held it, filling with fear, and then a big shaft of yellow light spilled in. Off in the corner a rat chattered and scurried into some unseen niche.

Someone had just removed the wide, loosened floorboard that was his doorway to the store.

An upside-down face appeared in the opening, eyes turning this way and that. It was the storekeeper.

Ben held perfectly still, not breathing. The light that came in didn't penetrate all the way to where he was, and he quickly realized from the continued turning of the inverted head and the movement of the eyes that the storekeeper didn't see him.

"Who's down here?" the merchant demanded. "Speak up! I know there's somebody here!"

Ben remained still as the darkness itself.

"I saw you come in here earlier today, you damned thieving interloper!" the storekeeper said. "Show yourself!"

Silence. Only the rats moved, hidden away in their dark and musky holes.

"I can make you come out of there, you know! I got a pistol up here—I'll shoot in all directions if I have to!"

Ben allowed himself to draw in the smallest of breaths, but made no sound nor movement.

The head pulled back up again. Without it to block the light, more came through, and Ben scooted silently back farther, all the way to the far foundation wall. He wondered if the storekeeper was really going after his pistol.

A shadow moved in the shaft of light; the head came back down again, but only far enough for the merchant to call in: "I'm dropping a snake into this hole! It's a copperhead—you'd best get your thieving vagrant hide out of there before my snake finds you!" A hand descended, holding to a twisting, writhing, living something that made Ben's blood turn icy inside him. The hand opened, the writhing thing dropped, the floorboard slammed back into place, cutting off all light, and the merchant's laugh was muffled and mocking from above.

Ben remained still, listening.

Something *was* moving across the earthen floor, making the faintest kind of slithering whisper. . . .

"Oh, God!" he whispered. "Oh, God, he really done it. . . ."

He headed on hand and knees for his exit, imagining the unseen snake after him, coiling up, aiming its strike. . . .

Ben Scarlett was half out of the hole when he saw the merchant come running around the store building. Light from the rear window of the store cast just enough illumination for Ben to make out all the relevant details. The merchant had a shotgun in his hands and a look on his face that combined bitter fury with the delight of a hunter who has outwitted his prey and is now ready for the kill.

Ben pulled himself the rest of the way out as the storekeeper leveled the shotgun. "You freeze right there, thief! Freeze like February! I'll kill you right here and now if you so much as twitch a whisker!"

Ben's arms lifted skyward. "Don't shoot me, sir. Please don't."

The merchant laughed. "It was only a black snake! No harm in it at all, but you sure did scurry out of that hole! I knew you would. I knew you'd never sit down there thinking there was a copperhead slithering about you!"

Ben felt foolish, though the truth was he probably would have come out almost as quickly even if he'd known it wasn't really a copperhead. He hated snakes of all kinds. They were in his view the worst of the banes of the kind of existence he knew, in which a man resided in holes and sheds and caves.

"I'm sorry I was down there. I was just taking shelter— I've got no home."

"You'll have a home now in a jail cell. It was you who broke into my store and took my whiskey—my medicine! It was you who stole the cigar from my desk! And I've been looking at my inventory—food missing, a bread box gone. It's been you, ain't it! How long you been living down there?"

"Just tonight, sir. I only found that place today."

"You're a liar. Get up."

Ben stood, arms still in the air.

"I'll be! You're one-handed. How'd that happen?"

"Well, sir, it's a long story. I was a soldier, you see,

trying to save the lives of some orphans about to be struck by this slow-bounding cannonball, and I stuck my hand out to—"

"Shut up. Turn around."

He heard and felt the merchant draw closer behind him. A long silence held. Ben tingled all over. Was the merchant going to crush in his skull with the shotgun butt? Was he going to shoot him in the back? Not knowing what to anticipate was terrifying.

The merchant's voice took on a snarling, snide, whispery quality. "You know what, you vagrant? I don't know as I'll fool with the police. I believe I might just deal with you myself!"

"Please, mister, if you'll just let me go I'll never come around anymore."

"Why should I trust you? It seems to me the thing to do is shoot you. No, no—too much noise. I'll crush in your skull and cut your throat. That'll do it."

A part of Ben said that this man was surely trying only to terrorize him thoroughly before letting him go, so that he'd be too scared to come around again. Another part wasn't so sure. There were some insane people in the world. A man like Ben Scarlett tended to run across more than the usual share of them.

"Yep, that's what'll do it! A knock on the head, a knife through the throat—*ssscccrrrrccchhhhhh!* Nobody would ever be the wiser, and you'd be stealing no more of an honest man's goods, would you!"

Ben was ready to believe the worst was really going to happen when a blessed sight revealed itself before his eyes. Another man appeared, emerging from the alley beside the church portion of the building.

"Lloyd," the man said. He had a quiet, even voice. He was tall and thin, with a pointed nose and an oversized chin that still looked oversized despite an obvious attempt to hide it behind a carefully groomed beard. "Lloyd," he repeated.

"Hello, Lloyd," Ben said. "I'm Ben Scarlett, and I'm pleased to meet you. I'd shake your hand, but I'm afraid the man behind me will shoot me if I lower my arms. He says he's going to kill me."

"Shut up!" the storekeeper said. He sounded completely different now that another was present. "I'm not going to kill you, never was. And that man ain't named Lloyd, you idiot. He was calling *my* name. My name's Lloyd."

The newcomer came a step closer, eyes on Ben. "My name's Gurney, the Reverend F. Victor Gurney. I'm the pastor of the congregation that meets in this building here beside us. The man behind you there is my younger brother. He's been kind enough to allow me and my congregation to use half of his building here for our church services since the Union army took over our own building for use as a hospital. My brother, you see, is under the illusion that he'll earn himself a heavenly admittance by allowing a church to meet on his property. It's his way of trying to buy off the Almighty."

The man behind Ben grunted unhappily.

Ben said, "He's really your brother?"

"That's right. And a rather intemperate, unthinking kind of brother he is sometimes, as he's demonstrated this evening. By the way, sir, you can lower your hands . . . your *hand* now. He won't hurt you." The Reverend F. Victor Gurney stepped around Ben to address the shotgun wielder. "Lloyd, what were you thinking? What if this man had died of fright?"

"I just wanted to scare him, Victor. He's been living under the store, sneaking up at night through a loose floorboard and stealing stuff. What are you doing here at this time of night?"

"The same thing you are, I suspect. I'd been growing suspicious that there was someone beneath the building, too. Noises and so on. So tonight I decided to stay in the building and see if I could detect anything for certain."

"Same here," Lloyd Gurney said. "But I'd already detected him. I saw him slipping in under the porch earlier today."

"Why didn't you call the police in?"

"I wanted to deal with it myself. It's me he stole from!"

"And you call pointing a shotgun at a man and threatening his life 'dealing with it'? It's a providential thing that

I came along. You might have gotten carried away and actually hurt this man." The preacher turned back to Ben. "You may go, sir. I think you've been punished enough for no more offense than trespassing under a building."

"Wait a minute!" the merchant protested. "What about the things he stole?"

"Well, there is that. Can you make any recompense, Mister . . . Scarlett, was it?"

"Ben Scarlett. Yes, sir, I can. I got a little money." He pulled out the coin and gave it to the preacher, who in turn handed it to the merchant. "That's all I got," Ben said. "Well . . . I do have a little Bible that a charity woman gave me today, if you want that, too."

"You keep the Bible. Read it, if you can. And now be off with you, and don't be hiding under buildings again. You can surely find a healthier place to live than that."

The storekeeper said in a challenging tone, "If you're so keen for him to have a healthy place to live, why not let him move in with you, Victor? Put some of that sweet Christian charity you blab about into action!"

"Well . . . I suppose that . . . there is the matter of the wife and the children, and the difficulty of keeping sufficient food on the table for—"

"Never mind," Ben said. "I don't ask nothing of you. If you'd just let me go back down there and fetch my possessions—and I'll give you back your bread box and such, Mr. Storekeeper—then I'll go on my way and you won't see me no more."

They agreed to that. Despite the snake he knew was down there, Ben descended a final time into the rough crawl space hole and dragged out his few goods. He wouldn't have done it had it not been for the fact that one of the things he'd come out without was the picture of Angel. He gave the storekeeper back his bread box and tried to give him back the two cans of food that still remained from the supplies he'd stolen from the store, but by now the manner of both Gurneys had changed. They both acted like men feeling rather guilty, and Lloyd Gurney insisted that Ben keep whatever food he had with him, and gave him back the coin as well. Reverend Gurney threw in a dollar of his own, and Ben held to himself the thought that if Lloyd Gurney was trying to buy his salvation through the donation of church space, as his brother had snidely charged, the Reverend Gurney himself was trying to buy away his own feeling of guilt at refusing to meet his brother's challenge to take in the pitiful specimen of humanity that was Ben Scarlett.

But in the end little of it mattered to Ben. All in all he had done rather well. For several nights he'd enjoyed the security of his under-floor dwelling. He had a bit of money in his pocket now, some food in his bag, and he had avoided jail. There would be other places to sleep. There always were. He'd get by.

He hoped that Angel, wherever she was, was getting by too, and that somehow soon he would discover a way to find her and reach her.

Chapter 29

Two days later Ben Scarlett felt that fate had transformed a bad turn into a good one.

Poking about near the river, he discovered a lonely, neglected little shed that stood within sight of the rear of the Southern Methodist Publishing House. Located in a dense thicket of scrub trees and ivy that not only hid the structure from the casual onlooker, but also helped hold it up, the shed had a sloping roof that didn't leak very much, and access through a rear door that was hidden from view from any direction. By good fortune the ivy that entwined the rear of the structure was not the three-leafed poison ivy, but the five-leafed, harmless Virginia creeper plant, so he could pass in and out without giving himself any rashes. Once again Ben Scarlett's talent for finding refuge had paid off, and as he dug through the trash in the shed, he discovered that more than refuge was here.

He found a Confederate uniform rolled up and hidden under a rotting crate. It was in surprisingly good shape, and, as best he could guess, had probably belonged to some reluctant rebel soldier who decided to desert sometime prior to, or perhaps during, Nashville's changeover from Confederate to

Union control in '62. Ben naturally tried on the uniform and found it fit quite well, though he decided it wouldn't be very prudent to wear it in a city under Union domination. But who could say when it might not make a handy disguise for some reason or another? Sneaking into Nashville in the tentlike dress of the poor, deceased Bertha Mae Trousdale had taught him the value of a good disguise. At the very least, the Confederate garb would make for a good underlayer of warm clothing once the weather turned cold. Hidden beneath his civilian clothes, it would be undetected and should pose no problem. He rerolled the uniform and placed it carefully into his bag of possessions.

He managed to sniff out whiskey, as well, which he purchased with the bit of money he had. But now the whiskey was gone, and the money too, and he was back at the place where the white-clad Bible women gave out bowls of soup, eating his fill at the long tables with a handful of other vagrants, and reading a new copy of the *Sage* that someone had left lying about. He was about to dump another spoonful of the thick soup into his mouth when he let out a little cry of surprise, came halfway to a standing position and let the spoon fall with a splash back into his bowl, then dropped onto the bench again.

A bear of a bald-headed fellow beside him was struck by some of the splashed soup. "Hey!" he protested in a low, grumbly voice. "Hey!"

"Look at that!" Ben said excitedly, shoving the newspaper under the big man's nose and pointing. "Read that right there."

"Don't want to read." He pushed the paper away.

"Just that part, that's all."

"Don't want to read! Hey!"

Ben only then realized the fellow couldn't have read it if he wanted to. "Oh. Well, you needn't read it, then. But you want to know what it says?"

"Yeah."

Ben's rapid-fire talk betrayed his excitement. "It's the editor's column, talking about how this governor fellow and a bunch of generals was touring around the city some days back, going through the hospitals and such. And listen to

this . . . 'Among those receiving the most attention during
the visit to Hospital Number Two was the beloved newly-
wed wife of this editorial pensman, the lovely Amy Deacon
Hanover, whose mounting rise to fame is evidenced by the
fact of Governor Johnson's familiarity with the details of
her remarkable story, and his ability to convey it, by the
very accounting of the tale's subject, with remarkable detail
to the fellow dignitaries in the touring entourage. The governor lingered for some moments in company with this
young and talented woman, who proved so staunchly the
opposite of her East Tennessee secessionist father, the late
Dr. George Deacon, and detailed to the generals with him
her brief but thrilling exploits as a Union spy, the tragic
wounding that she is even now continuing to recover from,
and her devoted voluntary activity on behalf of the Union
wounded in the military hospitals of Nashville.' " Ben put
down the paper. "You see? She's here! Amy Deacon is right
here in Nashville!"

"Who here in Nashville?"

"Amy Deacon is! Though it seems she's got married.
Sounds like to the man who puts out this very newspaper.
I ain't surprised she would marry a newspaper fellow,
coming from a newspaper family like she did." He looked
wistful. "Whoever she married, he's a fortunate man. I think
mighty high of Amy Deacon." He paused, frowning, and
snatched up the paper again. "Wounded? Did that story say
she'd been wounded?" He scanned through the words.
"Yep, that's what it said. Wounded! Lord, I can't believe it!
Somebody wounded Amy Deacon! It says she's getting
better, though. That's good."

"That's good. Who Amy Deakson?"

"Amy Deacon? Why, she's one of the finest, most beautiful, smartest, goodest, and bravest young women I've ever
known, that's who! I knew her in Knoxville. That's where
I'm from. And her, too. Knoxville."

"Oh. Knockville." The big man took another bite of soup
and waved at a fly orbiting his round, bald head. By some
miracle he actually caught it in mid flight, and held out his
closed hand, listening to the muffled buzz inside it. "Look
that! Hey! Look that!"

Ben didn't heed him, being full of reflection and also a growing inner pride to think that he knew someone prominent enough to visit with military governors and generals and get written about in newspapers. "I'm a personal friend of Amy Deacon. I once helped her on one of her spying efforts. She was a smuggler of counterfeit Confederate money, and I helped her get some of that money through Cumberland Gap one time. I knew she was going to Nashville then, but I had no idea she was still here." Ben realized just then that he'd been rash to reveal that he had helped a Union spy when he didn't know his listener's political sympathies. "Do you like the Union, friend?"

The man let the fly go and watched it fly away. "No, no, I don't like no onions. I don't like no onions in nothing. I don't like them in this soup. There go the fly. See?"

"Don't take no offense, but are you a half-wit?"

"Yes. Half-wit. I don't like no onions. My fly gone now." He took a big slurp of soup.

"My name's Ben. What's yours?"

"My name Daws. Folks call me Dummy." He ate more soup.

"You got a home, Dummy?"

"I live here." He gave a general wave, and Ben knew he was in the company of another man of the streets. Another of the shadow people who moved in the darker corners of society, rendered by alcohol or mental incapacity incapable of living in the brighter and bigger world.

Ben kept on talking just as if his listener could make sense of it. "Me, I don't favor neither North nor South. It don't matter to me. But Amy Deacon is strong Union. And an abolitionist, too."

" 'Litionist," Daws echoed. "Strong onion 'litionist. "

"Maybe I'll go see her," Ben said. "I wonder if she'd be glad to see me. I'd sure like to see her." He pictured meeting her, clasping her hand, hearing her warm greeting, meeting her husband, sitting down to discuss what had happened to both of them since last they parted, that being a day in Knoxville when Ben had left a letter for Amy, telling her how fine he thought she was. . . .

From somewhere, reality crept in. Ben looked around,

his little fantasy dissolving. He was nothing but a drunk, living on the streets in a strange city to which he'd come to seek a onetime lover who had become a common harlot. He was a man who lived under buildings and in sheds and ate charity soup in empty lots with half-wit companions. He couldn't call on Amy Deacon. The very idea was absurd. Why, if he approached her door, her husband would probably shoot him, and Ben wouldn't blame him if he did.

All his excitement died. He looked down at his soup, silent. The fly that had been Dummy's prisoner so briefly landed on the side of his bowl and dined. Ben watched it silently.

"Ben sad now," Daws said.

"Yes," Ben replied. "Ben sad now." He left the soup to the fly, took the paper and walked away.

Daws watched Ben until he was a block away and disappeared behind a building.

"Good-bye," Daws said aloud, and went back to slurping his soup. The fly buzzed away and didn't return.

Ben looked at the newspaper again when he was hidden away in his ivy-draped shed. He reread the portion about Governor Andrew Johnson and the touring military delegation meeting with Amy in that hospital room, and felt hollow and empty. He was a smart enough man to know that much of his ability to live with himself as he was derived from his ability to hide from himself what he was . . . and right now that wasn't working. The news that Amy Deacon was here, and apparently enjoying some social prominence, served to jolt him around to a clear and disconcerting picture of who and what Ben Scarlett really was. It was a short jump from there to self-pity.

I doubt she even remembers me. Why should she? What am I that I would be recollected by such a fine woman as Amy Deacon? He still remembered the gist of the lines he'd written in that letter he left at her hotel in Morristown: ". . . there is a sorry old drunk who thinks you are fine and wishes he was fit for you. I will always hold you dear in my mind and not forget you and I hope that you will think high of me as you can and not forget me nei-ther." It seemed foolish now. Probably she had laughed to read those lines. Somebody like him, asking even the remotest kind of affection from somebody like *her*? It was ridiculous.

I wish I had some whiskey. I wish I could get so drunk I'd forget about Angel and Amy Deacon and even about myself. If I was drunk there'd be nothing to worry about or feel bad about—

The thought cut off as he glanced down at the news-paper, which lay on the dirt floor, and saw a small, virtually throwaway editorial note at the end of a column. At the head of the column it said:

CYPRIANS ALREADY RETURNING FROM EXILE IN KENTUCKY; LOUISVILLE REFUSING BERTH TO CARGO OF "DOVES"

He blinked and read it again. Returning? They were *returning*? He snatched up the paper and began to read the smaller print beneath the headlines.

Word has been received that the latest effort of the occupying Federal army to divest itself of the problem of disease-bearing Cyprians who parasite themselves upon the Union soldiery of the city and its environs has little more chance of coming to useful fruition than the earlier attempt to cart off the quandary by railway.

We have learned that several of the ill-famed contin-gent so recently sent to Kentucky via steamer, said steamer, the Ivanhoe, *now being widely insulted among the cruder population by the likely-to-linger name of "The Floating W—House," have already begun to return from their exile in the Northerlands. Three of the sporting women, known best, to those who would know such things, by their working names of High Sal, Nectar Childs, and Babylon Flowers, were seen disembarking the most recent train in from Louisville. The news is that most of the women sent via The* Ivanhoe *to that distant*

*city still remain aboard it, the boat being refused port
and the right to divest itself of its unwanted human
cargo. The attitude of the military leadership of that city
is that no reason is seen why Louisville should make
itself a willing dumping bin for Nashville's problem citizens of female persuasion. Thus the Ivanhoe has been
sent steaming from one potential port to another, the
likelihood seeming to be that eventually it will turn
around and merely return to Nashville, soiled females
and all.*

*Those Cyprians who are beginning to reappear are
from among a few who managed to, in some manner,
depart the ship during one of its brief stops at port, and
who were promptly given railroad passes, compliments
of the United States military, back to Nashville. Thus
it seems that some other means of dealing with this
admittedly vexing situation must be found, even so
extreme a measure as licensing the sporting women of
the city and in this manner keeping a close eye upon
their activities and situations of health, in that the
spread of intimate diseases among the soldiers must certainly be stopped.*

*The attempt to deport the Cyprians has failed in any
case, whether all the deportees should return or not,
through a great influx of Negro harlots who are will-
ingly taking the places of their paler-skinned absentee
sisters. That white doves should be replaced by dusky
ones seems no solution, and we urge the authorities to
consider the possibility of licensure of Nashville's
Cyprian population—an option that might seem ill-
advised and morally repugnant in times of peace, but
which in the realities of wartime occupation might be
the only sane and sensible solution to a dilemma that,
prone to rouse joking through it may be, is far from a
joke in itself.*

Ben clutched the paper to his chest, forgetting self-pity,
forgetting even Amy Deacon. The Cyprians were returning,

and among those already here was the very Nectar Childs who was the friend of his own lost Angel!

Maybe Angel would return soon, too. Maybe she already had, and the newspaper had simply failed to note it. One thing was sure: He wouldn't find out sitting in his shed, moping and whining.

He had thrown off his hat when he came in earlier, but now slapped it back on his head, ripped out the relevant story from the newspaper, and exited the shed.

As rough and raw a life as he had led, Ben Scarlett was not accustomed to places such as this. His vice was liquor, not women, and it was to the standard saloons and backroom rotgut dens that he'd been attracted through the years. This place, located in a big, damp, and clammy cellar of a fire-ruined building near the river, had its liquor, to be sure, but the main attraction was women. Not many knew of this spot, and in fact it had been quite difficult for Ben to find out about it, for it was protected by those who treasured and frequented it. Here a man could find feminine company of the sort not shown to the parents and taken to the local church for a marrying ceremony.

Ben moved among the mingled humanity, the male portion of which included both uniformed and civilian figures, and felt the same sort of disgust that he himself roused in many who saw him. Curious as it seemed, Ben was a highly moralistic man where women were concerned. Had one of the white-clad, Bible-and-soup women stumbled onto this illegal, sprawling iniquity den, the disapproval she would have felt would have been no more severe than that being felt by Ben Scarlett. Her shock, perhaps, would have been greater, but not her disapproval.

A hand brushed Ben's arm; he turned and looked into the smiling face of a wrinkled, overly painted woman with bad breath and a yellow wig. "Looking for some love, mister?"

He pulled away from her, disgusted. "No, I'm not." He was about to tell her to go away, but remembered why he had come. "Is your name Nectar Childs?"

"No, honey, no." She didn't seem at all offended by his rebuff. Unattractive as she was, she probably received plenty. "I'm Babylon, and I live up to my name. Nectar, she ain't here. Me, I am." She reached out to stroke his arm again.

"Where would I go to find Nectar Childs?"

"She's in her rooms," Babylon said. "I'll leave it to you to find them. It's not my job to serve as a directory for her business."

Ben was not dismayed; he knew already where her room was.

"Forget Nectar," the painted face said. "It's me who can give you memories worth keeping."

He didn't want her. She sickened him. And he knew how to drive her off. "Hold my hand," he said, and extended his left arm. Without looking, she reached down for the hand but closed her hand around the rounded stump where the hand would have been. She looked down, her face filling with repulsion, and she pulled away, turned away. Good riddance as far as Ben was concerned. She lost herself in the crowd and he headed for the door.

He was relieved to be out of the place, glad to be out of its flaring, shadow-casting lights, out of its damp and piercing human stench. For once he, the embodiment of foul human smells, had encountered a rankness even he couldn't abide.

It was late; he did not want to be caught on the streets. With the utmost care he wound his way through alleys and passages and yards through a town he was coming to know increasingly well, until he reached the alleyway that led down to the street below where he'd been sent on his way by the soldier guarding the storefront. He wondered if the soldier, or some other, was guarding the spot tonight.

There was a soldier there, but because he was approaching through the alley, he was hidden from the sentinel's view. He climbed up the stairs very slowly, trying not to make them creak, and reached the closed door of the upper-story rooms. He closed his eyes, swallowed, said a prayer for Angel, and rapped very softly.

The door opened a few moments later and a woman looked back at him. In the way she painted herself, she was much like the woman who had disgusted him back in that dive, but this one was younger and not so ruined-looking, not so foul and spoiled. There was about her something that might have been pretty as recently as a year or two back. Whatever that something was, it was used up now. All this he noticed, but what he noticed most of all was that she had obviously been crying.

"I'm not receiving callers tonight, mister," she said softly. "Go away and come back some other time."

"Wait," he said just as she began to close the door. "Wait—I'm not here for what you think. I've come for news about somebody you know. Somebody I know, too."

She looked cautious. "Who?"

"Angel Beamish."

Her face changed. She began to close the door again. He put his foot out and blocked it.

"You stop that!" she whispered sharply. "Stop that or I'll scream, and there's a soldier down below!"

"I just want to talk to you. I'm trying to find Angel."

"You're Murphy! I know you are! You're Joe Paul Murphy, and I want nothing to do with you, not after the way you treated poor Angel!"

"I ain't no Joe Paul Murphy. I never heard of no Joe Paul Murphy. My name's Scarlett, Ben Scarlett, and there was a time I was engaged to be married to—"

He didn't have time to finish the sentence. The woman trembled and went limp, clinging to the door. He reacted just in time to step in and catch her. He half carried, half dragged her to a sofa on the other side of the room, went back and closed the door, and returned to her.

The fainting moment had been fleeting. Already she was on her feet, facing him. "You're Ben Scarlett? *The* Ben Scarlett? The Ben Scarlett who Angel was going to marry once upon a time?"

"Yes. And I've come all the way from Knoxville, looking for her." He fumbled in his pocket and pulled out the picture. "Because of this. I recognized her."

Nectar Childs took the picture—he noted the shaking of

her hands—and studied it. Her eyes filled with tears. "Yes, yes, that is Angel! I remember the day this picture was made. She and I, we went together, to the picture man, and he made lots of pictures of both of us. Some not so bad, like this one. Others . . . different, and worse. Oh, Angel! Dear Angel! How I wish you could be here! How I wish you could!"

"Where is she, Miss Childs? Still in Kentucky?"

She looked at him as tears began to stream down her face. Her lip quivered and it was a moment before she spoke. "She talked about you so much, Mr. Scarlett. She said you were so fine a man, so kind and good of heart, and how she wished she had married you all those years ago. She said it was drinking that made her not marry you."

"Yes," he said, fighting the urge to cry himself. The emotional intensity in the room was hot and overwhelming, the Cyprian's sorrow contagious even if he didn't know why. "Yes, it was my drinking. My drinking . . . my fault we never married."

"Oh, Ben, I feel like I know you. She talked about you so much! And the look of you . . . you're like I pictured you. Older, more rugged and tired, but your eyes, they're the eyes I knew would be Ben Scarlett's eyes. So gentle and kind!"

Now his tears did come, and an intuition. "She's dead," he said. It wasn't a question.

"Yes. She's dead. She died on the boat as we first reached Louisville. I was with her, and she talked about you. She was so sick at the end, out of her head. They never should have put her on that boat, sick as she was. She didn't want to go, but they made her. She got worse and worse, and at the end she was saying that she should have stayed in Nashville, because Ben Scarlett was coming for her there. She said you would come and take her away and marry her, and it would be like it should have been. She wouldn't have to sell herself anymore. She wouldn't have to be ashamed. I thought it was surely just the fever, nothing but foolish fever babble from a dying woman . . . but it wasn't, was it? You're here! She *knew*. Somehow she just *knew*."

He turned and leaned against the wall, hiding his face. The sorrow was welling up powerfully inside him, he knew he was going to lose control, and was ashamed for a woman to see him cry.

Chapter 30

Neither Ben nor Nectar Childs slept that night. They stayed up, huddling on the couch by the light of a single candle, then by no light at all when the candle burned out, and talked about Angel Beamish and themselves.

Many a long year had passed since the day Angel had told Ben that their engagement could not continue because of his growing tendency to drink excessively. He begged, pleaded, cried on his knees, promised to put away liquor forever, but Angel had been staunch. Her father and three of her uncles had been slaves of alcohol, and she knew the signs of it. They were all there in Ben Scarlett, and she could not have anything to do with him.

With Angel gone, Ben had seen no reason not to yield to the inner demon voice that urged him to drink. He became the very thing Angel had feared he would, and which he'd sworn he would never be: a full-fledged, addicted drunkard. From then on alcohol had ruled him almost entirely, with only occasional periods of shaking off its chains, and then only temporarily. He had never known what became of Angel; all he knew was that she left Knoxville after their engagement was broken. From then on he'd neither seen nor heard anything of her until the day he found the picture of her in the wallet of Curtis Delmer.

Nectar did not know the full biography of Angel Beamish, who was already an established prostitute, like Nectar herself, when they met. Angel was at first very quiet about her life, Nectar told Ben, but over time began to reveal a few details. Like the life details of so many women who fell into this ancient but tragic way of life, Angel's were details of difficulty and poverty, abuse by men who claimed to love her but didn't really know how. The worst of them had been a man named Joe Paul Murphy, whom Angel implied might have been a husband of hers at one time, whether legitimately or common-law, Nectar did not know. Murphy had beaten her badly; it was he who led her into prostitution. Angel escaped him, only to be found twice, once in Chattanooga, once in Atlanta. Since coming to Nashville, she hadn't seen him, but lived in fear of his return, and talked about him much.

But she had talked even more about Ben Scarlett, Nectar said. Especially lately, when sickness had come. Angel Beamish had said that she was wrong to reject Ben those years back, that had she gone ahead and married him, life would have been good for both of them.

Toward the end she developed a notion that somehow Ben would come to her again and make everything well. The years would be erased, the past washed clean.

Ben listened, tears coming frequently. When Nectar was finished telling all she knew, she closed her mouth and silence reigned awhile, she and Ben sitting side by side, staring across the dark room. Occasionally Ben would sniff and wipe at his eyes.

"How'd you lose the hand?" Nectar asked after a bit.

"I was fleeing toward Kentucky, running from the war," he said. "I cut it along the way and it mortified. Some stampeders come along and cut it off for me, and I suppose that's the only reason I'm still alive."

"You must be Union, if you was running North."

"I ain't Union or reb. I ain't nothing at all but me, trying to get by. I'm pretty sorry and no-'count, Nectar. It's a good thing that Angel broke off from me. I wouldn't have been good for her."

"If you'd married, you wouldn't have turned out sorry."

"Maybe not. I guess you can't never know some things, can you?"

"What will you do now, Ben? You've come all this way for Angel, and she's dead."

"I don't know what I'll do. I'll figure out something. What'll you do?"

"Just keep on like I am. It's the only life I know."

"It ain't a good life, Nectar. It'll kill you. Kills your soul and your body, too. Just like the life I live."

"You ever wonder if there's anything better? Anything that's really good?"

"I know there is. There's times that I've woke up in the night, and looked out . . . ah, it sounds foolish to speak it."

"No. Tell me."

"Well . . . I've looked out into the night, when everything's sleeping except me, and the moon's shining down, and such times as that I've felt the keenest kind of pang and wanting, you know. It's a wanting and aching that's so strong it hurts, yet you don't want the hurting to stop. Just a hot sort of longing for you don't know what, something that's good and pure and real, even though you don't know at all what it is and know you'll probably never really find it. Yet you know that, find it or not, it's *there*, and it's *real*, and if you don't ever find it yourself, at least somebody's going to. There. I told you it sounded foolish. You ain't never felt nothing like that, have you?"

"Maybe. I don't know. But it don't sound foolish. I'm glad you told me."

They sat silently for the next hour, when light began to spill in through the window. Ben, lost in deep and solemn thoughts, glanced to the side and saw that Nectar was asleep. He smiled sadly at her, reached over and patted her hand, and slipped out into the rising day, a hollow and sad man, missing a woman he hadn't seen in many years and never would again.

• • •

Ben was down near the river some days later when the *Ivanhoe* came back into dock and spilled out its bedraggled female cargo. At long last the inevitable had occurred, and the boat that was to have rid Nashville of its most ingrained vice had hauled the practitioners of that vice right back again. Ben watched the women as they passed. Some were laughing and joking crudely with the people who had gathered to watch them, others seemed weary and were quiet, staring straight ahead as they toted their carpetbags along the dock. Not a one of them, even the laughing ones, seemed happy.

Ben looked at every Cyprian face, hoping that somehow Nectar was wrong and Angel would turn up among the returnees, but she didn't. He hadn't really expected she would.

For the rest of that day Ben Scarlett existed in a state he had never experienced before. The deepest kind of contemplation fell upon him, taking away all desire for food, sleep, even liquor. He was able to step back from himself, view himself in an objective and dispassionate fashion and see clearly all the things he had tended to deny or ignore. What he saw made him ashamed, but this was a calm, objective kind of shame, a simple acceptance of the truth, and realization that he must not deny it any longer.

By the time darkness came he knew he stood at a crossroads, and that the path he chose would decide his fate once and for all. There had been a time when he had a chance for happiness with Angel, but he chose wrongly and lost it, and her. More than that, he lost the privilege of giving himself to Angel as her anchor and supporter, thereby providing her the basis for a life better than she had known. It hurt him to think of Angel having lived as she had, being beaten by this Murphy fellow and abused and degraded by God only knew how many men. The woman who had once seemed to him the epitome of all that was virtuous and good in womanhood had prostituted herself, lowered herself to a lifestyle he wouldn't have even wanted her to be aware of . . . and his neglect of the right and embracing of the wrong had contributed much to it.

He roamed the city by night, hiding from humanity, evading the patrols and the sentinels. In an alley he found a drunkard passed out, a bottle with a few shot glasses worth of cheap whiskey in it still gripped in his hand. The craving came and Ben slipped up to the fellow, took the bottle, and crept away.

At the end of the alley he lifted the bottle to his lips, but did not drink. He stared at the rim of the bottleneck for the longest time, then turned the bottle slowly up and watched the whiskey spill out onto the ground. It was the hardest thing he had ever done, but when the bottle was empty, he felt emotion rise inside, and it drove him to his knees, sobbing. He tossed the bottle away and put his single hand across his face.

"Oh God, oh Jesus, I'm so sorry!" he said. "I'm sorry about so many things, about everything. I didn't mean to live the life you gave me like I have. I didn't mean to become a drunk. I didn't mean to turn my back on everything that's good and take the bad and sinful in its place. I'm sorry, Lord. I'm sorry. I hope you'll please excuse me. I didn't mean to do it."

He wept until he was dry, then rose and headed to his hidden shed to sleep.

Part V

INVASION

Part V

Chapter 31

Confederate-held Cumberland Gap on
the Tennessee-Kentucky border

Julius Killefer had struggled against depression many a
time since coming to Cumberland Gap, where he served
in a light artillery company under the overall command of
General Archibald Gracie. Today was the worst. He stood
in formation with his fellow soldiers, many of them conscripts just as he was, and watched Mickey Cossit being led
toward a post erected in the center of a clearing. Poor
Mickey. He was trying hard to look courageous, but the fear
showed through. Julius wanted to close his eyes, but this
wasn't allowed. The soldiers, conscripts especially, were
here to see what happened to reluctant soldiers who made
the mistake of trying to run.

At the post they pulled Mickey's shirt from him and
exposed his white skin to the sun. Julius marveled at how
much weight Mickey's frame had shed; he had never known
a fellow could drop so many pounds in so short a time. But
who could hope to maintain any kind of frame when so often
the soldiers had to live on no more than a quarter pound of
poor bacon a week, and a bit of cornmeal and flour, along
with a bit of rice if they were lucky? Even the mountain

boys who had come into service already gangly living skeletons had lost pounds living on Confederate army fare.

Julius would not have expected Mickey Cossit, of all people, to try to run away. Mickey had always acted very frightened of rebel authority and had worried not only over every word he spoke, but every word he heard. Anything that sounded remotely seditious, mutinous, or even merely complaining, he had shied away from out of fear that reprisal would come down. Julius had expected Mickey to stick out his service until the end. But something had snapped within him, making him yield to the desire that burned in varying degrees within the breast of every conscripted soldier: the drive to run away.

A couple of other conscripts made their own earlier runs successfully. Mickey wasn't so fortunate. He was caught by a rebel patrol less than three miles from the point of desertion, lost in the woods.

Julius was relieved when he learned that Mickey would escape the punishment sometimes doled out to deserters: shooting by a firing squad in the presence of the entire company. He had hoped that Mickey would get by with the mildest punishment for deserters: ninety days on a ball-and-chain in the guardhouse, living on bread and water. Mickey wasn't that fortunate, however. He was to be whipped here today on the bare back, thirty-nine hard lashes with a leather strap about an inch wide. Such whippings broke the skin and left a man's back scarred for life.

Mickey was made to turn and wrap his arms around the post; his hands were lashed together at the wrists. Now Julius filled with a true dread. The whipping would be administered by one of the company. The punisher would be chosen by the lieutenant who was overseeing the unit in the temporary absence of the captain, who had gone to Knoxville. Julius knew the lieutenant didn't like him and was aware of his friendship with Cossit. He feared, intuited, suspected to the point of near certainty, that when the lieutenant passed down the line of soldiers to select the inflicter of the lash, he would stop before him.

The officer moved slowly down the line, whipping strap in hand, looking each soldier in the face. Julius stared straight ahead, watching the lieutenant only in his peripheral vision.

Out at the whipping post Cossit bit his lip and struggled to maintain his composure.

The lieutenant reached Julius and stopped. He stared into Julius's face, smiling slightly. The wait went on endlessly. Julius's heart hammered, but he refused to show any of his feelings on his face. "I believe I've found our man," the lieutenant said. "This whipping will be administered by . . . you." He handed the strap to the man beside Julius.

Julius felt such a wave of relief that he actually feared he would lose control of his bladder. But as the lieutenant and his unhappy designee walked together toward the waiting Cossit, Julius forgot himself and thought of his poor friend. He wished Cossit hadn't tried to desert; he knew now that even if his own sense of honor didn't keep him here, fear of punishment would. Despite all temptation to the contrary, he would never dare try to run away.

Cossit held out for the first three strikes of the lash. His body jerked with each slash of the leather and his eyes squeezed closed. On the fourth blow the flesh broke and he bit through his lip and drew blood. The screaming started on the seventh strike, and Julius stood there, light-headed and miserable, longing for it to be over and hoping he would not faint before it was.

That evening, Julius found time to read again a letter he had received in an attitude of joy two days before. Reception of mail was a time of excitement for all the soldiers at Cumberland Gap, for it came rarely. Newspapers made it in almost never. Julius had come to see that those fighting a war were often the poorest informed about its progress.

The letter was from Richard Weston, and the joy Julius felt upon receiving it was replaced by deep gloom when he read what it had to say. Why he was rereading the letter now, after such a sorrowful and depressing day, was something he couldn't have explained. Perhaps the misery of watching his friend lashed into unconsciousness demanded even more misery to keep it company.

He unfolded the letter and read it by the fading glow of twilight:

Dear Julius,

I hope this letter reaches you and finds you in good spirits
and health at the Cumberland Gap. Though we regretted
your wrongful conscription, we are pleased you were sent
there instead of to the sickly south country, from where
so many come back with the malary fever and such.

We bear you sad news. Your sister-in-law Susan is
dead, having hung herself. You were right about her
being off in her mind, for we often saw much sign of that
in the days after you were gone. She grew worse and
worse and talked often of a great weight of guiltiness
that bore on her, and when at last she took her life in the
barn, she left behind a letter telling what the guilt was
over, and I am sorry to tell that it was over the murder of
her husband. I am sorry to give you news in this way that
the brother whose welfare brung you to Tennessee and
into all this trouble, is dead by his wife's own hand. Also
the child of his loins. Susan wrote in her letter of death
that she had murdered both of them, and we are deep distressed to know this terrible thing.

She was a sad and wicked woman, and we grieve not
so much for her physical dying but for the dying of her
goodness and spirit that must have come first to allow
her to do such evil as she did.

Other than our suffering in this tragic affair we are all
well and good. Farewell Julius and know we keep you in
prayers and thoughts. We pray the soon end of this war
and that you will return well to your home, and we hope
as well that after that you will come and visit us when
you can.

                                    Yours very truly,
                                    Richard Weston & family

Julius folded the letter and put it back into the envelope.
Here at the day's close, with the sorrow of what he'd witnessed today mingling with the deeper sorrow of the news the
letter had brought him, Julius could understand how it was
that people sometimes ended their own lives, as Susan had.

Susan . . . the mere mental voicing of the name filled him
with fury. What could make a woman so wicked that she

would kill her own husband? And beyond that, and worse, her own child? It was inconceivable.

Julius thought about his parents, wondering how they would respond when they learned the truth. It might be enough to kill his father.

He looked at the darkening sky, longing for the war to end.

Old Forge region, near Elizabethton, Tennessee

Greeley Brown was more pleased than he would have been willing to admit. The damage his reputation had suffered after the theft of the money from his letter pouch hadn't been as insurmountable as he'd feared. After his return from the North Carolina mountains and all that unpleasant dutiful effort involving Nanny Josiah and her baby—an affair he resented more deeply each time he looked at his arm stump and realized how much the whole sorry business had cost him—he returned here to his Carter County home area and, with Sam, began recruitment of a new band of stampeders, expecting at the beginning to have much difficulty finding folks who would trust him. To his surprise, he found that his reputation, though damaged, had substantially regenerated itself, like a burned-over forest giving forth new life from what looks like a ruined landscape.

Or maybe it was the increasing desperation of the Unionists of East Tennessee that rejuvenated his career. The more time that passed, the more days and nights men had to spend hidden within their own home regions out of fear of the overlording rebels, the less particular they became about how they managed to get out and over to the Union lines. The eleven men now gathered by darkness at the same place from which he'd launched his last stampeder run with Spencer Cline, Ivy McDermott, and crew, were men who did not look like they could bear to stay another day where they were. Most astonishing, and relieving, to Greeley was that one of them, Henry Millwright Jr., known to all as Young Henry to distinguish him from his father, Big Henry, was the engaged beau of none other than lanky, hot-tempered July

Frakes, who was now hanging all over his neck and wetting his face with tears and slobbery kisses. Greeley didn't envy young Young Henry at all, July being far from an attractive young woman. But he did feel generally positive toward July at the moment, because earlier she had come to him, apologized for all the things she'd said during their last meeting, and told him she believed again that he was a trustworthy and good man. Greeley had actually been forced to wipe away a sincere tear when he heard that.

Before the stampeders set off, Greeley was the unwilling recipient of one of July Frakes's wet kisses. Weeping and intense, she put her hands on his shoulders, looked him in the eye and said, "Once again I want you to know how sorry I am that I accused you of being a sorry thief because of that money that went missing. I was wrong, I now feel sure. I believe in you again, Mr. Brown, and I want you to keep a close eye on my dear Young Henry while he's in your care."

"I will."

"Because if anything should happen to Young Henry, my life wouldn't be worth living."

"I'll be careful with him."

"And also because if anything should happen to him, I swear I'll hunt you down like a hen-killing fox and slice your throat wide open, ear to ear, and spit right down your neck."

"I believe you would do that, July. I really do."

They set off at last, the loved ones who had come to see them off returning to their homes, weeping in handkerchiefs and on sleeves.

"Will we make it safe, Mr. Brown?"

"Yes, Young Henry. We will if there's a thing I can do to make sure of it. In all my piloting runs I've lost only one man, and he killed himself accidental, running on a sharp stob in the darkness, thinking the rebels were chasing him. It shows the importance of keeping your wits about you. The man who runs from a true threat is wise, but the one who runs from phantoms is a fool, and sometimes a dead fool."

They headed on through the clear and windy night. Greeley glanced over, just to see Sam Colter at his side again. It had been too long since he'd been able to do that. It was good.

Chapter 32

They traveled fourteen miles that night, crossed the railroad tracks with great caution, and found a well-overgrown hollow in some woods to make a hidden camp come daylight. It was the month of August, and the Tennessee woods were dense and at places almost impenetrable, much more so than during Greeley's prior stampede run. Tennessee was that way: open woods and meadows in the spring and early summer, thick, junglelike mats of undergrowth by the summer's end. Where a man might pass with ease in June, he might have to hack a path through in August.

Greeley was pleased that his men passed the day without complaint in their brushy hollow. Many stampeders he had led complained like fussy children before they put five miles behind them. If this band held true to their present form all the way to the end, it might be one of the best and easiest stampedes yet, despite the fact that their number, with himself and Sam included, came to an unlucky thirteen.

Night fell and they proceeded, carrying their knapsacks between their shoulder blades and trudging along steadily and with little talk. Ten miles fell behind, then ten more, then another three or four, before they finally were at the

White Oak Flats with day just starting to break. Again they found a hidden place to camp and settled down to rest.

They were feeling the trail's effects. Young Henry's feet were badly blistered from walking in boots, passed down to him by Big Henry, that were a half size or so too large. There was no spring or stream nearby in which he could bathe his feet, and what water they had was in canteens and bottles and had to be preserved for drinking. Others were blistered and sore as well, and covered with briar scratches, and Holcombe Rankin griped so much about his aching leg muscles that Greeley was finally compelled to tell him to shut up and get some sleep.

They did sleep, being exhausted. Greeley was first to awaken. He roused them as the sun went down. They ate a bit of food, tightened up their footwear as best they could, and set out. Farther on they reached a stream and Greeley allowed them a few minutes to stop and wash themselves. Young Henry and Holcombe Rankin bathed their feet in the rushing water and declared it did them a world of good.

The terrain through which they passed next was extremely overgrown. Mosquitoes were troublesome. Greeley was displeased with their slow progress, but somehow they finally did reach the Holston River, where they stripped down, bundled up their clothing on sticks—Greeley used his rifle—and crossed over far too slowly to suit any of them. Greeley Brown never felt more vulnerable than when crossing a river with a bunch of stampeders, all naked as jays, in rebel country. When they reached the other side they came out, raced into the trees, and pulled on their clothing, cursing trousers that adhered to wet legs and struggled not to be pulled up.

They pressed on, drying out as they went, and reached the base of Clinch Mountain as the sun came up. Sheltered from view by the trees on the mountain spur, they continued traveling on up the slope until they reached a spot Greeley had encamped a time or two before. Though surrounded by trees, it was open to the sky, and the sun shone brightly in, warm and soothing. A few men ate, but most fell asleep almost at once, including Greeley. He pulled his hat down over his face and began to softly snore, so tired he forgot to mention to the others that they should take care to cover their own faces to avoid sunburn.

So of course most of them didn't cover their faces, and awakened in the afternoon with red and blistering countenances. Greeley had a little container of grease with him and shared it with them, having them smear their burned skin. Not a man had escaped some ill effect of exposure. Those who had no sunburn did not escape a hoarsening of their voices from sleeping on the bare ground.

By sundown they had eaten and were ready to go on. They crossed Little Poor Valley, Copper Ridge, Copper Creek, and an endless expanse of fields and cattle trails and hills and woods, until finally the night-blackened waters of the Clinch River rolled before them. Again they stripped and plunged in, and Greeley was halfway across before he realized that this time they might not be able to make it.

The water was swift and high; Greeley had to push up on his toes just to keep contact with the bottom. Young Henry, being shorter than Greeley—and far shorter than his fiancée—actually went under a couple of times and washed down the river and out of view, leaving Greeley to ponder frightening images of July Frakes slicing open his throat and spitting down his neck. But on the other side of the river they set up a frantic search and found that Young Henry had made it across in safety, washing up a hundred yards downstream from where he walked back up to meet the others.

They trudged until daylight began to pale the sky. By the first light Greeley saw, upon a road they had just reached, signs of a large number of horses having recently passed. Rebel cavalry, he was sure. He pointed out the sign to the others and it served the effect he wanted: Weariness seemed to vanish and they desired to put more distance behind them. On they proceeded, reaching the Powell Mountain spurs as the sun edged higher and full daylight came.

As before at Clinch Mountain, they continued on past daylight, making it all the way to the top of the mountain before finally giving in to weariness and settling down for a little food and a lot of rest. The journey was beginning to wear on them, body and nerve, but Greeley encouraged them by pointing out how close to Kentucky they now were.

The men made the best beds they could of leaves, knapsacks, and coats, and settled down for slumber, making sure
this time to stay out of the direct sun.

The coming of night sent them down the far side of the
mountain—a difficult effort because of the amazingly dense
laurel thickets that grew on the mountain slopes. No
humanly designed maze could have posed a harder challenge to a night-traveling band who could stay together only
with great effort under the best of conditions. Greeley kept
losing men, forcing a halt to progress while a search was
made, soft "Hallooo!" calls going out, vocal beacons raised
to be answered by the straying ones, until finally they would
be together again and proceed for a few more minutes until
someone else became lost and the whole process had to be
repeated.

Finally they made it through the laurel and down to the
mountain base. At Wildcat Valley they paused while Greeley
went ahead, looking for any evidence of potential trouble.
He saw none, returned, and they pressed forward again. At
Wallin's Ridge they encountered brush even thicker than
what had tormented and teased them coming down the
mountainside, and even Greeley was hard pressed to generate the will to attempt the climb by night. But they did
attempt it, and succeeded, though with hardly an inch of any
man left unabraded by the time they made the ridge top.

Moving along the top of the ridge for a while, they then
turned down it and headed for Powell Valley. The nearer
they came to the valley, the more they heard the barking of
dogs. Dogs . . . Greeley had come to hate them, thanks to
this valley. He would gladly take a shotgun to every dog he
could find, just to punish the species for all the trouble it had
caused him on stampeder runs.

Dogs aside, they were unmolested, and reached Powell
River quicker than expected. But the night was growing
old and short; they plunged into the water without pausing
to remove clothing, for there was no time to waste, and
once across, kept right on going, trailing great streams
behind them.

They were at the foot of Cumberland Mountain when
light came. Greeley was as gratified as he was weary; they

had made quite a fine run the past night. Climbing the mountainside by morning light, they turned and looked at the valley behind them, and saw from the smoke of morning cook fires evidence of a remarkable number of rebel encampments in the region they had just crossed. They had managed to blindly weave their way between camps without detection, and Greeley breathed a prayer of thanks for providential protection.

In a hidden spot on the mountain they sat down and ate the last of their provisions. Weary, torn, blistered, out of food, they were, even so, happy men. Cumberland Mountain was the most welcome of landmarks, the final barrier between them and Kentucky, and no one was in the humor for a long rest. "A few hours of sleep, and we'll get up and go on in," Greeley said. "And I believe we can consider ourselves pretty safe from the rebel threat right now. First time in many a month for most of you that you can say that, huh?"

They slept longer than they'd planned, but set off as soon as they awakened, passing from Tennessee into Harlan County, Kentucky, in the waning afternoon. They walked a few miles in, rejoicing to know they were away from Confederate-held lands. At length they settled down to sleep again, and passed a long night of much needed rest.

Greeley dreamed. He saw himself with a wife and a yardful of children, the youngest of whom he was tossing in the air and catching. He had two arms, two hands. It was a good dream, better than the reality to which he awakened all too soon.

Moving through Harlan County, they sought food from the locals but found it hard to come by. The people here were impoverished by raiders and others who had come by, taking from them what they wanted, but the Unionists among them shared what they could with Greeley and his men. It was far from enough.

Any of the men would have happily paid an exorbitant

price for a good horse or mule, now that they were past the rebel country and it wasn't necessary to be afoot for reasons of hiding and safety. It was all airy and hypothetical, however, in that hardly a horse or mule was to be seen. The livestock here in earlier times had been taken long ago by rebel raiders, and now ate grain in military stock pens in Powell Valley, or in some cases sizzled on the skillets of camp cooks.

"How far will you and Mr. Colter go with us, Greeley?" Young Henry asked.

"We'll stay with you at least as far as Manchester," he said. "From here I'd guess that's about seventy, eighty more miles. And there's a stop I'll need to make along the way, at the Greasy Fork. A family name of Killefer I need to call on."

"Friends of yours?"

"In a way. I conducted a young man of that family back into Tennessee earlier this year. He was looking for a brother who had gone missing. I've not seen nor heard from him since we parted, and I'm hoping that I'll find him safe and sound back home again."

The Killefer house looked ominously empty and silent as Greeley approached it alone. He felt the eyes of his men upon him, hidden and watching from the forest.

"Hello! Hello the house! It's a friend come to call, Killefers!"

No one answered. Greeley looked closely and saw that the front door was ajar. He strode across the clearing, squinting, trying to see into shadows and making sure he did nothing that looked threatening. Maybe the Killefers weren't here for some reason. Maybe no one was. Or maybe somebody besides the Killefers was in the house.

"Hello!"

He walked up more quickly, sure now no one was there. Pausing on the porch, he looked in through the slightly open door and saw a house that was for the most part empty. But not empty as if someone had moved out and taken their things with them. A few items of furniture remained, and a few dishes. This house was empty in the way a place was when it has simply been abandoned and various passersby and neighbors have helped themselves to whatever desirable goods remained, leaving the rest.

He pushed open the door, looking in on a dwelling obviously not occupied by humans for weeks. Something bumped about near the fireplace; he looked, and was startled by the vaguely human visage of a 'possum looking back at him in the somnolent manner of that creature.

"Howdy, 'possum. You seen the Killefers?"

He stepped back onto the porch, rubbing his chin. A glance down made him freeze. A dark stain marred the porch wood outside the door. He knew this kind of stain. Only blood left a mark like that.

"Caesar Augustus. I don't like the look of this at all."

He returned to his men and told them what he'd found. "These are folks I can't ignore. They were a help to me once, and I need to see what's happened to them. And young Julius, I'd like to know if he's come to harm in particular. I consider him a friend."

"What do you want us to do?" Sam Colter asked.

"Go to the house. Wait for me there. I'll go up to where Oman Killefer hides as an outlier, see if he's there. Don't be startled when you go in the house, by the way—there's a 'possum in there. Kill it if you want and we'll cook him up. Don't let anybody see you in there, though. There may yet be rebels in this countryside."

A few minutes later Greeley climbed along a path he'd last trod with the gun of Julius Killefer's mother aimed at his back. He didn't expect to find Oman Killefer in his hiding hollow. An instinct told him he was alone, that in some way the Killefers had come to harm, and that the bloodstain on the porch had some connection with it.

He stood at the head of the hollow and looked for signs of life. None. Advancing cautiously, just in case his instinct was wrong, he descended and approached the place where he'd first met Oman and Julius Killefer. He found their tent, broken down under a fallen limb. No one was inside and there were no marks to indicate anything other than animal life had roamed about the tent recently.

The Killefers were gone, no doubt about it. The bloodstain made Greeley figure that gone in this case meant dead. The enemies from whom Oman Killefer had been hiding must have gotten to him at last.

Greeley hoped they hadn't gotten Julius, too. Julius had probably made it back to Kentucky long ago, he figured. But he hoped he was somewhere else, safe, and that whatever ill had befallen his parents had managed to miss him.

They spent the night in the Killefer house and ate the 'possum for supper. Young Henry caught a couple of rats inside a cabinet and they talked about eating them, too, but no one had the stomach for it except Greeley, who had eaten rat a time or two when it was either that or starve. He decided not to do it this time, though, as the very notion seemed to disgust a couple of the men very badly, and the Killefers' apparent bad fortune had taken the edge off his appetite anyway.

They left the house by morning light and reached the Red Bird River, where Greeley found a man with food and supplies to sell. Though the price was high, Greeley paid it, and the men set out with spirits lifted because of the weight of new edibles in their haversacks.

Manchester, however, seemed a very long way off, and though they traveled hard, they made unsatisfying progress. Night found them deep in a remote, wild area, but they saw the light of a cabin in the trees and made for it.

Greeley approached it alone to begin with, spoke with the occupant, then returned to call up his men. "I've found us a place to stay tonight, and some supper . . . though I ain't sure I'm glad I found it."

"Why's that?" Sam asked.

"You'll see for yourself once you come in."

Two things greeted them when they entered the cabin door, the first being one of the most foul, organic smells that ever hung about a human habitation, the other the sight of a woman who was hardly identifiable as such.

She was old, though how old was hard to tell, and she sat beside her fireplace with a pipe made of corncob and reed stuck in her gums. Her mouth was a collapsed, lipless line in a face ridged with deep wrinkles and occasional hairy warts. Her hair was a mat of gray bristles, probably not washed in years, maybe never combed in her life. On her face was a crust of dirt that had become one with her and thickening down her neck to disappear under the ragged frock she wore. The frock was worn away at the bottom and the two thick legs that poked out beneath it revealed the same kind of dirty crust that covered her face. Her calves and ankles were the color of rust and scarred from the bites of many years' worth of fleas.

"Howdy," she said.

"Howdy," the intimidated group murmured back in rough chorus.

"My name's Nazareth Duck. Them there . . ." Here she indicated two equally befouled daughters, in their teens, who had stood until then unnoticed in the shadows, and now stepped forward into the light. ". . . are my girls. That one's Bethlehem. The other's Jerusalem."

"Howdy," the men murmured. The girls, very fat and filthy, wore terribly thin dresses and no underfrocks. What was revealed was enough to give blindness a good name. They eyed Sam in a way that made his skin crawl.

"The Ducks have said they'll see to our lodging tonight," Greeley said.

"Is there a Mr. Duck about?" one of the men asked.

"He's dead," Jerusalem Duck said in a flat and lifeless voice.

"In other words, the Duck has quacked," one of the stampeders whispered to another.

"He got drunk one night and choked to death in his vomit," the old woman said around her pipe stem.

Greeley eyed the two daughters and thought back to the fine-looking young women who had inhabited that cabin in Powell Valley where he and his followers had stayed the evening Spencer Cline died. It only went to show how varied were the fortunes of a stampeder pilot.

He had no idea whether Nazareth Duck had any notion of why this band of men was roaming in the night. She didn't seem to care, and whether or not she favored the Union was something Greeley was willing not to care about in turn, so long as she gave them what they needed. "Needed" was the proper word in this case. There was absolutely nothing inside this reeking cabin that any sane man could want.

The meal was horrendous. One skinny chicken, fried insufficiently in grease that had a strange, wild, gamey, thoroughly unpalatable flavor, provided the only meat. The balance of the food was corn bread made of spoiled and bug-filled meal, and mushy cabbage cooked, unwashed, with plenty of dirt on the leaves and a platoon of fat worms still inside. It was enough to make those two rats in the cupboard back at the empty Killefer cabin seem not so unappetizing to the stampeders after all.

Greeley, picking the worms from his cabbage and feeding them to the dozen or so dogs and puppies that circled the table throughout the meal, mentioned that he knew a family name of Killefer over about the Greasy Fork. Were the Ducks familiar with them?

Just then a new rank odor wafted across the table, mixing with all the others. "Warn't me!" Bethlehem Duck said, eyes flitting from side to side.

"It *was* you," Jerusalem said. "I heerd it."

"Warn't!" Bethlehem drew back a fist and knocked her sister onto the floor, then turned and began kicking her with bare feet.

"You gals, you quit that *now*!" the old woman bellowed, and the fight ceased at once. Jerusalem Duck got up and sat down beside her sister as if nothing had happened, and both went back to their wormy cabbage.

"I do know the Killefers, or did," Nazareth Duck said. "A sad tale."

"Why sad?" Greeley asked.

"They're dead," she said. "Killed by nobody knows who, right in their homes."

Greeley's stomach began to hurt, and not from the food. "Bushwhackers?"

"May well be. Nobody knows. They found him on the porch in his blood, the woman around back in the yard."

"Just them two? No more?"

"Just them two. They had two boys, but the eldest left home long ago, and the younger ain't been around for weeks and weeks. I heard it rumored he'd gone to Tennessee, looking for the older boy. Ain't nobody seen him since, far as I know."

Greeley shook his head, swallowing hard, feeling a knot in his belly that threatened to make his gorge rise any moment. "I'm sorry they're dead. They seemed good people."

"Oman Killefer prided himself on being a man of honor."

"I know. I know."

"Friends of yours, were they?"

"I knew them. Never had time to get to know them well."

The stampeders spent the night on the floor without cover, though beds and blankets were available. The beds crawled visibly with lice, and there was no question in any man's mind that bedbugs lived among the bedding folds. Morning came, and Greeley paid fifty cents per man for the food and lodging. No one was in the mood for breakfast. They set out just after daylight, glad to go.

Manchester, Kentucky

It was a most unexpected meeting.

Greeley turned at the sound of a familiar voice calling to him as he and his ragged stampeders walked through the town. Ivy McDermott was coming right for them, face as blotchy red as ever, and a crutch under his right arm. His right leg was gone from the knee down.

He came up quickly on the crutch, leaned on it and put out his right hand for Greeley to shake.

"Caesar Augustus, Mr. McDermott, what happened to your peg down yonder?"

"I took a bullet in it, first day I was out on patrol. Some sniper, probably a damned civilian with reb sympathies. Whoever they are, I hope they die soon and slow. I don't like this crutching about. It's no way for a man to live."

"Why are you in Manchester?"

"I live here now. I'm married. A widow woman. We got married only three days ago."

"I'll be! Congratulations."

"Thanks." McDermott looked around at the group. "More stampeders?"

"That's right. And this one here's a partner of mine. Sam Colter. Sam, meet Ivy McDermott."

"Pleased." They shook hands.

"You've come in at a good time," McDermott said. "There's a lot happening. Good things."

"What do you mean?"

"You ain't heard? It's happening at last, my friend: General Burnside is on the move. Has been for some days now. He left Camp Nelson on the sixteenth of the month with a good fifteen thousand or so men, heading for East Tennessee. They're going to invade, Mr. Brown. It's the day every good Union man in Tennessee has waited for. If you march quick, you might catch up with Burnside and see it all for yourself. I wish I could."

Greeley stared at his feet, then at Sam, then around at the others, all of whom stood with looks of joyous surprise on their faces.

"Caesar Augustus!" he whispered. "It's happening, men! It's happening at last!"

Chapter 33

The stampeder group broke up after the encounter with McDermott. Though all were equally thrilled with the news of Burnside's advance toward Tennessee, most of the band chose to continue on to Louisville to join the Fourth Tennessee Infantry, while Greeley, Sam Colter, Young Henry Millwright, Holcombe Rankin, and Jeremiah Neil, more adventuresome than the rest, opted to go after the advancing army itself. Greeley had waited for the liberation of East Tennessee for well over two years, and he wasn't about to miss this particular party.

As Greeley traveled southward, he did so with a lighter heart than in many a month. He felt like a boy on his birthday, or on the night before Christmas. Burnside was advancing! Every mark on the road left by the army moving unseen and ahead of them gave Greeley a burst of joy as he imagined what it would be like to walk again on native soil without fear of capture or conscription. If he'd known any steps, he might have danced down the road.

Occasionally he and his companions encountered evidence left by the advancing army, showing how difficult the march had been. There were broken vehicles, dead horses and mules, baggage of different varieties. "The mountains were hard on them," Young Henry observed.

The first Union soldiers they encountered were of the Twelfth Kentucky. Greeley gave them a big, grin-warmed greeting, and found himself and his companions promptly arrested as suspected spies. But it came around all right at the end: A brief interrogation and examination of the recruiting papers Greeley carried vindicated him and his friends, and the Twelfth Kentucky not only set them free, but filled their packs with food and supplies. They moved on.

Crossing into Tennessee, they found the army's track all the fresher. They began to meet other travelers on the way, local folks who had taken to the road in the army's wake because the soldiers had swept up every kind of forage they could as they advanced, and left the people with so little that many had decided to head into Knoxville in hope of finding refuge from the same Federal government that had just invaded them.

Greeley and his friends went to Kingston, on the Clinch River, and on to Lenoir's Station. Excitement grew. They pushed themselves almost as hard as if the rebels were chasing them, wanting to be in Knoxville when that city moved into Union hands.

Burnside's advance brought joy beyond measure to the thousands of East Tennesseans who held loyal to the Union, some openly, some secretly.

There was no joy for the rebel sympathizers of the region, however, as became very clear with the first insweep of blue-clad soldiers into Knoxville.

An advance detachment of cavalry under Colonel John W. Foster was the first to enter the city. Having crossed Cumberland Mountain at Winter's Gap, thereby bypassing the heavily guarded Cumberland Gap, Foster's Indiana soldiers made their appearance abruptly, while the people of Knoxville were distracted by an unusual problem. General Buckner's rebel soldiers had just left Knoxville, heading for Georgia and General Braxton Bragg, and in their wake a band of armed outlaws had made a raid into the city, sending the people into a state of shocked surprise and making them scramble to set up some means of defense.

Just at that moment, Foster came galloping in with his soldiers. The first man they encountered, ironically, was a Confederate sympathizing Swiss tailor named Straub, who ran from them and hid in the house of a friend. The soldiers went farther and faced down a lone civilian sentry in the midst of a street, while a gang of pro-Confederate women stood nearby and cursed them like sailors.

There were other encounters, pro-Confederates showing their spite, leading to some arrests. For a time all was quite confusing, inevitable in a war in which all contenders, except those in uniform, looked alike, sounded alike, and occasionally fudged the truth in moments when the truth might bring inconvenience.

By the time Greeley, Sam, and company reached Knoxville, confusion and hot-tempered encounters had given way to joy worthy of the advent of the millennium. Knoxville's Unionists, free at last from rebel domination, gave vent to more than two years' worth of stifled feelings, bottled emotions, smothered patriotism.

The Union soldiers, many from northern regions and unfamiliar with the South, had entered the city with little idea of what to expect. Though the overall Unionism of East Tennesseans was widely known, and in fact would soon spawn the formation of "East Tennessee relief societies" in Pennsylvania and other northern regions, few of the incoming soldiers, except those who were themselves East Tennesseans, had any notion of the level of welcome they would receive.

From the outskirts of the city on in, the Yankees were met by people who laughed, wept, sang, and waved American flags that had long been hidden under mattresses or beneath floorboards. Despite their poverty, the people brought out fruit, pies, cakes, beverages for the troops. Soldiers long away from their wives and girlfriends in northern towns and cities received more fervent feminine kisses than any that had come to them in their lonely dreams over the past months. Old men staggered out, leaning on their tottering canes with tears streaming down their faces, shaking the hands of men young enough to be their grandsons and acting as if they were the most honored of men to do so.

Greeley and Sam walked through Knoxville with grins that they couldn't have erased had there been any reason to try. The city rang with shouts: "God bless the Union!" "Three cheers for Old Glory and President Lincoln!" "God be praised, the Yankees have come!" "The old flag's back in Tennessee!" And as Greeley looked around and saw the beloved red, white, and blue banner hanging from porch rails and flying from every available pole, he could not hold back the tears. He glanced over at Sam Colter and saw that his situation was no different. Neither of them generally felt comfortable with sentimental displays. Today it hardly seemed to matter. The entire city was in tears, and if not for the cheers, laughter, and smiles that accompanied the crying, an unadvised newcomer might have thought some great tragedy had struck.

General Ambrose Burnside himself rode into Knoxville on September 3 and received a welcome worthy of a messiah. By his arrival, Knoxville was crowded not only with its regular citizenry, but also by at least half the population of the surrounding countryside. Joy was immense, almost universal, and seemingly unquenchable. Only those who had favored the Confederacy were in ill humor, hiding behind closed shutters and peeping out grumpily from behind curtains at the infuriating celebration outside.

Burnside's choice of a location for his headquarters provided a certain ironic satisfaction in itself. He moved into the vacated mansion home of John H. Crozier, at the corner of Gay and Clinch, and no one missed the fact that Crozier had been among Knoxville's leading Confederate supporters, and in fact had been one of the citizen volunteers who had helped man the defenses the day Colonel Sanders's artillery unsuccessfully hammered the town. Burnside took advantage of the balcony of the house to make speeches to the grateful citizenry. His words gave some comfort to the unhappy pro-Confederate citizens too, because he pledged fairness and accommodation even to them. Burnside's manner was warm and conciliatory. With his bushy dark sidewhiskers and balding head, Burnside made an impression not so much with looks as with his kindly but authoritative manner.

Greeley and his companions were eating at a common table in a Knoxville restaurant when they began to notice the beehive activity of an inordinate number of distracted waiters around the doors of a closed-off rear section, and realized gradually that dignitaries were surely dining back there.

"Reckon Burnside's in yonder?" Sam asked.

"Maybe," Young Henry said. "Look there . . . there comes a captain out of there. Laws! He's coming this way!"

"You fellows know him?" Greeley asked in a whisper, receiving quick head shakes in reply.

The captain approached the table and nodded. "Gentlemen." They made as if to stand, nodding greetings.

"No, no, keep your seats, and I beg pardon for the intrusion. Is one of you by chance Mr. Greeley Brown?"

"I am, sir," Greeley said, rising all the way this time.

"Mr. Brown, General Burnside is in this restaurant and has requested the opportunity to meet you, having heard that you were here."

"General Burnside wants to meet *me*?"

"That's correct. If you'll just follow me, I believe it will only take a few moments."

Greeley glanced at the others, feeling a hot nervousness that he hadn't experienced since the hour just before his marriage to his first wife years ago. He brushed a hand through his hair and wished he'd trimmed his beard. "Well . . . if the general wants to meet me, I'd surely be honored to meet him, too."

He followed the lieutenant off toward the rear room, giving one more glance back at his companions before he entered.

He came out again looking awed. Sam chuckled as Greeley slowly approached the table. "You look like Moses come down from the mountain, Greeley. What'd he say to you?"

"Not much. Just that he'd heard of me and my work, and how I'd brought in so many of the good loyal men of Tennessee to join the cause. He said he appreciated me and men like me, who've took so many risks just to give the opportunity to serve to men who otherwise would have maybe been drawed to the enemy for lack of any choice. He shook my hand, gents." Greeley lifted up his right hand and turned it, looking at it. "That hand right there, he shook it. I don't think I'll wash that hand no more. Imagine that! Me, Greeley Brown, shaking hands with Burnside himself! I wish my pappy was alive to see his boy."

"We're proud of you, Greeley," Young Henry said. "Good times, eh?"

"Good times is right. Right now I don't think there's another bad thing that could happen. What do you think about it, Sam?"

Sam shrugged. "You just never can't tell about something like that, I don't figure," he said, and went back to his food.

Chapter 34

Greeley Brown and Sam Colter stood on the railroad station platform at Knoxville and bade good-bye to the three stampeders who had followed Greeley on the trail of Burnside's army. Events had taken quite an odd turn for Young Henry Millwright, Jeremiah Neil, and Halcombe Rankin, who had anticipated only a flight into Kentucky and the Union ranks, not a celebratory expedition right back into the region they had fled.

All three, however, would still join the Union army. For all the celebration and perception of a long ordeal at last at an end, everyone realized that true liberation hadn't yet come. The rebels were driven back but not defeated, and they wouldn't relinquish East Tennessee easily.

After handshakes and farewells, Greeley and Sam boarded the train. They were oddly privileged: civilians given passage on a train hauling regular Federal troops of the 100th Ohio Regiment, who were bound for the reaches of the northeastern portion of the state. The right to accompany these soldiers had come through the efforts of Colonel James Carter of the Second Tennessee Mounted Infantry, who was among several old friends Greeley had encountered in Knoxville.

Because of his recruiting and piloting work, Greeley enjoyed a quasimilitary status, and very few strings had required pulling to give him berth on this train, and berth for Sam Colter too, at Greeley's request.

As the train chugged out of Knoxville and up the track, a spectacle much like the one that had greeted Burnside in Knoxville unveiled itself. Almost every mile of the way was lined, on both sides of the track, with joyous people, waving and shouting their welcome to the blue-clad soldiers, brandishing above their heads American flags that could now be safely flown in the open for the first time since the war commenced. The degree of Unionist sentiment displayed surprised even Greeley, and he smiled as he considered that possibly some of these joyous greeters were people who had prudently pretended sympathy for the rebel government and only now dared reveal their true feelings.

Strawberry Plains, New Market, Mossy Creek, Talbots, Panther Springs, Morristown . . . at every stop there were cheering crowds, baskets laden with fruit, pies, loaves of bread, hot biscuits—the Ohio soldiers had never received such fine treatment anywhere.

At Greeneville the train came to a stop and the soldiers spilled out to the most fiercely joyful welcome they had seen yet. Here in the seat of Greene County, one of the most staunchly Union counties in all the state, the crowd was immense and unusually vocal. People had come from all over the region and as far as western North Carolina to meet the soldiers and wave the Stars and Stripes. Only a few glum faces were seen; most of the pro-Confederate townsfolk were hiding away unseen in their houses. Greeley reflected with some ironic bitterness that those who now hid away certainly hadn't been hiding the day one Colonel Danville Leadbetter, who had been sent in by the Confederate government to rebuild the bridges burned by Unionist insurgents in November of '61, led two convicted bridge burners to an oak tree on a hill overlooking this very depot, and there hanged them before the crowd. The story went that rebel soldiers passing through the town after the hangings had paused to abuse the pitiful corpses, which remained up on display for a day or so. A warning to the Unionist populace.

At the Greeneville depot Greeley encountered several old friends, but this time it was Sam Colter, who had shaved off his beard in Knoxville and now looked more like his old self, who got the most attention. He'd worked in Greeneville in the downtown store of the late Hannibal Deacon, and most of the locals knew him personally or at least by sight. His hand was pumped heartily, his shoulder slapped by grinning men until it hurt.

"Who's that bunch yonder?" Sam asked one old friend, having noted a solemn-looking group of raggedly dressed people standing near the station platform, leading an ancient mule laden with a few packs and a very weak-looking, thin horse with a flimsy saddle strapped on its back. The people looked a little familiar, and Sam was sure he must have met them back during his store-clerking days in this town.

"Them? I don't know. My guess is they've come in from North Carolina. We get a right smart bunch of refugees from those parts coming through here. Times is mighty bad in them Carolina mountains, from all I hear."

Sam didn't have to be told that. He studied the group a moment more, then turned away as one of the youngsters in it caught him staring and stared back with a surprisingly dark, unnerving frown.

It seemed to Sam that he'd seen that face somewhere before.

Greeley discovered he was a famous and popular man around Greeneville. He'd led many a Greene County Unionist northward to the lines, and his reputation here seemingly had not been besmirched even temporarily by the episode involving the stolen money. Several boys too young to be soldiers approached him with pencils and pieces of paper and asked him to sign his name for them. He did so, feeling embarrassed to be treated as such a celebrity. In his mind, there was nothing all that special nor praiseworthy about being a Union pilot. To him, it was a grubby and hard life, nothing romantic about it.

Greeley was pulled by one of the autograph-seeking boys over to meet his family, and was separated from Sam when the yells and screams came. It took a moment for all to realize that these cries were not cheers; something had happened.

"He's stabbed!" a woman screeched. "He's stabbed bad!"

Greeley followed the rush of the crowd toward a scene of confusion over on the far end of the station platform. People blocked his way, cutting off his view. He cut to the right, worked his way through. Someone bumped his side and jolted pain through the still tender end of his amputated arm. He winced and pushed his way farther in, but could not reach a place to see who it was who'd been cut.

"Who is it?" he asked a man close by.

"A young man, can't tell . . . my goodness, I know that fellow! He used to clerk for Hannibal Deacon . . . what's his name? . . . Can't remember."

Sam. Greeley's legs became like wet putty. *Sam's been stabbed!*

Greeley shoved his way through the crowd, disregarding the protests this generated. It *was* Sam, lying on his back, eyes half closed, face pallid, blood covering his side and pooling. Helpless-looking men huddled around him, one trying to stop the flow of blood, the other babbling out to everyone that someone, anyone, should run find a physician, while a third kept declaring that it was "that boy that done it, that boy . . ."

"Sam, it's me. It's Greeley. What happened?"

"I knew . . . I'd seen that face before."

"Who, Sam?"

"In the mountains, that's where I'd seen him. . . . He watched while . . . we hung his father. . . ."

"Don't talk anymore, Sam. There's a doctor coming."

Sam kept talking, weakly. "I never saw him coming . . . didn't know nothing till I felt the sting of the knife. . . ."

"Hush, Sam. Please hush. You're going to be all right. You're going to be all right."

The stabbing of Sam Colter ended the celebration at the depot. A harried-looking physician arrived and began tending to Sam, while meanwhile a gray-haired woman who lived below the train station, and said she'd known Sam well during his clerking days, told Greeley that her house was available for him to rest in. They took him there. Gone was all Greeley's joy, even his awareness of anything outside Sam's condition. He fetched his and Sam's baggage off the train, went to the house where they'd taken Sam and shut out the war and the world when he closed the door behind him.

The train went on, bearing the soldiers past Greeneville and northeast toward Jonesborough. West of Telford, near an old stone house that dated to 1791 and was one of the area's best-known landmarks, they encountered resistance from Confederate soldiers and fought a tense little skirmish. The Confederates at length retreated, and the Federals pulled back as well to the whistle-stop of Limestone, a community built on the site of an old frontier fort and near the place where the famed Davy Crockett had taken his first breath. There, they left a battalion of the Ohioans to hold a blockhouse that had been built near the railroad trestle, and the remainder of the soldiers took the train back to Greeneville.

The Confederates weren't through, however. Their retreat at Telford had been a mere temporary pull-back, after which they were reinforced. Heading back down the track to Limestone, they took on the Ohio soldiers left there, fighting a moving battle along Limestone Creek, soldiers dropping and hiding behind the high banks, rising to shoot, dropping again.

And here the Federals, so flush with joy at their welcome to East Tennessee, faced the other side of the coin. The rebels were relentless, and eventually the Federals, running out of ammunition, were forced to surrender. Some 140 soldiers in blue, who shortly before had been grinning and waving at welcoming Unionists, found themselves captives of the Confederacy.

It was a minor fight, in one way, with fewer than twenty killed with both sides counted together. But it stood as evidence that the rebels were not going to be content to let the Union army penetrate East Tennessee unmolested.

Cumberland Gap

Julius Killefer doubted that in all the history of military activity, from the dawn of time until this September day, there had ever lived another soldier more eager to surrender than was he.

The way things were going, he suspected he would have a chance to do just that very soon.

He watched the flames eating away at an old mill that had been grinding corn endlessly for days, and did his best to look sad about it. That mill, now hopelessly ablaze and sending a great orange, leaping glow into the night, contained virtually all the rations stored to feed the Confederate soldiers occupying the Gap. *Let it burn!* Julius thought. *Give old Frazer one more reason to surrender!* Inside, Julius was singing, and his feet refrained from dancing only by force of his will.

The Federals had them in a squeeze, no doubt about it. From what the sentinels at the Gap had been observing through their spyglasses for the last few days, a huge number of soldiers and artillery pieces had been taking position on the Kentucky side of Cumberland Gap, while on the Tennessee side a brigade of some two thousand mounted Federals under General James M. Shackelford were in position. A demand for surrender had come in, and Brigadier General John W. Frazer, the Confederate now in command of the garrison defending the Gap, was reportedly giving strong consideration to it despite the official refusal he'd sent back. The surrender demand had come courtesy of General Shackelford.

So also had the mill fire, which in Julius's hopeful view could only enhance the odds of a quick surrender by Frazer, whom everyone said had not really wanted this command to begin with. Apparently, the guards stationed around the mill hadn't done much of a job, in that a band of Shackelford's soldiers had managed to sneak within their circle and get the fire going with blazing bags of wood shavings. Not only that, but they had safely gotten out again, the rebel guards firing in panic into the air, running like rabbits, and declaring that a major attack had just been launched against them.

The mill burned completely, to Julius's delight, and the next morning a new surrender demand came in. This one was from the commander of the Federals on the Kentucky side, a profane and severe Irish nobleman, Colonel John Fitzroy De Courcy. The demand was for unconditional surrender, which Frazer again rejected, but this time with a suggestion that perhaps a little more talking should take place.

Before long, rumors among the Cumberland Gap garrison had it that the talk was lubricated by an ample quantity of whiskey sent in to Frazer by De Courcy, via an emissary. If these rumors were true—and it would later be found that they were—then surrender seemed even more likely. Frazer reportedly enjoyed his whiskey and became quite a mellow man under its influence.

Julius turned at the tug of a hand on his elbow and looked into the face of a fellow soldier he'd seen only twice before. A newcomer, in his mid-twenties, to look at him, and very sallow and thin. He'd gotten that way as a prisoner of the Yankees somewhere up north, talk had it. He wasn't much to look at, to be sure, but the other soldiers thought him fine because he held that rare status of successful prison camp escapee. He'd made it out of his prison somehow and fled successfully all the way back to Tennessee, where he signed up again and was sent here to Cumberland Gap.

"Howdy," the man said. "My name's Bead Williamson. B.D., really, but everybody's called me Bead since I was a boy, and my baby brother run the sounds of the letters together. I'm betting your name is Killefer, right?"

"That's right. Julius Killefer." He stuck out his hand and shook Bead's. "How'd you know me?"

"From your looks. I took a look at you the first day I was in camp, and I thought, that boy there is a Killefer, sure as the world."

"You know my family?"

"I know your brother."

A dash of ice water in the face couldn't have struck with more impact. "What?"

"I say, I know your brother. Crowell. He is your brother, ain't he?"

"Yes. But . . . you must not have heard. Crowell's dead. His wife murdered him."

Bead Williamson laughed. Julius was too stunned by this to get angry.

"Murdered him? Where'd you get that notion? Crowell's in no situation to get murdered, at least not by his wife. He's a prisoner of war, up in Camp Douglas. Same prison camp I escaped from! Hey, friend, are you sick or something?"

Julius had staggered back, face growing pale. "I need to sit down. This can't be. It can't be! I got a letter that told me all about how his wife confessed she'd murdered him months ago. She even hung herself over it!"

"I'm telling you, Julius, your brother is alive. He was a prisoner even before I entered the camp. And he's still a prisoner today, unless he's escaped. And not many manage to do that. I was one of the few lucky ones."

"But if that's true . . . why would his wife have said she killed him? Why would she have hung herself over it, if it was all a story?"

"Well . . . I can't say I knew Crowell all that well so that we talked personal things much, but it was pretty common talk around the barracks that Crowell Killefer was open in telling everybody his wife wasn't sane. They say he used to joke that he was probably safer there in the prison than he would be if he was home with her."

"Crowell had to have been a Confederate soldier. . . ."

"That's right. A conscript, I think. I'm a volunteer myself, but I do believe Crowell was a conscript." Williamson grinned. "You're getting a bit of your color back now, Julius. Sorry to give you that news like I did—though I reckon it's good news, hearing that a brother you thought was murdered is still among the living!"

Julius smiled, then laughed. "It is good news. Grand news. I was just so surprised to hear it, when I was sure he was dead. But he's alive!"

"That's right. Or, he sure was last I seen him."

"Camp Douglas . . . where's that?"

"Chicago, Illinois."

"Is Crowell healthy?"

"He's got the usual prisoner complaints, but all in all, he's healthy. He surely does resemble you, Julius."

"I'd hardly know. I haven't seen him in a long time. I went into Tennessee looking for him, because we'd got a letter from his wife saying he'd vanished. I was conscripted by force while I was within the Confederate bounds, and now here I am, duty-bound by my oath to serve out my enlistment."

"You won't be serving much longer," Williamson said. "Before long you'll be a prisoner, just like your brother."

"You don't think the Yankees will parole us?"

"I wouldn't count on it. Me, I ain't staying around to find out. I'm slipping out of here before the Yankees have the chance to get their hands on me again. I don't relish being took prisoner again after having made one escape. You want to come with me?"

For a moment Julius was tempted. His emotions were thrashing wildly about inside him, one bumping away another only to be bumped away in turn by a third. He was joyous to learn that Crowell was alive, confused by how this seemingly solid bit of information could possibly gibe with what Richard Weston had written to him in that letter, and dismayed to hear that parole might not be in the offing once the Yankees retook the Gap.

The temptation to escape, however, had no prayer of overcoming the ingrained notion of personal duty of Julius Killefer's. He shook his head. "I'll take my chances and stay. I did make the vow, after all."

"Suit yourself, but the invitation stands, as long as it can. But the Yankees will be here soon, so if you change your mind, you'd best do it fast."

"I won't change my mind," he said. "Tell me again: You're for positive certain, swear to God, that Crowell Killefer, from Kentucky, son of Oman Killefer and husband of Susan Killefer in Tennessee . . . that's the Crowell Killefer you know is at the Camp Douglas prison?"

Williamson laughed again. "Swear to God. He's alive and as well as any prisoner can be."

Julius could find no more to say. He sat down on his rump in the midst of the camp, grinning like a fool, staring off into the sky. Williamson laughed once more. "See you later, Julius. Or maybe not. I'm gone from here real soon."

Julius didn't even hear him. His mind rang with the incredible news: His brother was alive!

The Confederate flags came down and the white flags went up over Cumberland Gap on September 9. Julius could hardly keep from crying in joy. He and the other soldiers marched to their stations, put down their arms, and gathered to await the official shift of power.

Not all of the garrison, however, surrendered. Some four hundred of those stationed in the more remote portions of the Gap simply vanished into the wilderness, as Julius had longed so badly to do so many times, only to be held back by fear of the whipping strap or the ball and chain. Two officers, Colonel Campbell Slemp and Major B. G. McDowell, were among those who disappeared. Julius saw Bead Williamson no more, and presumed he had escaped as well.

Those soldiers who remained to surrender had uppermost on their minds concern about what the terms would be. A happy tale began to spread that the soldiers would be offered parole and the chance to return to their homes. Julius prayed it was true. He longed to return to his Kentucky home and see how his family were, and to give the news about Crowell's circumstances, and Susan's death.

Among the company were some who were heartfelt rebels; these were deeply distressed at the turn of events and murmured, cursed, and kicked in a great show of anger. Julius was sorely tempted to smirk at them, but didn't.

In a while music caught his ear. At first he could not tell from where it came, but soon it grew louder and he saw a small military band come marching up the road. The music was "Yankee Doodle," and was sweet indeed to Julius's ears, though it made the sincere rebels about him all the more angry. But their fury mounted even further when the band came even nearer and struck up the tune "Dixie," which Julius thought was quite funny, but which the angry ones took as mockery. Then came the regular Federal soldiers, singing at the top of their lungs a popular ditty called "The Girl I Left Behind."

The Confederate soldiers assumed formation and stood watching as the bluecoats came in. A lean, distinguished horseman in a colonel's uniform came riding in through the midst of the soldiers, accompanied by a large guard, and asked of a sullen Confederate officer where General Frazer might be. Julius was intrigued by the accent, having never before heard a native-born Irishman speak.

"He's in his tent . . . sir," the officer replied, indicating with a wave the tent where Frazer had sat pouting and drinking for several hours.

De Courcy and his entourage rode to the front of the tent and called for Frazer to emerge. He did, looking very rumpled and bleary-eyed, snuff smeared across his face. De Courcy looked at him and smiled, then turned to one of his companions and said, "The whiskey has done its work." He spoke next to General Frazer. "I am happy to meet you today, General."

Frazer's voice was only slightly slurred. "Under the circumstances, I cannot say I am happy to meet you."

"I understand, sir," De Courcy said. "Please consider yourself a prisoner of war."

Julius closed his eyes a moment and breathed a prayer of relief. It appeared that the military duties of one reluctant Confederate from the Greasy Fork in Kentucky were about to come to an end at last, one way or another.

Events transpiring soon after the surrender of Frazer gave Julius a hint that not everything on the Union side of this affair had gone smoothly. The first hint came with the arrival of General Ambrose Burnside himself, who had come up on the Tennessee side to reinforce Shackelford and, apparently, with the intent of personally receiving the surrender of Frazer.

Burnside arrived at the surrendered camp shortly after

De Courcy's first appearance, accompanied by a finely out-
fitted and armed bodyguard of some two hundred men.
Julius had never seen such fine-looking soldiers, nor such a
welcome figure as Burnside.

Nor a more angry one. On his way toward Frazer's tent,
he looked at the Federal soldiers already on the scene, his
brows lowering. "What means this?" he bellowed. "Whose
men are these?"

The answer was given: De Courcy's men.

"De Courcy! Send for him—now!"

De Courcy arrived moments later, polite but cool toward
the general, whom he greeted without a smile.

Burnside's expression was withering. "Who gave you
permission to advance these men, Colonel? *Always* await
my orders before you advance! Do you understand me?"

"Yes, sir."

"Consider yourself under arrest, Colonel De Courcy. We
will discuss this more later."

Julius was in no position to understand immediately what
lay behind this odd and tense interaction between Burnside
and his subordinate.

The tension had begun the prior month, when De Courcy
was informed by Burnside that he would not be part of the
main body of Federal soldiers advancing into East Tennessee
in the long awaited invasion. De Courcy's role would be to
launch a direct attack upon the rebel garrison at Cumberland
Gap. De Courcy was the logical man for such an enterprise,
having served at the Gap while it was still under the control
of Union General George Morgan about a year before, and
thus knowing the country and the basic fortifications of the
Gap. But De Courcy was not pleased with the relatively
small force Burnside allotted him to carry out the enterprise,
nor the inexperience of a significant portion of that force.

His cavalry, for instance, was made up from the Eighth,
Ninth, and Eleventh Tennessee, most of whose enlistees were
inexperienced in battle and, in many cases, recent, untrained
civilians who had stampeded north from Tennessee. His
infantry unit, consisting of the 86th Ohio Volunteers and the

129th Ohio, pleased him little more than his cavalry, and he was particularly unhappy with the meager artillery provided him through the 22nd Ohio Battery: a mere half-dozen lightweight guns, hardly enough to knock out the Cumberland Gap fortifications. He had fewer than two thousand men in all, many of them so new to warfare that each counted for half a real soldier at best. All in all, De Courcy was convinced they lacked the manpower and firepower to have any hope of driving the Confederates from their Cumberland Gap fortifications.

So the rather mercenary-minded Irishman, a soldier since his mid-teens, decided that cleverness would have to substitute for strength. He would take this impossible assignment and turn it into a success—on his own, using his skill and his brainpower—and what glory was to be had in the victory, by heaven, he would claim for his own.

His plan was indeed a masterpiece of cleverness, all the more cunning by its very simplicity. The first portion of the great deception involved no more than mixing the regimental numbers on the hats of the soldiers he commanded. By creating new combinations, he was able to make the men appear to come from many more regiments than they actually did. By wearing these numbers before the camp followers and local merchants who came—with rebel spies among them—to sell wares to the soldiers during their march, De Courcy could virtually ensure that exaggerated reports of troop size and strength would get back to the enemy at the Gap. By playing about with the numbers of the 86th and 122nd Ohio regiments, for example, he was able to give the impression that their members represented not two, but eight regiments.

As he neared Cumberland Gap itself, De Courcy put the second portion of his ploy into the works. When he came in sight of the Gap's fortifications, he began a series of marches that seemed absurd to the men forced to take part in them, but had a telling effect on the Confederates who watched the movements through their field glasses. De Courcy divided his men into relatively small units with brief spaces between the units, and marched these units within the view of the Confederate watchers, then hurried them, under cover, back around to make precisely the same march again. Four times around the weary soldiers traveled, giving those who watched from a distance the impression that they were much greater in number than they were.

De Courcy pulled a similar trick with his handful of cannon, rolling them in, camouflaging them, slipping them out and around again, camouflaging them once more, and so on. Before he was finished, the rebels at the Gap had the idea that a devastatingly huge battery was aimed their way. It was a fine and effective piece of military sleight-of-hand.

De Courcy was certain that this great bluff would be enough to bring about the surrender of the Confederate garrison, but the arrival of Shackelford on the Tennessee side of Cumberland Gap threatened his grandstand play. Shackelford send word that De Courcy should make no surrender demands upon the garrison himself, that job being his own, by command of Burnside himself.

De Courcy, unwilling to have his chance at glory snatched away, was not cooperative. He intended that the surrender of Frazer should be handed to him and no other, and so it was that after he softened up Frazer with the whiskey he sent him and various bluff threats that he couldn't have possibly pulled off, De Courcy made his own surrender demands, setting a surrender deadline of two o'clock in the afternoon, September 9.

But in the meantime, Burnside had arrived on the Tennessee side of the mountains and sent word to Frazer that any further communication should be done with him and him alone. Burnside had then made his own surrender demand, and it was to this demand, not De Courcy's, that Frazer had finally agreed. But when the white flags went up, De Courcy took it as a signal to move in, fulfilling his goal of being the officer to accept Frazer's surrender—an honor Burnside had counted on being his own. And thus had risen Burnside's fury when he'd ridden into Frazer's camp, only to find De Courcy already there.

De Courcy's moment of glory had been sweet while it lasted, but it hadn't lasted long.

• • •

It was the same with Julius Killefer's blissful time of optimistic happiness. He'd happily accepted the story that he and his fellows were to be paroled at once, and thus was shocked when an entirely different word came the next morning and he found himself a prisoner of war. The paroles were not to come as quickly as expected.

On the eleventh of September, Julius was on the march, heading up a road already beaten into dust, up into Kentucky. There was little food, no protection from the elements, and scant available drinking water. He fell into despair and began to grow sick. But still he had to march, often moving in a kind of numb, sickly daze.

It went on for many days, and by the time he was at Louisville on the Ohio River, Julius was so weak and ill he could scarcely speak, walk, or even think a coherent thought. He did not know where he was going, nor did he care even to ask. Something in the back of his mind told him that death would be coming very soon.

The prisoners were ferried across the river and piled onto cattle cars, squeezed in like human lumber. They rode until the train stopped, and disembarked to find themselves staring at a great body of water. "What is that?" Julius asked an older prisoner beside him, his voice like that of a croaking frog.

"That's Lake Michigan," the man said.

Lake Michigan. Julius had heard of it, but try as he would, could not remember where that lake was. "Where's Lake Michigan?" he asked. Lord in heaven, but he felt sick! He felt he could tilt over and pass out at any second, and the prospect wasn't displeasing.

"Why, right there before your eyes, you fool!"

"I mean, where? What place is this?"

"Oh. Chicago. Chicago, Illinois."

"Chicago . . . you mean . . . we're going to be prisoners here?"

"That's right, boy. Camp Douglas."

"Camp Douglas!"

"That's right. Why the hell you grinning, boy? You think that's good news?"

Julius wasn't grinning now, but chuckling. Camp Douglas!

Of all the places he might have been taken, fate had brought him here, to the very prison where Crowell was held.

"I did it, Pa!" Julius said aloud, giving way to laughter. "I did it! I found Crowell, Pa!"

"Boy, there's something wrong with you!" the other declared. "I believe you're plumb out of your head!" The man reached out and touched Julius's forehead. "Lord have mercy! You're burned up with fever, boy!"

Julius was still laughing when his eyes closed of their own accord and he sank to the ground, consciousness fading out like a candle flame in a closed jar.

Greeneville, Tennessee

The look on the physician's face told the entire tale. Greeley stood, gazing at the old man as he came out of the bedroom where Sam Colter lay. He looked at Greeley, and it wasn't even necessary for Greeley to ask the question that had been burning on the end of his tongue since the doctor had gone in to make this most recent examination.

Greeley felt his eyes growing wet and red. The doctor shook his head.

"Is he . . . gone?" Greeley asked.

"Not yet. But it won't be long, and he knows it. He's asking to see you, Mr. Brown."

Greeley closed his eyes shut, forced back the tears. He didn't want Sam to see him weep. Sam didn't need that right now.

Caesar Augustus, but it was cursed unfair! Sam had gone through so much, survived so much, and now he was about to die because of a wound administered by a war-damaged boy. Greeley hated the irony of it. Most of all he hated the warfare that had caused it all.

"You'd best get on in," the doctor said.

Greeley sucked in a deep breath, steeled himself, and entered Sam's borrowed bedroom—borrowed death chamber, Greeley thought of it now—with a forced smile ghastly across his face. It died as soon as he saw Sam on the bed, more pallid than before, face sodden and cold-looking, eyes sunken as if he'd died already, breathing labored.

Greeley went to Sam's bedside and knelt there. "Sam."

He was almost surprised to see the eyes open. The whites of them now red and bleary, they turned in those dark and hollow sockets and locked onto Greeley's face.

"Greeley . . . glad to see you."

"Glad to see you too, Sam."

"I'm going to die, Greeley."

Greeley blinked; the tears, though, would not be held back. "I know."

"Something you got to do . . . for me."

"Anything, Sam. Anything."

"Amy Deacon . . . you heard me talk about her."

"Yes."

"I loved her, Greeley . . . I still love her."

Greeley nodded, wondering where this would lead.

"I want you to tell her that for me. Find her. Tell her what happened to me . . . tell her that when I died, I was thinking of her. Tell her I never stopped loving her."

"I will, Sam. I promise. Where is she now?"

"I . . . don't know. Find her for me . . . be sure she knows."

"I'll find her, somehow. I'll track her down. I promise you."

Sam closed his eyes; it seemed he smiled a little. "Thank you, Greeley."

"Glad to help, Sam." Greeley's voice quivered badly, and now that Sam had closed his eyes, he wept freely.

He can't die, God. It isn't fair if he dies.

Yet Greeley knew that all around him, in a vast and spreading circle of misery called the War of the Rebellion, others were dying in circumstances and ways just as unfair. Men, boys, women, children. Death upon death upon death, all over issues that seemed to matter very little here in this curtain-shadowed bedchamber.

He remembered words that Sam Colter himself had spoken after his first taste of true war: *I don't believe I care for it much.*

Greeley managed a very sad smile. *Neither do I, Sam. Neither do I.*

Sam's breathing became a bit more steady, and Greeley pulled a chair to the bedside and sat down in it, watching Sam's chest move up and down, grateful each time it did. He prayed hard, asking for a miracle, asking for Sam to somehow make it through, but knew the stab wound had been deep, and the doctor had told him earlier that much damage had been done internally.

Yet Sam breathed on, an hour, then two. Greeley leaned forward, resting his arms and his chin on the edge of the bed. Eventually his eyes drifted shut and he dozed.

He awakened; the room was dark. Standing, he went to the table and lit a lamp there. Cranking up the wick, he carried the lamp to Sam's bed and set it on the stand beside it. He looked down at his friend and partner for a minute or so, then quietly reached down and pulled the covers up and over the peaceful face.

Chapter 35

In a prisoner barracks, Camp Douglas

Julius knew he was quite sick, so it would have been easy for him to dismiss as mere dreams the vision he saw whenever he opened his eyes, but thanks to the information he'd received from Bead Williamson, it wasn't necessary. The face of Crowell Killefer leaning over him, intense with concern and looking, with that expression, more like their mother's face than Julius had ever noticed before, was no dream. Crowell was here, with him. Caring for the brother who'd come looking for him and found him in the oddest way and most unexpected place.

Crowell was bearded now, a new feature in Julius's experience of him. And he was thin, like all the men here.

"You rest now," Crowell told him the first time he appeared in Julius's blurry vision. "You've got the measles, but if you rest, you'll live."

He did rest, as much as the fever would allow. Every time he opened his eyes, Crowell was there, either already gazing down at him, or at his bedside. Crowell spoke to him often. Sometimes Julius heard what he said—encouraging words, always—but often as not the sound of Crowell's voice was masked behind a continual dull ringing in his ears.

• • •

Julius proved to be one of the fortunate ones. Few prisoners who contracted measles survived the disease, and the number of those in this camp who suffered from that malady was so high, he would later be told, that prisoners with measles weren't even taken to the camp hospital. There were far too many of them to be accommodated, and little that could be done for them in any case.

Yet Julius, against all odds, clung to life with a stubborn persistence, and came out of his illness with a vague memory of the moment he'd turned the corner toward health, a moment marked in his recollection by a hard-to-define awareness of something warm and good rising within him, and a subtle clearing of the mind for a moment or two. From then on, he made a slow and steady rise back toward his former condition, and toward the marvelous realization that despite the unhappy fact of being a Federal prisoner of war, the long-sought reunion had occurred. He was alive, he was there, and he was with Crowell.

When Julius was well enough and his mind fully lucid, he and Crowell talked, filling in the gaps of long separation. Julius told the story of the letter his family had received from Susan, and of his own hazardous and ill-fated pilgrimage into Tennessee, and finally the news of Susan's "confession" and suicide.

Crowell didn't seem nearly as surprised as Julius would have thought. "Susan never murdered our baby, any more than she murdered me," he said. "There never was a baby, Julius. All there was, was a woman with a diseased mind and notions she would get in that mind, and she had no ability to distinguish the false from the true. I don't know where it all came from . . . I believe there were things that happened to her during her girlhood that affected her. She talked sometimes about things, bad things. Mistreatment of the most foul kind by a neighbor man and his wife . . . things to break your heart and make you sick. Things no woman should have had to put up with, much less a girl."

Crowell looked around in the crowded barracks, leaned close to Julius and spoke softly. "I believe very strongly, based on things Susan told me in better times, that this neighbor man got her with child, and that she miscarried it early on, before her kin ever even knew about it. I believe she felt relieved and guilty about it at the same time. I believe it was that burden that ruined her mind, and came back to her from time to time and sort of intruded itself on to her grown-up situation, so she mixed up her present with her past. There were times, I feel very sure, when she would look at me and see that man who had misused her when she was a girl. Sometimes she just couldn't tell the real from the false, nor the past from the present." He paused and shook his head. "I'm so sorry she took her own life, though I'm not surprised at all. I half expected it, sooner or later. She was a burdened woman."

"Crowell, there was a cradle there in the house, just like there had been a child. She made me carry the cradle with us when we went to her kin in Greene County."

"Again, I ain't surprised. It fits with what I know of her. Even before we separated she had dreamed up the notion that she'd bore my child and murdered it. She asked me what I'd done with the cradle . . . but of course there'd never been a cradle. If she had one when you came to her, it's one she must have gotten after I was gone."

"Why were you gone, Crowell? I mean . . . I don't mean nothing bad against you by this question, but did you just leave her there, on her own, in the shape she was?"

"No, Julius, I didn't. I did leave her, yes, but with no intent of it being a permanent thing. She forced me out—threatened my life with my own gun, and I had to flee in the middle of the night. Left my clothes and everything behind in the house and went looking for help. I didn't know what to do, how to deal with her at all. But there was a conscription agent who had some bad blood toward me, and he got his hands on me before I could do a thing. Literally kidnapped me into the rebel army—I'm talking about getting knocked in the head, tied up, hauled away by force."

Julius nodded. "I know very well about getting conscripted against your will, because that's the very thing that happened to me—but this agent actually knocked you cold and tied you up? That's awful extreme."

"He had an extreme motivation. He wanted Susan. He'd been engaged to marry her before I came along, and he hated me for having taken his woman."

"So he got you out of the way so he could take her back. . . . But where was he? There was no man about the place while I was there, and Susan made no mention of one."

Crowell looked away, across the barracks. "Then maybe she rejected him. Maybe she did worse to him than that. She may have killed the man. Maybe that's where she got the notion she killed *me*. It would fit with how she confused people in her mind."

Julius remembered the unusable well, the odd stench of decay that rose from it, and Susan's claim that a "critter" had fallen into it and drowned. A chill shuddered through him. "So in her mind, maybe it was you she had killed, and when she wrote that letter to us, saying you had run off, she was trying to cover what she thought she had done."

"Perhaps. Or perhaps it was just more confusion. Her mind was always in a tempest, Julius. Nothing stayed the same in her perceptions for long. I lived with her enough time to learn that."

"There were times she would tell people you'd run off on her, and times she said you were dead."

"See? That's what I'm talking about. A tempest and a turmoil, one notion changing places with another, and back again. That was Susan. Poor, lost, crazy Susan."

"How'd you get to this prison, Crowell?"

"Got captured, that's how. I wasn't in the rebel army more than two days before I was sent out with a squad to patrol over near Nashville and got myself caught. Off I was sent, and here I am. Julius, tell me something: When you heard that Susan had 'confessed' to killing me, did you get that news to Mama and Pap?"

"No. I never had opportunity."

"We have to get to them, Julius. Me and you together."

"Hah! Wouldn't that be fine! But I doubt the Yankees allow folks to just up and walk out of this camp."

"No, but some manage to do it anyway, just like Bead Williamson."

A man walked across Julius's field of view between the foot of his floor-level bunk and the bunk right above him. The man had a long board tied to his back, across which was painted the words: ESCAPED PRISONER RECAPTURED. "Like that fellow there, huh?" Julius said.

"He was one of the unlucky ones. But some get free and never get caught. We'll talk more later on; a man has to be careful about his words. Meantime, you rest."

Julius looked around. "Where are the others who were brought in with me?"

"They're in the barracks next door to this one. They moved them over there a day or two after you came in. They kept you in here because I told them you were my brother and I wanted you to have my bunk, being sick."

"So I've been taking up your bunk?"

"Yes, but don't worry about it. I wanted you to have it. I wanted to be able to be close by you and get you through your sickness." He glanced about. "And I wanted you to be in this barracks, too. For reasons I'll tell you soon enough."

Julius wanted explanation, but Crowell shook his head and winked even before he could get the question out. "You'll see soon enough. Got to be careful. And that's enough talking for now."

Even though his health was back and he needed no more care from Crowell, Julius was never moved to the adjacent barracks with the rest of the prisoners he'd come with to Chicago. He and Crowell took alternating nights sleeping on the bed, the other making do on the floor. Meanwhile, Julius got to know the place to which he'd been brought.

Camp Douglas was a foul, wet, undraining prison camp, covering about twenty acres and surrounded by a tall, plain fence with a guard walkway built along the top of it. There was no decent system of waste disposal and the camp reeked of human filth; it was no wonder that sickness ranging from typhoid to measles thrived.

The camp was named after Lincoln's old political foe,

Stephen A. Douglas, who had once owned the land on which it had been built to house, primarily, Kentuckian and Tennessean prisoners. Standing close by Lake Michigan, subjected constantly to the fogs and cold winds off the water, and filled from fence to fence with stinking mud, the place had a terrible reputation. Prisoners had rioted in protest of the conditions, and there were official recommendations that it be closed. But it hadn't been closed, and in August new prisoners were swept in atop the old ones, and herded into barracks with big gaps in the walls and holes through the roofs.

The mysterious information that Crowell had promised to tell his brother was preceded with warnings given the intensity of some arcane society's rites.

There was a tunnel beneath their barracks. Not a full tunnel just yet, but a lengthy one, burrowing out under the muddy yard outside and toward the fence. It was being dug by night, a few feet at a time, the dirt being hidden beneath the barracks floor. Wood from the bunks was taken a bit at a time and used to shore up the narrow but lengthening tunnel, and so far no one but the residents of the Morgan Barracks had any idea such a tunnel existed.

It would be some time before the tunnel would be complete, and during that period, Julius tried to rebuild all of the strength he'd lost during his measles bout, and to avoid catching further maladies from the disgusting miasmas that rose from the slit trenches, where six thousand men emptied their wastes every day. As the weather grew cooler, the wind-permeable barracks, relatively comfortable in the summer, grew cold, and many of the men lacked blankets or proper winter clothing. Firewood given the prisoners, about a quarter of a cord per 120 men per week, was insufficient even to adequately cook the meals, much less provide heat.

Julius was among those who lacked adequate clothing, and ever since his measles, the cold bothered him greatly, but he held on by sheer will. The tunnel was getting longer each night. Some evening not too many weeks hence, it would extend beyond the wall, and on the first truly foggy night, the men of the barracks would finally be able to break away and lose themselves in the city of Chicago. Julius and Crowell vowed to one another that when that day came, they would not allow themselves to be recaptured, even if it meant death. Once they were free of Camp Douglas, they did not intend to return to it again. They would flee into Kentucky, vanish into the hills and mountains they knew so well, and make their way home again, or die in the effort.

Carter County, Tennessee

A grin spread slowly across Mathen Ricker's wrinkled face when he saw who had just appeared at his door, silent as a ghost. But he squelched the grin all at once and came to his feet at what seemed a good speed to him, but was in fact very slow.

"What do you mean, walking up on a man and trying to scare him!" he bellowed. "Greeley Brown, I might have shot you dead!"

"I doubt it," Greeley replied, stepping inside the cabin. "As slow as you are, Mathen, I could have hopped three circles around you on one foot before you could have reached whatever guns you have about this place."

The old man reached behind him and whipped out a small revolver, which he aimed at Greeley's chin. "Don't count on that, Lincolnite," he said, then grinned again and lowered the pistol. "Glad to see you, Greeley. I ain't laid eyes on you since your last stampeder run. Hey, how's that hurt arm?"

"Still not much feeling in it." Greeley wriggled the fingers again; this had become an instinctive and habitual move. "I'm getting by. Better a numb arm than a bad leg—at least a man can still run from the rebels with a numb arm."

"You may have to run from them. That Yankee invasion ain't done much for you Lincolnites in this part of the state, has it!" There was the faintest tone of triumph in Ricker's voice.

"I have to admit, it ain't."

In fact, Greeley might have truthfully stated that the

situation of the rural people in the far eastern Tennessee counties was perhaps worse now than prior to Burnside's coming. The changing tides of warfare in other areas had caused most of the Union invaders to be quickly pulled back out of the rural counties and concentrated around Knoxville, Chattanooga, and other more strategically important, populous areas. Thus, the rebels and their sympathizers, driven away or into hiding at the outset of the Federal insweep, now had a free run in most of the region again—and this time they were angry, and vengeful.

Greeley sighed. "You know, Mathen, just now I've reached the place where I hardly care who wins this bloody war. I just want it to be over, you know. I ain't sure there's any such things as winners in such a conflict as this. It's just people shooting each other, stabbing and murdering. People dying before their time."

Mathen Ricker looked probingly at his friend and saw in him a depth of sadness that was not commonly there. "Have a seat, Greeley. Tell me what needs telling."

A small fire blazed on the hearth, cooking Ricker's meager supper, which would be more meagerly portioned yet once he shared it with Greeley. Pulling up the stool, Greeley settled onto it and stared into the fire. "I lost a good friend and partner, Mathen. Sam Colter is dead."

"I'm sorry. How'd it happen?"

"He was stabbed at Greeneville, at the train station. A young North Carolina boy did it. Vengeance. He'd seen his own father hanged by bushwhackers. Sam being one of them."

"And so it goes," Ricker said. "One kills, another kills in turn, and another kills in answer to that one. On and on."

"Don't make much sense, does it?"

"Not a bit. And yet you can't stop it, somehow."

They both stared into the flames for a time, not talking.

"It's a sorry old war, Mathen."

"It is, Greeley. A mighty sorry war, and I've come to hate it more all the time."

Part VI

★ ★ ★ ★ ★ ★ ★

BITTER HARVEST

Chapter 36

Amy Hanover hadn't been squeamish even as a child, so the gore she'd seen in such abundance today did not much bother her. Her volunteer nursing at the various army hospitals had tempered her sensibilities even further; she was able not only to see the most gruesome war wounds without a flinch, but to touch, cleanse, and help stitch them closed. In recent days she had picked up and carried off many a shattered and freshly removed limb without a moment's hesitation, and wearily gone home several nights with blood staining her clothing yet almost escaping her notice.

Today, however, she was bothered. It wasn't the horrendous sights getting to her, but the accompanying din of human suffering. The clamoring wounded were everywhere, in great pain. Screams, moans, wails, sobs, pleadings rose all around, an atrocious symphony of horror rising from the throats of the Federal wounded from the terrible battlefield called Chickamauga. Amy had never seen this many freshly maimed men all in one place at one time.

The first trainloads of Chickamauga's wounded had begun reaching the Nashville hospitals earlier in the day, and since

then, new deliveries of the shattered and hurting had been
coming in steadily. Every army hospital in the city was past
capacity, every surgeon frenetically trying to accomplish
the impossible. Amy was stupefied and repelled by the sheer
volume of misery. She tried to remain mentally separate
from it all, businesslike and efficient as usual . . . but the
sounds, the screams, the cries for relief that couldn't come!
It was too much to endure, and several times she had felt
uncharacteristically light-headed and nauseous. Once or
twice the notion had come that perhaps something besides
the horrors surrounding her were contributing to her bilious-
ness, but there was no time to think much about it. She
swallowed down her qualmishness, closed her ears as much
as she could to the cries of suffering, and did her best
to follow the directions of the exhausted and overloaded
surgeons.

She had lost all track of time, and only an accidental
sighting of a wounded soldier's pocket watch made her
realize she'd gone for hours without food or drink. She had
picked the worst possible morning to skip her breakfast,
something else uncharacteristic, but today just after she'd
gotten up, the idea of food had made her feel queasy.

The realization that she was working without sustaining
nourishment generated no spirit of complaint in her. How
could anyone in the midst of all *this* feel anything but
grateful simply to be alive and in one unbroken piece? But
she did consider that her lack of food might be advancing
this nagging light-headedness, bordering on dizziness. . . .

"Mrs. Hanover, you should step outside a few moments.
Get some fresh air." She looked at the speaker, who gripped
her arm for some reason. Had she staggered? He was a
Yankee-accented surgeon named Masters, one of some fifty
such northern physicians who had come to Nashville to give
their service to the wounded. "Believe it or not, we've
finally caught up for the moment, and I believe we can spare
you briefly. You look terribly pale."

"I can keep at it as long as anyone here!" she said with a
touch of impetuousness.

"Out, Mrs. Hanover! Get some air. You almost fainted
right across this soldier."

She hadn't even realized it. Chided and surprised, she nodded and headed for the door.

The fresh air did help, as did the muffling effect of the walls, minimizing the moans and cries from inside. She found a stone beneath a blessed tree—Amy blessed all trees these days, because wartime demands on both fuel and security had stripped Nashville of much vegetation over the past year, giving its hills a barren look—and slumped down in rather unladylike fashion, legs sprawled and skirt bunched between her knees. Lowering her head, she closed her eyes and tried to make the buzzing inside her skull go away. *All those men, all that suffering . . .*

She looked up when she heard footsteps and saw a smiling Adam drawing near, a small covered basket in his hand. Happiness welled up, and admiration—he was such a handsome and welcome vision!—and she rose. To her surprise, she had to sit down again at once, dizzy.

His smile vanished, "Amy, are you sick?"

She pulled in a lungful of cool air and somehow conjured up a smile. "No, I'm fine. Just very tired. We've been overrun today. So many wounded! What a terrible battle it must have been."

"Yes, it was. I'm hearing rumors that soldiers from Nashville are in high numbers among the casualties. Oh my— Amy, you've got quite a lot of blood on you." Adam Hanover, unlike his wife, was not at all nonchalant about blood.

"I'm not surprised. It's been a butcher house in there, Adam. An absolute butcher house."

He made a disgusted face and held up the basket. "So much for you wanting to eat, then?"

"What are you talking about? I'm starved!" She nabbed the basket and threw back the cloth. The bread and cheese was a wonderful sight. "You came at just the right time. The surgeon sent me out for air because I was getting so weak. I missed breakfast today."

"I seem to recall you missed it a morning or two back, too. Are you sick, honey?"

"No. I'm fine." With cheese in one hand, bread in the other, she began to eat. A loud, hideous scream came piercing through the hospital wall, making Adam recoil, but Amy didn't seem to notice.

He looked at her fingers, wrapped around the bread and cheese. "I hate to think of what you've touched today, and now here you are, eating with no chance to have washed."

"You'd be surprised, Adam, how little difference things like that make when you've been in the midst of the kind of things I've seen today." She took the biggest bite of cheese so far, overwhelmed by the sheer goodness of food. She hadn't realized how empty she was. "I didn't expect to see you today. Why are you here?"

"Well, to bring this food to you, if I could find you, which I didn't think I'd do so easily. And to try to get some idea of the numbers of wounded coming into Nashville. I've gone from hospital to hospital, and it's so busy and confused that it's hard to get a half-reliable count. Is this hospital up to capacity?"

"Well beyond it. And it'll only get worse in a day or two," Amy said. "And I heard someone saying there'll be prisoners of war coming in from the same battle."

"Right. God only knows what they'll do with all of them. Some of them will be needing medical attention, too, I suppose."

The surgeon appeared at the door, fresh stains of bright crimson down the front of his apron. "Mrs. Hanover! You're needed again . . . a double leg amputation, and this one's a fighter. It's going to take several of us to keep him down." The surgeon paused a moment to draw in a breath or two of the September atmosphere, and looked longingly across the landscape like a chained dog yearning for freedom. "Oh, well, back to work, Mrs. Hanover. Let's go curse another man to the nickname of Shorty for the rest of his life." He glanced at Adam—"Good day to you, sir. Are you Mr. Hanover? Pleased to meet you"—and withdrew into the hospital.

Adam shuddered. "What a cruel joke! 'Shorty!' I ought to editorialize about the callous attitude—"

"You'll do nothing of the sort, Adam. Jokes are the way people under pressure keep from being crushed." She crammed another quick bite into her mouth, then gave

Adam a rather crumbly, crum-covered kiss and handed him the empty basket. "I'll see you tonight. It may be late."

"Amy, take care of yourself. Don't work too hard. You look a little pale to me."

"I'll be fine." Then she was gone. Adam left hurriedly so he wouldn't have to hear the pitiful cries that he knew would come when the double amputation began.

As Adam Hanover strode briskly along one of Nashville's busy streets, heading back toward his office, he passed a vagrant who huddled unseen in an alleyway, watching the traffic go by, marveling at the number of wounded men, feeling grateful that he was not a soldier himself, yet thinking that just now he might brave the fiercest of battles if only he knew there would be whiskey when it was over.

Ben Scarlett longed for alcohol, ached for it, needed it, grieved for it. But he had none, and even if he did, he wouldn't be able to drink it. In the emotional wake of the Angel affair, he had promised God Himself that he would never get drunk again. For him that was equivalent to not taking a drink at all, because even one taste would throw him out of control and make him imbibe more, and more, and more, until he was indeed drunk. Ben had to face it: He was destined to suffer through a total dry-out, all alone. He'd done it once before, but at that time some folks were about to help and encourage him. Nothing like that this time. It wasn't going to be easy.

"I don't know if I can do it, Lord," he said to the sky.

In his mind he could almost hear a booming, deep voice speaking back to him: *You must. You promised.*

He got up and walked toward his hidden shed, entered it, then five minutes later came out once more, paced around, and entered it again. The torment was setting in. Further, he was getting hungry, and had nothing to eat. He'd already gone by the place where the women in white served soup, and no one was there today.

The wind was getting up, and colder. Ben ducked back inside the shed and pulled out the Confederate uniform he'd found. Stripping down, he put the uniform on—it fit quite well—then pulled his baggy and threadbare civilian garments on top of that. At least he would be warm in his miseries.

He wanted liquor terribly, felt he would do anything to get it. He looked skyward. "I ain't fooling, Lord. I really don't know I can do this, especially by myself."

He imagined that voice again: *Then go get some help.*

Some help . . . who? Who did he know in the city of Nashville who would help a one-handed drunk sweat out his tremens? Nobody . . . except maybe Amy Deacon. What was her married name? Oh, yes, Hanover.

For a few moments he considered it. Amy was a terrifically kindhearted person, as wonderful a female as he'd ever known, and that not even excluding Angel. And he had given her some help that time, helping her smuggle that false Confederate money into Tennessee . . .

He scoffed off the idea. Him, go before Amy, like he was? Ben Scarlett had little pride, but what he did have he wasn't going to sacrifice by asking the female he admired most to hold his hand while he squalled and vomited and wet himself and swatted spiders that weren't really there.

Well, that ruled out Amy. So who else could help him? If the Lord was going to be making suggestions, he wished he would also give him some hints about how to go about carrying them out.

Well, there is that preacher who saved me from his brother. Maybe he'd help me, or know somebody who could. Or maybe those women who serve the soup could tell me a place I could go.

He knew already the soup women weren't about today. That left the preacher. It seemed a long chance at best, and he doubted he could even find the man, but looking would give him something to do, and perhaps he'd stumble across some food while he was poking about.

Ben stepped out into the wind and pulled his hat low over his ears. He was glad for the uniform under his clothing. It stopped the cold breeze quite nicely. He looked around, wished again for whiskey, and set off on long, fast strides, as tense and tight as an overwound watch.

• • •

The way Ben had it figured, the Lord was getting even with him for all the years he had wasted and all the wrong things he'd done. Why else would he be running him all over Nashville on an utterly fruitless mission?

The storefront church was occupied, but not by the preacher. The Federals had taken over the place as an overflow hospital; an ambulance wagon heading for it, hauling four bloodied soldiers, almost ran over Ben as he crossed the street. The driver cursed at him as he loped away.

He walked the streets for a while, counting the traffic of ambulance wagons until that got boring, and looked again for the soup women in that empty lot. Still none around. He stood pondering what to do. His whiskey thirst was growing overwhelming, and knowing that he could never slake it again was a torment upon a torment.

He would need help. Somebody to care for him and keep his spirits up. The first time he'd gotten off whiskey, it was with the help of a man he found beaten half to a pulp beside a road. He needed such a companion again. *If Angel were alive and I'd found her, I'll bet it would be easy to give up liquor. Having her again would be all a man could ever need.* He sighed and felt his eyes moisten. *Oh, Angel, I wish we'd never parted. I was a fool to let myself lose you.*

As he meandered along, he remembered something he'd overheard: In Nashville's Eastfield community there were reportedly huge numbers of refugees encamped, mostly East Tennesseans fleeing the rebels. Ben knew that some would surely be from Knoxville. Perhaps among them he might find a friendly face . . . though for the life of him he couldn't think of anyone in Knoxville, besides Baumgardner, who was generally friendly to him. Most people who knew him thought him a nuisance.

Still, merely having a new idea and someplace to go was encouraging, so Ben drew in his breath, looked around for errant ambulance wagons, and began walking in the general direction of Eastfield.

A couple of blocks down he saw Dummy Daws walking along, singing to himself and wearing a huge coat. Though

Dummy wasn't much to talk to, he could provide some company for a few minutes, so Ben accosted him. "Hey, Dummy! Hey, there! It's Ben!"

Dummy didn't hear him. He kept walking along, singing loudly, until he reached a firewood pile at the end of an alleyway beside a store building. He stopped, quit singing, and looked around from side to side in a suspicious manner. Ben almost hollered at him again, but grew curious. Dummy looked like he was up to something. Ben stepped behind a pole and peered around, watching.

"Ain't doing nothing! No, ain't doing nothing!" Dummy said it so loudly Ben could easily hear it all the way across the street. "Don't pay no 'tention! Ain't doing nothing."

He reached under the coat and pulled out a cloth sack with something inside. Peeping into the sack, he grinned, looked around again, and stuffed the sack into the firewood pile. He moved a few sticks about to cover it well, then chuckled loudly and said again, "Ain't doing nothing!" and walked on, singing again.

Ben waited until Dummy was around the corner and out of sight, then crossed the street and went straight for what had been hidden. He had promised the Lord to quit drinking, but his newfound sensitivity to personal guilt and responsibility hadn't gotten so far as the matter of theft yet. Maybe Dummy had hidden away some food.

Ben took the bag with him back a little farther into the alley and ducked behind the woodpile. Opening it, he looked in.

It wasn't food. It was a bottle of crystal clear home-brewed whiskey that Dummy had stashed.

Ben took the bottle in hand and stared at it. He began to tremble. Every bit of conscience he had, and there was more of it than there'd been just days ago, chided him, screamed at him, told him he should put that bottle back and go at full speed for Eastfield. He had pledged not to drink. God Himself was looking down to see if he would live up to the promise.

He gritted what teeth he had left and put the bottle on the ground. But he didn't rise and go. He merely sat there on his haunches, staring at it. He formed a mental image of himself picking up one of the firewood sticks and smashing the bottle, and told himself he really could do that. But along with that picture came another of himself picking up the bottle, pulling out the cork, taking a good, satisfying, burning swallow. . . .

I really could do that, too.

The moral battle raged a few moments more, but it was clear which side was losing. It was the side that had always lost when temptation grew strong for Ben. "I'm sorry, Lord," he said. "I just can't stand it. It'll be just this one time more, I promise you. After this, never again."

He picked up the bottle and removed the cork.

Chapter 37

September 25

David Calvin, a man with the most even-keeled emotions of anyone Adam Hanover knew, walked into the office of his publisher with an expression suspiciously like that of someone on the brink of tears.

"Good heavens, man, what's wrong?" Adam asked, laying aside the pen with which he'd been scribbling random notes concerning a new civic worry he had developed: fear that the Federal ammunition dumps scattered liberally throughout the city of Nashville posed a threat of fire or explosion, whether by accident or sabotage.

"Some better communications from Chickamauga are beginning to come in," Calvin said. "The numbers of the Nashville dead are likely to be staggering. General Maney's brigade is mauled terribly. General Cheatham's division has suffered ungodly casualties. It's going to be a terrible time for many a family here as the news starts to get out. It's a rebel victory, but one that this city in particular has paid dear for. So many of the dead ones came from Nashville."

"David, you're obviously agitated about this, but I don't quite understand why. These are Confederate losses you're talking about."

Calvin's expression iced over. "And Confederate dead don't matter?"

Adam replayed his own words through his mind and cringed. He'd done it again: Too many times he was so partisan that he let himself become heartless. He was a hopeless partisan. He'd never confess it to Calvin or even Amy, but one of the reasons he'd made such a stand against some of Andrew Johnson's policies early on was that he wanted to demonstrate to the public that he could be something other than a predictable Unionist reactionary, sometimes.

"Forgive me, David. I . . . misspoke."

Calvin stared at him, silent.

Sighing, Adam stood and turned to the window. "So a lot of Confederate families out there have suffered quite a loss, then."

"Yes. Including mine."

Adam turned, face inquisitive.

"I have three cousins under Cheatham," he explained. "We've heard that two died, but it's not official yet."

"I'm sorry. You know, I didn't even realize you had Confederate kin."

"Well, I do. Perhaps if you did, you might not be so cavalier sometimes in the way you . . ." Calvin trailed off. His chin quivered.

"You *are* upset!" Adam said. "I don't think I've seen you this way before."

"I'm growing sick of this war. Too many good people are dying, and sometimes I wonder if it's really worth their lives. It's easy to forget what we're fighting for."

"We're fighting for the preservation of the Union."

"I know. The preservation of the Union. Kill the individual, preserve the Union. Great and noble our cause!"

Adam gazed at him steadily. "You need some time off, David? You've been working awfully hard lately."

"No. No, I'll be fine." He looked at the floor a few moments, Adam's apple bobbing as he swallowed repeatedly and tried to calm down. "I'm sorry. I didn't mean to go on at you that way. It's just that I grew up with those cousins. We played together as children. Almost like brothers back in those days."

Adam mulled that and turned to the window again. "What you're saying brings to mind a possible editorial I might write," he said. With his back toward his editor, Adam couldn't see Calvin flick his eyes heavenward and lightly shake his head. Didn't everything inspire an editorial for Adam Hanover? Adam continued: "These Confederate deaths at Chickamauga are something like—pardon the cliché—the hens coming home to roost for our rebel neighbors. They've declared themselves rebels, sent their finest young men off to defend their provincial little notion of patriotism, and now those sons are going to be coming home in boxes or wind up in battlefield graves. The seed was sown, the plant grew, and now the bitter fruit is being harvested. Bitter fruit . . . bitter fruit . . . I like that. I'll use it." He turned back to his desk, grabbed up his pen and scribbled it down. "Bitter fruit. That's what I'll call it: 'The Bitter Fruit of Rebellion.'"

"Begging your pardon, Adam, but I don't recommend you do that just now."

"What? Why not?"

"Because of the human side of this. You've got to consider the sheer grief that's going to grip this city. I don't care how wrongheaded the rebellion is, it's not wise nor kind to preach at people while their grief is fresh."

"Oh, no, David, you're wrong. The very key to success is to get the point across to them while the pain *is* fresh. They'll grasp it better that way. If it hurts, I'm sorry. Truth has a way of bringing pain sometimes, until you get yourself onto the right side of it. That's what these foolish Secessionist people around here need to do. Get on the right side of the truth. Realize they were wrong to rebel, and understand fully that the personal losses they've suffered in their victory at Chickamauga and elsewhere are the direct result of their own foolishness. Quite a high price this precious victory had. It's the bitter fruit of flora they planted and cultivated themselves. I really do like that 'bitter fruit' phrase. Do you?"

"I love it to death."

Adam Hanover was in too big a way to catch the sarcasm. "Good, good. Well, we're in agreement, then. You

gather the facts, and I'll get started on the editorial. I had
something else here I was thinking of working on, having to
do with the ammunition depots around here, but we can hit
that later. The bitter fruit thing is what needs doing now.
You agree?"

"Whatever you say, Adam."

David Calvin turned and left the office. Before the
door closed behind him, Adam was already back at his desk,
head buried in his work, pen scribbling so fast that ink
droplets flew.

Ben Scarlett grunted and opened his eyes. "What in the . . ."
He sat up, blinking and trying to see. His head suddenly felt
like someone was inside it, trying to hammer his way out.
He reached down and felt something hot and wet on his
right leg—it was this that had awakened him.

"Looky there!" a boy's voice chortled. "Looky there at
him!"

Ben turned his squinted eyes toward the right and saw
three boys and as many dogs, standing back a safe distance.
The dogs barked at him as he sat up straighter, and the boys
danced and pointed mockingly, laughing. "Are you wet, you
old drunk? Are you wet?"

Ben touched the damp place on his leg and lifted his
hand to his nostrils. He looked angrily at the boys. "Did one
of them dogs pee on me?"

"Yes, he did, yes, he did!" the bravest of the mockers
said, lifting a leg, making a hissing sound, then shaking the
lifted foot. "Old drunk got himself peed on!"

"Go away."

"Let's all do it!" the lead mocker said. "One, two, three!"
They all lifted their legs and made the noise.

Ben came to his feet. He didn't get angry often, but these
boys had caught him at the wrong time, and the idea of
being peed on by a dog while he lay passed-out drunk was
humiliating even to him. He grabbed a rock and threw it at
the boys. He missed them but hit one of the dogs right on
the end of the snout. It yelped and ran off. The boys cussed
at Ben, and the other dogs barked furiously. Ben reached for

another rock. The mockers and their canine pack turned and ran after the injured dog, yelling abuse at Ben until they were out of sight.

Ben stood with shoulders slumped and tossed the rock to the ground. Looking down, he saw the big wet place the dog had left on him and was disgusted. "Look at that!" he muttered. "What makes boys want to be that way? I was never that way when I was little. Just like Curtis Delmer when he was a boy, them boys were. Just like him."

Ben pulled off his boots and removed the outer pants before the urine could soak through much to the Confederate uniform trousers beneath. He might have washed the stained trousers out in a creek somewhere if he didn't feel so sick and disgusted, not only because of what the dog had done, but because of what *he* had done. Despite his promise and good intentions, he'd gone out and gotten drunk again. Nothing had changed. Nothing would ever change. He was just sorry old Ben Scarlett, a man who dogs peed on and boys mocked, and who lay drunk on the ground at . . .

. . . Where? He looked around, not knowing where he was. He wandered when he was drunk sometimes, waking up in the oddest places.

He looked around, then stepped up to an evergreen bush nearby, pushed down a branch and looked beyond it. The rail yard. He had wandered to the rail yard and passed out.

A busy rail yard it was just now, too. A train had pulled in and unhappy looking men mostly in gray and butternut were being unloaded by Federal soldiers. Whole boxcars and flatcars full of them. They wore gray. Ben knew nothing about the Chickamauga fight, but it was evident to him there had been a battle somewhere, and the men being unloaded were Confederate soldiers captured as prisoners of war.

Ben wanted a better look. He pushed the branch down farther and started to step over it, but he was unsteady and fuzzy-headed and his muscles stiff from a night on the cold ground. He tripped, fell right across the bush, and rolled down a little bank.

"Yeow! *God!*" He barked out the cry in sudden pain, rolled around and up to a seated position, and yanked up his one good hand for a look. The area between thumb and forefinger was cut and gushing blood. He'd fallen onto some jagged old piece of scrap metal somebody had tossed out of the rail yard long ago, and it had sliced him like a blade. He felt faint and sick as he examined the gushing cut, which had bitten a good inch and a half into his flesh.

He spoke in panic to himself. "Oh no, oh no . . . I've got to get this seen to! I can't let this hand get mortified up like the other one. I can't lose the only hand I got!"

He tried to remember where he'd been headed when he found the whiskey bottle . . . Eastfield. He'd go there now, quickly, and get this hand tended to by some sympathetic East Tennessee refugee. No, no, there wasn't time. The blood was coming fast, and he was so afraid of infection that he fancied he could feel the wound already starting to fester up on him. How could a man live with no hands at all? How could he hold a fork to feed himself? How could a man hold a whiskey bottle without his hands? And how could he later lift hands to heaven to ask forgiveness for having drunk that whiskey if he had no hands to lift? Maybe this was God's ironic punishment to him for having failed his pledge.

He couldn't wait for Eastfield. He'd have to go to the nearest help he could, that being the Union guards below, who were still cattle-herding the rebel prisoners off the train. He started down toward them, but his coat hung up on a branch of the evergreen bush. In his rising panic he merely slid out of the coat and stumbled toward the guards. He fell and rolled, tried to get up and couldn't. In his perception blood was gushing everywhere, leaving him at a terrifying rate and quantity. "Help me!" he yelled. "Somebody help me, please!"

When he came to his feet again, he saw three Federals running toward him. "Help me!" he yelled at them. "I'm dying here, I swear I'm dying!"

Chapter 38

Amy laid down the day's copy of the *Sage* and stared across the room into the fire, her expression vaguely trancelike.

"Well?"

It took a moment for her to realize Adam had spoken. "Yes?"

"What did you think of it?"

"It's a fine edition. Plenty of news . . . so much of it dreadful, though. So many men killed."

"I was talking specifically about the editorial. 'Bitter Fruit.' You read it, didn't you?"

"Yes, I believe I did."

"What did you think of it?"

"Very well-written, as usual. You're a fine writer."

"Thank you. So much for what you think of the form. What about the content?"

"It was . . . very thought-provoking. Some excellent points."

"But . . ."

"But . . . maybe a little early."

"Early in what sense?"

"Adam, I don't want to be critical. Besides, the editorial is already on the street, so what's to be gained from hearing my viewpoint?"

"I want to know. I respect your opinion."

"Well . . . very well, then. I think it was a little . . . *hard* of you to preach about the 'bitter fruit' of rebellion while the bitterness is at its strongest. The editorial might have had more impact in terms of persuasiveness to the Confederate families here had it come after the dead had been buried awhile and the initial shock gotten over. As it is, I think it will only make them angry."

Adam looked at her straight-faced, then away and toward the fire. "I see."

"Oh, Adam, don't act that way!"

"What way is that, dear?"

"Hurt and icy. You asked me what I thought."

"And you certainly told me, didn't you!"

"You *asked*. I wasn't going to say a word on my own."

"That was kindhearted of you."

"Adam, I love you dearly, but when you get this way, I can hardly stand to be in the same room with you! How did a man become a newspaper publisher with such a thin skin?"

"A thin skin? I beg your pardon! Perhaps you've forgotten that I'm the man who dared to stand up to the military governor of the state, a man everyone expected me to support without question, and went to jail for my trouble!"

"No, I haven't forgotten that." She crossed her arms, looked away from him, and added, "How *could* I forget?"

"What does that mean?"

"Nothing."

"No, no. Tell me what you meant! Are you implying that I'm braggadocious?"

"I'm implying nothing! All I mean is that you are proud of having done what you did—rightly so, I might add—and you aren't likely to go very long without finding some reason to mention it."

"In other words, braggadocious."

"You're impossible!"

"And braggadocious. Don't forget that. Impossible, braggadocious, and hard-hearted for not thinking enough of the feelings of the poor bereaved rebels—rebels whom, I might point out, have themselves brought this war to our nation and bereaved many a good Union family through it. Or perhaps that doesn't count for anything. Perhaps, in this sad time of grief for so many poor bereaved Nashville rebel clans, we're not to look at the broader picture."

"I've never seen you so scornful, Adam! My goodness, why ask for my opinion if you don't really want to hear it? Or maybe you only want to hear me agree with you, like a good and faithful little wife. Well, let me remind *you*, sir, that I grew up the daughter of a man who never expressed one view I could agree with, and not only did I have to put up with that, I had to actually serve as his surrogate writer! I spent many long months putting into words views that repelled me, and I have no intention of ever hiding my true viewpoints again! So if you don't want to hear them, don't ask!"

He stood. "I believe I'll go to bed early tonight. Maybe read awhile. More peaceful in the bedroom than in here . . . and not nearly so cold. I do believe I see icicles beginning to form on the furniture."

"Any coldness in this room comes from you . . . and from this cold editorial you are so proud of." She slapped the paper with the back of her hand.

His face reddened, he opened his mouth, but nothing came out. Wheeling, he stormed away to the bedroom and slammed the door.

He was still awake two hours later when Amy opened the bedroom door and slipped in. He watched her enter and said nothing. She went to the bed, sat down on its edge, and lifted from his hands and off his chest the facedown open book he'd been reading, but without seeing a single word.

"I'm sorry," she said.

He looked at her. "Me, too. I made quite an ass of myself, didn't I?"

"That you did. I almost expected you to bray at me."

He laughed and lifted his arm to wrap around her. She leaned down and put her head on his chest, looking up at his face from below. "You're quite handsome, you know."

"Yes, yes. We impossible, braggadocious, coldhearted types are often very handsome."

"I don't know how that argument even got started. It's kind of a blur."

"I suppose I started it. I admit it: I was trying to get you to say you agreed with me and were glad I'd published it when I did, and all that. Because of David Calvin, really."

"What's David got to do with it?"

"He made some of the very same points you made downstairs, when I first brought up the idea of writing the editorial. He said we should wait, not salt the wounds of the bereaved . . . basically the same thing you said."

"Two against one. You felt like everyone was ganging up on you."

"Worse. I felt like maybe you and David were right, and I was wrong." He gave her a squeeze. "Amy, if I was coldhearted in writing that editorial, I didn't mean to be. It just seemed the right time to me to make those points."

"Who can say? Maybe it will do some good."

"Maybe. Oh, well. What's done is done. If I make a few rebels mad, it's not like they don't already despise me anyway. I'm convinced that half our circulation consists of people who buy the paper just so they can cuss at it while they read it." He chuckled. "Like last Sunday. After services, four . . . no, five different men came up to me, mad as hornets, telling me that I'd 'missed the mark' on this or 'spewed outright lies' on that. Five men, five different things they were mad about! I swear, I can keep things stirred up without trying, just by doing my job."

"That's probably because part of the job of a newspaper publisher *is* keeping things stirred up." She brought her face toward him and kissed his chin. "I'm hungry. Want to go downstairs and have a bite to eat?"

"Hungry again? We had supper not all that long ago."

"I know. It's just that I didn't eat breakfast again, and didn't have much during the day, either."

"I'm worried about you. What's this thing of not eating breakfast and all?"

"I believe there's a good reason for it."

"What?"

"You might say that something inside of me is causing me these problems."

He almost came out of the bed. "My lands . . . you don't mean a parasite, do you?"

"Oh, heavens no!" She laughed. "A *parasite*?"

"Well, you're around all those fleabitten, wormy old wounded soldiers all the time, fresh in off the battlefields with every kind of parasite in the world crawling on them and through them and . . . wait. What *do* you mean, 'something inside' you?"

"Think about it. What do you think? Not able to eat in the mornings, light-headed, queasy when I've never been that way before . . ."

He looked at her and his eyes began to brim. "Praise be!" he said. "Praise be! Are you sure?"

"Pretty much, yes. Every sign is there. And my monthly hasn't bothered to come along for a good while now." She laughed to see tears roll down his face. Adam Hanover always prided himself on never being emotional. She kissed him again, on the lips this time. "What do you want? A boy or a girl?"

"I don't care. I don't care at all." He hugged her, squeezing her shoulders until she thought he'd break them. "I love you, Amy. I love you so very much! I want to be with you a lifetime . . . you, and our little one."

"I love you too, Adam." She looked at him. "And I'm ready to show you right now just how much I love you."

His tears ceased and a slow grin split his face. "Does that mean what I think it means?"

"Yes. Adam Hanover, right now I'm going to . . . go downstairs and fix a big plate of food, then bring it back up here and let you feed it to me!"

"Why, you little scoundrel . . ."

She ran from the room and down the stairs, laughing all the way to the larder, before he could get out from beneath the covers in time to grab her.

"You just wait!" he hollered.

"I'm afraid it's *you* who are having to wait tonight, my dear!" she called back up.

"I love you, Amy Deacon Hanover."

"I love you, too."

At the corner of Spring and Cherry streets, Nashville

Adam Hanover, with David Calvin at his side, looked up at the big, broad, unfinished new structure called the Maxwell House and thought that this was just the fine kind of edifice a city like Nashville deserved. Yet it was also frustrating to observe such a superb building while knowing that it was being put to what Adam considered a menial and inappropriate—though probably unavoidable—use.

It wasn't the first time the Maxwell House had been used as something other than the hotel its builder had intended it to be when construction began in 1859. The outbreak of war had halted work on the building, which was five stories tall, made of brick, and covered a 175-by-160-foot parcel of excellent street-corner property. The rebels had taken it over as a place to quarter troops, calling it "Zollicoffer Barracks" in honor of the Confederate general and former *Nashville Banner* editor of that name. When the Confederates had left Nashville and the Federals had come in, the building, with its rows of tall, arch-topped windows, was again utilized for military purposes as a convalescent barracks. Now, with Nashville being swamped by an influx of prisoners of war from the Chickamauga fight, the fourth and fifth floors of the Maxwell House were being used as military prison space, packed well beyond safe capacity.

That situation had Adam thinking, as usual, about writing an editorial. The problem was deciding just what the editorial should say. Certainly prisoners had to be kept somewhere, and perhaps the Maxwell House was the best place . . . but he sensed there was something worth writing about this overcrowded situation, if only he could come up with it.

"Adam, I really think there's no coon up this particular tree," David Calvin said. "I mean, what could the authorities do? Drive wounded soldiers out of their hospital beds to make room for prisoners of war? The Maxwell House seems as good a place as any to me."

"You're probably right about that. Still, I have this notion, just a feeling, that there's the potential for trouble here. The building isn't even finished, after all, yet it's being stuffed to the gills with humanity."

"Just a bunch of rebels. I wouldn't worry about them."

Adam didn't miss the subtle barb in his editor's comment. Calvin hadn't quite gotten over the insult he felt from Adam's attitude at the news of the Chickamauga rebel casualties, even though, at Amy's suggestion, Adam had made a point of admitting to Calvin that just maybe he'd been a bit wrongheaded on that one.

"Well . . . maybe there's nothing to do but keep an eye on the situation. I'd like you to come around here some over the next bit of time, keep your ears open, find out how the situation is in there. Meanwhile I'll see if there might not be some other space around Nashville that could be put to holding some of these prisoners. If there is, perhaps the *Sage* can provide some helpful suggestions along that line."

The two journalists turned and headed toward Adam's parked buggy. He seldom utilized it. Being a brisk and enthusiastic walker, he found he could generally get where he needed to go more quickly on foot. With several stops to make today, however, he had opted for a vehicle.

Shifting off the Maxwell House subject, Adam began telling Calvin more of his thoughts about the dangers of powder depots around a busy city, when someone called to him. "You, sir! Yes, you!"

He stopped and turned to a heavyset, whiskered man who came striding rapidly toward him with cane in hand.

"Hello, sir," Adam said. "What can I do for—"

"You are Adam Hanover?"

"Yes . . ."

"Publisher of the *Sage*?"

"Yes, I am. Can I help you in some—"

"Are you the author, then, of the recent editorial called 'Bitter Fruit'?"

"Indeed I am. If there's a question about—"

The man, without another word, lifted the cane and brought

it down hard on Adam's shoulder. He was lifting it a second time when David Calvin intervened, putting himself between the man and Adam, who had staggered back at the first blow, as much out of surprise as anything. He stood gaping for a moment while Calvin struggled with his attacker, but then Calvin was pushed away and onto his rump and the man came on again.

He got in three more blows, all across Adam's shoulders, before others on the street made it over to break up the brawl. Three burly fellows grabbed the cane-wielding man and held him. "You want the police, I reckon?" one said to Adam.

"No . . . no." Adam rubbed his shoulders, wondering how bad the bruising would be. "No . . . let him go. He was merely expressing his viewpoint in a rather boorish way."

"Expressing his . . . Mister, it looked to me like he was trying to beat you to death."

"No," said the attacker. "Had I wanted to kill him, I would have done so. I merely wanted him to learn that not only rebellion has its 'bitter fruit.' Sometimes a foolishly written, heartless bit of newspaper rubbish, good only for increasing the pain of those who have suffered too much pain already, can generate some very rancid fruit of its own."

"You lost someone at Chickamauga?" Adam asked him.

"My son," the man said. "My only son. And I shall lose my wife because of it too, because this whole business has destroyed her health within a matter of a few short days. That blasted editorial of yours did nothing but make it worse. Damnation! Would you brutes let me go? I'll not hit him again."

"Let him go," Adam said.

"You sure, sir?"

"Yes. Let him go."

The man lifted a fat finger and aimed it at Adam's nose. "You, sir, had best learn a bit more about common human decency. You blasted Lincolnites may have control of this city, but the time will come when the situation will change, and it may be *you* tasting the fruits of your foolishness! Good day to you."

Adam watched the man stride away. David Calvin said, "You could have him charged. That was assault, straight out."

"I know. But what would that gain? He has it out of his system now, and perhaps some good can come of it. I want you to write this event as a story, David, and we'll publish it, front page."

"Why? You want to encourage more of the same?"

"No, I want to discourage it. Count on it: If there's one man willing to take his cane to someone, there's a hundred more who are thinking about it. Let's let them have some vicarious satisfaction, finding out that I've already gotten my comeuppance. They can say their serves-him-rights and forget about it."

David Calvin grinned. "Good thinking, Adam."

"That's the first grin I've seen from you in far too long, David. I believe you're proving my own theory: You saw me take a beating and now you feel better for it. Admit it! I can see it in your face!"

"I do confess that you might have had it coming. That editorial was poorly timed."

" 'Cold.' That's the word Amy used. 'Cold.' Oh, well. Let's get out of here." He looked at the now-distant figure of the man who had caned him. "There he goes, off to some smoky tavern to brag about how he laid it to that fool Lincolnite editor! The rebels will be eating Hanover hash over this one."

They went to the buggy and left the Maxwell House behind.

Chapter 39

Adam and Amy Hanover had just finished dressing and were sitting down to breakfast together—the first shared breakfast in many days—when they heard a rush of footsteps on their porch and someone hammered the door. Amy wiped at her reddened eyes; she'd been crying some this morning, emotional in the hormonal upheavals of pregnancy and over the terrible-looking bruises that marred her husband's shoulders as a result of the caning he'd received.

Adam began to get up. "Who in the name of—"

It was David Calvin, and he didn't wait for Adam to admit him before he came in. Even before Adam got out his sentence, Calvin burst in through the unlocked front door, looked around wildly, then spotted Adam coming his way and ran to him.

"You've got to come, Adam. I just heard that the staircase at the Maxwell House collapsed. You were right—too many prisoners in there. They were lined up, coming down to breakfast, when it gave way."

"Any killed?"

"I don't know yet. Probably. They say it's a scene of chaos over there. Hurry! I knew you'd want to see it yourself."

"I wish the buggy was rigged—"

"I have a buggy already—my neighbor let me borrow his."

They were on their way in less than a minute.

Apart from the fact that only six had been killed outright, it was about as bad as it could have been.

The staircase on the top floor had gone first, dropping heavy wood and human beings onto the staircase below, which had given way, adding its own weight to the load that then crashed into the stairway beneath it, and so on down to the second floor. More than seventy men were hurt. The entire Maxwell House corner was aswarm with people in various states of agitation, and injured prisoners were being led or carried out, depending on their condition, and placed on the ground while surgeons called to the scene inspected them.

The volunteer nurse in Amy wouldn't let her stand by idly, and she quickly went to give what assistance she could. Adam and David, meanwhile, talked to witnesses, took notes, and did their best to ascertain just what had happened.

In the midst of the tumult, Adam felt a hand on his arm. He turned to see a wide-eyed Amy looking back at him. "Adam, come quick!"

"What is it?"

"Come here! There's someone here . . ."

He could hardly keep up with her. She ran between two rows of the injured and literally leaped over one of them to enter the next row, where she knelt beside an unconscious man. Adam took a more dignified approach and picked his way through the row Amy had leaped, came to her and knelt at her side. Amy had taken the injured man's hand in hers . . . the only hand the fellow had, Adam noticed, and it was tightly bandaged.

"Adam, I know this man. I've told you about him. This is Ben Scarlett!"

"Ben Scarlett . . . that drunkard from Knoxville?"

"Yes! Yes! He's a good man, Adam, despite his drinking and so on. A good and dear man, and I want to help him."

"Help him? I'm sure they'll tend to him along with the others."

"No, I want to take him in. I'll tend to him myself."

"Take him . . . you mean into our *house*?"

"Yes. Adam, this man is a friend. I know that sounds odd, but he is. I may be the only friend in the world that he has, and it's my duty to do what I can for him. He helped me smuggle that money, at risk to himself, and now I can return the favor."

"Amy, I don't know. A drunk, in our house? And are the rebels down to enlisting drunkards off the streets now, I wonder? You're sure it's him?"

"Yes! I want to take him in, I mean that. We have influence with the authorities, both of us. I know we can arrange it. I'll go all the way to Governor Johnson himself if I have to."

"You really do mean it, don't you!"

"I do. Let's take him in, Adam, if the surgeons say we can. We can take responsibility for him, see that he doesn't flee. I can't believe he's a soldier! There's something amiss in all this. Can't we take him, Adam? Won't you agree?"

"You make him sound like a stray pup."

"Adam, please!"

He looked at the supine figure of a man who looked like he had known the worst side of living for more than his due of time. Sallow, wasted, thin, he didn't appear to be long for this world. Most likely the surgeons would examine him and say he required hospitalization.

"Amy, if the surgeons say he's fit for it, I'm willing to take him in, at least for a time. He did help you, after all."

She smiled and kissed Adam, then looked down at the face of Ben Scarlett and wondered if it was impending death that made him look so sallow and wasted.

Adam Hanover walked toward his home a couple of nights later, deeply lost in thought. Who would have thought it? Ben Scarlett, as sickly and terrible as he looked, wasn't nearly as bad off as he seemed. He had a cut on his one hand, but that was healing, and the only injury he'd received in the fall of the staircase had been a very insignificant concussion and one bruised rib. As for that sallow, pallid look, the surgeon didn't think that meant much. Some people just look that way, he said, especially those who've lived inebriated lives and haven't had enough of the right kind of food. If the Hanovers wanted to take this fellow in, that was fine with the physician. He'd probably fare much better in a comfortable domestic setting than in a crowded military prison facility.

As for the military authorities, they didn't put up any fuss at all, somewhat to Adam's chagrin. The Hanovers wanted to take a prisoner off their hands? Fine with them! This fellow had been claiming he wasn't a soldier anyway, that the uniform he'd been wearing at the rail yard was a castoff he found, and the guards who had herded him in admitted they couldn't figure out how a true prisoner of theirs could have gotten away from the train. Furthermore, the head count of transported prisoners on that load came up one extra when Ben Scarlett was thrown in.

And so now Ben Scarlett, who had regained consciousness even before they left Maxwell House, was a resident of the Hanover dwelling. Propped up on the fine bed in the spare bedroom, he had it pretty good for a fellow who apparently had gone through a round of very ill luck.

Unwilling host though Adam was, he had to admit that Ben Scarlett was interesting. Amy seemed to hold him in very high regard; something about the man touched her. Master of words though she was, she hadn't been able to explain it completely to her husband. She knew Ben was no more than a vagrant and drunkard, that he'd wasted his life and probably was overdue for the grave, but still, she declared, there was something about him, and in him, that was pure and good. She admitted it made no sense. How could a man like that be good? What was even remotely pure about a person who had drunk his life away and probably stole half of whatever living he made? Maybe, she speculated to Adam, what she sensed in Ben was the ghost of what he might have been, not what he was. Or maybe she was even sensing the kind of man Ben Scarlett yet could be.

Realistically, Adam had his doubts about that. A man

who had lived Ben's kind of life for as many years as he had wasn't likely to reform. When Amy said she detected the good and pure in Ben, what she was probably feeling was mere pity, supplemented by a sense of appreciation for the complimentary and loving things he'd said about her in that letter he left for her once.

Adam found only one flaw in that theory: When he was around Ben, he detected the very same vague things Amy did, and that certainly didn't come from any past experience with the man. It was instinctive, intuitive . . . he could just sense that somewhere in the blasted wasteland that was Ben Scarlett's life, there remained a hidden Eden that was not yet spoiled, and might yet blossom.

More mundanely, he also believed that he just might be able to get a story out of the man. Bit by bit, Ben had related to them a moving tale of coming all the way from Knoxville, alone and mostly on foot, right through the heart of war-torn Tennessee, to find a lost love who apparently had become a Nashville prostitute and died on the steamer to Louisville. Ben declined to say how he'd learned she was in Nashville, saying that there was a "certain picture-taking fellow I don't want to get in trouble." Even without that detail, there was much to give the story merit, not by importance so much as its merely human side. It was a story that was something like Ben himself seemed to be—tragic, failed, and sad, yet capable of stirring the heart.

It also had a timely element, for the Cyprian issue was back in the public mind again, with the Federals having decided that since they couldn't oust them, they might as well register and regulate them. Thus in Nashville, Tennessee, for the first time in the history of the United States, prostitution had been given legal standing, with "soiled doves" signing up on a registry, undergoing physical examinations to ensure they were free of venereal diseases, and if they were, receiving a license to practice their trade.

"You there, mister."

Adam stopped. A young man stepped from behind a tree. "Let me ast you something. You the newspaper fellow who writ them bad things about the rebel folk of this city?"

Adam wasn't in the mood to take another beating, especially from someone who looked no more than sixteen at most. "Step aside, young fellow."

"No, sir. I asted you if you was the newspaper fellow."

"If you want to talk to this 'newspaper fellow' you keep mentioning, I suggest you go to his office and see him during business hours. Good evening."

"I asted you who you was!"

"You may have 'asted,' but I'm under no obligation to answer everything you 'ast.' Good night."

He walked past the young man, who turned and watched him for a few paces.

"You'd best watch yourself, newspaper man! You'd best learn to be careful what you say 'bout folks!"

Adam walked on, ignoring him.

"They's a lot of people mighty mad 'bout what you writ! They's some of them mad enough to kill you! I'm a-warning you!"

Adam called back over his shoulder: "And I'm a-going home. I suggest you be a-doing the same."

He felt the young fellow's stare on the back of his neck, and knew he'd been imprudent to be so mocking. He couldn't help it, though. He was tired of people who believed the way to carry on public debates was with canes and threats on the streets.

If he had it to do over again, he would have never written that editorial.

While a somewhat unsettled Adam Hanover was covering the final few blocks to his home, Amy was lifting her hand from Ben Scarlett's shoulder and saying, "Ben, if it's a friend you need to help you get past the liquor, then a friend you have. Two friends—me and my husband, too."

Ben wiped a stray tear from his eye. Ever since he'd come into Amy's presence again and been treated so kindly, he had been more shaky in his emotions. He'd just laid out before her that night of longing and pledges that he had believed was a turning point . . . until he found Dummy's hidden bottle of whiskey. He told her there was no hope of him making it out of the whiskey bondage without the help and support of a friend, and Amy responded as he had dared hope she would.

"You're too kind to me, you and your husband both," he said. "I don't deserve it, Mrs. Amy." That was his tag for her: Mrs. Amy.

"If we only got what we deserved in this life, we'd all be in pretty bad shape, Ben," Amy replied. "Listen . . . I don't know much about dealing with someone who is coming off his liquor, like you will be. I don't know what it will be like except from what I've heard. I know that it isn't easy, or pleasant."

"I went through it once. It was pure hell, if you'll pardon my French. I don't relish the idea of you seeing me go through it."

"You must understand, Ben, that I've been working as a volunteer nurse in the Federal hospitals. There isn't much I haven't seen. I've always been a strong person . . . I'm stronger now than I ever was. I'll help you get through it, if you really want to do it, and if you'll promise me you'll not turn around and go right back to it when we're through."

"I already promised God, and I broke that promise real fast. I'll try to do better with you."

"I don't want you to try. I want you to *do* it. Trying means nothing unless it succeeds."

He thought about it, nodded. "I'll do it. I really will. And when I'm through, I won't go back."

She reached down to squeeze his hand, but remembered the wound. "How's the hand feel?"

"Doing good. Healing up nice. I was afraid it would beal up on me and I'd have to get it cut off, too. I'd hate to go through life with no hands at all."

The door opened and closed downstairs; Adam's voice rang up through the house, announcing his arrival.

"I'll go down and greet him. And I'll tell him what we've been talking about."

"I hope he won't toss me out of here."

"He won't. He's a good man, Ben. If he wasn't, I wouldn't have married him. If you want to get off the whiskey, he'll be glad for it. I promise you."

"God bless this family, both of you."

She was about to go out the door but paused and grinned back at him. "Not just two of us anymore. There's a little one, not yet born."

His eyes brightened. "Why, Mrs. Amy! That's a wonderful thing! I'm so glad to hear of it! A little girl, I'll bet, just as pretty as you!"

"Maybe so! Good evening, Ben. Come down and join us later, if you feel like it."

Adam listened to what Amy had to say and arched his brows. "A drunkard, drying out right here in our house . . . Amy, I don't know what I think about it. I had an uncle who went through that years ago, and I saw a little of it. It's a terrible thing. Does Ben really mean it? Does he know what he's getting into?"

"He does. He's been through it once before."

"Ah! And went back afterward, obviously."

"He swears he won't do that this time. I have to believe him."

"Who do you intend to keep with him? He'll require somebody close at hand, especially through the worst of it."

"I'll do it."

"No. I'll not have that. He might become dangerous. There are things they see, notions they get, and fears . . ."

"I believe I can handle it."

"You truly want this?"

"I do. I want him to have the chance to live. If he doesn't do this, he'll be dead in a year. I'm sure of it. God only knows why he isn't dead already."

Adam thought about it. "I'll go along, then, on one condition."

"What?"

"That you let me hire someone—a man, somebody big and strong and capable physically of dealing with Ben if he should get violent on us. I'll not have you hurt for Ben Scarlett's sake, especially with the baby to consider."

"I can accept that." She smiled. "Thank you."

He smiled and shook his head. " 'Thank you,' she says. As if it was ever really my decision! I've figured out something about you, Amy: What you want you generally get."

She smiled coyly and made no reply. There was no point in contradicting the truth.

Chapter 40

It could have gone much worse than it did.

Ben Scarlett was as good as his word. In all the miserable days of letting his system fight off the addiction that consumed him, he never once even asked for a drink. Nor did he grow violent, though sometimes he did see horrible images that weren't truly there and would thrash and flail as he recoiled from them. The man Adam hired to see Ben through the worst times, a burly former slave now living as a "contraband" in Union-held Nashville, had a relatively easy job of it. And then, one night, Ben came downstairs, looking like he'd just fought the devil and won. He looked at both Hanovers, smiled, and said, "I think I done it."

It was a happy time for Amy, one her husband didn't mar by letting her know of the threats that continued to come to him. He was surprised and disturbed that the feelings stirred by one mere collection of ill-advised words were lingering so long, and actually seeming to worsen. There were letters that came to the paper, some to the house—he made a point of trying to collect the mail personally, before Amy could see—and once there was a flaming rag tossed onto the porch. Fortunately, he was home at the time—Amy gone off to do some volunteer work at Hospital No. 2—and stomped the rag out before it even blistered the paint. Ben Scarlett was there too, however, and Adam was forced to take him into his confidence and confess that he was worried about his safety.

Ben asked for a job the next day. All he'd ask in return would be food and board, and the latter he could take right at the newspaper office, on a cot in a back storage room. He could sweep up the place, learn how to help with the printing and distribution, and act as a night watchman, "just to make certain the place never was bothered by nobody." Adam took him up on the offer and threw in a small wage besides. Given the threats and so on, he'd been thinking about hiring a night guard anyway, and certainly Ben couldn't keep on living there in the house. He was staying true to his pledge and keeping away from liquor, and was beginning to fatten up and look downright healthy, but the boredom of simply being at the house wasn't good for him. Boredom was more likely to drive him back to drinking than any other single factor. A job was indeed just what Ben needed.

So Ben became an employee of the *Nashville Sage*, and made of himself the best one-handed floor sweeper in the state, until the day that Amy surprised him with a gift: a shining metal hook on the end of a cup designed to fit over a handless wrist. It was a fine fit, and after Ben got past the stage of unfamiliarity, during which he was lethally dangerous, swinging the hook about mindlessly, he became adept at using it.

Another natural benefit of Ben's newly sober, industrious life was that he began to learn. He didn't consciously try to; it just happened. He'd been literate for years, but didn't read much, mostly just scanning through stray copies of old newspapers that blew through his trashy world. Now he began to read the *Sage* quite carefully. Quite a few times he picked up on spelling errors and "things that just don't read right, Mr. Hanover," and Adam Hanover expanded Ben's duties to include proofreading. Ben was so proud when this happened that he shed tears, reached up to dab them with the wrong arm and almost hooked off his own nose.

For once the events of the war began to come together in Ben's understanding. He glimpsed the overall strategies being pursued by the various armies, though of course many details of these were withheld from the press and public and came clear only after the fact. He developed a great interest in how matters were progressing, or regressing, depending on the individual case and viewpoint.

From the Unionist viewpoint, regression seemed to be holding the day around Nashville. Though the city was held by a strong Union force, rebel activity, much of it performed by free-roaming irregulars, increased greatly. These activities sparked many an eager rumor among the strongly rebel populace. Typical of them: Wheeler and Forrest are coming to Nashville with cavalry, to liberate the city from the Union! Before long Nashville will be in Confederate hands again!

These major events didn't come about, but some lesser ones did. Though Forrest and Wheeler never showed up in Nashville, nearby Murfreesboro did get swept by a force of several thousand rebels who ripped up railroad tracks, destroyed water tanks, and burned bridges. And at Lebanon, just a skip and a jump from Nashville, bands of rebels appeared, moving through the countryside, derailing trains and stirring up both trouble and more rumors of bad things to come for the Union in Middle Tennessee.

East Tennessee saw its share of autumn activity, too. Colonel John Carter, Union, faced off with Brigadier General John S. Williams in a skirmish at the Greene County town of Blue Springs, then fell back with the rebels to the east of town, the Yankees farther west at the town of Bulls Gap. Burnside left Knoxville by railroad, hauling trainloads of Ninth Corps soldiers with him, and settled in at Bulls Gap to direct the Union side of the fight. It turned out to be quite a brisk and wide-ranging battle, centering mostly on Blue Springs, but with related action taking place as far away as Rheatown, several miles on the far side of Greeneville. When the Blue Springs Battle was over, however, the lines of both armies were not sitting much differently than when they had started.

In mid-October, General Ulysses Grant, newly named

head of the Union armies in the West, arrived at Nashville on his way to Chattanooga, where he removed General Rosecrans from command of the Army of the Cumberland and put General George Thomas in to replace him. Adam made a strong effort to obtain an interview with Grant during his brief Nashville stop, staking out the St. Cloud's Hotel in hopes of seeing him, but it came to naught.

Meanwhile, the threats against Adam continued, becoming worse the more rebel activity increased in the region, and also harder to hide from Amy, who wasn't easy to deceive in any case.

Ben, who knew about the threats, watched Adam struggling under the pressure of them. Adam threw himself into his campaign against the dangerous powder depots in the city, voicing much criticism of the Union's handling of that matter. Ben, growing more perceptive as his mind cured itself of the effects of drinking, figured out that Adam was deliberately trying to show the world he was capable of criticizing his own team, maybe to stifle some of the mounting hatred of him among the pro-Confederate populace. It didn't seem to be working. The stories and editorials about the powder dumps generated a bit of controversy and discussion, but nothing major.

And the threats continued. Ben, sleeping at the newspaper office, began seeing suspicious movements by night outside the windows, and often slept lightly, worried about arson.

Amy said nothing about it, but Ben could tell that she realized what was going on. He began accompanying Adam as much as possible whenever Adam walked through town, and used the cooling weather as grounds to encourage him to use his buggy more. The real motive was to make Adam less visible to the public. Adam, accepting the cool-weather argument as his pretext, did begin forsaking the walks in favor of the buggy, but everyone, including Amy, knew why he'd really made the change.

As the physical atmosphere of Nashville made the slow degree shift from autumn moderation toward winter cold, so also did the psychological atmosphere. The city began to feel different, to seem a more hostile and dangerous place to be.

Out along the river hidden snipers began shooting at the boats plying the river between Nashville and Louisville, usually doing little damage, but creating an aura of danger that ate at the nerves of boatmen. The military response was to clear trees from the banks, and to give permission to boat crews to shoot at any person seen lurking suspiciously along the banks. Thus the aura of danger spread to encompass not only the river itself, but the area surrounding it.

More rumors began among the rebel population: The Union was going to force every private household to use its extra rooms to house East Tennessee Unionist refugees and—even worse in the mind of the white-skinned public— Negro "contrabands." Adam and David investigated this rumor and found it false, but few were inclined to believe what was written in a Unionist newspaper. Adam realized that as time went by and factional bitterness grew, his newspaper was becoming less tolerated and more ignored. He began worrying, second-guessing every decision. The newspaper's quality suffered. Circulation began to drop, then advertising.

Meanwhile, the threats did not drop. They increased.

So did guerrilla activity around Middle Tennessee. Rebel regulars and irregulars rode in Cheatham and Dickson counties. There were shootings, in one case, at least, with the shooter being Unionist and his victim a pro-Confederate civilian. This only hardened Confederate feeling against the occupying Federals.

Adam, growing more fearful and still seeking, consciously or not, to appease the rebels who hated him, urged an immediate, thorough investigation of the shooting of the Confederate civilian. The campaign won him no new friends. Readership continued to fall off, and advertising, too. Adam heard rumors of a boycott of his newspaper by businesses who themselves were being threatened of boycott by the Confederate public if they didn't withhold their advertising.

David Calvin grew increasingly quiet and withdrawn,

writing less and not as well. He gave his notice early in November and disappeared, not saying where he was going or why. Ben figured the threats had reached him, too. Amy began working in David's place, though she was an ineffective substitute because Adam wouldn't allow her the freedom of activity David had enjoyed. He worried about her, and the baby.

In mid-November Confederate General Longstreet launched an effort to retake Knoxville from Burnside's army, setting up a battery on the Tazewell road and lobbing shells into the city. The siege continued for days, but in the end Knoxville would remain in Union control, and Longstreet would withdraw into the northeastern end of the state, to spend the winter headquartered in the tiny hamlet of Russellville, between Morristown and Bulls Gap.

The bloody apex of the siege occurred on a fog-shrouded Sunday morning in the fight for Fort Sanders. And on that same morning, miles away in Nashville, Ben Scarlett awakened to the sound of a shot outside the office. Rising, throwing on his trousers, he scurried to the front window and peered out.

"Oh Lord, no, please Lord . . ."

He went out, shirtless despite the cold, and knelt beside the bleeding and blankly staring figure of Adam Hanover, who lay crumpled on the edge of the street. Why had he come here on a Sunday morning? Why had he walked rather than taking the more protective buggy? Why?

"Adam!" Ben all but shouted into his face. "Mr. Hanover, can you hear me?" The eyes moved, blinked, but color was fast draining from Adam Hanover's features.

Ben intruded himself into the line of Hanover's blank gaze. "Adam, it's Ben. I'm going to get you help. You hear me? I'm going to get you . . ."

He trailed off. Something had changed in Adam Hanover's face even as he spoke. Light had faded out in the eyes and a long, slow exhalation that wasn't like that of a living breath had escaped the unmoving lips.

"Adam?"

This time there was no answering twitch, no blink or motion of the eyes.

"Mr. Hanover, can you hear me, sir?"

Nothing.

Ben stood and gazed down in disbelieving silence. He understood, but he did not accept. It couldn't be true.

Adam Hanover couldn't really be dead.

Chapter 41

Nanny made her escape from the Thornwell Estate after hearing that the Union general named Burnside had come into Knoxville. She planned and prepared carefully for several days, stealing food, clothing, a knife, and everything else she could think of that she would need to survive a lonely trip over the mountains into Tennessee. She wanted to steal a pistol from Phillip Thornwell's collection of guns, but the opportunity never arose.

She would not take the baby; that, she'd decided almost from the beginning. A trip through the mountains with a small child would never succeed, and besides, Little Joel was well cared for here. There was food, good shelter, plenty of people about to see to his welfare. They could do for him more than she ever could, and could love him better. Nanny was not blind to her weaknesses. She lacked the ability to love as deeply as most people, and accepted this. In its own way, it was convenient not to love very deeply. Love raised hurdles to hold a person back from what they wanted for themselves. She saw love as an inconvenience, and perhaps a form of slavery in itself. And Nanny hated slavery.

The escape itself was manifestly simple. She merely rose in the night, gathered her goods, packed them into a haversack she'd improvised from blanket fabric, and left. She was confident she could reach Knoxville with relative ease, and not become lost in the mountains. But this was the confidence of inexperience, not experience; Nanny had never been more than five miles from Josiah House her entire life, until Greeley Brown led her to the Thornwell Estate.

She reached the edge of the property and stopped, looking back at the big house where Thornwell slept, then at the slave cabins. For a moment her heart stirred; she thought of Little Joel lying in there, asleep. *What if I never see him again?* The thought was more deeply jolting than she would have expected. But of course she would see him again. When the Union won the war and all the slaves were truly free, she could come back here and get him, and they would be together. Or maybe it would be best if she didn't. Another slave woman here was taking good care of him now; he was happy with her. Maybe it would be best if she just let it all stand as it was and didn't come back at all.

So Nanny fought off the maternal tug that drew her back toward the slave cabins and her child. She would accept no bondage any longer, not of slavery, not of motherhood. Turning, she left the Thornwell Estate without another backward glance and headed into the mountains.

From now on, no matter what, she would be free.

Three days later Nanny admitted to herself that she was lost. The mountains were an endless maze, every place looking the same, every creek winding and twisting and cutting through terrain that she could not follow. And the cold . . . she had not been prepared for such a biting, cutting, painful cold. Her food was dwindling, and forbidden thoughts were rising: *I should go back. If I don't go back, I'll die.*

Yet she didn't know how to go back. That direction was as lost to her as any other.

So she walked, trying to make her food last, trying to follow the sun and the waterways, hoping she would somehow strike civilization. She did come upon one small community, revealed to her at dusk by the faint twinkling lights of cabin windows down along a waterway in a valley far below her. The happiness of seeing this, however, faded as she realized that she could not go there. She was a runaway slave. They would recognize this at once and take her back into bondage.

She had a little food left. She would go on. Maybe Tennessee was just over the next mountain.

All she found over that next mountain, however, was another mountain and another winding maze formed by ridges and narrow valleys. She did locate a path and followed it onto a mountain road too narrow even for a wagon, but the sound of horses coming around the bend behind her sent her into hiding. She watched a hard-eyed gaggle of armed men, led by a broad-bellied, auburn-bearded man, ride by, knew they were bushwhackers and huddled in terror until they passed. She'd heard stories among the slaves both at Josiah House and the Thornwell Estate of the terrible things bushwhackers did, especially when they were rebel at heart and their victims were straying Negroes. Nanny didn't know what breed of bushwhackers these were. She would take no chances.

A night later, her food nearly gone and her stomach empty and heart heavy, she sat down on a log and wondered how long it would take her to die. Looking up, she thought she saw smoke rising from the top of a peak . . . or was it merely a trick of the clouds at twilight? Standing, she looked more closely, and was sure that indeed there was smoke. She kept her eye fixed on that peak as darkness came, and before long she made out the faintest distant glitter of firelight. Someone was there, maybe more bushwhackers, maybe outliers or Home Guards or conscript dodgers. Whomever it was, she decided, come morning she would go to them and trust to fate that they would be helpful and benevolent, not dangerous.

They saw her long before she saw them, and when she finally did become aware of them, they were already positioned around her so she could not run. She made them out

the way one often makes out a silent, still deer in a thicket—
slowly, the lines and features taking shape a little at a time
until the mind finally gives an identity to the form it's
seeing.

Nanny knew what these men were. Indians. Cherokee,
she supposed. They carried rifles and wore gray Confederate uniforms.

One of them stepped forward and faced her. "Who are
you?"

She was grateful he spoke English.

"My name is Nanny."

He looked her over. "You're a runaway?"

She would not answer that directly. "I'm going to
Knoxville."

He evaluated her with his eyes and spoke to the others in
what to Nanny was a mere guttural babble. They moved in
together and looked at her, a mere handful of swarthy, lean,
uniformed men, their hair long and tied up behind their
heads. They kept their eyes on her while they talked to one
another, and Nanny was afraid. And angered. She felt helpless, knowing they were discussing her without her being
able to understand. Being helpless always made her angry.

The one who had first confronted her spoke again. "Are
you hungry?"

"Yes," she admitted.

"Come to our camp. You can have food."

She nodded her acceptance. "Who are you?"

"We are soldiers of Thomas's Highland Legion. Cherokee. We watch these mountains for men trying to flee to the
Union lines. We've never caught a runaway until you."

Caught . . . What did he mean? Was she to be taken
back, or turned over to someone else? Should she run? She
was afraid to run. They would shoot her, or catch her.

"What is your name?" she asked.

"What is yours?"

"Nanny."

He mouthed the name to himself, then said, "My name is
Jim Matoy."

• • •

She entered the camp not knowing what they would do to her. Anything seemed possible; these were Indians, and over the years and among the slaves, she'd heard lots of fearsome talk about Indians. For all she knew, they would kill her and eat her. Maybe take her hair and torture her. Perhaps violate her and dispose of her when she was used up.

As it turned out, all they did was feed her.

Jim Matoy was the only one, apparently, who spoke English well enough to converse easily with her. He asked her many questions about where she'd come from and why she was going to Knoxville. Too tired and mentally weary to lie, she simply told the truth, or part of it, saying nothing of her baby or about Josiah House. She didn't want them to know of her ties to that place. If they took her back, she would rather go back to the Thornwell Estate, never again to Josiah House.

To the question about why she was going to Knoxville, she could only answer that she was going there to be free.

She could not tell what the other Cherokees besides Matoy thought of her. They had unreadable faces and deep stares, and muttered to one another in their own tongue, sometimes laughing and gesturing at her openly. Matoy didn't join in the laughter. She found she liked him. He seemed kind and gentle. In her mind he became the protector, the others with him the unknown and fear-inspiring. She ceased to look at them, looking only at Matoy.

The food, game the Cherokees had provided for themselves and bread baked in the coals, filled her and gave her strength. When she'd eaten, Matoy came over, took her pack, and silently began packing what remained of the bread into it, provisioning her though she hadn't asked. When he was through, he handed her the pack.

"There is someone I'll take you to. They'll not hurt you. They'll show you the way to Knoxville."

She didn't know why he was helping her. He was a rebel, but he was going to help her escape. Unless he was lying and this was a trap . . .

She had no alternative, of course, but to assume the best of him and go along, because she could never run away. He gathered up his rifle and haversack and with a jerk of his head gestured for her to follow.

Nanny was hard-pressed to keep up; he moved through the woods like a ghost, seemingly unimpeded by any obstacle that came before him. He was but one more of the legion of phantoms haunting the mountains, one more of the unseen but eternally present human ghosts conjured by wartime.

Somehow she was able to follow, though she often fell far behind and he was forced to wait for her, impatience on his face.

He brought her to a low cabin on a hillside, and beyond the frayed bear hide that hung inside the entrance in lieu of a door, she was presented to a humped and ancient figure, obviously Cherokee, yet so old and wrinkled and plainly dressed that she did not realize for a long time that this was a woman and not a man. Matoy talked to the old woman for a long time in Cherokee, then turned to Nanny.

"She says you can call her what the white people call her: Polly Swan. Don't think that because she's old she can't help you. She'll take you to the end of the mountains. From there on you'll be alone; you'll have to find your own way to Knoxville."

"Why are you helping me?"

"Because you want to be free. I believe in being free, too. Even a soldier can believe in being free."

"Thank you."

He nodded his acceptance. "Good-bye." He ducked out under the bearskin and she saw him no more.

Nashville, early December

Ben could tell from the way Nectar looked at him that she didn't quite recognize him. He grinned at her, cocking his head, and said, "Have I changed that much since you seen me?"

Recognition dawned. "Ben? Ben! Ben Scarlett! My goodness, look at you!"

He was standing on the landing of the stairs leading into

her rooms. It was noon, but Nectar obviously had just gotten up from hard sleep. "You going to let me come in?"

"Why, surely, of course . . . but Ben, what's happened to you? Look at you—dressed nice, fleshed out . . . and look there! You've got yourself a hook for a hand! Why, ain't it nice! So shiny and all."

"I polished it before I come over. It was a gift to me . . . I'm proud of it." He lifted and turned it, displaying the glint. "Kind of pretty when the light catches it right."

He came inside; she directed him to be seated on the couch. "Ben, I've got whiskey. Can I get you some?"

For a moment the temptation was strong, burning, promising a familiar but rejected pleasure that he knew could be his again within a few sips. He ground his teeth together, steeled his spirit until the demon quit urging so strongly. "No. No thank you. I've give it up."

"You have? No lying?"

"No lying. I sweated it out. I don't aim to go back to it. And I've got a job . . . well, had one, but the newspaper is closed now."

"Newspaper? You was a newspaperman?"

"I swept up at the place, helped with the press and such. Did some proofreading," he added proudly. "That means looking for wrong-spelled words and such."

"Lord, ain't you done well! Me, I can hardly write my own name, and can't read nothing much but a few signs and things. 'Laundry' and 'Restaurant' and such as that."

"I hear they registered all the Cyprians with the army. Are you registered?"

"Yes . . . but I been thinking I might give it all up. It's no way to live. It's dangerous. And it's wrong. I know that sounds peculiar, coming from me of all people . . . but it *is* wrong. You live my life for a while and you'll see how wrong it is. Nobody has to tell you. You just know it."

"But what will you do?"

"I'm going to leave here, I think. I have a couple of old maid sisters in Lexington. I'd like to go to them, if they'll have me. After that, I'll find something to do. I don't know what."

"Best of luck to you, Nectar. Is that your real name, by the way?"

"No. My real name is Laurelleen. Laurelleen Finchum. That's a beauty, ain't it? I like Nectar better. Sounds like a sweet name, you know. Nectar."

"It's a pretty name, yes."

"Why are you here, Ben?"

"I wanted to give you something." He reached into his pocket and pulled out the picture of Angel. Glancing at it for a couple of moments, he then handed it to her.

"You're giving me this?"

"Yes. I want you to keep it. You can remember her when you see, and think of me, too."

"Why are you giving it to me? You should keep it."

"No. I have a picture of Angel I will keep." He tapped his brow. "Up here. I like to think of her like she was when I first knew her, not like she was when she turned to . . . you know, the kind of bad things she turned to."

Nectar smiled and held the picture to her bosom. "I'll treasure it, Ben. Thank you."

"Oh, and I wanted you to have this." He produced a small packet of money. "Ain't much, but I figure you could use it. I earned that money through regular work, no stealing like I used to do, and so it's mine to give."

"Why me?"

"You were Angel's friend. I can't do nothing for Angel now, but I can do something for her friend."

"Ben, you're a good man. The best man I ever met."

"I ain't good. No. Far from it."

"I think you are good . . . and I believe Angel was lucky to have knowed you."

Ben shook his head. "No. I did the wrong things with my life. I turned to drinking and let that drive Angel away. It was a fool's choice. If I hadn't made it, if we'd married and I'd kept sober and worked hard, Angel would still be alive today. She'd never have turned to whoring. We'd be together and happy. It was me who turned away from all that. All my fault."

Nectar did not argue. It was Ben's place to assess himself

and his life, not hers. "Did you say your newspaper closed down?"

"Yes. The publisher, a good man name of Hanover, was shot by somebody, we'll never know who, because they didn't like him writing some of the things he'd wrote. He's dead. He died with me kneeling beside him. And now his widow—a fine, fine woman she is, too—has decided to leave Nashville. She's going back to Knoxville, figuring she'll probably open up the newspaper there, instead of here, now that the Union has Knoxville again. I'm going with her."

"Knoxville is your home, ain't it?"

"That's right."

"You'll work for the widow, just like for her husband?"

"Yes." He laughed. "Lord have mercy—and it's a good thing for me He does!—the folks in Knoxville won't know what to think, seeing old Ben Scarlett wearing decent clothes, working, staying sober, reading books, going to church. . . . It'll be right fun, watching them watching me."

Nectar smiled, stepped forward and planted a kiss on his cheek.

"Thank you," Ben muttered, suddenly bashful.

"I'm glad I got to meet you, Ben. I hope you have a good and happy life from now on."

"I hope the same for you. And you be careful, going to Lexington. Don't let the war get you."

"Maybe it'll all be over soon."

"I hope." He nodded, grinned with his lips pursed so she wouldn't see them quiver, and said, "Well, time to go. Good-bye, Nectar."

"Good-bye, Ben."

His eyes dropped to the picture still clutched in Nectar's hand. *Good-bye, Angel. Good-bye.*

He left, slipping on his hat, trotting down the stairs to the street, letting the hook scrape down the wall just so he could hear the noise it made, to please the boy still hiding within the man. Nectar watched him from the landing until he was out of sight, then stepped back inside and closed the door.

Chapter 42

He had to get out, sometimes, away from Amy, so she wouldn't see what a burden it was on him to watch her grieve. She tried to hide it—stoicism was natural to her— but she didn't succeed. Ben knew that a part of Amy had died with her husband there on that street in Nashville, and whatever life she made for herself here in Knoxville would not be as complete a life as she'd known for those few months.

At least there was the baby. A bit of Adam Hanover still living in the unseen, developing body of another.

In another way, Ben figured, Adam would also live on in the newspaper Amy would begin publishing. Sometime next year, the plan was, though so far Amy hadn't done much toward that goal. The wound was far too fresh, the pain too great. Work would come later. Amy was a well-off young woman, thanks to inheritances, and under no economic pressure just now. She was even paying him his old wages, even though there was no newspaper yet in existence.

Ben had already picked up rumors that Parson Brownlow, Knoxville's premiere Unionist newspaperman, was not at all pleased that Doc Deacon's widowed daughter was back in town and about to launch a publication that would tread on what he saw as his own exclusive territory. No doubt the parson's famous verbal fire would soon turn on Amy Hanover, bitter with sarcasm at this young female upstart. Well, let him have at it, Ben thought. Amy was strong. She could handle it.

Meanwhile, Ben read Parson Brownlow's newspaper every time it came out, looking for ways Amy might do him one better whenever they got the *Sage* rolling again. He'd read an interesting Brownlow editorial today, he reflected: something about the need for greater security at Federal prisoner of war camps. This need, Brownlow asserted, was illustrated well by an escape that had occurred at the first of December at the Camp Douglas prison in Chicago. An entire barracks full of captured rebels had been emptied via a long tunnel dug beneath the camp fence. Exiting on a foggy night, the escapees had vanished into the city of Chicago even before their guards knew they were gone. An entire barracks of prisoners, vacated! Brownlow thought it was shameful.

Ben didn't. Reading that story he'd laughed. He knew about being trapped and captive. He believed in escape. Rebel, Federal, civilian, it didn't matter to him. A man had the right to strive to be free of whatever held him, whether that be the high wall of a prison camp or the glass wall of a whiskey bottle.

It was a Saturday afternoon, and Ben wandered without hurry. The streets of Knoxville had called to him, as had a certain fresh tomb in the same old Knoxville cemetery that held the body of Amy's deceased father. Ben pushed his hat low onto his head to keep his ears warm. With hand and hook in pockets, he set off on his long stride for the cemetery.

The stone was a beautiful one, a simple marble spire with a Bible verse carved at the bottom. The name chiseled into it in all capital letters was that of Daniel Baumgardner. Ben stood by the grave for a long time, looked around to make sure no one was in earshot, and spoke to the spirit of his departed friend, dead now since shortly after Ben had left for Nashville on his quest for Angel Beamish. His heart, folks said. It just gave out one night in his sleep, and he was gone.

"Mr. Baumgardner, I wish you could see me like I am now. You wouldn't know me. I ain't drinking no more, I been working with some good people. My clothes are clean and I've even taken to wearing underwear. I comb my hair and go to church and read the newspapers. I intend to find me some schoolbooks and learn some about ciphering numbers and history and so on. I'm going to make of myself the kind of man you were always telling me to be. I wish you could see me. You'd be proud, I think."

He left the cemetery so he wouldn't get too choked up and red-eyed, and made a tour of the city, every street so familiar, yet so different because he was different. At length he reached the empty old fire-damaged Deacon warehouse, and headed around to the rear of it. Hard to think now that this had been home to him mere months ago. Months! Yet it might have been years, as different and cut off from that old life as he felt now.

He couldn't resist it. Glancing from side to side just as he used to do, he went over to the hidden ladder that still leaned against the wall, climbed it slowly, and pushed open the makeshift doorway. It was growing dusky outside, so little light spilled in. He crawled through the opening, trying not to muss his clothing too much. Now that he had decent clothes, he wanted to take care of them.

He propped the wall-panel door open with a stray piece of wood and stood in the midst of what had been his "room." Memories of the wasted life that had been most of his life overwhelmed him, and he sniffed and struggled with tears. Hands in pockets, he looked around, up and down . . . and paused, cocking his ear, suddenly aware. . . .

"Who's there?" he said. "Somebody's in here! Who are you?"

Movement in the dark nearby, movement of a shadowed, slender figure, a glinting of the meager infiltrating light on the edge of a blade . . .

"You get away from me, sir, you leave me be! I'll kill you!"

Ben backed away from the figure, whom he could barely

make out. "Easy there, I didn't know this was your place. I wouldn't have come if I'd knowed. Who are you?"

"My name's Nanny, but it ain't none of your affair. You just leave me be! Get away from me. Get out of here. This is *my* place. *I* live here."

"Fine, fine. I understand. This used to be my place, you see. There was a time I lived right here, just like you."

She stepped closer; he could see her better now, though the light outside was fading fast and darkness would soon enshroud everything. She was black-skinned, thin, emaciated, dressed raggedly, a woman who had suffered an ordeal.

"You lived here?" she said.

"Yes. When I was drinking. Lived here just a few months ago."

She looked at him. "I don't believe it. You dressed too good. You ain't never lived like this."

"I did, I swear. But I've put away the whiskey and got myself work. And there were people who helped me. Lent me a hand." He paused. "Maybe you could use a hand yourself just now. You got food?"

"No." The knife, still in her hand, did not go down. "Why? You aim to give me some?"

"I got none to give just now, but I'll take you to a lady who will be glad to feed you. Her name is Hanover. Mrs. Amy Hanover, she used to be Miss Amy Deacon, the abolitionist. You heard of her?"

"No. Abolitionist . . ."

"That's right. She despises slavery. Used to write for abolition newspapers and sneak slaves to freedom on the Underground Railroad. You know about the Underground Railroad?"

"Yes."

"Are you free, or slave?"

"I'm free. I got nothing, no food, no money, no nothing, but I'm free. I'm free forever." She began to cry. "I'm going to die free. Going to starve, I 'spose, right up here in this hole, but when I do, I'll starve a free woman. Ain't never going to be a slave again."

"You won't starve. I'll take you to meet Mrs. Amy.

You'll like her. She's good and kind, and she'll take care of you just like she did me."

The knife lowered and fell to Nanny's feet. "I'm so hungry," she said. "I'm so, so hungry."

"Come on," Ben said, reaching toward her. "Take my hand. I'll help you onto the ladder. Then you and me, we'll go see Mrs. Amy. We'll get you some food."

"Why you help me?"

"Because I was a slave, too. Different kind of slave, but a slave, sure as the world. Come on. Let's go. You can trust me, I promise."

"What's your name, sir?"

"Ben Scarlett. Just call me Ben. No Mister, no nothing. Just Ben."

He got her onto the ladder and watched her weakly descend. When she was safe on the ground, he turned and slipped down onto the ladder himself. Turning, he looked one more time into the black depths of the place he had known so well so recently. "Farewell, Ben that used to be," he said, softer than a whisper. "You made it through, old fellow. Nobody would have ever thought you would, but you done it."

He reached the ground and, with Nanny at his side, led the way back through well-known streets, imagining that he could see in every darkening alley the ghost figure of the man he'd been, looking back at him through hollowed eyes, lifting in greeting to him, as he passed by, a wrist without a hand.

"Are you cold, Nanny?"

"Yes."

"You won't be for long. There's a big old stove where we're going, just as hot as a summer sun. Come on. Let's hurry."

AFTERWORD

THE PHANTOM LEGION, second volume in THE MOUN-
TAIN WAR TRILOGY, is a novel strongly rooted in fact.
Though its foreground characters are mostly fictional, the set-
tings, scenarios, and circumstances in which they live and
move substantially reflect historical realities.

Further, several of the characters themselves are based,
at least partially, upon historical figures. Some aspects of
the experiences and personality of the character Julius
Killefer, for example, derive from the true-life story of a
young reluctant Confederate soldier named Newton
Dobson, a Unionist who was forcibly and illegally conscripted into the Confederate army in his native Greene
County, Tennessee, and stationed thereafter at Cumberland
Gap. When the Gap was taken by the Federals just after
Burnside's celebrated invasion of Knoxville, Dobson's
unusually strict sense of personal honor, which stemmed
from his devout Christian beliefs and innate strong personal
character, led him to stand by the Confederate loyalty oath
that had been forced upon him, though his personal senti-
ments remained as Unionist as before. This strong sense of
duty cost him an opportunity for parole and freedom, leading

to a trying period for the young man as a prisoner of war at Camp Douglas. Dobson, unlike Julius Killefer in THE PHANTOM LEGION, remained a prisoner until the war's end, not participating in the escape mentioned at the end of the novel, and later went on to become a rural physician in his home county back in East Tennessee.

As already stated in the Afterword of the first volume in this novel trilogy, THE SHADOW WARRIORS, the Greeley Brown character is inspired by the true-life "Union pilot" of Carter County, Tennessee, Daniel Ellis. Though Ellis's personal circumstances were quite different than those of Greeley Brown, he possessed a similar drive, dedication, courage, and skill at his unusual but important service. Ellis's published memoir provided many of the details used in this novel to describe the "stampeder runs" of Greeley Brown, including routes followed, circumstances met at various places along the way, and even several of the character types encountered.

The Merriman Swaney character is based upon no one historical figure, but is a composite portrait of the typical quasi-military Carolina/Tennessee mountain bushwhacker. Men such as Swaney operated on both sides of the conflict (though in the mountains, where conflict inevitably grew personal, the war sometimes seemed to have more sides than just two). War was truly hell in the mountains, where children were raised to live at peace with others, but when attacked, to strike back hard. The mountain fighting spirit was, in the words of one old North Carolina mountain woman, to "die, die like a dog, with your teeth in a neck."

The storyline involving Ben Scarlett's search for his old lost love in Nashville touches upon one of the war's more odd and obscure affairs, that being the efforts of the occupying Federals to deal with the widespread prostitution problem plaguing that city at the time. The scenario involving the deportation via Kentucky-bound steamer of many of Nashville's resident prostitutes actually occurred. It failed rather abysmally—the prostitutes simply returned to Nashville at first opportunity—and the Federals, in effect, shrugged, fell back, and punted. Rather than trying again to ban the prostitutes, they set up a registration system for them and issued prostitution licenses. The duly licensed prostitutes, in exchange for being allowed to practice their trade without harassment, were required to have medical examinations to ensure they were free of transmittable diseases. In effect, the occupying Federals had, under the pressure of wartime realities, created America's first system of legalized prostitution.

The celebration that accompanied Burnside's invasion of Tennessee occurred as described in the novel, and perhaps more than any other incident of the Civil War in East Tennessee reveals how widespread and deep-felt was Unionist sentiment in that region. The wild cheering of citizens and the profuse offering of foodstuffs and other gifts to the incoming Federal soldiers, this despite the poverty of the citizenry at that time, were so ardent, emotional, and impressive that recountings of the experience made their way into many a soldier's journal. One thing was clear to all who witnessed the Burnside invasion: East Tennessee was indeed a most reluctantly Confederate region, the majority of its people staunchly pro-Union, and so eager to again live under the Stars and Stripes that they viewed the triumphant Burnside in an almost messianic light.

This fervent Unionism of East Tennessee set it apart from the middle and western sections of the state. Similar differences remain today, showing up most clearly in politics. While Democrats dominate in modern-day West and Middle Tennessee, East Tennessee, still heavily populated by descendants of Unionists, is predominately Republican, still overwhelmingly supporting the "Party of Lincoln," still standing widely apart from the rest of the state. Old-timers of East Tennessee, and even some not so old, can recall relatively recent days when the links between modern political lines and the Civil War were still starkly clear; one Greene County anecdote collector recalls a man who, speaking in 1935, declared he would never vote for a Democrat: the Democrats, he said, had killed his "Pappy." The passing of seven decades had done nothing to blur in that man's mind the identification of Democrats with the Confederacy, Republicans with the Union.

The saga begun in THE SHADOW WARRIORS and

continued through THE PHANTOM LEGION will go on in the final volume of the trilogy, SEASON OF RECKONING, telling the further story of Ben Scarlett, Amy Deacon Hanover, Greeley Brown, Nanny Josiah, and the other denizens of this tale. Look for it in the book racks this fall. As the Mountain War builds, so does the adventure.

CAMERON JUDD
Greene County, Tennessee